Advance Praise for *Lost in Las Vegas*

"A fantastic, funny, and fast read! The Vegas underbelly as if presented by the Coen brothers. Bravo!"
— Kevin Pollak, co-star of *The Usual Suspects, Casino, A Few Good Men*; named by Comedy Central as one of the top 100 comedians of all time

"The funniest, truest account of Vegas life I've ever read. The verbal exchanges between John and Ludo are priceless. It's *Pulp Fiction* meets Pulp Vegas."
— Jim Mauro, former editor, *Spy* magazine

"This book ranks with *Fear and Loathing in Las Vegas* as an unforgettable comedy, ranking with such classic novels as *Catch-22* in its originality and use of humor . . . brilliant in its use of language."
— Edwin Silberstang, author of *Nightmare of the Dark* and *Abandoned*

"Astonishing! Avery Cardoza has crafted a classic gambling adventure that grabbed me from the very first page and wouldn't let go. The words are incredibly vivid and there's rhythm and thought woven into this that goes way beyond what I expected."
— Mike Caro, The Mad Genius of Poker, author of *Caro's Book of Poker Tells*

"*Lost in Las Vegas* is a rollercoaster of a novel that takes the reader on highs, lows and everything in between. Like the city of Vegas itself, it is filled with madcap adventure and fun."
— Gabriel Packard, Assoc. Director, Hunter College Creative Writing MFA Program

"I love it, I love it, I love it! A classy piece of literature."
— Vitaly Babenko, Director of Publishing, Club 366 Publishers, Moscow

"Of the many books written about Las Vegas, this one ranks right up there with the best. It has levity, comic-drama, and enough interesting characters to fill the city. Great fun."
— Leonard Wise, author of *Diggstown* and *The Big Biazarro*

"In *Lost in Las Vegas*, Avery Cardoza provides the darkest and craziest tour of this craziest of cities ever to see print. I laughed my ass off!"
—Arnold Snyder, Gambling Legend, Charter Member of the Blackjack Hall of Fame

Lost in Las Vegas

Two regular guys, one desperate dream — get the hell out of Vegas!

Lost in Las Vegas

Two regular guys, one desperate dream
— get the hell out of Vegas!

avery cardoza

cardoza publishing

Meet the author, watch videos, and get extras at
lostinlasvegas.com

Notes on the Hardcover Book
In a tribute to the past when printed books were works of pride, this hardcover edition is printed on 13 signatures of uncut paper and contains illustrations created specifically for this book. This book is a work of fiction. With the exception of recognized locations (some of which have been altered for fictional purposes), the places where events are depicted are derived solely from the author's imagination, and any resemblance to persons living or dead, incidents, or places, is purely coincidental.

Acknowledgments
Many thanks for helpful manuscript suggestions to Jim, third draft; Joyce, third-and-a-half and fifth drafts; Julian, fourth draft; Mark Brayer, cover art and layout; Paula B, copy editing; my fantastic editor, Dana Smith, thirteenth and final draft; and the wonderful illustrations by Anna Wilkenfeld.

ISBN 10: 1-58042-313-2
ISBN 13: 978-1-58042-313-7

CARDOZA PUBLISHING
P.O. Box 98115, Las Vegas, NV 89193
Toll Free Phone (800)577-WINS
email: cardozabooks@aol.com
www.cardozabooks.com

In mid-September, 2001, in Brooklyn, I saw a leaf take its fall from a tree and hang suspended in the air, catching light and glowing resplendent in autumnal colors. I watched as it drifted to the ground to fade and later crumble into dust and scatter to the winds. I can still see that leaf in its ephemeral moment of majestic beauty, brilliant in its being. This memory I hold and cherish, and it keeps the colors of that leaf alive. With this memory, one day, I will die.

This book is dedicated to my mother Bascia; it's a work she never lived to see.

Preface

A plane rushes westward at 533 miles per hour. It is packed, and the passengers can barely wait to charge into a fantasy they have been anticipating for days, weeks, years. And now, just a matter of hours.

The excitement is palpable. A vacation here is a dip into the unadulterated pleasures of flesh and soul, where visitors emboldened by free drinks become bigger than the selves they left behind. Imbued with the spirit of wild abandon, revelers will walk taller, drink harder, and become more grandiose in their manners as they get sucked into a fast-paced, nearly sleepless orgy of hedonism. Amid the tantalizing pleasures that dance day and night live the seven deadly sins—lust, anger, sloth, vanity, envy, gluttony, and avarice. Line up each initial, add "sex," and the letters spell: Las Vegas.

The plane speeds closer to its destination. Alcohol flows, and blackjack and Texas hold'em are dealt on food trays while players ride the emotional vicissitudes of luck with every turn of a card. Bets made with miniature pretzels, peanuts, coins, and bills are accompanied by bursts of excitement as winners claim their manna. The losers, no less feverish after the setback, wait for the first two cards of the next deal— then the flop, turn, river, and showdown.

Buzz, buzz, buzz. Soon the real action will be upon them. A red-faced man pushes all-in with hard cash—all he has on him. The plane starts its descent. A precipitous one.

Viva Las Vegas.

Chapter One

"Homes, this thirteen thing going to be hanging over us like a curse, like some bad voodoo dust or something," Ludo Garcia says, shaking his head. "Thirteens are bad luck, man. Everyone knows that. I got a bad feeling about this."

John Howard-Hughes paces back and forth watching travelers haul their bags off carousel thirteen at McCarran Airport in Las Vegas. He sighs and faces his best friend. "No matter what we do, where we go, you always find a thirteen somewhere. I don't know what's with you."

"I don't find them, they find us. Starting to remind me of that Mexico trip. Started the same way."

"Let's not talk about that."

John shoves his hands into the pockets of his khaki trousers. A not-quite-matching beige dress shirt buttoned to the top sits under a blue blazer, a contrast to Ludo's red polo shirt, black high-top Converse sneakers, and Bermuda shorts in a dizzying pattern of reds, oranges, yellows, and blues. On his head, Ludo sports a dark red paisley bandanna.

They watch an oversized green bag wrapped with two frayed straps spit out from the bowels of the luggage hold. A relieved passenger, the only other one remaining, grabs it and hurries away. The immediate area around John and Ludo is empty and, except for the squeaking and grinding noises of the conveyer belt, strangely quiet.

"Hey, homes," Ludo says after two long wordless minutes.

"What?"

"I hope you like what you're wearing."

"Why's that?"

Ludo nods in the direction of the conveyer belt, the apparatus bereft of any luggage.

"There's nothing coming off that thing!" John says.

"Not looking good, homes."

Like dogs dazed at their own reflections, the two friends watch the empty carousel as it goes round and round and round, their introduction to a city where the night can be as bright as day and the day can be as dark as night.

"Great start to a vacation," John says. "What else can go wrong?"

Chapter Two

John and Ludo search among the tuxedoed chauffeurs, about to give up on their free hotel pick-up when they spot an obese man dressed in a stained white T-shirt and brown drawstring pants settled deeply in a chair holding a piece of ripped cardboard, their names scribbled in pencil. He leads them outside to the open-air garage. After two halting pauses to expunge spit of a frightening greenish hue, he stops in front of a dark orange car, a jagged dent stretching along the passenger side and ending above a balding back tire missing its hubcap. The car is coated with dirt and grime, and there is a gap where the missing side-view mirror has been knocked off. Two gritty wires, green and red, protrude from the hole.

"Why are we in the parking lot, Ludo? Don't they usually pick you up at the curb?" John whispers as they squeeze into the tight space behind the prodigious girth of the driver. The temperature in the car is barely cooler than the stifling air outside it, even after exiting the airport, despite the wheezing efforts of the overmatched air-conditioner. John stares horrified at the conduit of dripping sweat gathering in the folds of the driver's neck and then disappearing down the fleshy surface of his back. "And what happened to our shiny black limousine? They're supposed to send one, right?"

"Maybe it broke down or something, they sent this one instead," Ludo says. "I don't know, homes."

As the car navigates traffic on Las Vegas Boulevard—the Strip— John and Ludo take in the dizzying collection of eye candy that defines the Las Vegas skyline, a parade of one-upmanship and gaudy opulence— Disneyesque castles and spires, façades of the Brooklyn Bridge and Empire State Building, a half-sized version of the Eiffel Tower, soaring fountains cascading out of an eight-acre man-made lake, mock pirate battles, and volcanic eruptions—all the ostentatious displays that color the Strip. Lights sparkle, glitter, and pulsate, the neon magic of Las Vegas in full resplendent bloom dancing before their eyes.

"This is something else, eh, homes?" Ludo says. "Look at them fountains. That the Bellagio?"

"Yeah, I think so. It's supposed to be the best or one of the best here," John says, shifting uncomfortably behind the driver, his knees pressing against the seat back and aching from the pressure.

"The one we staying in, just as good?"

"Top of the heap. That's what the travel agent told us," John says.

The taxi abruptly stops after turning east on Convention Center Drive, blocked by a man in a dark full-length coat missing half a sleeve. He is holding up his oversized trousers with one hand and he pushes a cart overflowing with swollen garbage bags across the street, oblivious to traffic. His beard is clotted with knots and streaked with gray, and he has the frightened expression of a lost duckling that can't find its mother, a scared man-child the sun hasn't yet been able to wither and take away from the promised land.

He passes and the taxi continues on, a dichotomy of Vegas revealed. In this town, where life can be profoundly altered by the turn of a card, a spin of the wheel, or the roll of the dice, reality and illusion get blurred. The illusion may be the reality, and the reality the illusion. Like Halloween, when dusk settles into night, Las Vegas can be the trick or the treat, the rush of the first dice roll or the devastation of the last one.

It is here, a city where day and night juxtapose and fate intertwines with the gods of chance, that two vacationers just off a plane are on their way to find out which part of Las Vegas awaits them.

Chapter Three

The taxi grinds to a halt outside the Hidden Treasure Casino and Hotel, a four-story structure with a peeling and unimposing façade. In front, a plaster canopy trying to pass itself off as a decorative touch is supported by two thin columns of an indeterminate color somewhere in the rotted-white, muted yellow, and dying puke family, the color unevenly worn by the elements, almost begging for a fresh coat of paint. The entrance, two plain tinted doors with horizontal metal bars that push to open, sits thirty feet from the street.

"Hey, buddy," the driver calls after John. "That'll be thirteen dollars."

John leans back through the window. "They said the limo ride was included. We bought a first-class package!"

The driver glances at the hotel, then back at his car, his eyebrows knitted together in a quizzical expression.

"Never mind," John says, handing him fifteen dollars and telling him to keep the change.

"And don't start with me on that thirteen again," John says, raising his right hand and avoiding Ludo's gaze.

"Damn," Ludo says, rubbing his neck and waving away billows of

blue-gray exhaust left by the departing vehicle. "Where this guy learn how to drive? He gave me, like, whiplash, working that gas pedal like an air pump." He kicks a stray pebble off his high-tops, thrown there by the departing car, and watches it roll toward the curb. "This is the top of the heap that travel agent sold us? I thought first class was Bellagio, Caesars, Mandalay, one of them. This ain't the top, just the heap. Don't them fancy places here all have fountains and everything?"

"Maybe first class is on the inside," John says. "You can't always tell from the outside."

"I don't know about this."

John and Ludo push hard on the reluctant doors of the casino and step inside. Banks of slot machines and a cacophony of noise greet them: gamblers whooping it up with small victories or cursing their bad luck; keno runners and change girls hawking their wares; the clicking of chips from blackjack, craps, and roulette tables; the spinning reels and pounding of coins into metal wells of video poker and slot machines; and the sucking and gurgling of coins from players who feed the old-fashioned beasts with the regularity of a psychotic metronome. The air is heavy with smoke and the odors of stale beer, foot-long hot dogs, cheap mustard, buckets of yellowed popcorn, and soiled dollar bills oozing human sweat.

They make their way along a faded reddish-brown carpet, its pattern barely discernible, and stand between maroon theater ropes frayed and worn to a dull color, waiting for the receptionist to finish chatting with an ancient janitor. Ludo presses on the carpet with his foot, wondering if the Italian polished marble he had expected is somehow underneath.

"What are you doing?" Ludo says after John checks his watch for the third time.

"This is taking forever."

"Maybe things a bit slower out here, but whatever. Man, I told you, you got to chill out a little, you going to get a heart attack one day."

"I know, you're right," John says, sighing heavily.

"Start with this." Ludo points to the top button on John's shirt. "Let a little air in."

John undoes the top button of his shirt and then a second one when Ludo points again.

The receptionist finally waves them forward. He is well tanned and his thick bleached-blonde hair is combed to perfection, giving him the appearance of a surfer from Southern California.

"Welcome to the Hidden Treasure, your home away from home," the receptionist cheerfully announces through perfectly aligned white teeth. "Your name, please?"

"John Howard-Hughes."

"Fine. Thanks, sir," the receptionist replies, his gaze lost somewhere over John's head.

"John," John enunciates carefully, holding the syllable for an extra second, "Howard-Hughes."

"How am I? Still fine," the receptionist replies. "And the name is not John, it's Joe." His moon-shaped fingernails tap a laminated nametag pinned to his chest identifying him as Joe from the state of Montana. He starts humming, his eyes dreamily scanning the ceiling. He has not yet made eye contact.

"There's got to be a way," John mumbles to himself. He looks carefully at the receptionist, hoping to attract his attention to sea level.

"Let's try again. My first name is John and my last name is Howard with a hyphen attached for Hughes—not *yous*: That's John Howard-Hughes. You know, like the famous billionaire?"

"*The* Howard Hughes?" the receptionist intones, looking directly at John for the first time. The humming stops and a nervous energy transforms him, his face a pool of twitches.

"No relation," John says.

"Really? Come on, you can tell me."

"None, Joe, I assure you," John says, annoyed. "I hear it all the time. It's just a similar name."

The receptionist suspiciously glances around the lobby. The words come out in a low whisper through clenched teeth; anyone out of hearing range would be unaware he was talking. "Your secret is safe with me. I'll call you 'Johnny' to throw *them* off. Johnny, Johnny, Johnny."

"John will do. I never go by Johnny."

"Johnny, Johnny, Johnny, Johnny, Johnny." The receptionist's voice is deep and low, as if possessed.

"Joe, is there some way we can get past the name so I can check in already? You ever get called 'Joe Montana,' you know, the football player?" John makes a passing motion with his arm.

The receptionist stares blankly at John with no visible sign he has heard him speak.

"I have a prepaid trip. Maybe that's written down?"

"Ooooookay," Joe Montana says, slowly dragging out the word. His eyes shift wildly in their sockets, scanning the lobby, before they drop to his reservation book. He speaks so quietly that John can barely hear him. "That's right, indeedy. I see you'll be with us for three nights. 'First class,' it says here."

Joe Montana loudly clears his voice, then starts coughing raucously and lustily stamping his feet. "Yesssss," he says, "you've got the very last room available."

John and Ludo look at each other, unsure what to make of the receptionist. Joe Montana motions John to lean in closer.

"What is it?" John whispers, drawn in by his secretive manner.

"Johnny, Johnny, Johnny, Johnny, Johnny," the receptionist whispers back, his eyebrows flipping up and down with each "Johnny."

John pulls the key from Joe Montana's outstretched fingers, quickly moving away from the check-in area.

"Mr. Howard-Hughes, Mr. Howard-Hughes," Joe Montana calls out in an urgent whisper.

"Yes, Joe?" John turns to face him.

"Never mind," Joe Montana says, waving both hands side to side and furiously shaking his head.

"Something wrong with him," Ludo says to John as they head across the lobby.

John leads the way down a narrow corridor on the third floor, the carpet uneven under their feet, its plywood base warped and creaking. Naked bulbs cast odd shadows on the walls, barely illuminating the hallway. The last door is smaller and different from the others.

"This don't feel right to me," Ludo says. "Three-thirteen? We ain't even got into the room and already we're triple stacked on thirteens. Too many coincidences to be coincidences, you know what I'm saying?"

"Oh, come on! How many times do we have to have this same argument? What, a thousand times?"

"I only bring up the obvious. And I'm right those thousand times."

"I don't know why I let you suck me into these things. A number is a number. What's the big deal about thirteen? It's a good thing you don't gamble; superstition and math don't mix."

"Thirteens never mix with anything. You accountants think a number is a number, but you ain't looking at when a number ain't a number."

"What sense does that make? How could a number not be a number?"

"See, that's what you never get!" Ludo says.

"Never mind."

Ludo enters the room and flicks the light switch, ducking as a moth darts past his head. The central bulb, hanging naked from a cord with no fixture, barely illuminates the room, which reeks of mold and mildew as if not occupied for months. Just a few feet separate two single beds, making the room look more like a glorified maid's closet than guest quarters. The sole window, situated near the ceiling, is just two feet wide and one high. A thin drape, the color of faded urine, hangs limply in front of it.

"What is this place?" Ludo says, reclining on a bed that sinks down half a foot and creaks with his weight.

"They snookered us," John says. "Something didn't feel right when that travel agent said he'd throw in first class for free, but only if we booked it immediately. 'The last package remaining,' he said. Talk about the bottom of the bad-pickle barrel. Remind me not to believe those ads on late-night television."

"When something is for free, it's usually not for free, you know what I'm saying?"

"Hey, don't get too comfortable." John glances at Ludo sinking deep into the bed. "You close your eyes, you'll never get up. Of all things, why did you do a graveyard last night?"

"You know how it is at that hospital. Triple shift Dr. Kroll made me do to bust my balls. Four years there, homes, and Kroll still hasn't figured out that my job description is orderly, not whipping boy."

"Yesterday wasn't a picnic for me either," John says, his intestinal acids gurgling—they do whenever he thinks about his overbearing sister and father at the family accounting firm where he's a junior partner who was never made a junior partner—and he subconsciously rubs his stomach, recalling the acrimonious months-long battle to get time off for this trip. He considers taking a swig of Pepto-Bismol to relieve the discomfort—but it is buried in luggage that hasn't arrived, which makes the acids churn even more.

"I hear you," Ludo says, kicking off his shoes and pulling the blanket over him. When his weight shifts, the springs groan like three hoarse trumpets played out of tune.

"I'm going to take a quick shower, freshen up," John says.

"Homes, why don't you hang your clothes in the closet first so they don't get wrinkled?"

"Very funny, Ludo."

———

John barely finishes lathering his head with shampoo before the water turns frigid, cutting his shower short. When he steps back into the room, Ludo is wrapped tightly in the blanket and snoring.

"Ludo! Ludo!" John shouts, pushing his shoulder.

"What is it?" Ludo says, his eyes half closed.

"You fell asleep!"

"No, man, I was just thinking."

"Come on, get up."

"Don't worry. I got plenty of energy. Big night ahead of us. Big night. Just let me rest my eyes a few seconds." Ludo's eyes close and his breathing gets deeper.

"Ludo!"

Ludo's eyes snap open. "What?" He looks around, startled. "Homes, can't get a moment's peace around you." His voice slurs as he sinks back into a dreamlike state. "You too worked up. Got to relax a little, you know what I'm talking about?"

"Come on," John says, shaking him again. "Let's get out and cruise the Strip, see what's going on."

"Just let me close my eyes for a few minutes, homes," Ludo replies, his voice barely audible. He turns on his side and the bedsprings creak like a rusty symphony.

Instantly, with almost two sleepless days dragging their weight on him, Ludo is dead asleep, neon deep in dreamland.

Chapter Four

Unable to rouse Ludo from the bed and excited to see the city he has heard so much about, John heads downstairs and asks a taxi to drop him off at Bellagio. He tips the driver two dollars and retreats from the long entranceway of the property to the walkways out front, pausing a few minutes to watch the elaborate fountains dance up and down. John heads north along the Strip, passing Caesars Palace, where on New Year's Eve in 1967, daredevil motorcyclist Evel Knievel disastrously jumped the fountain and crashed, breaking nearly every bone in his body, and then he reaches the Mirage, with its volcano spewing manufactured fire into the sky.

Though fascinated by the sights, John feels closed in by the dense mass of tourists along the sidewalks and decides to escape from the claustrophobic immediacy of the pedestrians around him. Walking rapidly, he passes the jostling crowds watching the volcano show and hurries into the Mirage.

The cool air inside the casino is refreshing, especially after the uncomfortable stickiness of the hot desert evening. But better yet, there is room here to breathe without a constant swill of slow-moving humanity crowding his space and bumping into him.

John aimlessly wanders past the atrium with its spectacular plants and soaring skylight, and follows the meandering walkway past the table games and slots and into the shopping area, turning to stare at a man who appears to be the living reincarnation of Elvis Presley. His jet-black hair, brightly oiled with brilliantine, is long and combed straight back in the style kept by the King. The man's thick sideburns, cherubic face, and charming smile—a look the impersonator must have practiced for thousands of hours in front of a mirror—perfectly captures the persona of Elvis. The clothing is right-on as well: His brightly patterned bell-bottoms flare broadly over black cowboy boots tipped with silver, and he wears a garish shirt open to reveal a chest full of black curly hair.

Spellbound, John watches the impersonator swagger down the walkway. Distracted, he bumps headfirst into a strikingly beautiful woman in her mid-twenties, knocking her Gucci handbag to the ground. The soft fabric of her silk sundress clings tightly to the woman's trim and voluptuous frame, revealing ample breasts and luscious skin.

"I'm sorry," they both say simultaneously.

John instinctively goes to pick up her handbag, as does the woman, and their heads meet in the middle, banging lightly.

The woman's long, dark hair, parted to the side, swings across the middle of her back as she stands back up, rubbing her head.

"Don't move!" John says, holding out both his hands. "Let me pick up your purse without us crashing into each other again—if you don't mind."

John carefully retrieves the bag off the ground and hands it to her. "Here you go, mademoiselle."

"Thanks, that was nice."

"It's the least I can do after running you over and almost cracking your head open! I'm John, by the way," John says, extending his hand.

The woman laughs. "Hi. I'm ZZ. Nice to meet you." ZZ shakes the hand offered and smiles, revealing perfect white teeth and wide sensual lips.

"Are you okay?" John asks.

The woman rubs her head again. "I'm okay, but I can see you have a hard head!"

"Let me take a look." John looks at the spot where their heads met, and softly runs his fingers over the scalp. "Maybe you'll get a little bump, but that's about it. Doctor McDreamy officially says you'll live."

"You're a doctor?" ZZ says.

"No, I was just kidding."

"You're funny." ZZ smiles and their eyes meet. "Can I call you Doc for short? I like that!"

"Really," John protests, "I'm not a doctor. Just call me John."

"No, I like 'Doc!' That's what it will be. You live here?" she asks.

"No, I gave up living in the shopping arcade last year. Now I prefer housewares." When she stares at him blankly, he says, "Actually, I'm visiting from New York with my high school buddy, Ludo. I'm just here on vacation."

"New York? How exciting! I've never been there."

"Yeah, it's a great place. Actually, I sort of live in the suburbs, in Brooklyn, but it's technically part of the city."

ZZ smiles, her lips glowing softly. "Do you want to walk around with me a little?"

"Sure," John says. "You can give me the official tour."

"I love wandering around stores, just seeing all the new products they have. It's fun."

She touches John lightly on the shoulder and leads the way into a store selling cosmetics. John obediently follows behind, his blood quickening with the electricity of her touch. He is thrilled by this charming, beautiful woman, and cannot remember ever feeling so entranced.

ZZ passes by the Chanel and Clinique counters and stops in front of Borghese. She picks up a bottle marked "tester," unscrews the lid, and squirts a palm-full of thick white cream on her hand, lathering it thickly on her arms. She takes another liberal portion from the container, bends down, and vigorously rubs the lotion onto her shapely legs. A small amount of cream is left on her hand.

"Ummmm, this is nice. You want to try some?" she asks. Without waiting for a reply, she rubs the remaining lotion onto his arm, the feeling of her palms soft and sensual to his skin.

ZZ turns to a smiling young woman behind the counter, dressed almost like a nurse in a starched white uniform, her bobbed hair a throwback to an older generation. "Do you have any free samples?" ZZ says.

The woman, happy to have a few customers to break up the tedium of a long day, reaches under the counter and hands ZZ a few small containers.

"Here you go," the salesperson says.

"Thanks!" ZZ takes the samples, her face flush with excitement. Giggling like a little girl and energized by the stash of free goods, ZZ grabs John's hand and pulls him over to the next counter, where various products are displayed along the top. She squirts lotion from a pink-colored container into her hand, but not liking the smell, wipes it off on a tissue paper, and moves on to the following counter. She squeezes out big gobs of lotion into her hand from a Tommy Girl tube. John looks down, embarrassed, as ZZ thickly covers her arms and legs with the cream.

"I like this one!" she says excitedly to John. "See if they have any free samples. Ask her for me, okay?"

John hesitates, uncomfortable about approaching the stern-looking woman behind the counter. "You don't want to ask her?" he says tentatively.

"I'm asking you to do me a simple favor. What's the big deal?" ZZ says, raising her voice.

John is taken aback by the outburst and is grasping for words when ZZ's cell phone rings.

"Excuse me," she says to John. ZZ checks the phone's caller ID and picks up the call after the first ring.

"What is it now?" she yells into the phone. "You didn't do it? . . . What?" ZZ pulls the phone away from her ear and screams into it, "Fuck you, you asshole!" before slamming the lid shut. Her eyes flutter like confused butterflies caught in a maelstrom and her hands shake convulsively.

"Are you okay?" John says after a few seconds.

ZZ doesn't respond, her stare lost somewhere within the hard case of her cell phone.

"ZZ." John waves his hand in front of her eyes. At first, she appears to look right through his hand as if it were transparent glass and not really there. "ZZ?" John says again.

"That fucking prick!" ZZ finally says, her eyes slowly focusing on John's hand. "I'm sorry, it's my ex, he's a really bad person. Really, really bad."

"Sorry to hear that."

"Well . . . whatever."

"Do you want to talk about it? I don't know, maybe you can bounce some things off me, and I can give you some insight to help."

ZZ's pupils contract into dark pinpoints and dart about like a spaceship reentering at the wrong angle and careening wildly off the earth's orbit. Though she is looking at John, she doesn't appear to see him.

"Maybe I should go," ZZ says quietly, looking down.

John glances around nervously, this magic encounter with ZZ slipping out of his grasp. "Hey," John blurts out, "can I invite you for lunch or something?"

ZZ's eyes blink rapidly as if washing away the remnants of old thoughts, a late-afternoon tide carrying loose pieces of sand back into the ocean. John is about to curse his luck at the bad timing of ZZ's disturbing phone call, when her face suddenly lightens up.

"It's eight forty-five at night, how could we eat lunch?" ZZ playfully answers.

She starts giggling, and John, startled at another precipitous mood change, scrambles to put his thoughts together.

"How about dinner then?"

Chapter Five

The taxi drops John and ZZ in front of an unassuming Italian restaurant tucked at the end of a small commercial strip mall several miles east of Las Vegas Boulevard. The interior is long, narrow, and dimly lit by recessed bulbs. Small candles on every table provide an intimate and private setting for the patrons with just enough extra light to illuminate the surroundings.

The restaurant reminds John of the Sicilian Social Club in the Bensonhurst area of Brooklyn, where a few years earlier, mistaking the club for an authentic Italian cappuccino house, he had waltzed through the doors to be greeted by two monstrous and brooding men who had made it perfectly clear that it was a private club and John had made a mistake. Flashes of the fright John had felt stayed with him for weeks and intermittently for months, causing wrenching pains in his stomach, the episode eventually disappearing from his consciousness.

Until now.

When the manager, a barrel-chested man in a finely tailored Italian suit, sees them enter, he heads in their direction, biceps and triceps pushing hard against the fabric of his jacket.

"Welcome to the Amiga Bella," he says in a thick Brooklyn-Italian accent. His voice is so low, it is almost menacing. He eyes ZZ askance as if there is something about her that triggers a memory he can't quite get at. "Just the two of you?"

After looking at John a little too hard for his comfort, the manager picks up two patent leather–covered menus and leads the way to a small table set for two. He pulls out a chair for ZZ, the furniture like a toy against his big frame, and tucks her in when she sits.

"A waiter will be right with you," he says as he hands them menus and continues on toward the rear of the restaurant.

"Looks like a *Godfather* movie in here," John says, uncomfortably glancing about.

Pictures of Venetian gondola scenes adorn the walls. There is also a large oil painting of Venice, with the paint gobbed on in thick strokes, the artist having used generous portions for each motion of the brush. Purple and green bunches of plastic grapes and red apples hang from either side of the picture.

"They're just a bunch of fake Mafia wannabes, believe me," ZZ says.

John involuntarily shivers with ZZ's mention of the word "Mafia," remembering his chilling experience back in Bensonhurst, a memory not undone by the manager's hulking presence. He feels a swirl of pain in his stomach as the acids that form when he gets tense begin to work their nefarious magic.

"You know how it is in this town," ZZ continues. "Even *he* thinks he's something with that fake Ver-sash-ee, Ver-sakk-ee or whatever."

"Ver-sach-ee?"

"V-E-R-S-A-C-H-I," ZZ says, spelling out the letters.

"You mean, the suit?"

"I'm talking about the manager, aren't you listening to me? Yes, the suit he's wearing. He thinks he's a big shot, Mr. Versachi, you can see by looking at him. That suit probably cost him ten dollars on the street or something."

John nods his head and glances toward the rear where the manager is ostensibly busying himself with the rearrangement of a few folded napkins, but appears more to be studying something else, as if trying to figure out a pattern buried in his past, fragment by fragment.

"Anyway, the food should be yummy here," ZZ says. "I heard this place has the best veal. The best! Shall we share a few things?"

"Sounds great. Why don't you just order for us and what we get, we get."

"Okay," she says and quickly scans the menu. "Do you like seafood?"

"I like everything. Order whatever you feel like. Don't even ask. I just don't eat meat or fish, and can't stand pasta, vegetables, or salads, but everything else would be just great."

ZZ looks at John, puzzled.

"I'm just kidding," John says. "Everything is good for me. Order whatever."

"Oh," ZZ says, distracted. "Waiter, waiter," she impatiently calls out across the room. A waiter, his back to them, is taking the order from an elderly couple a few tables over.

"We're ready to order. Can we get service here?" ZZ continues, undeterred by the man's back.

The waiter, a tall gaunt man in his late fifties with hair graying on the sides, turns and acknowledges ZZ with an annoyed nod of his head. He finishes taking the couple's order and heads over to the table, a slight limp noticeable in his gait. He is dressed in traditional waiter garb, black trousers and a black jacket over a button-down white shirt. His uniform sits on him as if he were born into the profession and had been thirty years plying the trade.

He stands between ZZ and John, pulls out a pad from his back pocket, and stands ready, pen in hand.

"You're ready to order, ma'am?" the waiter says.

"Duh! No, we're just enjoying reading the menu," ZZ says.

The waiter shifts his attention away from the table, looking off at the far wall as he lets the remark pass. After a quick deep breath, he returns his gaze to ZZ.

"Go ahead," the waiter says. John notices that the "ma'am" is dropped this time around.

"I want to try the first nine appetizers."

"Excuse me? All of them?" the waiter asks.

"Yes, that's what I said. We'll share them. And for the main dishes, he'll get penne alla vodka, light on the sauce, and I'll take veal parmigiana, also easy on the sauce, but with extra cheese. Everything to share. Extra cheese on the parmigiana. I like cheese."

"That's a lot of appetizers! Don't you think that's too much food?" John says.

"Let's try them," she says lightly. "It will be fun."

"But still, don't—"

"Should we not get them?" ZZ shoots back. Her pupils flare as if ready to dance on the edge of a fire. "Should we just forget about it? We don't have to eat if you don't want to, you know."

The waiter watches impassively, his pen hovering over the pad like a stick insect frozen in flight.

"No, that's okay, no problem," John says, watching ZZ carefully. "I want to eat. I'm sorry, ZZ, I didn't mean anything."

"If it's a problem," ZZ says, pushing her chair back slightly, "let me know now. I—"

"No really, take it easy, let's get them, okay? But how about a tenth appetizer?" John says to ease the tension. "There's one you missed."

"Are you being funny?"

"I'm just kidding," John says. "Nine's enough."

"Anything to drink?" the waiter interjects.

"Just bottled water, non-sparkling. One large bottle. And lots of lemons," ZZ says. "Extra lemons."

"I'll get this order to the kitchen," the waiter says, turning toward the back.

"Extra cheese on the veal. Lots of cheese," ZZ calls after him. The waiter continues toward the kitchen without responding, his left leg dragging slightly behind the right.

"He's snotty, isn't he?" ZZ says to John. Her eyes dart about the restaurant like a machine gun strafing an open field before she locates a busser two tables over.

"ZZ, you have—"

"Busboy, excuse me," ZZ calls out. The busser is conversing with two silver-haired men drinking espresso, and the three of them look over.

The busser, an eager, pimply teenager about eighteen years of age, excuses himself and hurries over to ZZ.

"Ma'am?" the busser says.

"Can we get bread and butter, please?" ZZ says. The busboy nods his head. "And two glasses of water. Right away. Lots of lemon. The waiter didn't bring them yet."

John glances toward the kitchen in the rear of the restaurant. The waiter is quietly conferring with the barrel-chested manager and his hands flap around like panicked birds in a cage. The men look in his direction as they speak, but when the waiter makes eye contact with John, the waiter quickly looks away, giving John the same eerie feeling he had upon entering the restaurant.

──────────

The waiter arrives with a large round tray hoisted on his shoulder and heavily laden with plates of steaming food. He sets the tray on a stand he unfolds, and carefully rearranges the water glasses, vase, and condiment containers to make room for his delivery. One by one he unloads the bounty of food until all nine appetizers are squeezed onto the table, the waiter barely fitting each dish in the small space. He steps back and looks at the table packed full of food, grimacing slightly, before casting a last furtive glance at ZZ. The waiter then picks up his tray, collapses the stand with a sharp click, and retreats back toward the kitchen area.

"This looks good, ummmmm," ZZ says. She picks up John's plate and puts a portion of each of the nine dishes on it—asparagus tips, fried calamari, bruschetta, fried zucchini, mozzarella caprese, roast peppers and tomato, thin-sliced prosciutto, three mushrooms in oil, and artichoke hearts—and then serves herself the same nine portions.

ZZ tries the fried calamari first, chewing slowly, and looks over at John. "What do you think of the calamari?" she says.

"I'll get to it in a minute. I'm working on the mushrooms. What do you think?"

"It's like rubber, too chewy, they cooked it too long. I've never had one this overdone. You should send it back."

"Don't worry about it," John says, his face coloring. "What's one more dish to the tab?"

"We shouldn't pay for food that is no good. That's not right. I've had calamari all over this town—this is the worst yet. It's like rubber."

"It's no big deal," John says. "So we'll pay for one extra dish. Not a problem."

"Doc," ZZ says, warning him, "are you going to start arguing with me again? I can't be with someone who's going to argue with me about every little thing. You have to learn how to relax."

"Okay, alright, we'll send it back."

John nervously watches ZZ cut the zucchini in small bite-sized portions and nibble on one of the pieces.

"What's with this dish?" She makes a face. "It's horrible. Try it."

"If it's so bad, why would you want me to try it? You really don't like me, huh?"

She giggles. "You're funny! But really, it's no good. You would never know it's zucchini."

"Waiter, waiter," she yells across the restaurant. The waiter is taking dessert orders from two diners several tables over, and he turns around. "Here," ZZ calls over and waves her hand wildly. The waiter turns back to the couple and finishes taking their order. From behind, John can see the back of his head shaking involuntarily.

"This guy is half asleep," ZZ complains. "Someone has to wake him up. Really. I don't know what his problem is."

"Listen, you need—" John starts, but is interrupted by ZZ, whose attention is completely focused on the waiter.

"Waiter, waiter!" ZZ rings out again to his back. This time, the waiter, still busy at the other table, doesn't respond, though John sees his back stiffen.

ZZ turns to John and says, "They're slow around here."

John is about to say something, but ZZ's focus is so fixated on the waiter's back that he realizes she wouldn't hear a word and he holds his thoughts. Until the waiter limps over, about thirty seconds later, a disquieting silence reigns at the table.

The waiter positions himself at ZZ's left and looks down at her from his tall perch. His hair appears grayer than earlier and his face is knotted in tension.

"May I help you?" the waiter says superciliously.

"This calamari tastes like rubber. He doesn't want it," ZZ says, indicating John with her forefinger.

"Would you like me to have the chef cook you another order?"

"Not after this! We don't want it, right, Doc?" she says rhetorically, glancing at John, and then back at the waiter. "I don't know why the cook would even serve food this way. It tastes like rubber. And the zucchini is too salty." She indicates a plate of fried zucchini. "He doesn't want this one either."

"No problem at all," the waiter replies. "I'll take them back to the kitchen." He picks up the two plates and heads toward the rear.

"The calamari is too chewy, taste it yourself," she calls after the waiter.

"I think he got the idea," John whispers to her as the waiter heads off with the two discards.

"We shouldn't pay for them," she says irritably. "He was real snotty about it also. He's got a real attitude problem."

"Don't yell at me. I'm on your side!" John says.

"You tasted the calamari. Wasn't it like rubber?"

"ZZ, you ever hear the saying 'Beating a dead horse?'"

She giggles softly and playfully pinches John on the arm.

ZZ sends back two more appetizers, carefully explaining their shortcomings to the barrel-chested manager in the hand-tailored Italian suit when he comes over to check on their meal. He listens quietly, displeasure printed on his face like indelible bullet holes in a frozen carcass, while the waiter stiffly marches the rejected plates back to the kitchen, his left foot slightly dragging behind him. John gets that same bad feeling from the manager—he still can't get that image of the two goons from the Sicilian Social Club in Brooklyn out of his head—and is relieved when the Versace-clad man leaves the table.

A few minutes later the waiter returns with the main dishes. He sets to work rearranging the remaining appetizers and water glasses, pushing them to the edge of the table to make room. He sets the veal parmigiana in front of ZZ first, and then the pasta in front of John, placing them carefully as if he were an artist putting the finishing touches on a canvas.

"Light on the sauce and lots of cheese as requested," the waiter says, a hint of sarcasm coloring his voice. The portions are large, and ZZ's veal parmigiana overflows with cheese.

"I hope these meet with your satisfaction *this* time," the waiter says.

"Looks good to me," John says quickly, hoping to distract ZZ's attention from the waiter's last remark. The tension between her and the waiter is decidedly uncomfortable, as if they were two boxers at a prefight weigh-in holding such animosity for one another that their patience to wait until the official ringing of the bell to begin the violent festivities is cast in grave doubt.

"Can you bring some Parmesan cheese on the side?" ZZ says to the waiter. "He likes lots of cheese. And more lemons for the water."

The waiter rubs his hands together and briefly looks over at the pendant grapes hanging by the Venetian gondolas as if wondering whether wine could be made by stomping on them with his feet. "I'll have it sent over right away," the waiter says brusquely before departing.

ZZ spikes a piece of veal onto her fork and begins chewing on it when her phone rings. She checks the caller ID, makes a disgusted face, and turns the power off on the phone.

"Asshole," she mutters.

"Your ex?"

ZZ nods her head and takes a bite of the veal. "This is pretty chewy," she says, pointing at the veal with her fork.

"Why does he still call you?"

"I don't know. We have a business together," she says, still working the veal in her mouth. "He still runs it, but I don't have anything to do with it anymore, except he sends me a profit check every month."

"What kind of business?"

"It's an Internet company," ZZ says, her voice drifting off as she spies the waiter coming in their direction.

"Here is the cheese," the waiter says, approaching the table. He puts a silver cup filled with grated Parmesan in front of ZZ. "Is everything okay here?"

ZZ makes a face and says, "I don't like the veal. It's not tender. Can you take it away and have the chef prepare a better piece?"

The waiter snaps the plate off the table, and without uttering a word or looking at either one of them, returns to the kitchen holding the plate of food in front of him as if he's carrying a dead raccoon.

"Nasty thing, isn't he?" ZZ says.

John shrugs, hoping to divert her from the subject before she gets worked up. Her screaming fit in the cosmetics section flashes in his mind. He would shrivel in embarrassment if she embarked on another tirade in this quiet restaurant.

"What kind of business is it?" John innocently asks.

ZZ is distracted again. She watches the waiter limp toward the back and stop off to the side of the swinging doors that enter into the kitchen. John follows her eyes and sees the waiter and manager again conferring in the back. However, this time when his eyes meet John's, the waiter doesn't avert his look. Neither the manager nor the waiter is smiling. In fact, the manager is staring hard at John.

John looks back at his plate and picks at his food. He waits uncomfortably for ZZ to speak, barely containing a gasp of pain from the acids churning harder in his stomach, and unconsciously drops his left hand to press against its surface. ZZ is now watching the busboy chat with one of the silver-haired men, who glances back at the table, and waits for the eager teenager to turn in her direction so she can get him in motion with her next set of requests.

The atmosphere is heavy, as if the waiter, manager, and ZZ are careening on an unavoidable collision course already set in the fates of the evening, three cars hurtling forward, pedal to the metal. John hopes the outcome of the meal is more benign than the building tension suggests, but so far, he sees no armistice in sight, especially considering the way ZZ and the waiter are baiting one another. Meanwhile, ZZ's mien makes it clear she is unapproachable, at least until she gets hold of someone on the wait staff.

"I really don't like that waiter," ZZ finally says, her eyes fixed on the busboy. "What did you say?"

"What kind of Internet company do you have? Like selling stuff or—"

"Can we change the subject? Okay?" ZZ says. "I don't want to feel like I'm being integrated."

"Interrogated?"

"Whatever."

ZZ pulls a mirror out of her handbag, puts on a fresh coat of shimmering, faintly pink lip gloss, and replaces the metallic tube into her bag. Her lips smack together as she works the application on evenly, further highlighting lips that are full and sensuous. ZZ opens her mouth to call out to the busboy, but when he heads in the opposite direction, she turns her gaze back to John, looking at him for the first time in what seems like minutes.

"Do you want dessert tonight?" she asks, beaming.

"Is it okay if I finish dinner first?" John says, stunned at yet another mood change.

ZZ starts laughing. "You're so funny! But would you want some?"

"I think this will do it, ZZ. That was so much food, I'm about stuffed. I couldn't eat any dessert. Not a thing more."

ZZ's face turns dark and she puts down her knife and fork. "I have to go to the bathroom."

"What's the matter?" John stammers. "Is everything okay?"

"I'm fine."

"You seem upset."

"I said everything is fine." ZZ abruptly pushes her chair back and stalks off to the restroom, leaving the chair jutting three feet into the aisle.

The waiter comes by and pushes it back toward the table. "The veal will be out in a few minutes. Can I take any dishes away?"

"I'm not sure, maybe it's best to leave them for now. You can get rid of the bread basket though. I don't think we'll need that. Let me ask you," John says, trying to ingratiate himself with the waiter, "what's the best show in town, something I have to see?"

The waiter puts the butter into the bread basket and lifts it off the table. "Well, that all depends, of course. Siegfried and Roy at the Mirage was a long-running Las Vegas standard, but that dreadful and unfortunate tiger incident ate that one up, so to speak. However, you could see one of the Cirque du Soleil shows—those are always terrific." The waiter leans his other hand on the back of ZZ's chair. "You staying on the Strip?"

"Well, right off it. A buddy of mine and myself are staying at the Hidden Treasure. We just got here a few hours ago. I'm pretty much right off the boat."

"The Hidden Treasure? Really?"

"You from here?" John queries, ignoring the waiter's reaction.

"Heavens no, nobody is. From Chicago originally, been here seventeen years now. Housing and food are cheap, wages are good, lots of nightlife, everything can be had twenty-four hours a day. Works for me."

"This must be a weird town to live in. With all the gambling and the fast life, must be people of questionable character everywhere, I guess."

"You have to watch yourself at every step, if you know what I mean," the waiter says, clearing his throat a few times and looking into John's eyes as if his throat-clearing contained a deeper message than shifting phlegm in his respiratory system to a different location.

John isn't sure what the waiter is getting at, but decides he'd rather not know. He is about to ask about restaurant recommendations when he sees ZZ coming back from the bathroom at a frenetic pace.

"Enjoy your stay here," the waiter says, making sure to leave before her arrival. He walks off with the bread basket, taking a circuitous route out of ZZ's path.

"What were you talking about with that loser?" ZZ says, sitting stiffly in her chair.

"Nothing really. Do you want dessert?" John asks.

"Why would I want dessert?" she snaps back, her eyes glowing like freshly fanned embers in a campfire.

"I don't know, it seemed like you might have wanted to try something before."

"Not after what you said."

"What did I say?"

"You know what you said."

The waiter comes by with another veal parmigiana, slides it in front of ZZ, and moves on to another table.

"I don't know," John says. "I really don't know."

"You don't remember what you said?"

"Of course, I know what I said, but what exactly of what I said that's bothering you, I have no clue. We've been here for more than an hour!" John says exasperated. "Please tell me."

"Don't play dumb, you know what you said." ZZ's voice rises. She takes a bite of the veal, chews on it a bit, and pushes the plate away.

"ZZ, I have no clue what you're talking about. Please, tell me what's the matter. What did I say?"

John groans and puts his fork down as well. Suddenly he feels the potential void of a girl who has put some light and movement in his boring and static world of long numbers and long hours. A depth of despair quickly engulfs him and moves off, swirling above his head, a rain cloud that touched down but still hovers nearby, threatening. This marvelous high-strung woman is nothing like anyone he's ever met, and he is entranced and already sees himself being drawn into the embrace of her web. But he can also see it all slipping away, irrevocably, with the wrong comment.

John rubs his hand back over his hair and takes a long drink of water.

"Well, maybe *I* wanted to get dessert," ZZ says.

"Well, go ahead, let's get some." John turns around and waves to the waiter.

"I don't want dessert anymore."

"Why not? I don't understand."

"Why should I want dessert after you slammed the door shut on me and said you didn't want any?"

John is incredulous. "You only asked if I want any, you didn't say *you* wanted dessert!"

"Whatever." ZZ is staring off to some spot about a foot above and wide of John's head.

"I'm sorry. I didn't understand that you wanted dessert. I thought you were only asking me if I wanted to order some."

"You already told me that. I heard you the first time."

"Come on," John says, "let's get something, okay?"

"Didn't I just tell you five seconds ago that I didn't want dessert? Are you paying attention to me or thinking about some girlfriend back home somewhere?" ZZ turns in her chair so that she faces completely away from him.

John sees the waiter approaching and waves him away. "That's not fair. I'm sorry, ZZ, I didn't mean to, you know, start anything. Can we make up?"

ZZ is lost in thought, staring blindly across the restaurant as a heavy silence descends over the meal. Her face is bathed in harsh shadows, and her eyes, black orbits floating in pools of dark light, appear to balance delicately on a precipice between hard darkness ricocheting in dangerous currents and soft light bathing in stilled water.

John looks down at the table and fiddles with his fork, apprehensive about the reaction that will emerge from the swinging pendulum of her moods. He becomes painfully cognizant of the sounds around him: a man ripping open a sugar packet, a spoon slowly stirring the sweetener in a double espresso and grating harshly against the bottom of the porcelain cup, the low whirling hum of an overhead fan, and the slight whip of his fork as it turns in his hand.

The busser passes in front of ZZ and she doesn't seem to notice, the first time the eager teenager has had a free pass from her all evening.

"Okay then!" ZZ exclaims after some seconds pass. Like the flick of a switch, the darkness that shadowed her eyes disappears and ZZ's engaging and infectious smile, framing perfect white teeth, explodes with happiness. She licks her lips playfully and serves up more appetizers onto his plate. John, riding her moods like a car in stop-and-go traffic, feels the heaviness around them dissipate, and he smiles too.

"These are good, uhm," she says, reaching across while John opens his mouth and accepts the proffered food. "Uhm. Fresh string beans. The best." She fishes another string bean from the plate with her fingers and dangles it teasingly in front of him.

"Open big," she coos and slides it into John's mouth, her fingers softly brushing against his lips.

ZZ cuts a big slice of veal and chews on it without remark, apparently finding this new portion more to her liking. She smiles at John as she lifts up her glass and pours a liberal amount of water over her hands, rubbing them together vigorously. Water cascades down through her fingers and over her veal and a small stream spills onto the table, creating a large wet spot next to the plate. ZZ quickly dries her hands with a napkin and dabs at the corner of her lips.

"Let's go!" she whispers fervently to John, her face flush with bursting energy.

"You don't want any coffee or tea or whatever?"

"No, let's go," she says, a strange excitement in her voice.

"I'll get the check." John raises his arm, catches the waiter's attention, and makes a scribbling motion. He pulls out his wallet and tosses a credit card on the table.

ZZ abruptly stands up and heads toward the door. John watches her stride across the restaurant. She pauses by the door and turns back toward him, flashing a mischievous smile full of bright, white teeth and lots of promise.

John—flustered, bewildered, and confused—looks back at the perturbed face of the barrel-chested manager in the hand-cut Versace suit and then back at ZZ, poised at the door, ready to fly like a bird freshly out of a cage, on the cusp of freedom. John has a decision to make.

It's now or never.

Chapter Six

He goes for it.

Everything happens quickly, a blur on fast-forward. When ZZ strolls out the exit, and the whoosh of the closing door behind her reverberates softly in the air, there's a moment of eerie silence before an explosion of noise, as simultaneously, as if choreographed by a master, John, Versachi, and the waiter come alive in a whirl of movement.

John stands up quickly, but in his panic, his thighs violently collide with the table's edge when he neglects to push his chair free, sending the furniture over on its side like a toppled pole struck by a car. The waiter crashes hard to the floor with the upended table, his round tray sailing off his hand like a flying saucer. It spins over a neighboring table and into a wall, its contents splattering loudly against its surface. Fresh, steaming food, the colors of the Italian flag—ravioli pesto, fettuccini alfredo, and eggplant parmigiana—gets tossed and strewn in all directions, painting the surface of the white walls in a patriotic Italian fresco of greens, whites, and reds.

John looks about for a moment, stunned at the sudden chaos around him, and makes a mad dash toward the exit. The tablecloth, which he had inadvertently tucked into his pants along with his napkin, ludicrously trails behind him like a long white tail. Crystal glasses, plates topped with partially eaten appetizers, and silverware trapped on the linen clatter on their magic carpet ride like the magnified and frantic sounds of vigorously shaken dice at a craps table.

In feverish pursuit, the manager hurdles over both the downed waiter and the table, surprisingly nimble for such a big man, and lands on the tail edge of the tablecloth trailing behind John. The hard yank of the cloth sends him tumbling sideways, and the big man and a nearby table go down in a flurry of falling objects. More glasses, silverware, plates, flower vases, and salt and pepper shakers scatter about the floor in an explosion of jarring sounds. Two more tables go down like dominos, their contents spewing across the floor as well, with a third one pushed back and tottering, its salt and pepper shakers whizzing off the edge like two fallen ice skaters skittering across a frozen pond.

On the opposite side of the cloth, the brakelike action caused by the weight of the manager landing on the cloth and its sudden release snaps the tablecloth free from John's pants and propels him forward into an ancient-looking vase by the entryway, sending both objects to the floor. The vase shatters into pieces and a profusion of old dust, like a mini–mushroom cloud from an atomic explosion, rises from the crash. The tablecloth, now free, lays benignly on the floor, expressionless, an innocent party to the pandemonium surrounding its wild adventure. On either side of its ends, separated by a dozen paces, two men sprawled on the floor frantically clear their heads and scramble to their feet.

John, up first, quickly reaches the front door, opens it, and is out and running for all he's worth. The big manager, knocking shards of butter plates, glasses, and flower petals off his clothing, is up two seconds later and in full pursuit. Out the door, about a hundred steps ahead of John, ZZ races down the street, her head held high, a wild mare that has just shot through the confines of captivity and gained the freedom of the open range. Her hair flows bountifully behind her and her arms pump up and down exuberantly, a purebred born to run. In seconds, the sprinting form of ZZ disappears around the corner and out of John's view.

The barrel-chested manager with the hand-tailored Italian suit emerges from the restaurant like a matador's bull bursting out of its holding pen and into the stadium, screaming profanities in mixed English and Italian at the fleeing customer. John soon wins the corner, and glancing back as he turns, sees the manager halted outside the restaurant, red-faced and waving his fists in anger.

Well down the block, ZZ barely slows as she makes a right-angle turn down an alleyway. John sprints after her, struggling for breath as he runs, with nine appetizers, two glasses of wine, and a good portion of penne alla vodka hanging heavy in his stomach. He reaches the alleyway where he last saw ZZ and heads down it, throwing a last glance behind him to confirm he is not being followed. At the end, gasping for air, he ducks behind a large green garbage bin, utterly exhausted and unable to go any farther. If they're going to catch him and do what they have to do, well, he can't go another step. That's it, that's all he's got.

But where did ZZ go?

John sucks hard for oxygen as he assesses the situation. He can't believe what just occurred, this sudden bout of insanity, the wanton destruction in the restaurant, and the wild flight down the street away from a massive mobster. Of all things, John Howard-Hughes, the accountant who never so much as stole a bar of candy, is now hiding like a two-bit criminal behind a trash bin in a Las Vegas alley.

What the hell did he just do?

Chapter Seven

Bad enough John has just made himself into a common criminal in a mad compulsive act so far out of character he cannot believe what just transpired; now he has also lost ZZ into the night! There is no way to contact her. He has no idea where she lives or works, and he has no phone number for her. In fact, he knows almost nothing about her. What he does know is that he had more fun and thrills with her this brief evening—and managed to get in more trouble—than he can ever remember in his entire life.

But at what price?

John's breathing echoes hard off the concrete. He feels lost and empty in a god-forsaken alleyway in a strange city that just got that much stranger. In frustration, he bangs his hand hard against the side of the dumpster, the resounding echoes of the metal reverberating like a sonorous wail. John cradles his head in both his hands, covering his eyes and rubbing them with the heels of his palms.

What happened to that magical girl who, in the mad flight out of the restaurant, disappeared into the night? John is so distraught and confused that he thinks he hears giggling mixed in with the heavy echoes of pounded metal, and in frustration he bangs the dumpster again.

"Boo!" ZZ yells out, appearing as if by magic from behind a wall, her chest heaving up and down, her face red with excitement. She is exhilarated.

"Wasn't that fun?"

────────

While John peeks around the alleyway to see if the coast is clear, ZZ brazenly motors past him onto the street and turns left, heading back in the direction of the restaurant and the main thoroughfare.

"Come on, let's go," ZZ calls out. She is already several strides past John and moving like a car jammed into fifth gear.

"Geez, you're so crazy," John says, feeling foolish with his cloak-and-dagger peek around the bend.

"Hurry up!"

"Hold on," John says with alarm, hurrying after her. "We can't go that way."

"They're already back inside. Stop worrying."

"ZZ, wait," John runs a few steps to catch up. "That was crazy in the restaurant. Why did you do that?" he asks.

"Do what?" ZZ snaps back.

"The rest—"

"You really should chill out a little sometimes, Doc. Take some Valium or something. I don't know what your problem is. No wonder you haven't had a girlfriend in two years, three years, whatever you told me before. I mean, really."

"That's not—"

"Doc," ZZ says, saying the word in an upward lilt, like a warning.

"Okay, you're right." John sighs as he quickens his pace to keep up with her brisk walk. "You know, I really have fun hanging out with you. I'm glad we met."

ZZ brightens up like a light switch flicked on. "Me too!"

A taxi appears down the street, facing away from them and idling at a red light. ZZ grabs John's hand and they start running to catch it.

"Wheeeeeeeeeee," ZZ shrieks giddily, her hair flowing in the breeze.

ZZ takes John to an apartment in a semi-upscale two-story complex several miles from the Strip, near the intersection of Russell Road and Mountain Vista. This part of Las Vegas, where few tourists have occasion to visit, is a sprawling suburbia of one- and two-story southwestern and ranch-style homes, mostly in small gated communities, mixed in ubiquitously, as elsewhere in Las Vegas, with big empty lots awaiting development, in development, or recently built as the city and suburbs of Las Vegas push their way farther into the desert. Scattered between the housing communities are two-story low- to middle-income apartment complexes, the architecture of one resembling the other, with the same light colors favored in the southwest, featuring pools, desert landscaping dominated by salmon-colored rocks, mesquite, incongruous green grass, and covered outdoor parking to protect the inhabitants' vehicles from the punishing rays of the sun. Not that long ago, even as little as two decades earlier, this area was parched desert land dotted by occasional ranches and homesteads, and before that, empty desert, a state of existence it had endured for tens of thousands of years. But the fervor of gambling and the hand of man, inspired by the rattling of six-sided red dice and the mad spirit of chance, carved up and remolded the landscape into a man-made mirage.

John and ZZ sit close together on a very soft, light tan Italian leather couch. John is sipping out of a tall glass filled with a strong screwdriver, the second one that ZZ has mixed for him, the color a soft plush orange. He is content to wind down and relax for the first time since his early-morning start back in New York. Reflecting over all the things that went wrong in this tumultuous day—the delayed takeoff from JFK, the lost luggage, his and Ludo's disappointment over the ride in a cramped and dirty vehicle when they were expecting a limousine, and subsequent bigger disappointment when their first-class accommodations weren't first class at all but a miserable shoebox of a room in a dumpy hotel with a very strange receptionist. And finally, the debacle at the Amiga Bella restaurant—the nine appetizers, the parade of food going back and forth to the kitchen, ZZ's volatile mood swings, their skipping out on the bill and wrecking the restaurant, and the hasty flight from Versachi, the brooding and massive manager. John has trouble believing that the events of this day, easily the most insane of his life, have occurred in such a brief span of time.

His ruminations float with the vodka, his thoughts dulled and slowed by the alcohol. The evening, the whole day as he ponders it, feels more like a dream or a movie he's watched from outside his skin than his own reality. He looks over at ZZ. She sits quietly holding a glass filled with water, a few ice cubes, and two lemon slices. This is the first time he has seen her tranquil, as if the high-powered energy of her turbulent charge through the day had expended itself and the forces of gravity and resistance had slowed her to a halt, the full throttle of her fifth gear downshifted to a steady, calm hum, a smooth idle in neutral.

"Is it okay if I slip into something more comfortable?" ZZ asks.

"Sure."

"I'll be right back, okay?" she says and walks into the bedroom, gently closing the door behind her.

John takes the opportunity to look around the apartment. Outside of a couch with end tables, a low and long iron and glass table in front of him, and a small television perched in a simple entertainment center, there is little in the way of furniture or knickknacks to suggest that anyone permanently resides here. He notices no personal effects—no photographs, birthday or holiday cards, magazines, clothes, or other items lying around as he would expect. The walls are bare except for a few unremarkable prints in plain frames, decorated no better than a cheap motel room. The only item John can see that varies from the generic is a small well-stocked bar in the corner, though that piece of furniture could be considered as generic as anything else.

John wanders over to the kitchen. He is greeted by more basics, again seeing nothing that implies that an individual has put his or her personal touch on the apartment. Even the refrigerator, bare of the magnets, corkboards, and little notes one typically expects in a woman's kitchen, suggests nothing resembling a feminine touch. Finding nothing interesting, John returns to the couch and takes another sip of his screwdriver.

The door to the bedroom opens and ZZ steps out. She is ravishing in a one-piece red nightie that barely reaches below her upper thighs. The clinging fabric is sheer across the midriff and cut to reveal the curvaceous swell of firm, well-formed breasts. She has a big smile on her face and her eyes are lowered and turned downward, as if bashful.

"Shall I model it for you?" she asks quietly.

"Wow, you look great, ZZ."

On the radio, a sultry Whitney Houston song, "My Love is Your Love," plays softly. After John's long stressful day, the relaxing vodkas, ambient light, and soothing tones of Houston's song are perfect for the evening.

"Well?"

"Yes, of course," John says.

ZZ giggles, starts turning around, then changes her mind. "I'm shy," she says, smiling coyly, and returns to the same spot as before on the couch.

Something in the back of John's brain, like an incessant knocking on the door that is being ignored, has been rattling around his skull and bothering him. He leans forward, finally getting a handle on it, and realizes what he couldn't put together earlier. He abruptly puts his drink on the table, stands up, and pulls his wallet out from his back pocket.

"Oh my god!" John says as he riffles through his wallet.

"What's the matter?"

"I don't have my credit card!"

"You don't have it?"

"No, it must be in the restaurant. I think I left it on the table when I took it out."

"Are you sure?"

"I'm pretty sure. If it's not here," John says, emptying the contents of his wallet on the table and examining each item individually, "I don't know where else it could be. I think I left it there. Actually, I know I did. On the table, that's where I put it."

"That was dumb. Why did you do that?" ZZ says.

"Everything happened so fast. One minute we're eating, the next I'm being chased by some ape two hundred times my size, and then I'm hiding behind a dumpster. I don't even know what happened."

John wipes his head as if sweating, but his hand comes away dry.

"What's the big deal? You can still charge things. You have another credit card, don't you?"

John remains quiet.

"Really, what's the big deal about one credit card?" ZZ says. "Just get another. You have to chill out. You make such a big deal about everything."

"ZZ, the Mafia guys there, now they know who I am! I'm screwed."

"Don't worry about things so much! We already talked about that. You said that guy you call your friend told you that also."

"But they know who I am!"

"Shhhh, sit here," she says to John and pats the spot next to her like a toddler would do. John obliges and she nods for him to sit closer. Their legs touch and John feels the warmth radiate from her bare skin.

ZZ moves closer to John so that they sit side by side. The sweet, alluring fragrance of her perfume enticingly wafts in his nostrils and the fingers of her right hand dance on his leg. She reaches back to lower the lamp, casting the light of the room into soft shadows. She undoes a pin on her head, placing it on the coffee table in front of them, and shakes back her long, luxuriant hair.

"I love this music," John says.

"Do you really?" ZZ purrs, her eyes far away. "Have you always liked it . . . " Before John can answer, she swings her legs over his lap and straddles him.

John drinks in her subtle perfume, breathing deeply as he feels the warmth of her body spread through his. His skin, extra sensitive now, tingles. ZZ runs her hand through his hair, and firmly gripping the back of his head, pulls her pulsating body to his.

Ludo is snoring methodically in the hotel room when a violently ringing phone interrupts its steady pattern. As yet, he does not awaken, but lies fitfully in a half-dreamlike state. It is ten-thirty at night and he barely has much sleep invested into the evening. The phone rings three more times before Ludo fully awakens. Startled, he sits up in bed and looks around to get his bearings. It is dark in the room, and for a moment Ludo has no idea where he is. As unfamiliar objects start to take shape in the darkness, he remembers: He is in a hotel room in Las Vegas, on vacation with his buddy, John Howard-Hughes. By the fifth ring, his last dream, a nice fantasy about a ride in a red convertible filled with four beautiful young women, has faded away.

He reaches over and picks up the receiver. "Ludo's Pool Hall, Eight Ball speaking," he says sleepily.

There is silence for a few seconds.

"Hello. Hello?" Ludo says.

A thick Brooklyn-Italian accent comes over the line. "Howard-Hughes, please."

"He's not here, man. Can I take a message?"

"When will he be back?"

"I'm not sure, maybe an hour, I don't know. Shall I tell him who's calling?"

"I'll call back, thanks."

Ludo groans and drops back into the comfort and warmth of the bed. Within seconds, he is back in the convertible, and dreams of everything beautiful envelop his every sleeping sense.

Like ravished rabbits making up for lost time, John and ZZ plunge into the night and enjoy each other's company. Pent-up passions penetrate deep into the aura of their souls; flesh meets flesh, fire meets fire. They work their way from the couch to the bedroom floor and then to the bed, traversing their way around the apartment in a night of deep expressions. Clothes are hastily flung off in various directions and are strewn about the apartment, with the last items scattered across the bed and surrounding floor. Music plays softly and two candles, having run their course to the end of their wicks, cast their last flickering shadows against the bare walls and expire within a minute of one another. The gods walk with these humans this evening, taking them places well beyond their comprehension. Time goes slowly, blissfully, and after expending deep psychic energies, John's breathing becomes fuller and rhythmic, and his eyes close.

It is eleven-thirteen in the evening, a little more than thirty minutes after the first call, when the phone rings again in the hotel room. Ludo instantly awakens, jarred by the invasive noise that shakes him from a troubled sleep. This time, without lifting his head off the pillow or opening his eyes, he reaches blindly and picks up the phone on the first ring.

"Yo," Ludo says.

The voice on the other end has a familiar accent. "Howard-Hughes, please."

"Still not back. You want to leave a message?"

"Just tell him a very good friend is calling. I'll try later."

Ludo opens his eyes and looks at the clock. He sees that it reads 11:13, but he can't figure out if it is morning or night. He replaces the receiver in its cradle and leans his head back on the soft pillow. It is not long before consciousness turns over its keys to the subconscious and the sounds of snoring and deep breathing fill the room.

ZZ watches John's sleeping form for some minutes, then closes her eyes, but remains awake. They hold each other closely, arms and legs wrapped around one another. Restless, and preferring to see rather than imagine, ZZ opens her eyes again.

"Doc," ZZ whispers into the night, waking John up.

John opens his eyes and sees ZZ's face inches from his. Her eyes are dark and deep, and the wildness that rollicked in her pupils during the day is nowhere in sight. Instead, a stillness prevails, and it is then, John realizes, that her beauty emanates from the warm depth of her eyes, a magnetic force that draws him deeper into whatever manifestations and mysteries a man's soul finds in a true meeting with a woman.

"Yes?" John says.

"Nothing."

There is little other talk this night, and none is needed. The communications between ZZ and John are sent wordlessly, by touch, by mood, by the many gifts of human expressions. In the middle of a city of lights that are too bright, where bad realities crash head-on and destroy the weaker or more unfortunate, two denizens of the earth, dropped onto the planet for some reason far beyond their ken and tossed together by the winds of fate, share a magical evening bathed in the inviting warmth of halcyon darkness.

It is but a brief respite from the dark edges of this city, and for now, they savor it, soak it in like a weary body enveloped in hot bathwater. It is safe where they are and how they are, and in this protected harbor, the night licks and salves their inner wounds. However, when the morning sun arises in the desert, as desert thorn bushes, tumbleweed, cacti, wild sage, and scorpions heat up with the sun, and as the garish neon-lit beasts of the city turn off their glow, somewhere in Las Vegas, a rooster will crow its early-morning call.

And it will be a new day.

Chapter Eight

John is in the middle of a disturbing dream in which he is savagely thirsty but cannot reach the oasis before him. Mutant scorpions taller than a man jealously guard the sparkling waters and chase the human intruder, moving awkwardly on hairy and gangly legs. John runs, but the repulsive beasts are faster. He feels their hot breath and hears the clacking sound of their shell-like skeletal feet on the hard desert floor directly behind him. Just as one beast's clammy appendage grabs his shoulder, John abruptly awakens, breathing heavily and in a sweat. ZZ has shaken him awake from this nightmare and stands over him next to the bed. The sun has not yet risen and the light from its impending arrival has just started coloring the sky with pastel hues of soft yellows, lightly brushed oranges, and faint pinks. John glances at the digital clock by the bed and watches a new minute click before his eyes. It is exactly five thirty A.M. ZZ is already dressed for the day, wearing pink cotton shorts with a matching halter top that exposes a flat, tanned stomach. She is holding a glass of orange juice that she offers him.

"Don't you sleep?" John asks as he sits up to take the glass.

"I love you," ZZ says. She is smiling, but her eyes have a troubled look, a haunting distraction to them that John recognizes from the day before.

John takes a long swill of orange juice and swallows loudly. He hands the glass back to ZZ and drops back on the pillow.

"Aren't you going to say something?" she says.

"I'm sorry. The orange juice is delicious. It's wonderful. Thank you."

"You know what I mean."

"We just met," John says.

"Go ahead." ZZ puts her hand on John's leg and nods her head as if to manually move John's lips.

"Okay. Me too. I love me also," John says.

"Come on, silly. Just say it once and I'll be happy."

"I like you a lot."

"That's not funny." ZZ removes her hand from his leg and her back stiffens.

"Okay, okay, okay. I love you."

ZZ's face breaks out in a radiant smile. "I've known you less than twelve hours," she says, her eyes bright. "Doesn't it seem like forever?"

———————

As evidenced by a few weak rays clawing their way through the small window high up by the ceiling, it is morning in the hotel room where Ludo, after a night of tossing and turning, floats somewhere between consciousness and sleep. He is resting on his side when the phone rings. Ludo yawns deeply before answering it.

"Bankrupt and Louie, Accountants, Zero Balance speaking," Ludo says thickly.

The same heavily accented voice from the night before is on the other end of the line. "Did Howard-Hughes get back yet?"

"Out of luck. Sure you don't want to leave a number? I don't know when he's coming back."

Ludo glances at the clock. It is six forty-five in the morning and he wonders where John is. Probably trying his blackjack system, he figures.

"I want to surprise him," says the voice on the other end. "Thanks anyway."

"Suit yourself."

The phone line goes dead, disconnected on the other end. Ludo replaces the receiver, yawns mightily, and turns over on his other side.

———

ZZ, full of energy and looking like a greyhound ready to spring from the opening gate at the races and madly pursue a mechanical rabbit, stands over John with her hands on her hips and impatiently watches him put on his shirt. It is five forty-five in the morning and John, exhausted from just a few hours of sleep, moves sluggishly. ZZ keeps looking at the door as if expecting someone to enter at any minute, and her eyes dart madly about the room.

John finishes buttoning up his shirt, but discovering that he is a notch off, he undoes the arrangement and starts again. This time John begins from the top button, methodically lining up the buttons and holes carefully.

"Hurry up, let's go!" ZZ says.

Any residue of tranquility from the night before is gone; the stick shift is out of neutral and jammed into fifth gear. ZZ is in motion.

"You have to get to work?" John asks.

"Just hurry, I like to get an early start on the day," she says. "I'll wait by the front, but hurry up."

———

It is a few minutes after six o'clock in the morning when John alights from ZZ's car in front of the Stardust Hotel and Casino, one of the oldest gambling houses in Las Vegas. He is barely out of the car before ZZ speeds off with the passenger-side door still open, waving goodbye as she races down the street. John watches the car turn sharply and leave a thick black stain on the first corner, the screech of rubber on cement crisp in the early morning. He wonders if ZZ is actually in a rush or knows no other velocity than that of a rocket hurtling forward.

John pulls out his cell phone and tries the number ZZ gave him, questioning whether it is legitimate. It is. ZZ answers on the first ring.

"Hi Doc," she says brightly. "You miss me?"

"All the way, that's for sure. You know, you almost took off my arm when you left, you lunatic. Jesus, ZZ, let me at least close the door to the car next time before you drive off!"

"I thought you were out of the car," she says laughing. "I have to go, I'm on the phone. Call me later, okay? Bye," she says a little too quickly and hangs up.

John pauses, his lips pursed to say more, but the connection is gone. He feels slightly disconcerted by the abrupt termination of the call, but at the same time relieved that ZZ has provided him with the correct number and that he will be able to contact her again.

John stares at the last vestiges of the surreal neon glow of the casinos' marquees along the Strip backlit against the oncoming glow of the desert morning, a strange juxtaposition of real and unreal. He walks along Las Vegas Boulevard for a bit, getting a feel of the Strip when it is sedate. Then, taking one last breath of the fresh morning air, he retraces his steps and enters the Stardust, figuring he'll kill some time before he heads back to check on Ludo, maybe win a few bucks on the way and take his mind off the conflicting thoughts rattling around in the back of his brain.

The casino is quiet this early in the morning. The late revelers have mostly called it a night, and it is still too early for the compulsive gambling locals, the ones who play until their money dries up like water splattered on the 115-degree asphalt and then anxiously wait until their payday arrives to repeat the weekly grind. The early birds, who are just now getting up or preparing to hit the buffets, have not yet migrated to the tables either.

After circling the blackjack tables twice, like a shark closing in on an impending meal, John finds a table he likes, joining a bleary-eyed lady somewhere in her seventies. A massive stack of chips is spread in front of her across three spots like a treasure chest of spilled coins. Seeing the old woman's overflowing pool of green and black chips, John figures the table has been kind to her so far, and better to ride with good luck than with bad. As John situates himself at the table, he sees that his first impressions of the woman belie a deeper and sadder truth: It is not luck the woman is riding, but an unraveling weave of deep desperation and loneliness, of ennui and apathy, a beast of burden no longer able to carry the psychic load. The bleary-eyed woman wearily pushes out a flat three hundred dollar bet after every loss, or pulls back a stack when she wins so that the same three hundred dollar bet is made on each hand, regardless of the previous outcome. Her face, deeply drawn by lack of sleep and bloated by untold amounts of alcohol and coffee, has no more emotion in it than the clay-composite chips she mechanically pushes out hand after hand. Win or lose, her expression stays the same, as if winning or losing has no bearing on anything relevant to her—which, apparently, it doesn't.

At the table adjacent to John, three male gamblers in their mid-twenties with two small piles of red five-dollar-chips in front of their positions congregate around a single betting spot. They barely hang in there against the forces of sleep deprivation, trying to get every last ounce out of their big night, though it is clear, even from where John sits, that between the exhaustion of their long binge and the copious amounts of alcohol they have so obviously consumed, that they can barely make out the pips on their cards. It also seems clear, given the mismatch at this point in time, that it will be the casino that will win and suck every last bit of juice out of their drying fruit, rather than them making a dent in the casino's ocean of resources. And apparently, judging by the third drunk hanging on to the back of one of his friend's chairs, the first of the three players' bankrolls has already been laid waste. Maybe the second's as well.

The young men trying futilely to preserve their five-dollar red chips might be skunk-high drunk, but the woman at John's table, comparatively, is levels beyond and past them in a state of inebriation, appearing to be just a few drinks away from a comatose state. When the waitress brings John a cup of coffee, she whispers to him that the woman has been playing and drinking for thirty-six hours straight, not leaving the table once to take a break or even go to the bathroom, a remarkable feat in itself. It is a scene unlike anything John has ever witnessed or could imagine happening anywhere else but the gaming hells of Las Vegas. The old woman's face, fixed in an unflinching granitelike expression, and her robotic, sparse movements would be a marvel if they weren't so haunting. Her hands, perfectly manicured and elegant, ironic against this tawdry scene, seem to be the only visually functioning part of her body. They move only to handle her cards, her bets, or her drinks, or to reach back with a red five-dollar toke each time her whiskey is delivered, which is often. The woman never looks at the cocktail waitress, letting her know when she wants another Jack Daniel's, served straight up on the rocks, by tapping her glass with her long red fingernails, nor does she look at the dealer—just her cards, her chips, and her drink. Her head never shifts an inch in either direction, not left or right, not up or down, as if it had been created and welded into a semi-permanent position specifically for the purpose of overseeing wagers and viewing cards. She has the look of a woman who has lived around a lot of money and obviously still has a pile to play with, but it is money that has somehow gone bad for her. And now, mired in a history that has overwhelmed her present, she seems to be drowning her sorrows in a painful and obsessive ritual of self-flagellation.

"It is one of the saddest sights I ever did see, I'm telling you," the waitress whispers to John in a voice paved with layers of nicotine and tar and raspy from decades of hard smoking. Her hand rests briefly on John's shoulder, dry and unnaturally light to the touch, feeling like a parrot's claw. "I'm wishin' I had her money to burn like that. Good luck, honey," she says, looking at John incisively before continuing, "with everything."

The waitress clears her throat and moves away, a smell of stale whiskey from her last words left hanging in the air.

John glances back at his neighbor, the old lady plastered into a world of hazed oblivion, who doesn't even have the good fortune to lose so that this sad and grotesque spectacle can end. Nothing short of dropping from exhaustion or dropping dead itself would get the woman off that chair and away from this grueling contest before all her chips were gone. That was clear. The casino wasn't going to suggest she take a break, nor did the woman volunteer to move, if at this point she could even do so. She was going to play her hand for all it is worth, right to the very end. She was the customer and wanted to play; the casino wanted to get its chips back. It was a maudlin match with time on the casino's side. Though the old woman was riding a remarkable run of luck, it was going to turn, as it inevitably did. Already, thirty-six hours into this marathon gambling session, the woman has exhibited amazing physical fortitude and stupendous luck.

John is reminded of the old movie, *They Shoot Horses, Don't They?*, in which depression-era couples, struggling to be the last ones standing, danced till they dropped, hoping for the big prize that would pave a way out of their financial desperation. Only here, with the bleary-eyed lady, there was no prize in the end, only the end itself. And there was no dancing partner, just a slow waltz on a hard, lonely slab of time and bad fortune. John makes a mental note to check the following day's paper; he has a bad feeling about where this macabre dance might end.

Sure enough, the woman's card luck carries over to John. Chips begin piling in front of him in small, neat stacks as he wins hand after hand. Betting between five dollars and twenty dollars per hand, he knows without adding up the chips that he is, at the very least, several hundred dollars ahead. But the long night and previous day's travails take a toll on his energies. Around eight o'clock in the morning, John realizes that he has lost his concentration and is too exhausted to continue with any effectiveness. Taking the advice of his blackjack book—to quit when ahead or when too tired to play optimally—he gathers the chips in front of him and stands up to leave. He takes a last sad look at his erstwhile table companion. The woman, having lost a hand, mechanically pushes three hundred dollars more onto her betting spot, taking no more notice of John's departure than she did of his

arrival. After more than two hours at the table, John has not heard the woman utter a word, change her bet, or even look in his direction, and he walks away from the blackjack game wondering if the woman even knew he was there at all.

He goes to the back of the casino where the casino cage is located, glad to stretch his legs a bit, and pushes the red and green chips across to the cashier, getting U.S. greenbacks in return. He stuffs the cash in his front pants pocket and heads out of the exit.

After the long night, the fresh air and morning sun outside the Stardust feel good on John's face. He tips the doorman a dollar and hops into a cab, letting the driver know that the Hidden Treasure Hotel and Casino is his destination. The taxi arrives quicker than John would have liked, about eight hours quicker—a good night of sleep's worth. The few minutes' worth of nap in the cab is woefully too short and makes him feel more exhausted than before he had closed his eyes in the first place. John pays the fare and wearily drags his body out of the cab, into the hotel, and to his room at the end of the hall on the third floor, room number 313.

Ludo is watching sports highlights on the television when John enters the room. He is wearing bathing trunks he stored in his carry-on knapsack, and his bare feet are propped up on the bed.

"What up, Ludo?"

"Hey, what up, stranger?" Ludo says, and uses the remote to shut off the television. "It seems like the phone rang every time I tried to get a good sleep running, but you ain't looking like the freshest daisy in the field either. Long night, huh?"

John drops a pile of money on Ludo's bed.

"What'd you rob a convenience store?" Ludo says.

"Three hundred and eighty-seven dollars! A little blackjack donation from the casinos."

"Not bad, big boy," Ludo says. "So that blackjack system you talk about works then?"

"All the way."

"Good, moneybags, you're treating for chow downstairs."

———————

It is eight forty-five in the morning, predawn for revelers and gamblers who run the night right into the morning in Las Vegas, and late morning for reformed gamblers who've had their livings and possessions whipped out of them in years past and now use the morning sunshine as the start to a new day as opposed to the end of a miserable one in settings they now avoid like the black plague. The breakfast customers talk in hushed morning voices, waiting for the ample food portions of the diner to kickstart their day. While the hotel itself has fallen into disrepair over recent years, this unpretentious eatery attached to it through the central lobby has been serving up solid food for more than three decades. Locals like this coffee shop, not only for the rich history of stars who had once patronized its doors, but also because it is a great place to eat anonymously, a hidden getaway near the action yet away from the star-struck tourists.

John and Ludo, looking like two more of the all-night soldiers who march hard through an evening's revelries, sit in a red-backed cushioned booth across a speckled beige Formica table rimmed with polished metal around its edges. They are exhausted from their interrupted sleep patterns, which reveal themselves in darkened furrows under their eyes.

John stirs a spoon in his black coffee even though there is nothing to mix; he hasn't added anything to the dark liquid. When he finishes this futile exercise, he taps the spoon a few times on the cup's lid and places it on the saucer. He wraps both his hands around the steaming cup, letting its warmth sink into his palms and the insides of his fingers.

"Something on your mind," Ludo says, sipping on an herbal tea sweetened with honey. "Talk to me."

"I'm just sitting here. What makes you think something's up?"

"All I got to do is look at you." Ludo raises one hand, palm up. "Well?"

John puts his coffee cup down and turns it around a few times. "I'm in deep, Ludo. It's not good," he says.

"What's going on, bro? You're not worried about work again?"

"No, it's not work. You don't want to know. You really don't want to know."

"I know I don't want to know, that I know. But I got to know if we're going to have any kind of meaningful conversation here."

"Trust me, you really don't want to know," John insists.

"If I didn't want to know, I wouldn't ask you. And if you didn't want to talk about it, why the hell are you talking about it?" Ludo throws up his hands. "So stop saying 'I don't want to know' and give me the *know* already, or let's change the subject to something we both can talk about. You starting to act like that nut job at the reception, acting suspicious all over the place."

"It's a mess," John says. "Not only do you not want to know, but I don't want to know."

A man behind John with a lisping, high-pitched voice, interrupts. "You two knuckleheads going to keep on with this stupid conversation, or we going to find out what's going on with this story? I can't listen to this nonsense much longer."

"Look, little sister," John says over his back, "why don't you mind your own business?"

"Cool it, man," Ludo whispers to John, frantically motioning with both hands.

The man in the booth behind John, whom Ludo can clearly see from where he sits, is a very big man with arms powerful enough to knock over a horse with one blow. Ludo recognizes the face from television. This is not the type of man John or anyone else, regardless of size, would knowingly taunt.

"Why should I?" John says indignantly to Ludo. "Let the fruitcake mind her own business."

Ludo groans and continues motioning with his hands. "Cut it out, homes," he says through gritted teeth, his eyes pulling sharply as a signal to John to peek over his shoulder.

"Excuse me," says the man in the other booth, his voice soft and girlish, but with a decidedly irritated edge, "you calling me a fruitcake?"

"You're asking me if I'm calling *you* a fruitcake?" John says, smirking. He turns around and finds himself staring into the broad, stern face of Iron Mike Tyson, ex–heavyweight champion of the world, not six inches away from his own.

"Holy mother in heaven," John says, his face coloring a deep shade of crimson. "I was, uhm, you know, ah, I was talking about, uhm, about my friend's sister over here. I mean, my friend over here, of course, his sister's not here. Oh my god."

"I don't have a sister, homes."

"Shut up, Ludo."

"Is that right?" Tyson says to John, his voice as soft as the sharp edge of a guillotine.

Mike Tyson gets out of his seat and stands over John. From up close, his arms and chest looks more massive than they appear on television, which is substantial and quite imposing from just a few feet away. John looks over at Ludo and seeing no help there, looks back at Tyson. The ex-champion looks down at John, his face as serious as if the bell had rung and the referee had backed away to leave his loose-lipped opponent at the ex-champ's mercy.

John audibly groans. The black eyes of the fighter stare into his own, and John, with fear coursing through his pores, tries to say something, but when he moves his mouth, no words come out.

Tyson's face suddenly breaks out into a broad grin. "It's cool," Tyson says. "I was just funning with you a little bit. You guys take care now," he says with a wink, and walks past their table and out of the coffee shop.

John continues staring at the spot Tyson has just vacated, his face blank, like his brain is overloaded and can't take in the information.

"You got to learn to relax, homes," Ludo says. "You keep arguing with everyone, you going to get us into trouble. Or get an early heart attack or something. You lucky that guy didn't relocate your head to another galaxy. Yo, were you never told not to play with explosives?"

John lets out a big sigh of relief and turns toward Ludo. "I thought he was going to kill me."

"It looked like that. That boy swing, homes, you on your way past the moon right now. Be visiting Jupiter or something. Of all people for you to mess with on the entire planet, Mike Tyson, man. You too much sometimes."

John exhales deeply, his lips pursed like a tropical koi at feeding time. "I've never been so scared in my life, Ludo. My body just broke out into one giant sweat when I turned around and saw him."

"You ain't the first, homes."

"Wow," John says, banging the side of his head with his hand, still trying to get it clear. "I almost crapped in my pants there. Man, oh man. Oh, Jesus. I think I'll go back to the room and take a long cold shower after that. Maybe a hot one, I don't know."

"Keep your head straight, homeboy," Ludo says, standing up and banging fists in solidarity with John, "I'll catch you out by the pool."

———————

The early morning desert sun in Las Vegas burns fiercely in the summer, and as the clock hand turns a full rotation marking the time as ten-thirty in the morning, the temperature has already soared high into the nineties, the air outside heating up like a freshly fired oven reaching its stride.

Ludo reclines in a cushioned chair by the pool, his face glistening with sweat. He wears bright yellow swimming trunks that hang below his knees and dark sunglasses that tint everything a deep shade of crimson. The top layer of the tropical drink on the table beside him is frothy and white. A wedge of pineapple hangs off the rim of the glass, gathering shade under the tiny purple umbrella impaled in its rind as if taking shelter from the withering heat of the oppressive rays. Ludo has a newspaper unfolded in his hand and is perusing the sports section as John approaches.

"You missing some good sunshine here, man, good views too. The pool is *the* place. That's what I'm talking about." Ludo nods in the direction of two women in their early twenties sunning themselves on the other side of the pool. One is wearing a pale blue bikini and slowly spreading lotion on her flat, tan abs. Her companion lies on her stomach, a red thong barely visible against her skin. Her tanned buttocks, luminous in the sun's rays, shine with a fresh coat of tanning oil.

"Feels like it's a hundred degrees out here," John says.

"Almost there already. The weather people say it's going to reach one hundred and thirteen degrees today. Can you believe that? Can fry eggs." Ludo nods over at the bikini-clad girls and winks at John. "Hey, no word yet on the clothes?" Ludo asks, slurping nosily on his cocktail.

"What clothes?"

"Man get lost for an evening, he don't know where he's at. Love written all over you, like, like, ah, a wrapper on a piece of gum, man, like ah, a light bulb and a sardine in a tin can."

"What are you talking about, Ludo?"

"Our suitcases, man, I don't think the airline found them yet."

"What? They said we'd have the bags this morning. And we don't have them, do we?"

"It's still early, maybe they'll come up with them yet. Don't sweat it. Nothing we can do about it anyway."

Ludo wipes the sweat off his forehead and takes a sip from the long straw poking out of his drink. "Yeah, you ain't exactly dressed for the beach, man," Ludo says, pointing to John's long slacks. "Lucky I kept a few things in my side bag. I bet you'll trade in last night for them shorts, hey homie?" Ludo playfully punches John on the arm.

"You might say that," John says. "How do you know?"

"It's written all over you, home town," Ludo catches the eye of the girl in the red g-string bikini. She has just sat up, and they exchange smiles across the pool. She is fanning herself with a pink visor inscribed with the words, "Keep It Real." Ludo turns back to John. "What's her name?"

"ZZ."

"That's cool, Casanova, very cool."

"Everything clicked so perfect, I can't even describe it." John reaches over, grabs Ludo's drink, and takes a sip. "Pretty good," John says, shaking his head with approval. "She's just a little crazy and a lot of trouble. But I had a great time."

"A little bit of trouble is good, man." Ludo turns a page in the paper, stares intently at an article for a few seconds, and puts the publication down. "Man, it's hot out here." A small drop of sweat rolls down the side of Ludo's face and, amused, he watches it fall to the ground and evaporate almost instantly.

"I mean, *a lot of trouble*," John says.

"What you talking about?" Ludo says with a sly smile as he catches one of the girls' eyes and she smiles back at him. "They all a lot of trouble," he adds, laughing softly and enjoying the sun warming his skin.

The girl in the red bikini has dived into the water, going the full length of the pool underwater. Ludo follows her progress as she gets out on the shallow end, towel dries her perfect body, and shares some giggles with her friend.

"To getting rich in Vegas," Ludo says, and holds up his drink. "Feels good to get away, homes. I mean, really, life should be one long vacation. Should be just like this every day. You know what I'm saying?"

"I hear you." John nods to a spot behind his friend. "See that guy over there?"

"Who you talking about?"

"The guy on the lounge chair, toward the back."

Ludo peeks over his shoulder. "The guy combing his hair?" Ludo says, opening up a small bag of potato chips and stuffing a handful in his mouth.

John shakes his head in assent.

"What about him?"

"Well, what's he doing?"

"He's reading a magazine, man."

"No, not that."

"Okay, he's sitting down."

"That's not doing anything at all. That's just sitting."

"It look like he's doing something by sitting to me," Ludo says. "Alright then, you tell me. What's he doing?"

"You give up?"

"I'm not giving up, I'm just tired of this nonsense. You being ridiculous again."

"Just like that? That's it?" John waves his hands around.

"Breathing, blinking his eyes," Ludo says, raising his voice. "I don't know what the fuck you think he's doing."

"Okay, if you don't want to know, then that's that," John says. He shrugs, and with his right hand, smoothes down the front of his shirt.

Ludo pulls a few chips out of the bag and noisily crunches on them, staring hard at an errant potato chip that has fallen to the ground. After a few seconds, he breathes deeply and faces his friend. "Okay, what was he doing?"

"He was combing his hair," John says. "I don't know what it is, but people are always combing their hair around me."

"He was combing his hair?"

"You saw that, didn't you?"

Ludo looks at John. "The first thing I say is, 'The guy combing his hair,' and then you want me to guess that he's combing his hair when I already said that. Something wrong with you, man, too much arithmetic or something with that accounting you do. I don't know where you come up with this stuff."

"Well, he was combing his hair, wasn't he?"

Ludo stares dumbfounded at John. He reaches into his bag of chips and finding it empty, loudly crumples it into a ball and tosses it into a garbage can a few feet away. "That's the dumbest thing I ever heard."

John is looking at something over Ludo's shoulder. Ludo turns around to see another man combing his hair, then turns back to face John's smug look.

"Don't start with that," Ludo says.

"I didn't say a word. I'm just sitting here."

"But you looked knowing I would look. Same thing."

"I looked 'cause I looked. I can't help where you look."

Ludo looks at John suspiciously, shakes his head, and takes a long sip of his drink, licking his lips where some drink has spilled over.

"Okay, so, you be liking this girl, homes, eh?"

"Yeah, she is pretty special. It's a weird feeling, I really can't explain it, but it's special. You know, I'm really comfortable with her. I mean, you never know where things will go."

"You crazy? You already talking about the big pie in the sky and you don't even know nothing about this girl? No disrespect intended, homes, but you just met her *yesterday*. Last night! The lord made the world in six days. You got just one evening under your belt. You ain't even created the animals yet."

"Everything starts somewhere. Hey, it beats hanging around with my sister Bella."

"Wrestling hungry lions or petting African crocodiles beats hanging out with her. Hey, you going to have dinner with ZZ tonight, or you going to find some Elvis preacher and head over to the wedding chapel instead? Where we at, lucky boy?"

"Ludo, you're impossible. Can't take the New York out of you."

"Damn right, bro. I'll fly the colors till I'm horizontal." Ludo raises his right fist and leans back in his chair. His attention shifts to the two girls on the other side of the pool, their tanned, oiled skins shimmering in the sun.

"Talking about weird things and everything," Ludo says, "they got this 'Knuckleheads of the Week' show I saw this morning on the TV, and check this out. This yo-yo goes to a restaurant, stiffs them on the bill, and wrecks the joint. Is that dumb or what?"

"Sounds just like another petty crime. What's dumb about that?" John says.

"The dope leaves his identification on the table. I mean, how dumb is *that*?"

"Pretty dumb, I guess," John replies in a barely audible voice as the story sinks in.

"Man, there some stupid people out there. Can you believe the idiot just leaves his ID? Why don't he leave his phone number and the best time to call also?"

"Alright, alright, enough Ludo," John says.

"What the fuck is eating you?"

"Nothing."

"Chill out, man, I'm just talking."

Ludo pulls the straw out, sets it on the table, and drinks directly from the glass, licking the white froth off his lips. "Meanwhile, the guy busted up some fifty-thousand-dollar vase or something. Imagine, fifty thousand dollars for some little knickknack?"

"Fifty thousand dollars?" John's throat is suddenly dry, as if he has just swallowed a teaspoon of sand.

"Yeah, fifty thousand dollars! That's what they said. That's a lot of money for some old clay."

John mumbles something.

"What's that?" Ludo says.

"What did the guy look like?" John says in a hoarse voice, wondering if he is now a household face on network television.

"The camera was too far away to tell. Just one of them cheap security deals they put in there to knock down insurance rates or something. I guess someone at the security company made a few bucks selling it to the news. You can't see much through them, you know what I'm saying? Funny though, the guy had a sport coat like that blue one you wear."

Ludo finishes off the drink with a big slurp and licks his lips clean. "That hit the spot." He places the empty drink on the table and says to John, "Hey, you alright? You're not looking too good."

"I'm fine, Ludo. I guess they didn't mention my, ah, ah, his name?" John watches the ripples in the pool, mesmerized by their too-short journey to the water's edge.

"Nah, this old Italian guy, the owner I guess, said he didn't want to get the police involved, he wanted to keep the matter an internal thing. Man, it looked like he was going to punch the cameraman before he drove off in his car. He was pissed! I know one thing: I wouldn't want to be in that knucklehead's shoes if he's caught. That place looked like a little Mafia joint." Ludo pauses and looks at John. "Oh, by the way, someone keeps calling for you."

"Huh?"

"I said, someone's been calling for you."

John perks up. "A girl?"

"No, a friend of yours says he wants to get together later for a bite. We could all grab dinner together tonight if you want."

"Outside of ZZ, I don't know anyone here, Ludo."

"You must know *someone*. He's calling you, not me."

"Well, who was it then?"

"He didn't leave a name. I could barely understand what he said anyway. I was half asleep. Kept waking me up. Hey, you hear about the Yankee game?"

John sighs heavily and lays down on the lounge chair without a word, looking drawn.

"What's with you, man, you don't like the Yankees no more?" Ludo says and shrugs his shoulders.

Chapter Nine

John is apprehensive as he enters Lilly D's Casino at five minutes before noon. ZZ has agreed to meet him here, at a bar most of the way into the casino, but the brief conversation they had earlier disturbs him. She talked about the possibility of having lunch in a way that suggested they wouldn't, and of getting together in a way that suggested it would be the last time. ZZ had seemed far away, her mind elsewhere, as if a voice outside of her was talking to him. Judging from her monosyllabic tone, it feels like this get-together might be more like a goodbye than a hello.

John makes his way through the one-story casino with the same sinking feeling he felt huddling behind the dumpster in the back alley the day before, fearing that his budding relationship with ZZ will wilt before it has a chance to take hold and bloom. That this might be their last meeting makes his heart heavy, a prisoner to a chain struggling to drag a seventy-pound iron ball across the casino floor. The possibility of losing ZZ—the most exciting woman he has ever met, if even so briefly—sends an indistinct pain coursing through him, a loneliness like a prisoner pulled from the general population and sentenced to six months of solitary confinement. John's only serious relationship had been a while ago, and he feels a special connection with ZZ, a shared emotional background of sorts that can't be put into words. It is magic; he couldn't describe it any other way.

John passes a long bank of slot machines. The players at this local grinder's casino, mostly solitary women in their fifties, sixties, and seventies with bland faces and bland hair, quietly punch buttons, disinterestedly watching reel after reel spin, their expressions constant regardless of the result, as if winning or losing spins are of equal value to them—or worse, of no value. And the beat goes on. Push the button, watch the reels, push the button, watch the reels. A few men are there as well, faceless figures dropping coins into inanimate objects. Mostly washed-out specimens with no other place they can think to go or with nothing better to do, these players are killing time until their next event, perhaps a meal, perhaps back to their lonely apartments and desolate lives, or perhaps a disconsolate stroll down memory lane to contemplate how the promise of their lives has ended up in a meaningless pursuit of three cherries or five suited cards ace through ten, or a bunch of video keno numbers. Pushing buttons on a machine, and pushing them again and again. And again. Just killing time. Or vice versa.

This off-Strip gambling house, especially busy on paydays, is a far cry from the typical Strip casino frequented by better-heeled tourists, where the action is upbeat and patrons on vacation are having fun. Here in this local grind joint, players are serving hard time for being dealt bad cards in life, a constant flow of second- and bottom-pair hands against ace-high flops, always showing down the ignorant end of a straight to boss straights and flushes, or small two pairs to bigger two pairs or trips. The few aces they are dealt get bad-beaten to kings or snuffed out on the river to a runner-runner longshot.

John looks into the first lounge he passes, a gaudily decorated affair with a semi-circular stage large enough to comfortably hold a band of eight musicians. Other than a few stragglers nursing beers at the bar, it is quiet. When the band kicks in later, the lounge will be jumping, but that's later, when the locals come in after work for a little relaxation before their evening's grind at the machines, or after they've gambled away their bankroll when about all they've got left is their Bud or Miller money.

There is no ZZ here so John heads to the adjacent bar, finding ZZ sitting quietly at a table drinking a tall glass of iced tea through a straw. Two lemon slices float in the dark liquid. She is the only customer.

"Hi ZZ, how's it going?"

When John bends down to kiss her, she turns her face so that the kiss lands on the cheek. Her skin is cool and foreign against John's lips, like he's kissed a chilled shrimp.

"Hi Doc, what's going on?" she says flatly.

"Not much, just seeing if you're still up to having a bite." John sees the answer in ZZ's eyes before she responds.

"This is not the best day for lunch, Doc, okay?" ZZ looks at her iced tea as she speaks. "I'm meeting my ex in a few minutes, and it's not a good idea that you two meet right now. He's a little upset about things."

"Listen, ZZ, I really need to talk to you. It's important."

"Can't this wait until tomorrow?" she says.

"I wouldn't ask if it wasn't urgent. Some things have come up. It's really important."

"You sure?"

John nods his head. He feels awkward standing above her, but given her standoffishness, it would feel even more awkward to sit. While she contemplates the possibility of meeting John, ZZ looks down at her hands, picking at a chip of red polish on her fingernail. Finishing that, she twirls the thin gold bracelets on her right wrist a few times, the metal clanging softly. She looks up at John.

"Okay," she says resignedly. "The only time I can meet today will be later, for a little bit. It's not the best place to meet, but you said it's important. We'll meet later at the Silver Cactus in room eight-thirteen. Upstairs."

"The Silver Cactus Hotel and Casino?"

"Yes, Doc." ZZ sighs. "At three o'clock. There might be a few people hanging out there, but don't worry about them. They're a bunch

of losers. And don't tell anyone there anything. All they have to know
is that we are just business friends. Even better, just say acquaintances
if they ask. The less they know the more it suits me. I don't like gossip.
Three o'clock. Okay?"

"Who are these people?" John asks. Something about the way ZZ
describes them makes him anxious. And why can't they know that ZZ
and John are friends, even more than that? "Are they—"

"I told you," ZZ says, cutting him off. "They're just a bunch of
losers. Ignore them."

"But—"

"Doc," she says in rebuke, her voice rising, "do we need to talk
about the same thing over and over again? Look, it's not the best time
to talk now. I'll see you later, okay?"

ZZ looks around nervously, as if expecting her ex to show at any
minute. Her pupils, dilated wide in the dark bar, are like pools of liquid
onyx.

"Room eight-thirteen, three o'clock," John says. "Thanks, ZZ, I
appreciate it. I know it's not a good day for you. See you then."

John walks away with a weak wave and turns back at the exit.
ZZ sits there, like a forlorn tree in a vast wasted field, picking at her
red fingernails, and quietly, as best John can surmise, contemplating
something in her life that deeply disturbs her.

———————

Ludo and John are sitting at a semi-circular booth in the coffee
shop with dessert plates in front of them when Mike Tyson walks in.

"Hey champ, what's going on, bro?" Ludo says, signaling him
over.

"How's it going, fellas?" Tyson is carrying a newspaper opened to
the sports section and is clean-shaven and dapper in a freshly pressed
white dress shirt.

"Why don't you join us?" Ludo says, moving over toward John and
making room for Tyson in the booth. "Just hang out and read the paper

here. Do your thing, man. Don't worry about us or nothing."

"Okay, if that's cool with you. Just want to catch up on a few things in sports if you guys don't mind. I like coming around here to grab a cup of coffee, nobody bothers me."

Tyson sits down next to Ludo, orders a cup of coffee from the waitress, and focuses his attention on the paper.

Ludo has already devoured most of a large slice of chocolate cake and plays with the remaining piece, a bite-sized morsel that he pushes around the plate as if reluctant to finish the last of his dessert and be left with nothing. He stares rapaciously at John's plate, where a large slice of apple pie sits untouched.

"What is it, Ludo?" John says in a cutting tone.

"I don't know what you're talking about."

Ludo turns his head away from John's plate, but his eyes remain fixed on the pie.

"Something is on your mind," John says after a few seconds of silence.

"Ain't nothing on my mind. Just chilling."

"Go ahead, Ludo, say what you're going to say. I know what it is anyway."

"Man, you make such a big deal out of everything. I was just wondering if you were gonna eat that pie, nothing more than that," Ludo says defensively.

"Aha!" John exclaims. "I knew it."

"You didn't know nothing." Ludo points to the pie and lifts up his palm. "Well?"

"I'm just not hungry yet," John says.

"So why the hell you order it?"

John shrugs. "You said we're getting dessert, so I got dessert. I don't know."

"But if you're not going to eat it, why order it? It's wasteful, you know, starving children and things."

"What are you saying, you want my pie?"

"I just don't like to see waste, that's all. So what about that pie?"

Ludo asks through a mouthful of cake, his last piece now history.

"I'll eat it."

"Hey, don't get testy with me. I'm just being your big sis on this trip. Making sure you eat your food," Ludo says laughing.

Mike Tyson peeks around the edge of the paper, then pulls it higher so that his face is hidden behind it.

"Only thing is my sister doesn't stare at my food while I'm eating it like a skinny wolf looks at a fat chicken." John crosses his arms and stares hard at Ludo. Ludo leans back and crosses his arms as well.

"You saying I'm staring at your pie?"

"You're sure not flirting with it."

"Now I might stare at a chick, but not at a pie. I'm just looking at the pie because it's there. There's a difference."

"I think you got that reversed, because you're staring at my pie, and you're staring at my pie because you want it. Chicks, on the other hand, you look at."

"This is a dumb discussion," Ludo says, "and none of this means nothing because you said you're gonna eat it. So why we talking about it? And I wasn't staring at your pie, just looking—man, it's right in front of me. What? I got to look at the other side of the room like a backwards-headed goat?"

"Do you want it, Ludo? Simple question."

"I was just asking if you were going to eat it. I didn't say I wanted it. And you already said you wanted it. Discussion done."

Mike Tyson sticks his head out from the paper, loudly turns the page, and retreats behind it again.

"For someone who don't want it, you sure talking about it plenty," John says, raising his voice.

"You talking about it equally as plenty," Ludo says in a louder voice.

The waitress comes over to the table and stares at the two. "Is there anything else I can get for you gentlemen?"

"Yeah," Tyson says, looking up from his paper. "Bring two big, fat corks and a bowl of Super Glue."

John turns to the waitress. "He does this every time. He'll stare at my food and rather than saying he'll eat the food if I don't, he plays these games like I don't know what he's up to. But I know what he's up to and he knows I know, so I don't know why he does it just the same. Am I right, ma'am?"

"Just 'cause I ask him if he's eating it," Ludo says to the waitress, "it doesn't mean I want to eat it, that's all I'm saying. Am I right?"

"I'm out of this one, fellas," the waitress says. "I just take the orders and bring the food around here. My duties don't extend to conflict-resolution discussions about apple pie."

John raps on the table. "Ludo, I thought you said this discussion was done. Nothing to talk about, right?"

"Right. It's done," Ludo says. "I was just checking to see if you wanted it, that's all."

The waitress sighs and walks away from the table.

"Aha, so you do want it?" John says loudly. "Just admit it and simply say, 'Can I have your pie?' and be done with it. Free yourself, let it all out. And stop freaking out the pie by staring at it."

Tyson looks up from his newspaper. "Do I have to listen to you fuckers do this again? Just eat the pie—or don't eat the pie and give it to him. What's so complicated about that?"

"Mike's right, just take the pie," John says, annoyed, and pushes the plate toward Ludo.

Ludo pushes the plate right back and raises his voice as well. "I'm not freaking out your pie. How can you freak out a pie, man? What's wrong with you? It's just a piece of pie."

"That pie is so freaked out, it has an identity crisis now. It doesn't know it's an apple pie anymore, it thinks it's a peach pie."

"You ridiculous, man."

"No, you're ridiculous," John says, raising his voice even louder.

"No need to get so testy. All I was seeing is if you're eatin' it or not. No biggee."

"How can I eat the pie when all I'm doing is arguing with you about if I'm going to eat the pie?"

John and Ludo stare at each other belligerently, their faces red, the veins on their necks taut. Tyson has pulled the periodical so close to his face, no one could tell who is behind the paper.

"I'm just asking if you want it, homes. No need to make such a big deal about it."

"When it comes to food, you're never just asking. You're asking with a *purpose*. Do you want the pie, Ludo?"

Tyson groans from behind the newspaper.

"So, do you want it?" John persists.

Ludo raises his hands in the air. "You just tell me if you're eating it or not and stop being so childish about the whole thing."

"You're the one being childish. If you want another slice, why don't you just order one?"

"I don't want to order another slice."

"But you want this one if I don't eat it, isn't that right?"

"No mas, I had enough," Tyson says, tossing a five-dollar bill on the table. "Here's for the coffee. I can't take this crap."

Tyson stands up and folds his newspaper. "See if you two can work it out somehow," he says, shaking his head and lumbering away from the table.

Chapter Ten

You can stare at a situation in fright for only so long before fiction becomes fact and develops a life of its own. John and Ludo pause outside room 813 of the Silver Cactus Hotel and Casino. They stand side by side staring at a simple wooden hotel door like two miscreant children outside the principal's office, afraid to knock because an angry headmaster awaits them on the other side.

Ludo leans forward, pressing his ear against the door, but he cannot make out any words through the wood, just the sounds of husky male voices and muffled conversations. He shrugs and looks at John.

"I don't understand why we're meeting her here," Ludo whispers out of the side of his mouth. "This is a strange place to meet her privately, you know what I'm saying? With a room full of people? What kind of private is that? I don't know about this."

"I don't know either," John says in a hushed voice. "This is where she told me to meet her."

"Room eight-thirteen? You sure?"

"This is it," John replies, his voice coming out hoarse. He notices a slight trembling in his hands and clasps them together to control their shaking.

"Number eight-thirteen, man, not a good number. Bad luck. Why does everything we do around here seem to end in the number thirteen?"

"Thirteen again?" John says tremulously.

"Right there in front us again, homes. I don't feel good about this, bro. I just don't. What the fuck is going on inside that room? And who the hell are these people?"

"We're in the middle of a casino. What could possibly happen? What, we get gunned down in a hail of bullets?"

"Yeah, that and other things," Ludo says. "And this is not the middle of a casino, let me remind you. It's a closed room. Ain't no impartial witnesses behind that door. And we both know that girl is trouble, and since she brought us here, that's what I think—it's trouble. More of it."

"Like what could happen?" John asks nervously.

"Whatever 'what' might be, I don't want to be 'what-ed,' that's what."

Ludo crosses his arms for emphasis and they look at each other. "Hey, homes," Ludo whispers, "what do you know about this girl?"

"You'll laugh, Ludo, the place we went last night, I don't know if that's where she really lives and I don't know what she does. Hell, I don't even know her last name. But I'm telling you, it feels right."

"Nothing about this feels right," Ludo says, "and I ain't laughing."

Ludo looks down the hallway; it is deserted and quiet, as if there are no other occupants on the floor. Neither speaks or advances a plan to get through to the other side of the door. After a few long seconds, John softly clears his throat.

"What?" Ludo says.

"Well, I guess we should knock on the door."

"I suppose so."

"You're closer," John says.

Ludo steps back. "Now you're closer. You knock on that door, hombre. This whole thing is your thing."

"What's the big deal? This is just a meeting place. To say hello and whatever. You'll get to meet ZZ, and we'll be in and out and downstairs in no time at all. Go ahead, knock."

"If it's no big deal, why don't you just knock on the door instead of staring at it?"

"You're such a child, Ludo."

"Is that so?"

"Really, you're so childish sometimes. Like now."

"I may be a goddamned child, but you're knocking on that door," Ludo growls. "Bad enough I have to be standing here in front of a number thirteen. Them number thirteens like a tornado twisting all over us and wrecking everything in this town."

"Okay, then, I'll do it." John raises his hand to knock, but instead, pausing in midair, pulls his hand back and drops it to his side. His palms are moist with sweat, and he rubs them against his pants to dry them.

John and Ludo huddle next to each other in the hall like scared herd animals, the number 813 in simple gold letters staring them in the face.

"Here goes nothing," John says, raising his hand. He looks over at Ludo one last time, sees no encouragement there, and sighs. John meekly taps on the door, hitting it twice. The door immediately opens, as if the knock was expected at that very moment and no time was to be wasted. John's hand is still suspended in the air, and he drops it sheepishly to his side.

A tall, narrow-shouldered man in his sixties, with a full head of gray hair immaculately combed straight back, stands there measuring them as if they are livestock being sized up at an auction and found to be inferior. He wears a tuxedo that hangs off his gaunt frame like an ill-fitting curtain, and his face, narrow and drawn, has the look of death, the mien of a mortician presiding over a funeral. Hopefully, not theirs. The man peers over the top of his half-rimmed glasses down the hall behind John and Ludo, and then at their shoes, taking in the whole situation with one penetrating look. He rests his stare disconcertingly about one inch over John's eyes, where a bullet to the forehead might be aimed in an execution, and addresses him in a guttural voice that scrapes out of his throat.

"May I help you?" the man asks after a few very long seconds.

"We're here to meet ZZ," John says anxiously, his voice catching in his larynx.

The man, still peering over his glasses, unsmilingly steps aside, and without another word, allows the two to enter.

As John and Ludo squeeze past the mortician into the room, the door quickly shuts behind them. The harsh sound of the bolt slamming into its lock startles and unnerves them further and, instinctively, like trapped animals facing the salivating lips of a drooling predator, they move closer together. The room, a few seconds earlier boisterous with noise, becomes deathly quiet, the silence hanging heavy and oppressive, as if a man had emitted his last gasp to a sober crowd of witnesses and still swings on the gallows.

There are eight occupants in the room: six grim-looking men sitting around a poker table, all of whom turn toward the door; the mortician who allowed them entrance; and a short, creepy-looking man with a bulbous nose sitting by himself in the corner, chain-smoking cigarettes and watching the action with beady eyes. The players at the poker table drop their cards and silently stare at the two visitors standing dumbstruck before them. Seconds, ephemeral pieces of time, drag slowly as eight sets of eyes from around the room burn into John and Ludo, laser beams that scour them like Brillo pads scraping burnt crud off a frying pan. Dripping in their own nervous sweat, John and Ludo feel skewered by these piercing looks, as though their very souls are glass windows and a bunch of killers is scrutinizing them through the clear panes.

Upon finishing their ominous inspection, the men turn back toward the table and resume their game. The oppressive silence of moments earlier is replaced by the ambient sounds of shuffled cards, chips tossed into pots or being idly played with, and snippets of words being bandied about by the participants.

John and Ludo let out a collective sigh of relief, thankful that their silent ordeal is over and nervously taking in the situation. Looking around, they see a room that looks like a converted hotel suite, but with no beds or other hotel-type furniture. Instead, a green felt-topped poker table and chairs, positioned close to the door, dominate the main part of the space. In the far corner of the room, by a window that overlooks the neon lights of the Strip, is a wet bar fully stocked with multiple bottles of alcohol and mixers on its counter and a small brown refrigerator underneath. The room appears to be the permanent gathering spot for this private poker game, a special arrangement, no doubt, negotiated by someone with substantial juice in the Silver Cactus.

The smell of cigars, cigarettes, whiskey, and stale sweat permeates the air. Above the table where the men are playing hangs a dense cloud of stagnant smoke fed by a steady stream of reconditioned nicotine from the players below it, all of whom smoke.

"ZZ will be back in an hour," the gaunt doorman says to John. "She's expecting you. Until then, make yourself at home. There's drinks and mixers in the corner there and beer in the fridge if you like." The mortician points to the far side of the room. "Feel free to pour yourself a few."

"I think we'll take you up on that," John says, grabbing Ludo's arm.

"No fooling around, man, I don't like this place," Ludo whispers to John as they walk over to the bar. "Let's get out of here while the gettin' is good."

John leads the way to the bar, fills two glasses with ice, and pours each of them a healthy shot of Jack Daniel's. They unenthusiastically click glasses. While John takes a sip from his glass, barely wetting his lips, Ludo downs his drink in one gulp. The frightening reception at the door has rattled him, and he holds his glass out to John for a refill.

"I got a bad feeling about this. It's bad news here," Ludo says. He looks over at the creepy-looking man sitting by himself in the corner, puffing on a cigarette and eyeing them obliquely. "I don't like it. One hour, he said?"

The gaunt doorman in the tuxedo approaches them with long

strides. His thin frame and long legs make him appear cadaverous, an upright apparition gruesomely marching their way. "They're playing one-five large-dollar seven-card stud over there," he says in a deep voice, as if a helping of gravel had been shoveled down his throat, "if any of you would like to join them while you wait. It's spread-limit, bet anything from one dollar to five dollars on any betting round."

"ZZ told me that she'd be here right around now," John says to him. "You sure she's going to be one hour?"

"If you can't wait, I can let her know when she returns," half-glasses says, smiling broadly and exposing small, uneven teeth, but there is as much warmth in that smile as in a day-old corpse. He then turns and in long, loping strides reaches his hard-backed chair by the door, where he sits, stilled, like a sphinx, as if guarding an ancient tomb and its treasures. His rigidity makes him look as if he had been planted there all along and hadn't moved or spoken, as nondescript as the other fixtures in the room.

"That guy gives me the creeps," Ludo says.

"No kidding."

"I don't get it." Ludo says, nodding toward the poker game. "How can they play for dollars and be so serious about it?" He downs the rest of his whiskey in one gulp, fills up John's glass and then his own. "It's funny about people. They worry more about paying two cents extra for a gallon of gas or a nickel extra for a carton of milk, than, like, a thousand dollars extra for, like, whatever, something big, you know?"

"You got that right," John says.

"And these guys are playing just for dollars? It looks like a funeral over there. I thought people supposed to have fun playing poker. Makes no sense to me, homes. Why play the game then?"

"Yeah, they look tense. I'll tell you something, when poker players get like that, you know, tense and uptight, they become easy marks if you know what to do. As long as we got some waiting to do, maybe I'll kill a little time at the game. Get us a little lunch money. You mind?"

"Suit yourself, but I still think we should get the fuck out of here." Ludo looks at the creepy-looking man in the corner, and the man looks away. "Everything is wrong about this place. Even the number. Thirteen, man, it's no good."

"Ludo, stop with this thirteen nonsense and take it easy. I'll see if I can pick a few feathers from these Vegas show birds. It's just a tourist town, what the hell do they know about big-city poker?"

"Okay, then, go ahead and knock yourself out. I'll hang here. Free booze, I can keep myself busy. But really, homes, aren't they awful serious and everything?"

"It's just a one-to-five-dollar game, that's what he said. Can't be too much to worry about. They're the type, as you said, that get worked up about the two-cent gas money and get tense about pocket change. It's not like the game is life or death or anything."

"Beats me with all this stuff, I'm no gambler," Ludo says as he pops opens a beer and takes a swig, "but why would anyone waste time on taco money? Really. I'd rather put my money into the cold stuff. At least you get something for your money, you know what I'm saying?"

John approaches the poker table. "I guess I'll sit down with you guys if it's alright?"

"As long as you can handle the action," a wiry man with a heavily scarred face says gruffly. "We're playing one-dollar chips. Large."

John looks at the chips and shrugs. They appear regular-sized to him.

"I think I can handle that," John says, pulling up a chair and sitting down. "A large dollar is about the same size as a small dollar the way I see it. George Washington's first words as President of the United States, you know, referring to his weekly poker game, was 'In our new country, all dollars are born equal.'"

John laughs at his own joke, but as he looks around, he is greeted by blank faces—no one has joined in. He shrugs, pulls a few bills from his wallet, two twenties and a ten, and confidently flips them on the felt, eliciting dry laughter from all the players except one, the man with the deep scars on his face, whose expression doesn't change from a hard fixed stare. John doesn't get what's so humorous, nor does Ludo watching from the bar, and the two glance at each other uneasily.

"That's funny," says the player to his right, but the man doesn't smile.

"This is a gentleman's game. We settles up at the end," the dealer says. He shuffles the cards as he speaks, riffling the deck with skilled flourishes. "Youse can put your money away."

"Fine by me," says John. Everybody's eyes are on him as he self-consciously reaches over to retrieve the three bills, feeling like a circus animal on display. Apart from the sounds of cards being shuffled, the room grows silent again. With shaking hands, John inserts the money in his wallet as six sets of eyes track its progress, and then he replaces the billfold into his back pocket.

"In this game, we trusts people for their credit," the dealer says, breaking the silence. "We figures youse have to be able to afford the action to get your heart pumping. Who wants to play small dollars anyway?"

John laughs and again no one joins in with him.

"Yes, that's right," the scarred man responds dryly.

"We usually buys in for a minimum of fifty chips," the dealer says, deftly shuffling the cards as he speaks. "Each one worth a dollar. Does that works for youse?"

John nods, and the dealer, a broad-shouldered man sitting directly across from him, counts out three stacks of ten chips each and one small stack of four five-dollar chips. His enormous chest reminds John of a ridiculously overstuffed chair back with two arms and a head attached, a powerful mass of flesh and muscles. When he leans forward to push the piles of chips over to John, the buttons on his shirt become so taut, straining against their holes, they look like six projectiles primed to be released from a tightly drawn bowstring.

"Let me introduce youse to the table," the dealer says.

The big man stops shuffling the cards and looks to his left. "Nexts to me here," he points with the deck to the man with the heavily scarred face, "is Johnny Wonderbread. Nexts to hims is Apples," indicating a very heavy man sweating profusely. "Then betweens Apples and youse is Joey Cleaners." Joey Cleaners is the best-dressed of the group, wearing a gray tailored suit and a silver silk tie with darker silver lines criss-crossing it, and a matching handkerchief sticking out of his left breast. Cleaners' face is pockmarked, as if measles had ravaged the skin when he was young, and he wears a grimace that looks molded and frozen on him like hard plastic. While Apples and Cleaners nod slightly in recognition, Johnny Wonderbread, the scarred one, stares across the table at him as if nothing has been said.

"On the other side of youse," continues the dealer, indicating John's left, "is Rock, and then youse got Joe Popcorn."

These two also nod in greeting to John.

Except for one eye that is slightly drooped and appears to be blind, Joe Popcorn has unremarkable features with the exception of his head, shaved clean and oiled, and his luminous eyes, which glint like lethal laser beams. A bowl of popcorn rests between him and the dealer. John watches Joe Popcorn slowly work a few kernels between his powerful jaws and instantly is reminded of a *National Geographic* special where the host describes the manner in which African crocodiles move their mouths as they crunch the bones of large mammals that have fallen victim to their powerful jaws. John gets the uneasy feeling that Popcorn is figuratively picturing him as his next meal, a kernel of popcorn primed to be crushed between his teeth. Rock, who sits just to John's left, is another massive bruiser as big as the dealer. He restlessly toys with his stack of chips as though he wants to crush them—or something else—in his thick hands.

John notices that outside of the dealer, not one of the players has spoken a word in greeting. Johnny Wonderbread didn't even acknowledge his presence when introduced, and the others simply nodded. Something is strange about this group. There is none of the light-hearted banter typical of a casual home poker game. These players are deadly serious. But just the same, the forum is poker, and John is going to show these local yokels what happens when a player from the big city sits down with small time opponents at the table.

"They calls me Knuckles," says the dealer. Knuckles balls his big hands into fists and sticks them across the table in John's direction. Tattooed in cheap blue ink above the knuckles on his thickly scarred left hand are the letters L-O-V-E, one letter per finger, and on his right hand, the letters H-A-T-E.

Love and hate.

Seeing John's shocked expression, Knuckles breaks out into a wide, toothless grin, a macabre smile that suggests more the pleasure he would have beating someone to death with his scarred fists than showing off his prison tattoos.

John breathes out heavily and feels his hands become damp. This intimidating group of men is getting him more frightened by the minute. He leans back in his seat to contemplate the players around the table. What kinds of people have congregated to play this poker game?

"The guy in the corners there," Knuckles says, indicating the short, shifty-looking man sitting by himself and chain-smoking cigarettes, "that's Harry. He runs the game."

Harry lights a cigarette from the end of the one he has smoked down to the butt, takes a deep drag, and watches the escaping smoke from the recently crushed tobacco rise slowly from the ashtray.

"How do we know you by?" Apples says, rolling his prodigious head to the side as he speaks, but not quite looking in John's direction. This is the first time another player at the table has addressed him since he received his chips.

"Jjj-" John starts and then stops.

He thinks better of using his real name at this table full of nicknames and aliases—Wonderbread, Cleaners, Popcorn, Apples, Rock, Knuckles—and nervously racks his brain for a name to fit in with the machismo of the menacing men surrounding him. His eyes desperately scan the room for a clue. Panicked and with his thinking abilities out of kilter—like a train knocked off its tracks and skidding on the rails—John's eyes alight on a platter of baked goods dominated by a cluster of cupcakes in waxed paper wrappers and topped with bright pink frosting. Everybody is staring at John, waiting for an answer. His train now fully derailed, he is in full panic mode from the simple act of Apples asking him his name. He just can't think. A few more seconds tick by, long hands of time dragging heavily in the thick air. As if hypnotized, John can't take his eyes off the bright pink topping of the pastry.

Before he realizes what he is saying, John blurts out "Cupcakes."

"Cupcakes?" Joey Cleaners says.

John immediately bemoans the effeminate moniker he has saddled himself with, but it is too late. Cupcakes it is.

Of all things to come out of his mouth—Cupcakes!

———

Harry, the short, shifty-looking man with the bulbous nose and yellow teeth, gets up from his corner seat and walks over to converse with the cadaverous man sitting sphinxlike at the door. They talk quietly, and then Harry, his yellow teeth peering out from under his beady eyes, walks across the room to the bar where Ludo is standing.

"Hi," Harry says, his voice filled with false bravado and thick with sleaze, a little man's complex evident in his loud greeting. He is wearing slacks and a brown button-down shirt pushed out in the middle by the twenty or thirty extra pounds he carries around his waistline. His arms, too long for his short frame, hang at his sides like an orangutan's. More precisely, he has the appearance of a two-legged rat mutation gone awry.

Harry holds out his hand at a downward angle, and Ludo has to reach down to shake it. The hand is gummy and weak, like the flaccid skin of a dead fish. Ludo quickly removes his hand and rubs his open palm on the back of his pants leg, as though trying to remove the sodden film of decayed flesh.

"You must be ZZ's friend. I'm Harry," he says.

"Actually, I'm her friend's friend. I don't know her. Her friend is at the table." Ludo is reluctant to mention John's name to this creature, lest more than his hand gets soiled.

"So you're not ZZ's new friend?" Harry says, and turns to get a good look at John sitting at the poker table.

"If you're looking for ZZ's friend, Cupcakes is here at the table," Apples calls over from the game.

"Cupcakes?" Harry says quizzically. He pulls a Camel from a crumpled pack, lights it, and takes a long pull on it before offering the pack to Ludo.

"No thanks, I don't smoke," Ludo says.

Harry replaces the pack in his shirt pocket and stands in a cloud of cigarette smoke, an expression resembling grim befuddlement on his face.

"So, where you guys from?" Harry says.

"Brooklyn. We're just here on vacation."

"Is that right?" Harry says, inhaling deeply and letting a few ashes fall to the floor. "Your friend know ZZ long?"

"I stay out of his business. I don't ask, he don't tell." Ludo is uneasy around this creep and is hoping he'll go away so he can enjoy his beer in peace.

"Let me ask you," Ludo continues, "how do these guys know each other?"

"They're all killers and use this game to blow off some steam once a week," Harry says, a dull glint reflecting off his yellow teeth.

Chapter Eleven

After playing for about ninety minutes, John gets up to stretch his legs, walking over to the window where Ludo is sipping on a beer. The room has a sweeping view of the Strip, and beyond it, the looming hills of Red Rock Canyon farther off to the west.

"Quite a view, huh?" John says.

"What fucking stakes you playing?" Ludo asks curtly.

"One dollar up to five dollars a bet. Small stuff. Why?"

"One dollar to five dollars?" Ludo repeats.

"Yeah, one dollar for the low bet up to—"

"I know how it works, Cupcakes," Ludo says sarcastically. "What I mean is, what *are* the stakes?"

"What are you taking about?"

Ludo lowers his voice to a whisper. "Where you at, man? Nothing is like it is on the surface is this town. Behind all this neon and lights and fountains and volcanoes and artificial crap all over the place is a city full of sleazy people and we're deep in the shit of it, right here in this room—"

"Wait, Ludo," John interrupts, "you don't think that the stakes are what I think they are over there?"

"I don't know what the fuck they're talking about with this one dollar large shit, and popcorn and apples and all that other crap, but I don't think they're talking about popcorn and apples, you know what I'm saying?"

"Give me a break. It's just a dollar game," John says. "I'm just killing a little time. ZZ should be showing up pretty soon, so I may as well make a few bucks while we wait. These patsies are paying for our drinks later."

"Maybe so, but I'll tell you something else, homie," Ludo says, first glancing over his shoulder to make sure no one else is listening. "This whole thing feels bad. I told you that before we even walked into this room. This whole fucking thing feels bad. Hurry up and let's get the fuck out of Dodge, like pronto, man. Like pronto fucking pronto now! You know why they call scarface, over there, Wonderbread? I already got the scoop from that yellow-toothed rat."

"Why?"

"It's because of all the slices from a knife fight—and not because of what was done to him, but what he did to the other guy." Ludo points his index finger at John and lowers his voice to a whisper. "And do you have any idea what these fine fellows you're playing cards with do for a living?"

"Come on, Cupcakes," Apples calls over from the table. "Cards are being dealt, you're up."

John hesitates before he walks back to the game, settles back into his chair, and uneasily looks around again at his tablemates. He folds early the next few hands, forfeiting his one-dollar antes while he composes himself. Something Ludo said is weighing on him, but he can't quite figure out exactly what it is. It hovers just outside his mental grasp. Was it that bit about Wonderbread and his knife fight, John wonders, glancing at him out of the corner of his eye; the part about what these men do for a living, which Ludo didn't get a chance to mention before John headed back to the table; or was it his friend's inference that the stakes of this game might be different than what he thought and that he is playing in a game way over his head? Or is he simply uneasy that ZZ is late and he is insecure as to its significance? In any case, something *is* bothering him. The acids boiling in his stomach affirm that.

ZZ had warned him against meeting here and had tried to arrange their get-together in another location. But he had insisted. What was that about? And why not here? And then again, why here? Even so, why isn't ZZ present now?

As Knuckles counts out more chips for both Joey Cleaners and Rock with which to replenish their stacks after they busted out on the same hand, John takes advantage of the brief respite to collect his thoughts. By no stretch of the imagination could this collection of hard-edged men be called a bunch of regular Joes. No, something is too serious about this group, too awfully serious: Knuckles, the massive dealer with no teeth and prison tattoos etched onto his fingers who just seethes violence; Popcorn, a menacing presence whose merciless stare could strip paint off the wall; Apples, with the oversized head that never quite looks right at you, who would probably kill for the thrill of it and casually smoke a cigarette while he admires his handiwork; Joey Cleaners, with the hard-molded plastic face and humorless demeanor (what exactly *does* he clean?); Rock, massive, short-tempered, and mean, who looks as vicious as a junkyard dog when an intruder has trespassed; and Johnny Wonderbread, with the knife-scarred face, who looks like a messenger of death, maybe the scariest of the bunch.

And that is saying a lot.

What kind of game has he blundered into? Finally he sees what Ludo was getting at before Apples called him back to the game. Sure, it has to be—these guys are a bunch of cold-blooded killers for hire, men who smoke out their victims' lives with no more remorse than if they had snubbed out the butt of a smoldering cigarette, dispatching others to a place they would never return from. Murderers, hit men, sadists, snuffers, squelchers, killers by trade. He already has an idea what Johnny Wonderbread does to his poor victims, but Apples, Rock, Cleaners, Knuckles, Popcorn? What gruesome methods do they use? And what is Harry's relationship to this group? But even more important, what is ZZ's connection to this sordid den of murderers? How does she know these guys? Through work? Through acquaintances? Is she an accomplice? Too many troubling questions with answers that might not be pretty cycle through John's head, a spinning merry-go-round with no good horses on the poles.

"Hey, Cupcakes, you with us?" says Cleaners in a toneless voice. "You can daydream all you want when you kick the bucket or someone kicks it for you. But for now, why don't you see what you've been dealt?"

John snaps back to reality, picking up and examining the cards dealt to him. He is getting fed up with the aggressive intimidations of the thugs at the table and makes a decision. Enough fooling around. He is determined to bludgeon his opponents out of this pot with bluffing and heavy betting. It's a poker game, nothing more, nothing less. He'll show these macho brutes that poker is his arena, not theirs, that he's the big carnie in this circus. After all, he owns the weekly home stud game back in Brooklyn, winning seven times in a row even, and has done well in the few years he has been playing with some old high school friends and their friends. The stakes in this game are a little higher than what he and his friends like to kick around in—the minimum bet in this game is one dollar instead of the ten cents he is accustomed to playing back home—but so what, it's not like it's going to break the bank, and seven-card stud is seven-card stud.

He holds three hearts with the ace of hearts face up on board, the right upcard to push these players around and equalize the machismo factor at the table. It is the highest upcard on board. He'll show them.

John throws a chip into the center of the table and aggressively announces, "One dollar to play." Like a pigeon with a puffed-out chest, he looks around to register his bluster with the other players. John is counting on the strength of his ace and his forceful demeanor to chase some of them out of the pot and narrow the field. While a one-chip bet in a friendly home game has no impact, this group of players takes every chip wagered very seriously. But then again, there is nothing friendly about this game.

Rock, the next player to act, reexamines his cards and studies John's face carefully. "I'll play," he says throwing a chip into the pot, calling the bet. One by one, all the other players call the dollar bet and casually flip their chips into the pot.

Knuckles deals a second face-up card around the table. Each player now has four cards, two cards face down, hidden from view, and two cards face up and exposed to the other players. Apples has the high hand showing on board for this round, a pair of jacks, and he bets two dollars, a sizeable bet that is considered aggressive and duly respected in this game. Joey Cleaners folds and flips his cards face down to the dealer, Knuckles hauling in the discards and pushing them off to the side.

"I raise you two dollars," John announces, flinging in the original two-dollar bet plus his two-dollar raise.

Rock calls, placing four chips into the pot, and play moves around to Popcorn. He stares at John while contemplating his action.

"You bluffing me out of this pot with crap, I'll cut off your balls and fling them out the window to feed the birds," Popcorn says. He grabs an uncooked kernel of popcorn and grinds it slowly and loudly between his teeth, never once removing his eyes from John's.

John doesn't know what to say and drops his eyes to the felt. He squirms uncomfortably in his seat and feels his bluster deflate like an air mattress with its plug pulled, convinced that Popcorn is not the type to joke around. A sudden rush of heat envelops him and his pulse quickens. He is not sure what to do. The players are quiet for a few moments, the threat hanging over John like a hovering bomb.

"Don't worry, Cupcakes," says Apples, breaking the silence. "He's just kidding. He only works with baseball bats." Apples wheezes out a quick laugh, then rolls his head on the thick skin coiled around his neck until his eyes come to rest on the money in the pot.

"I fold," Popcorn finally says. With the index and middle fingers of his right hand turned horizontally, he imitates the cutting motion of a pair of scissors. He accompanies this mock cutting motion with a clicking sound and a malevolent smile aimed at John. Knuckles and Wonderbread also fold. The betting comes around to Apples. He calls the two-dollar raise, closing the betting for the round. John, Rock, and

Apples are the only players left in the hand, and Knuckles deals a fresh card face up to each of them.

Apples' two jacks are still the high hand showing, and he goes first. "Check to Cupcakes' aces," he says.

"Three big ones to Apples' jacks," John replies, nonchalantly flipping three chips into the pot.

"Is that supposed to be a funny?" Apples asks, incensed.

John is studying the chips in the pot and doesn't realize that Apples is talking to him until Apples slams his hand on the table, causing the chips in the pot to jump.

"Don't ignore me, boy," Apples screams out, pointing a fat finger at John. "You calling me a drunk?"

"What?" John snaps to attention, terrified. "You talking to me?"

"You called me a drunk. Nobody calls me names."

"The only thing I said was three chips to Apples' jacks."

"There, you said it again," Apples says, slamming the table harder, this time with both fists. "You called me applejack. You think I'm a home-brewed pigeon, is that it?"

"I-I-I didn't mean anything," John stammers.

"Then why did you say what you said?" Apples screams.

John looks around helplessly, afraid to say anything more. There is no telling what might set these people off. Apples glares at him with one eye, the other one aiming at the money in the pot. A blanket of silence hovers over the game, magnifying the imagined sound of John's own heartbeat.

Popcorn mercifully breaks up the tension, cracking a kernel between his teeth.

Now it is Rock's turn to act. He stacks six chips in front of his cards. "Three more," he announces, raising John's bet and making it six chips to play.

Apples folds without hesitation against the raise, tossing only his two hole cards and one of the jacks to Knuckles. The other jack, a jack of spades, he holds in his hand, staring at its markings and nodding his head, a vicious cut creasing his forehead. He makes a motion to toss this card to the dealer, but instead, stops his arm in midair, looking at the picture card as though he is going to crush it to death. Suddenly, he rips the black jack in half, and, Frisbee style, whips the two pieces through the air at John's head. One piece glances off John's forehead and lands on the floor; the other, the head of the jack, lands face up atop John's chips, balanced perfectly on the clay pieces, an inanimate Cirque du Soleil performer strutting its stuff. John keeps his head down, facing the ripped jack that, ironically, stares up as if mocking him.

John is more scared than he's ever been in his life and figures the safest policy is to keep his mouth shut and his eyes away from Apples. The man is a dangerous psychopath on the brink of violence, and John doesn't want to engage the madman in any way that might push him over the edge.

Rock and John are the only two players left in the pot. This is only the second raise that Rock has made, and John is convinced he has nothing, that he foolishly thinks this big raise will force John to fold. John nervously slides the ripped jack off his chips, averting his eyes from Apples, and pushes out six chips, three to call Rock's raise, and three more to reraise—a bold move and a clear message that he wants this pot. John fully expects Rock to quietly fold his cards as he has done time and again when facing raises, thinking his big reraise should be enough to shake the last coconut off the tree and give him the pot uncontested.

John is smugly counting chips in the growing pot, seeing what a win might bring him, when Rock shocks him with an unexpected move.

"Reraise," Rock says, throwing six more chips in the pot.

What's this?

John studies his opponent's cards anew. Rock has two eights and a queen on board, plus two down cards hidden from view. John's three hearts on board are backed by two more in the hole, a flush. Rock can easily see that John is representing a flush and he still raises with his probable hand of perhaps, John guesses, three eights? One of John's hearts is a queen, so that is one fewer card available to Rock's queen on board, and he has seen an eight go out of play earlier, so he knows Rock can't hold four eights. At best, he could be drawing to a full house or already have one, but that seems unlikely given that at least two of the cards he needs are out of play. If that thinking is correct, Rock is dead in the water. But still, Rock's shocking reraise gives John pause, so he simply calls the three-chip reraise, halting the betting for the round.

Knuckles deals the fourth open card to each player. This round, called sixth street, marks the sixth overall card each player receives. There will be one more card dealt and one more betting round after this one. John gets dealt the jack of clubs, which incites Apples to slam on the table again and start muttering; Rock receives the two of hearts. Neither player has improved on board. Barring a last-minute lucky draw by Rock on the next card, the seventh and last one that will be dealt, John feels he is well positioned to win. Maybe Rock doesn't believe he has a flush, figuring he'll beat John with whatever garbage he's holding. He'll soon find out.

"You be careful what you say about that jack," Apples warns, pointing an accusatory finger at him.

John can feel the glare from Apples' eyes, two laser pinpricks on his forehead, and he hopes the man's simmering emotions don't spill over into something worse than a further tongue-lashing. He fears that the next item Apples hurls at his head will be something more lethal than two halves of a plastic playing card, and he tries his best to maintain a low profile. He is afraid that Apples is looking for any excuse to make something bigger of this.

John doesn't check his two down cards, but notices something troubling: Rock doesn't either. Rock is a creature of habit who has checked his hole cards religiously each time a new card was dealt, and that he doesn't this time sends off alarm bells. Maybe Rock has a better hand than the two pair or three of a kind John suspects? In poker, when a player breaks a pattern, it's a *tell*, a giveaway that reveals information about the strength of a player's hand. In seven-card stud, when a player doesn't check his downcards after doing so religiously, it suggests he has already received the cards he needs—which is why he no longer has to check them. In Rock's case, that better hand would be a full house, which beats John's flush every day of the week.

John starts thinking that he should have played this hand more conservatively, but it is too late to change anything now. His chips are already in the pot.

Rock goes first and bets. "Five dollars," he announces, the largest bet he has made, and he throws five chips into the pot.

It's up to John. "That's five dollars?" John says, buying time to think. A five-dollar bet from Rock seems to confirm his worst fears.

"You have a hearing problem?" Rock turns sideways to face him. He has a slight lisp and John almost doesn't understand him. "Do I need to speak more clearer for you or do we have a problem here?"

"No problem, I'm sorry," John says quietly.

"If I say five dollars and throw five dollars in the pot, that means I'm betting five dollars and I don't need to be questioned about it."

John looks down and nods.

"Did you hear me?" Rock raises his voice, and the thick veins on his neck swell. "I didn't hear you say anything."

"Yes," John says, his eyes lowered.

"Don't ask me then, got it?"

"Yes, I got it," John says, and meekly puts five chips into the pot, calling the bet.

Knuckles deals the last round of cards. This card arrives "down and dirty," the seventh card dealt in seven-card stud.

"Up to you," John says quietly.

"That'll be another five," Rock says, confidently tossing five chips into the pot.

John pushes five chips toward the middle, calling the bet. The betting is over, and now there is no more maneuvering. Simply, the best hand will take the money in the pot.

"Show 'em," Rock says.

"You bet first, so you show them first," John says. "Those are the rules."

"What did you say to me?"

John hears Popcorn's mandible loudly crush a raw kernel, making a cracking and then grinding sound between his teeth, and it unsettles him even more. Another chewing sound, a louder one, comes from across the table. John can't believe what he sees: Apples has bypassed the normal process of eating fruit by the bite and has stuffed an entire crabapple into his mouth. His cheek billows out into a giant ball as he chomps loudly on the green fruit, with bits and pieces of apple spilling out of his mouth as he chews.

John is too frightened to challenge Rock, and now he is equally frightened by how the killer might react if John wins. The man is clearly riding on the edge, and John fears that the slightest provocation might trigger him, or trigger Apples, who is still simmering over the incident with the pair of jacks. Unlike Apples or Popcorn, Rock has no snack to chomp on and crush; he might let out his frustration in a different way, at something bigger, alive, and closer by—like himself, John Howard-Hughes, who conveniently happens to sit an arm's length away, within easy throttling distance of Rock's lethal hands.

Being prudent and taking the path of least resistance, John decides to show his hand first. The last thing he needs is to incite this short-tempered brute into an unholy rage by arguing the finer points of poker protocol.

"I have a flush," John says hesitantly, not sure if he's rooting for his hand to win or lose, given the frightful anger of the man next to him. John turns over two hearts to go with the three hearts showing on board. The flush is a strong hand, but a loser if his opponent has that full house he is worried about. He peers at Rock out of the corner of his eye, afraid that looking at him directly might be seen as an affront.

Rock stares at the flush like it's his pet dog lying dead at John's feet, his face an exercise in internal restraints and convulsing emotions that want to explode in mayhem. His right thumb slowly fans a small pile of chips. A deathly pall hangs over the table, the only audible sound the clicking of Rock's chips, one upon another.

John tensely sits, his heart pounding heavily, waiting, along with everyone else, to see what Rock will do. Rock, however, says nothing.

He just sits there riffling chips, silently brooding over John's flush. A few more seconds pass, and John, emboldened by the delay and convinced his hand is the winner, reaches across with both hands to grab the pile of chips in the pot and haul them back to his stack. He is suddenly buoyant. His thinking was right on: Rock didn't have the goods and is obviously surprised that John indeed holds a flush, exactly as represented by his upcards. John's strong hand has clearly taken the wind out of the big man's sails.

"Looks like it's mine," John says, breathing a sigh of relief and exhaling air out slowly through his lips. His fingers rest on the pile of chips for an extra moment, reveling in the win. The chips are cool against his fingers, soothing, and feel good. It's a huge pot, and he psychologically needs this win. In the back of his mind, Ludo's doubts about the real stakes of this game make him nervous. And while John is pretty sure that one dollar is the price of one chip, he would feel a lot better having more than the fifty chips he began with rather than having fewer.

Like an eagle swooping out of the sky and nailing an exposed hare in the field, Rock's big hand slams down on top of John's, pinning it to the felt.

"Not so fast," he says.

He lets go of John's hand, leaving a huge red mark on the skin. Rock turns over his hole cards to reveal the hand he has held since his fifth card, three eights and two queens. A full house. It is the hand John feared—and it's a winner. Rock's face breaks out into a childlike grin. Only seconds before, this giant of a man had worn the menacing countenance of an angry killer whose composure was about to self-destruct; now he sits gloating like a toddler who has successfully bullied the prized toy away from his weaker brother.

"When he raises, he's always got the goods, Cupcakes," says Popcorn. "Always." Popcorn rolls his head around, his eyes aiming somewhat in the direction of John. "Why do you think everyone got out of that pot so quick?"

"That's why we call him 'Rock,'" Joey Cleaners chimes in.

John looks at the huge pool of chips being pulled in by Rock—the largest pot of the evening—and shakes his head in disgust. What the heck was he thinking? His final hand, a flush, was obvious, right there for anyone to read. But more importantly, he had ignored raises from a player who had raised only one other time all night, when four deuces, a monster hand, had been held. It was obvious to Rock that John had the flush; it should have been equally obvious to John that Rock had a full house.

It's a cardinal rule in poker to play your opponents and not your cards, and John, a fool trapped in his own misguided thinking, ignored the obvious, driving through the hand like a drunk motorist recklessly and arrogantly propelling his vehicle through red lights. He had tried to be tougher than these killers in a surrogate way, bludgeoning them with aggressive bets and a tough posture, but essentially, all he had done was run another red light, an inopportune one, and get crushed by a bigger object, a huge tractor-trailer that could be seen for two hundred yards down the road. Sure, he had a flush, a hand normally strong enough to win, but in poker, strength is relative. Like the others, he should have folded when that first raise from Rock came down. There is a rule of the road that every experienced driver knows: Yield to bigger moving objects when they're in your path. In poker, it is no different: Respect the rock.

What was he thinking? "Rock" is the standard time-honored poker nickname for tight players who only play premium hands, and there is usually one of them in every game. A rock is the most predictable of all the poker-playing types. Unless you've got the goods yourself, you fold when a rock bets. Every poker player worth his salt knows that.

What an idiot!

John stares at his decimated pile of chips. He has just lost a monster pot, twenty-seven chips, almost half of the chips he had stockpiled before that hand was dealt. No longer is he on the winning side with a cushion. Now, he is well behind the eight ball and feeling pressured. The big loss to Rock rattles him, and John, who had steadily and confidently built up his winnings earlier, plays scared, afraid to lose another big pot.

His opponents sense John's weakness and play aggressively against him, raising when he bets and chasing him out of pots he would otherwise compete for. Like Rock, he has become predictable, an easy mark for his opponents.

John adds up his chips for the third time, as if not believing his accounting the first two times. It doesn't take long. Only thirteen chips of his original fifty-chip buy-in remain. Thirteen chips. He has been sucked into the mentality of this game where every chip is contested and played for as though it has far greater value than a simple dollar.

"This is crazy," John thinks to himself. "I have become as serious as the rest of them, and I'm down a measly thirty-seven dollars. Not even two twenty-dollar bills!"

John looks over at Ludo. He is standing by the bar, a worried look on his face, sipping from a can of beer. When their eyes meet, Ludo shakes his head and turns away. He's obviously upset and John can understand that. While things don't appear bad, John's just a few bills down—what's the big deal?—they *feel* bad. And they feel dangerous. Three players have overtly threatened John: Apples, with his violent ripping and throwing of the jack; Popcorn, with his threat of cutting off his balls and throwing them out the window; and Rock, clearly on the edge, waiting for any excuse to inflict violence. The others—Knuckles, Cleaners, and Wonderbread—are like a gurgling vortex of boiling lava hovering inside an angry volcano, poised to rain misery on the villages below.

Every remark these players make seems to revolve around some overture of violence, death, and killing, and it frightens him. Events are spiraling out of John's control, like he's a spinning top that threatens to hop off the table and crash wildly to the floor, with all four sides of the table close and dangerous. John tries to remember what Ludo said to him earlier, but his concentration has been shattered by the loss to Rock and the threats against his person. He can't think clearly—and it's not from the alcohol. Strangely enough, for all the drinks John has consumed during the afternoon—two shots of Jack Daniel's and three screwdrivers—he's not the least bit drunk. If anything, he's stone cold sober. But at the same time, the room feels suffocating, like the air-conditioning vent is pumping out heat rather than cool air and the vent is a reverse air exhaust sucking all the fresh air out of the room.

John loosens his top button and downs a full glass of ice water, but it doesn't cool him off much. He's still hot, too hot.

"How long you guys normally play for?" John asks no one in particular. His voice comes out embarrassingly high-pitched, like a squeal from a teenaged girl. John wishes he had just kept his mouth shut, but it is too late now.

"Usually until you're broke or dead," Cleaners responds in a raspy voice. This remark causes Popcorn to break out in a high-pitched laugh, but like a candle snuffed out by two pinched fingers for the very last time, the laughter stops just as suddenly.

"Why, you got other plans, Cupcakes?" Wonderbread adds, the long scars on his face reflecting dully in the light.

———————

A few minutes later, down to his last eleven chips, John holds a big hand that looks like a winner. Only John and Wonderbread are left to contest the pot. The last cards have now been dealt and each player sits with his final hand. Wonderbread holds the high hand on board, three fours and a six, and flips two chips in the pot to open the action on seventh street, the last round of betting.

John is feeling pretty good about his chances and pauses for effect.

"Time to get out, rookie," says Wonderbread.

"Why, you got another four hidden?" John asks, emboldened by his hand, a full house.

"One more down here," Wonderbread says, tapping on the cards he has face down in front of him. "Is it enough?"

"I don't think you have it. Make that two more," John says, pushing four chips into the pot. He now has seven chips invested into the pot, with his last four chips not yet in action. John is certain that the powerful hand he holds will beat Wonderbread and deliver him the money in the pot, but he doesn't want to bet all his chips for fear of scaring Wonderbread out of the pot. If he wins the hand, it will replenish his dwindling stack of chips. The other players have folded, leaving behind their antes, and their third- and fourth-street bets, so the pot is big. And, as poker players like to say when they break even or go ahead after being down, it will allow him to "get well."

Johnny Wonderbread stares across at him. His eyes are pools of dead light, and his lips, set tight like a knife rammed into a body clear up to the hilt, are pale, as if all the blood has drained out of them. A long scar runs from his temple across his cheek and all the way down to a spot just above his jaw. There, it meets a smaller, shallower scar to form a tiny carved X on his face.

"Mama told me never to tell lies," Wonderbread says. In precise motions, like a medical examiner carving up a cadaver, Wonderbread picks up six chips, raising John's two-dollar raise by four more dollars, and neatly puts them in the pot. He never takes his eyes off John's, watching him carefully, as if this were a gunfight in the Wild West and a split-second's hesitation could mean the difference between acting fast and drawing life, or the wrong end of a speeding bullet and the stopping of a heartbeat.

"I call," John says quickly. He puts his last four chips into the pot and turns over his cards, three sevens and a pair of kings, a beautiful and powerful full house. It's a very strong hand that doesn't come often.

But is it strong enough?

Wonderbread turns over his down cards one at a time. First an ace. Then a five. Neither of these cards means anything. Then he looks squarely at John, slowly turning over his third down card. It's the four of clubs, the last four in the deck, giving Wonderbread quad fours. It's a monster hand. The four is the one and only card that can beat John's hand.

"Forty-four, magnum force," Wonderbread says. "I win, you lose."

John undoes another button on his shirt. The room has become hotter, and he has trouble drawing enough air into his lungs.

"Looks like youse out of chips," Knuckles says. "Youse wants in for some more? If not, youse settles up with Harry over there."

John looks over at Rock, still gloating from his earlier win; at Popcorn, who is making a cutting motion with his fingers; at Knuckles, flexing his big scarred fists, love and hate dancing in cheap blue prison ink; at Apples, still parboiling with anger, who spits a seed out of his mouth and pings it off the glass ashtray in front of him; at Cleaners, something savage expressing itself in his plastic face (is that skin real?); and at Wonderbread and the deep, dead scars running across his face— and he shakes his head in decline.

John picks up a crumpled napkin, already moist with his own sweat, and wipes a few more beads of perspiration off his forehead.

Chapter Twelve

Harry waits for John at the bar, swirling his whiskey in ice cubes that clink off the glass. Though he doesn't look at John directly, Harry follows his progress across the room. John walks past him, picking up a handful of ice from the bucket sitting next to the liquor bottles, and dropping them into a tall glass. He turns the faucet on cold and watches the water cascade out of the fixture before pushing his glass underneath and filling it to the top. He feels Harry's shifty eyes on him as he downs the cool water in one long gulp.

Ludo stands a few feet away, looking out on the Strip and gripping his can of beer tightly, as if it were a life preserver that he couldn't afford to let go. From the corner of his eye, he sees Harry's beady eyes studying John's profile, one apelike arm dangling by his side, the other bent at the elbow, his nicotine-stained fingers wrapped around his drink.

Harry hesitates before addressing John, turning slightly in his direction but not quite looking at him. "So you're ZZ's friend?" he says, letting that thought float in the air while he examines his drink. "You know her a long time?"

"Oh, less than a year or two," John says, looking away. He is uncomfortable talking to this loathsome creature, let alone supplying any information to him.

Harry thinks on that for a few seconds, shaking his head in thought. "I see," he says. "So you sort of know her well?"

John shrugs, waiting to see where Harry is going with this.

Harry's decaying teeth peek out from his mouth while he lifts his glass to drink. "Be careful with her, and don't say I didn't warn you," Harry continues. "She's not what she seems."

"What do you mean?"

"Just take it from me," Harry says, turning to face him. His shifty eyes move around the room and come to rest on John's shoulder. "You ready to settle up for the game?"

"That's fifty dollars?" John queries with a shaky voice, somehow feeling the amount isn't right.

Harry looks at him silently, and one at a time, he cracks the knuckles on each hand. His eyes, like a rat's, are beady, and they peer at John from an oblique angle. John feels his heart pounding in his chest, and in the silence he counts off ten long heartbeats. Harry's gaze is fixed on the smoke drifting up from his cigarette as he ponders John's statement. Over by the door, the cadaverous gray-haired man sits motionless, his eyes watching every move closely.

"This is not a laughing matter," Harry finally says. He lights another cigarette from the end of the one he is smoking and crushes the old one in an ashtray filled with butts worked down to the filter. He takes a deep drag on the fresh cigarette, letting the blue-white wisps creep out through his nose and mouth before he exhales and blows a funnel of smoke off to the side. Harry's simian arms drop, hanging limply by his sides as he looks up into the cloud of nicotine exhaust he has just blown out of his mouth.

Knuckles takes a break from the game and walks over, muscles bulging from his massive upper body. His legs, built like tree trunks, look near to bursting through his linen slacks. If Knuckles looked big sitting down, he looks even bigger standing up.

"He thinks he owes fifty dollars," Harry says to him.

"Youse thoughts we was playing for snack money, youse little shit? Whadaya kiddin' me? It's five grand, cash money," Knuckles says.

"Wait a second," John protests, "you just can't—"

"What's it gonna be?" Knuckles says.

John pulls out his wallet, thumbs inside through a few bills, and looks pleadingly over at Ludo.

"I don't know, man," Ludo says quietly.

"Gives me the wallet," Knuckles says, grabbing the billfold from John's hands and handing it to Harry. John stares numbly as Harry pulls out all the money inside and counts it carefully.

"You're a little short here, Cupcakes. I seem to get only sixteen hundred and twenty-seven dollars in my count. You think my math is a little off?" Harry asks.

"No," John says weakly, eyeing his gambling stake, blackjack winnings, and vacation money about to go away in one fell swoop.

"How about your friend here. What does he got?" Harry says.

"I wasn't playing," Ludo says. "Don't look at me."

"I's looking at youse," Knuckles says. "Now, he's asking what youse got."

Ludo pulls a dark green leather wallet out of his pocket. "I don't have much. Just food money."

Knuckles takes the wallet from Ludo's hand before he can protest and turns it over a few times with great interest, like he's examining a strange new species of frog.

"Hey, that's my wallet," Ludo says.

"Is that so?" Knuckles says in a voice so soft and sedate, as if talking to a little child, that it makes Ludo shiver involuntarily from fright. "What, youse want it back?"

Ludo, not sure how to respond, simply shrugs in a noncommittal fashion, fearful that any kind of response will be taken the wrong way by the seething brute—and with bad consequences.

Knuckles fishes out five crisp one-hundred-dollar bills, Ludo's food and entertainment budget for the trip, and a driver's license—the entire contents of Ludo's wallet—and hands these items to Harry.

"Here, take it," Knuckles says, and flips the empty billfold back to Ludo.

"That's five hundred dollars more," Harry says, counting the five bills, "for a total of twenty-one hundred and twenty-seven dollars they've given us."

Knuckles rubs his hands together, looks at John, and says, "Then youse owes us some money, ain't that right, Cupcakes? Now, youse not holding out on me, are youse?"

"That's it, I swear to God, that's everything I have with me," John says, "I—"

"Don't interrupts me," Knuckles says menacingly. "I wants my money and I wants it soon. Do youse understand what I's saying?"

"I—"

"I told youse not to interrupts me. The first thing youse gonna do is comes up with a plan to makes things right—and comes up with it fast. Am I clears on that?" Knuckles looks hard at John.

"They should make things right," Harry says. "That's a good idea. What do you think, Knuckles?"

"That's a good idea," Knuckles concurs, his eyes a glint of hard polished stone. "I thinks that's a good idea."

"I don't know what I can do so fast," John says. He looks over at the table. The players are watching the confrontation with grim expressions.

"Youse better get a whole lot more optimistics in a hurry, Cupcakes. I's an optimistics guy myselfs and I got faith in youse. But don't make me feel pessimistics about things. That wouldn't be good."

"What do you think I been telling you all along?" Ludo says to John. "You too pessimistic about things. You gotta look at the up side of things. He's right, man."

"Shut up, Ludo," John whispers out of the side of his mouth.

Harry studies John while he pulls long and hard on his cigarette, a full half-inch of tobacco burning down while he inhales. His fingers, stained a dirty shade of ochre from decades of smoking cigarettes down to the butt, hold the filter near its edge.

"Knuckles," Harry says, "he says that what he has here is all he can get right now. That's what he says."

Knuckles takes a long look at John, scotch and a solitary ice cube swishing around in his glass. The knuckles on his right hand, where "hate" is tattooed, are gnarled and scarred, making the tumbler of scotch look like a thimble in his beefy hand. Without another word, Knuckles, with a slight smile that sends shivers up John's back, returns to the poker game.

Harry digs further into John's wallet and removes his driver's license and a few scraps of paper. "So I got twenty-one hundred and twenty-seven dollars in my hand, which means you owe me twenty-eight hundred and eighty-three dollars."

"Hey, it's only twenty-eight hundred and seventy-three dollars," Ludo says. "You're ten dollars off."

"Jesus Christ, what's the matter with you?" John says. "What's a goddamn ten dollar difference?"

"Ten dollars is ten dollars, that's what the difference is. Exactly ten dollars. You the accountant, man, why you asking me?"

"Ludo, now's not the time for this nonsense. Ten dollars doesn't matter here."

"Ten dollars is ten dollars. I don't care what you say," Ludo stubbornly persists.

"You don't understand—"

"Why don't you two shut up? I'm getting irritated," Harry says. He pulls out some papers from John's wallet. "I see we have some plane tickets here for a Ludo Garcia and a John Howard-Hughes."

Harry looks at each of them in turn, then returns his attention to the wallet. He pulls out a business card and reads it out loud: "Howard-Hughes, Howard-Hughes, and Howard-Hughes, Accounting Services. Brooklyn, New York. I see," Harry says, dragging deeply on his cigarette. A full inch of ashes hangs precariously off the end of the butt, a red glow showing between the dead ashes and the unspent tobacco. "I think I'll hang onto this so I know where to collect my debt. That's a good idea, isn't it, Cupcakes?"

John silently looks down at his feet, the impact of these killers knowing where he works hitting home.

"Howard-Hughes, Howard-Hughes, and Howard-Hughes, Accounting Services," Harry repeats.

"Wait a second, there," Ludo says. "Five hundred dollars of that money is mine."

"Is that right?" Harry looks at Ludo thoughtfully, and places the plane tickets in a neat pile with John's driver's license, scraps of paper, business card, and cash, adds Ludo's driver's license and money to the stack, and stuffs the whole pile into the breast pocket of his sport coat. He hands the empty wallet back to John and says, "Why don't I hold these couple items as, how do you say, insurance? That's your business, isn't it?"

"No, it's accounting, like it says on the card," Ludo volunteers.

"Will you shut up, Ludo?" John says in a low voice through gritted teeth.

"Oh, by the way," Harry says after taking a small sip of his drink, looking obliquely at John, "your lady friend called to say she can't make it." With that pronouncement, Harry picks up his drink and swallows the rest of it in two gulps.

While John and Ludo let this new development sink in and try to figure out their options, Harry chomps down on a large ice cube, noisily crushing it into small pieces.

"Let's get out of here," Ludo says.

As they turn to go, Harry grabs hold of John's arm. His narrowed eyes look at John from an awkward angle, and the overgrown nails of his stained fingers hang on to John's sport coat like an eagle's talons.

"Let me give you two pieces of friendly advice, Mr. Howard-Hughes, Howard-Hughes, and Howard-Hughes, Insurance. First, watch out which women you hang around with in this town. You've already been warned on that score. And two—and listen to me carefully, Cupcakes—don't make an optimistic person pessimistic."

Harry pauses for a few seconds, smoke drifting up from the cigarette he has dragged deeply on, and he blows the smoke off to the side.

"You get what I'm saying?"

Chapter Thirteen

John and Ludo leave room 813 in a daze, dragging their feet down the hotel corridor as though they were shackled to leg irons, two chain gang prisoners just out of sentencing and on their way to serving hard time. They're like dead men walking, feeling not only like they lost all their money, but their fight as well. The gravity of their predicament adds weight to their chains, making their silent march down the long narrow hall to the elevator seem to take forever. They stand next to each other in front of the elevator door on the eighth floor of the Silver Cactus Hotel and Casino.

"I heard about getting yourself caught in a whole bunch of shit, man, but you found the fucking cesspool," Ludo says. "The fucking big pond, man. 'Cupcakes!' What the fuck was that all about?"

"What are we going to do?" John cries. "Twenty-eight hundred and eighty-three dollars. They got our licenses. They got our tickets. They got my business card. My business card! They know where I work, where my family works for God's sake."

"Two, eight, seven, three," Ludo says.

"What the hell is that supposed to mean?"

"It's only twenty-eight hundred and seventy-three dollars. He was off by ten dollars."

"Come on, not that again," John says. "This is a disaster! What are we going to do?"

"I told you I didn't feel good about this. Room eight-thirteen, man, you should have listened to me."

"I don't need to hear this now. Please."

"You don't need to hear this? We're here twenty-four fucking hours and you already digging a hole to China. Damn! You know what twenty-eight hundred and seventy-three dollars means?"

"Yeah, the cost of our funeral, discounted because there's two of us. What does it mean, Ludo?"

"The thirteens not only divide evenly in there, but it's how many times they divide with each other—one hundred and thirty-one times. That's one-three-one."

"I don't need to know that to know we're in deep trouble."

"But what you do need to know is that one hundred and thirty-one times is one-three-one. That's thirteen going forward and backwards, all in the same number. You get thirteen whether you start with the one and middle with the three or end with the one with the three in the middle. They all twisted around each other now."

"What are we going to do, Ludo? What are we going to do?"

"Beats the fuck out of me, but this is the doozy of all doozies. I have to hand it to you," Ludo says, shaking his head in disbelief. Seeing John's distraught face, Ludo decides to let it go. "Alright, homes, alright. Let's just get a bite and think things through. Eating is always a good way to let things resolve themselves, you know, food, with all them qualities in it and everything."

John stares glassy-eyed in front of him, shuddering at the thought of where this vacation has headed. And Ludo doesn't even know the half of it. "Where the hell is the elevator?"

"You didn't push the button."

"Well if you knew I didn't push the button, why didn't you push the button?"

"Well, I thought you were going to do it," Ludo says.

"No, the way it is," John says, irritated, "is I thought you were going to do it."

"But obviously I didn't, so seeing I didn't do it, I don't know why you didn't."

"Okay, now that you know I didn't push the button, you can push it, okay?"

"Why don't *you* push the button?" Ludo says. "That's the real question."

John and Ludo stand silently until a girl about ten years old, wearing a simple pink dress with lavender trim and an oversized Minnie Mouse watch, walks down the hall and stands between them. After a few seconds, the little girl checks her watch and calmly resumes staring at the elevator door. John and Ludo glance over at her, but she makes no move to push the button.

"Nobody pushed the button," Ludo says to the little girl.

"I'm in no rush."

"Okay," Ludo says.

Another few minutes go by and the three of them stubbornly stand there, quietly facing the elevator. No one has made a move to push the button, and as yet, no elevator has alighted on the floor. Soon, a family of five arrives and stands behind John, Ludo, and the little girl. Right on their heels, another couple comes by, and they too take their place facing the elevator. The party of passengers waiting for the elevator grows to twelve people as another couple joins the group. As if taking a cue from John, Ludo, and the little girl in the pink dress with lavender trim, the rest of the waiting group stand with hands clasped in front of them, either ignorantly or stubbornly, leaving the button unpressed.

The father in the family of five, standing directly behind John and Ludo, unclasps his hands and pulls out a comb. He smoothly runs it through his thick hair with careful strokes, making an elaborate procedure out of the motions. John glances behind himself for a second, and then over at Ludo, who can see the man combing his hair out of the corner of his eye. John raises his eyebrows as if to say "I told you so," and then they go back to staring at the elevator door.

A few minutes later, as startled guests in the lobby look on, twenty-seven people explode out of the elevator and into the lobby like a split pomegranate showering seeds through the air.

Chapter Fourteen

"These guys are going to come after us if we don't come up with the money soon," John says, staring at the back of his friend's menu. They're in the Railbird diner on Tropicana Avenue near Pecos, sitting across from one another.

"Uh-huh," Ludo says absentmindedly, studying the menu.

John contemplates the options and just doesn't see any way out of this mess. Even if he were back home, there is no money in his bank account to pay this debt. Heck, he doesn't even have a bank account, a fact his sister reminds him of every week with the same refrain: "You're an accountant and you not only can't keep track of your own finances, you don't even have a bank account? And you're broke all the time? *Really*?" John had used all his spare money for this trip and the one place to turn, his best friend Ludo, is also a dead end—he's stuck in this predicament right along with him. As it is, John still owes his sister four thousand dollars for a five-thousand-dollar used car he bought that had gotten stolen before he had a chance to even put seventy-five miles on the odometer or get insurance. His sister is below the absolute last resort. Bad enough he still hears every day about the debt he owes to her, the last thing he needs in life is to call her for another loan—or to call his father, which would be worse—especially under these circumstances.

"Those poker players are a bunch of hired killers, every single one of them. They don't look like the most patient group of people."

"Right," Ludo grunts.

"You have any ideas what to do?"

Ludo doesn't respond from behind the laminated list of food offerings.

"Ludo, are you listening to me?"

Ludo pulls down the menu and looks at John. "Yeah, you just asked me if I have any ideas what to do. Man, it's not easy with these big menus. I'm thinking about pork chops or maybe just plain old spaghetti and meatballs. I'm not convinced about their turkey plate. Why, what are you thinking of getting?"

John balls his fists in frustration. "We were almost killed back there and you're wondering what I'm thinking of eating?"

"Well, yeah, a couple of tough choices, hard to figure the right order here."

"Do you realize that those killers are going to be after us if we don't come up with money we don't have?"

Ludo looks up. "I keep telling you, homes—don't worry about things you don't have to worry about until you have to worry about them, you know what I'm saying? It's the old Ludo Rule, I been telling you this for ten years. See, them other problems gonna be there just the same whether we eat now or yak our heads off like two old ladies all day long. The difference being that if we order the food, we can eat it, and the problem hasn't changed from beginning to end. The other way around, we don't order and we don't eat and that problem still there and now the ending and the beginning all confused with each other, they don't know what to do, and we still hungry. That's what I'm getting at." Ludo glances at a steaming plate of food passing by and licks his lips. "So, what do you think?"

"I don't know," John says dejectedly. He picks a stray hair off the table and tosses it on the floor.

"Just pick something out, man, don't make such a big deal about it," Ludo says, running his fingers down the menu and considering another choice. "Just some food."

"Do you ever think of anything besides food?"

"When I'm hungry, I think about food. When I'm tired, I think about sleeping. You make things too complicated, man." Ludo puts down the menu and bangs on it with the bottom of his hand. "Life's all right in front of you."

"The only thing in front of us is the life expectancy of a flea, Ludo. If one of those hoodlums doesn't do us in, another one of them will." John covers up his face with both hands and groans through his fingers. With his eyes closed, John pictures a larger-than-life image of Knuckles' gnarled and scarred right hand with the word "hate" tattooed above the second joints.

"We got all meal to talk about it," Ludo says, reaching over and patting John on the shoulder. "Let's just order up a little food. What are you getting?"

"I don't know, Ludo." John shrugs and throws up his hands. "How about you?"

"I asked you first."

"Why do I have to tell you first?"

"'Cause I asked you first, that's why," Ludo says. "How can I answer something you haven't even asked yet? Do I have to guess every question you going to ask before you ask it?"

"But you have it figured out already, so why don't you tell me first?" John says. "Then I can figure out what I want and tell you."

"Because I asked you first, homes." Ludo crosses his arms and leans back against the chair, digging in his position.

"What if I had asked you what you were having first?" John says.

"But you didn't, you asked second, so it's not a practical question. It's still your turn first no matter which way the water goes upriver, you know what I'm saying?"

"Ludo, water can't go upriver. By definition, it can only go downriver."

"You telling me water can't reverse itself? How about toilets flushing one way up here and a different way down in South America?"

"What does the Coriolis effect have to do with it?"

"See, there you're getting off on all that college-educated nonsense and we just trying to order food. You so busy with Plato, Aristotle, and like Jennifer Lopez and whatever stuck up your learning ass, when all you got to worry about is, like, hamburgers or whatever. And—"

"Ludo," John interrupts, "I took accounting classes in junior college, not politics."

"Whatever. But the bottom line, homes, and you know it, and I know it, and Aristotles knows it, is I asked you first!"

"Aristotle is dead. Somehow I don't think he knows it."

"Alright, Jennifer Lopez then. She's alive."

A short, thin man with long, stringy black hair flings open the swinging kitchen doors and marches over to where the manager of the diner is standing, one table over from John and Ludo. The man's face is tense with anger, and water drips off his arms. He removes his dishwashing apron, which is also wet, and flings it into the manager's chest.

"Screw you, Virgil, I'm out of here," the man says, and stalks toward the exit, his short feet looking silly making long strides. "Wash your own goddamned dishes."

"You sucked anyway," the manager yells after the dishwasher, his face turning the same color as his curly red hair. He bends over, sticking out his ample rear end, and repeatedly pats his buttocks with exaggerated and emphatic sweeps of his right hand. "Kiss my ass," the manager screams across the diner, "my big hairy ass."

The dishwasher gets to the front door, turns around, flips the manager his middle finger, and continues on outside, slamming the door behind him.

A woman with two small girls throws a bill on a nearby table and hurries out the door, a look of disgust on her face.

"Screw her too," the manager mumbles. He is standing next to John and Ludo. "These dishwashers are all goddamned lowlifes anyway, every last one of them," he says to them, and walks back to the kitchen through the swinging doors.

John watches the door to the diner close and throws up his arms. "How can I think about food now? These guys are going to kill us if we don't get them money!"

"Don't change nothing whether we going to die tomorrow or in fifty years, we still got to eat today. Just get something basic like meatloaf and French fries, lots of country gravy, and some greens on the side. It's good with that gravy. And there you go, problem solved, Mr. Accounting."

"Problem solved? That's what you want!"

"I'm just trying to help, man," Ludo says.

"My point is this: You're ordering what you want for you, as if you were eating it—in addition to what you are going to get—so it's like you're ordering twice for you and no times for me."

"I'm trying to do the best I can sitting over here. If I was me, inside of you over there, I could order what you wanted over there. But I'm me over here so I can't figure out what you want over there, except from the way I see it over here looking at you over there."

"But you're over there and not putting yourself over here, instead of putting yourself over here from over there. You end up getting me an over-there order instead of getting me an over-here order."

"You thinking too much again. I try to step in your shoes from my shoes, but you like, switch your feet, so your shoes don't know which way they're pointing," Ludo says. He holds a fork in his hand, and John is getting dizzy watching its progress through the air. "And from what I know over here of what you might want over there—" Ludo pauses when he hears a woman clear her throat.

The waitress is standing in front of them and sees the two going at it again. She rolls her eyes and releases a big sigh. "Do you guys ever stop?"

Ludo bypasses the two menu items he had been contemplating and instead orders the special of the day: fried chicken cooked extra crispy, with sides of macaroni and cheese, collard greens, and cornbread. The meal arrives on an oversized plate with the food piled high, steam rising lazily from the hot food. Ludo tucks his napkin into his collar and lustily digs into the generous portions of food, licking his lips at the hearty repast spread before him.

John orders the meatloaf Ludo recommended, but after fifteen minutes, his portion sits in front of him virtually untouched. Now and then John pushes the food around the plate or picks around the meatloaf like it's infested with worms. But he is just going through the motions; his stomach is too twisted into knots to ingest food anyway.

One table over, a few cops on break sip coffee and share a crumb cake. Behind them, incongruously, two heavily tattooed bikers wearing white T-shirts and leather vests emblazoned with gang colors dig into a meal of hamburgers and milk shakes. They talk softly, quite aware that in the booth adjoining theirs, the other side of the law sits within hearing distance.

"Well," John says, "I guess the bright side is that they didn't kill us and throw us out the window."

"Not yet, anyway," Ludo says with a mouthful of food. "Hey, if you're not eating that meatloaf, can I try a piece?"

"Go ahead."

"Thanks." Ludo spikes a chunk with his fork. "Your fries look good, though I think you would have been better off with the mashed potatoes. Can I try them too?" John nods his head and Ludo grabs three fries and stuffs them into an already packed orifice. "Don't tell me you gave that big-nosed, two-legged rat every penny you had."

"Of course I did. You were there."

"That was dumb. You mean you didn't hold back at least fifty dollars, twenty dollars, five dollars, whatever?"

"He didn't exactly give me a chance to sort out my money before he took my wallet."

"Nothing like 'fleecing a few local yokels in a little game of poker.' Isn't that what you said? What happened to that, big boy?"

"Okay, okay, okay, don't rub it in." John sighs and pushes two French fries around his plate. "Didn't you hold back any money? You know how you sometimes keep a few bills in your pocket?"

"I had only that five hundred dollars, didn't even get a chance to break a penny of it in yet! And that fine fellow with the prison tattoos on his knuckles wasn't overly encouraging about me starting a savings plan."

"Ludo, we just got cleaned out of everything we have here with us. It's nothing to joke about."

"I'm not joking, man. Believe me, I'm not," Ludo says. He dips two more fries in ketchup and halves them with a crisp bite. "So he took your business card, your driver's license, your money, all that crap, even those scraps of paper you always keep in there? All of it, right?"

"And our plane tickets also."

"Our plane tickets? I forgot about that. Damn! That's fucked up on top of being fucked up." Ludo grabs three more fries, dips them in ketchup, and chews them slowly. "So how do we get back home?"

"I don't have an answer to that one, Ludo. I really don't." John shakes his head. "I think we got other problems too."

"How could we possibly have any problems other than having absolutely no money between us, no debit or credit cards, no plane tickets to get out of here, and blahty, blahty, blahty, blah?" Ludo says. "Oh yeah, excuse me. And a yellow-toothed creep, one mortuary-looking skeleton, and six murderers who gonna be vacuuming the town looking for us to get their poker chips back?"

"You know how you're always talking about worrying about what you got to worry about only when you have to worry about it?"

"Yeah?"

"Well, remember how you said there was no other money in your pocket?"

Chapter Fifteen

Thirty minutes later, John and Ludo are still in the diner, only this time they are not seated comfortably in a padded red vinyl booth enjoying food and ample air-conditioning. Instead, they are toiling over soiled and crudded pots, pans, glasses, bowls, plates, silverware, and refuse, learning the basic functionality of the diner's dishwashing equipment while it mercilessly pumps out heat. Ludo wears an apron and is vigorously scrubbing a blackened pot in the big sink as John enters the kitchen with a heavily laden tray balanced tentatively on his right hand.

"Remind me to put this on my next resume," Ludo says as he watches John place a stack of dirty dishes on the counter. "Lots of fun, man." He is rinsing a large soup pot, and finishing it, pushes it off to the side.

"Boy, were we in luck that the dishwasher got fired today. If that job didn't open up, the manager said he was going to put us in jail. And those two cops were looking at us. Did you see that?"

"Oh, we're just full of luck, homes," Ludo says as he grabs another pan. "Piled up with it."

"How about you freeloaders stop working your mouths and start

132

working the dishes," the manager yells from across the kitchen. "We got lots of dishes to do."

"You better treat me good or I'm going to quit," Ludo yells back, winking at John.

"You better shut your mouth or you'll be making beds downtown in the jail with the other vagrants instead of washing dishes," the manager warns. "Since you can't afford bus fare, I can always go get those cops inside to give you a ride."

"Your momma still make your bed, Virgil?" Ludo calls over.

"Keep talking," Virgil says, staring across at Ludo, "just keep talking."

"Ludo, keep cool, we got enough problems," John whispers.

"Just riding him a little, that's all."

"We can't afford to lose this position."

"I don't know how we could afford to get into this position. You're right, though, this is such an upwardly mobile job, I would hate to blow this opportunity. Maybe I could make assistant busboy next. Homes, remember how I told you that I hate washing dishes?"

"Yeah."

"Well, I hate washing fucking dishes."

"There's another table needs clearing," Virgil calls over to John. "You think you can shake your cute little ass over there after you're finished chatting with the dishwasher?"

John mutters under his breath, "Asshole."

As John leaves the kitchen, the manager stops him and asks, "By the way, what *is* your name?"

Ludo calls over, "He goes by 'Cupcakes.' I'm Ludo."

"Will you shut up, Ludo?" John calls back.

"Cupcakes?"

John and Ludo listlessly watch the second hand snake its way around the face of the round clock on the wall above the slop sink. They sit, slumped over on two upturned milk crates next to the dishwashing equipment, exhausted from a long, arduous, and harrowing day, feeling as energetic as melted wax on a candle holder. It is twelve o'clock, midnight, and they have been working in a stuffy, hot room since six P.M. without a break. And they are beat.

Virgil strolls into the kitchen and heads over to where they sit, a smug expression on his face, looking like a mother goose lording over her goslings. "We're even now, puppies," Virgil says to Ludo, counting out and stuffing five ten-dollar bills in Ludo's shirt pocket. "You and Cupcakes can be on your way."

"It's been real," Ludo says.

"Y'all come back if you need some more work. We'll keep the light on for you," Virgil says.

"Somehow I don't think you'll see us again," John says wearily.

"Guys like you always find a way."

"Hey, you think we can grab a cup of coffee for the road?" John asks.

"I don't think so," Virgil says. "We had enough charity for the evening. But catch me tomorrow at the homeless shelter. I'll put in a good word for you on the food line, okay, Cupcakes?"

Ludo takes off his apron and flips it to the manager as he heads through the swinging doors of the kitchen. "Fuck you, Virgil."

The hapless pair waits twenty minutes to get a taxi back to the hotel, reluctantly parting with ten dollars for the ride—a good chunk of their money—and don't make their way to sleep until almost one o'clock.

Their repose doesn't last long.

———————

At two-thirty in the morning, a loud banging on the hotel door awakens them, and John shoots bolt upright in his bed.

"I think they came to get us," John whispers. "We're screwed."

"Don't get the door. We ain't here," Ludo whispers back.

Three more loud knocks on the door follow. Outside the door, the muffled sound of shuffling feet and whispering can be heard.

"What are we going to do? Knuckles probably lost patience, or they sent Rock," John cries. "They're going to take us out to the desert!"

"Shhhh," Ludo cautions, holding his finger up to his lips.

There is more banging and a few seconds of silence. A girl, giggling and slurring her words, says, "Open up already. Come on!"

"Who you looking for?" Ludo calls back.

"Brett?"

"I think you got the wrong room."

A flood of giggles and the loud raucous laughter of a man is heard. "You got the wrong floor, dodo," a man calls out to the girl. There is a thump against the door, some more laughing, and then the voice of the drunk girl. "Oops, sorry," she calls out. "We got the wrong room. Sorry."

"Why you get me all nervous for?" Ludo says. "Just a bunch of drunks."

For the next hour, John tosses and turns, too wound up to sleep. Thinking he hears something, he sits up and strains his ears.

"Go to sleep, man," Ludo calls over.

"Did you hear that?' John says.

"The only thing I hear is you making a racket for the last hour. I can't sleep if you're going to spin around like a caterpillar making silk. I'm tired, man. I need some sleep."

"What time we go to bed?" John asks.

"Like one-thirty or something. Why?"

"No reason."

At five in the morning, Ludo, who has been unable to fall back asleep, looks over and sees John staring in his direction. "What the fuck's the matter with you?" Ludo says. "I can't sleep with you staring at me and all. Givin' me the heebie-jeebies or something. Look somewhere else."

"I can't sleep either. I'm thinking about what they're going to do to us."

"They're not going to do anything. They wouldn't have let us out of that hotel room if that was the case," Ludo says. "We can't bring them any money if we're dead."

"I guess that's true," John says.

"Now go back to sleep. Damn!"

Sometime after dawn, the somnolent sound of Ludo snoring lulls John to sleep; however, their REM cycles don't last long. A loud knocking awakens them again. John pops up and looks over at the source of the noise. Some light filters through the small window and bathes the room in a yellowish glow, but stare as he might, John cannot see through the wood of the door.

"Ludo," John whispers. "You up?"

"Of course I'm up. I don't think I slept two hours all night—and lousy ones at that."

"Ask who's there."

Ludo opens his eyes, sits up and gives John a searing look. "Just as easy for you to do it without asking me," he whispers back.

"Just do it. I'll explain later."

"You got a lot of things to explain about later."

There is another loud knock on the door, this time with more force.

"Who's there?" Ludo calls over.

"Room service."

"Room service from where?"

"From the hotel, where do you think?" they hear from behind the door. It's a man's voice, gruff and businesslike.

"We didn't order nothing, did we?" Ludo asks John. John shakes his head no.

"Hold on," Ludo yells out.

Ludo walks over to the door, opens it, and is given a silver food tray from a bellman. Ludo is about to close the door, but the bellman hasn't moved.

"Yeah?"

"Is there anything else?" the bellman says.

"No, that's it. Why?" Ludo tries to close the door, but it is stuck at the base. The bellman has edged forward and has lodged his foot in the frame.

"Well?" the bellman says.

"Well, what?"

The bellman clears his throat, but doesn't move or say anything further.

Ludo looks at the man's arched brows. Now he gets it: The bellman is looking for a tip. "We'll get you later," Ludo says to him and forces the door closed, squeezing out the bellman's foot.

"What kind of place is this?" Ludo says to John.

Ludo places the silver tray on the edge of a dresser. "Let's see what we got here," he says, rubbing his hands together. "Maybe a little extra free breakfast with the trip?" With his back to John, Ludo opens the lid and sees two pastries inside. He shrugs his shoulders, picks up one of the pastries, and takes a bite. "This is pretty tasty, man. You want one?" he says over his shoulder to John.

"What is it?"

Ludo turns in John's direction, his face a mask of confused thoughts.

"Cupcakes."

Chapter Sixteen

Las Vegas is a twenty-four-hour city where virtually anything and everything is possible at any time. It's an orgy of hedonism: Eating, drinking, partying, and gambling are partaken of with a fervor and passion unmatched and almost unimagined back home. In the casinos, the palaces of sin that the city is built around, it's a different world with new rules or no rules, an adult playground in another dimension, an anomaly where clocks are no longer the purveyors of time, as there are none; daylight is not a point of reference, as there are no windows; time doesn't exist in an accustomed manner, but is held spellbound within the walls and artificial lights; cash is not the currency used at the tables, it is chips; temperature is not subject to the vagaries of the sun, the winds, or the baking heat, but is carefully climate controlled. Eating? More like gorging at gluttonous buffets with food shoved in by the plateful. Drinking? Water is not the elixir of life in this desert, it is booze and more booze. The dice, the cards, the wheels, the machines— it is all about the trials of luck and the chance to catch a jackpot or the big roll.

Once players are inside the grip of the gambling house, it is a new world. And all it takes to play is money.

"Lucky we have some leftover cash from the diner to get something to eat," John says.

It is seven forty-five in the morning. John and Ludo are exhausted after a night of worrying and tossing and turning, and have given up on getting sleep. Instead, they trudge down to the hotel's coffee shop to grab a bite to eat and think things over. The waitress has just placed the twenty-four-hour-a-day Cowhand Special featuring pork chops, mashed potatoes, and house salad—John's meal choice as recommended by Ludo—in front of John. Ludo sits with a triple-decker chicken salad sandwich served with added bacon, the bacon cooked extra crispy to his specifications.

Ludo takes a big bite of his sandwich, puts it back on the plate, and mechanically works his mouth up and down, slowly chewing on the food. His eyes are fixated on a piece of bacon that has slipped out of his sandwich and fallen on the plate. He examines the bacon as it were a divination symbol containing all the answers to this disastrous turn in their lives—and then picks it up and eats it.

"Well, are you going to say something?" John says, staring blankly at the mashed potatoes on his plate. His elbows are propped up on the table, and he holds his head in both hands as if his neck alone won't support the weight.

"What the hell were you thinking?"

John looks up. "Jesus Christ, I don't know. Didn't you ever do anything dumb, like really stupid that didn't make sense?"

"Yeah, homes, but not *that* dumb. Whatever happened to the concept of money management, you know, not losing all your eggs to one omelet? Didn't you tell me all about that with your blackjack stuff?"

"I thought they were playing for one dollar a chip, not one hundred dollars!" John moans, chasing an olive around the plate and trying to stab it with his fork. "I don't know, ZZ inspired me in some weird way, made me temporarily insane. What can I tell you?"

"You better watch out for those inspirations, homeland. Your next inspiration may be to rob a childcare center of its crayons or something. This must be some chick. Already I don't like her. That whole thing didn't add up, you know what I'm saying? Was she setting us up in there with that guy Harry?"

"I don't think so."

"But it's possible, right?"

John doesn't respond, so Ludo continues. "Tell me what else you know about her. What kind of work she do?" Ludo takes a big bite of his sandwich and nods his head in satisfaction from its taste. A thin piece of lettuce catches and hangs from the corner of his mouth. Ludo removes the stray lettuce with his finger, looks at it, and drops it into his mouth with the rest of the food.

"I don't know what she does."

"How about where she lives? You stayed over at her place, right?"

"Well, her apartment, that's the thing. I don't think it was her apartment. I mean, that's the weird part I can't figure out. There were no decorations, nothing feminine about the place at all. Or even personal. I don't even know if she lives there. Maybe she just borrows the place or something. So where does she live? I really don't know."

"So you don't know anything about where she lives, works, her last name, nothing?" Ludo says, looking incisively at John. "All we know about her is that crowd she hangs around with—Harry, Knuckles, Wonderbread, and the rest of those wonderful folks. Something is not right with this picture. I mean, I don't know if you're picking up on that. You know that thing about how you judge people by who they associate with? What is it, 'Birds of a feather, flock together' or that other one, 'Where there is smoke, there's fire?' Well, I be looking at lots of smoke, homes, columns of it, you know what I'm saying? Columns of it," Ludo repeats, throwing his hands in the air.

"I got us into this mess, not her."

"But she just seems to be all around the action, doesn't she? Listen, homes, I don't mean to be getting down on you or nothing, but this girl sounds like a real lot of trouble, like she the fuse for one stick of dynamite after another. I think you're in over your head, you know, like playing a baseball game with footballs and hockey sticks or whatever, or knowing the rules they be playing with. Or I should say 'we,' since I seem to have become weaved into this mess like cheap thread on ah—what do you call it—ah, like, whatever, you know what I'm talking about? Face the facts, we're neck deep in loose shit."

John moves some food around his plate with his fork, but isn't eating any of it.

"Go ahead," Ludo says.

"What?"

"There's something you're not telling me," Ludo says. "I can feel it."

"What else can there be?" John says innocently.

"I don't know, but there's something else going on here, an undercurrent. Something to do with that girl."

"What?" John says, figuring Ludo couldn't possibly know of his disaster at the Italian restaurant, but he is wary nevertheless.

"Something else bad went down. What is it?"

"Can we not talk about her anymore?" John is looking down at his plate again. "How about all that stuff about being positive, not negative about things?"

"Alright, alright, yeah, you right, being positive. That's what it's all about," Ludo says, looking suspiciously at John before stuffing the rest of the sandwich in his mouth. He works the last of the bread in with his hand and then gulps it down with some water. "Listen, homes, we gotta deal with your stress, right now. Starting right now." Ludo works the air with his two hands as if molding clay thoughts in front of him. "Forget that other shit for a minute, that mess be waiting on us just the same. The Ludo Rule, man, it makes a lot of sense: Only worry about what you have to worry about when you have to worry about it. Right now we're eating, that's what we dealing with right now."

"We got bigger problems, Ludo, I—."

"Easy, man. Relax for a minute, like I said, we don't got to deal with it right this second. Let's get back to basics." Ludo chomps on a pickle slice and licks his fingers clean. "You gotta realize that stress and food, it all tied in together. Yin, yang, dog, cat, bread, crackers, all that shit."

"What?"

"Yeah. Remember we were talking about health food and all that and I was thinking, you know, that that health food thing is a good idea for you, man? Clear the thinking out." Ludo illustratively taps on his head with two fingers, then passes his hand above the food in a wavelike motion. He ends with a small flourish, as if tossing away the problems. "All that food, man, if it's the wrong stuff, it don't let the stress out. You know what I'm saying? Clog it all up inside."

Ludo eats the last pickle on his plate, wipes his mouth clean with a napkin, and then pushes the empty plate off to the side.

The waitress comes by and John waves her away. "When I get stressed out all that aggravation goes right to my stomach," John says. "You know that. Indigestion, cramps, stomachaches, the whole works. At work, this guy next to where I sit calls me the Pepto-Bismol Kid because I'm drinking that pink stuff half the time."

"That's no good, man."

"I've been thinking about doing something about my stress for a long time, and well, why not now?" John bangs the table with his hand for emphasis.

"That's it, hombre," Ludo says, slamming his hand down as well. "Eating the wrong things and overeating is the plague when you got that nerve thing going. You gotta eat right and eat light."

"I'm feeling better already. At least a little, anyway."

"That's it, homes, you getting there!"

"Let them kill me," John says with a smile. "At least I'll go out doing the Ludo!"

"Yeah, let them kill us," Ludo repeats halfheartedly, without thinking. "Wait, homes! Let them kill us? You nuts?"

"Hey, they can only kill us once. No need to worry about it now, like you said," John says with a shrug. He dips his fork into the mashed potatoes, the utensil filling with a fluffy white pile, and he lifts it off his plate.

"What the hell you talking about? It already going to your head, this stress," Ludo says. "You're not making sense. We really got to deal with this stuff right now. Let's start with them mashed potatoes. No good with all this stress going on and everything. Too heavy. You know what I'm saying?"

"Yeah, I guess so." John longingly looks at his fork filled with mashed potatoes, hovering in the air like a plane frozen in flight, and puts it back on the plate. He's hungry, but like Ludo says, his health is more important.

"Gotta stick with the program. Push that stuff away from you, right away," Ludo says in a commanding voice, indicating John's plate with his hand. "Avoid that Roto-Rooter clogging stuff, that's right. Get your head back in your head and you'll be thinking with your head, that's what I'm talking about."

"You're right," John says. He puts down the fork and pushes the plate away. "I can do this."

Ludo picks up John's fork filled with mashed potatoes, and puts it into his own mouth. "It's all about willpower, my friend," Ludo says through a mouthful of food. "Making a statement to yourself, man, 'cause that's the most important person. Yourself." Ludo puts another helping of John's food in his mouth and gesticulates with the fork. "You gotta do yourself right, because no one else will. It's about philosophy, psychology, physiology, philanthropanthy—"

"Philanthropanthy? Is that a word?" John asks.

"Whatever. But life is like a maze, man, not like a straight street. It goes around itself and comes out somewhere, and it might do this and it might do that, but it is like, ah, you know what I'm saying?"

John stares back confused. Ludo has polished off John's mashed potatoes and then finishes off the pork chop on John's plate, lustily sliding the last piece into his mouth. "Mashed potatoes aren't a good idea for me now, right?" John says plaintively, rubbing his stomach.

———————

Joe Montana is manning the early morning reception desk when a barrel-chested man enters the lobby, walks over to where he is standing, and looks him in the eye. He is wearing a finely tailored Italian suit and addresses Joe Montana in a deep voice.

"Is Mr. John Howard-Hughes here?" the man asks.

"I'm sorry, he is out at the moment."

"Can I leave a message for him?"

"Yes, I can take a message. That's Mr. John Howard-Hughes you want? Yes . . . and whom may I say it's from?" Joe Montana asks.

"Just give him this," the man says, handing Joe Montana a sealed envelope with "John Howard-Hughes" written on it in red ink. "He'll get that, right?"

"I'll make sure he does," Joe Montana says and watches the big man lightly glide across the lobby and out the front door.

———————

John exits the coffee shop and enters the lobby of the hotel with Ludo trailing behind him. He proceeds to the reception desk where the keys in this old-fashioned hotel are kept in wooden slots behind the counter. John takes the room key from Joe Montana's outstretched arm and starts toward the elevator when he is halted by the voice of the receptionist.

"Mr. Howard-Hughes," Joe Montana calls out.

"I'm fine," John calls back without turning around.

"No, Mr. Howard-Hughes, you have a message. It was dropped off earlier."

"A message?" John stops as if a warning shot had been fired, then immediately turns around and returns to the counter. Joe Montana hands him a small sealed envelope, holding it by its edges as if it were offal from a contagious leper. John rips open the envelope and pulls out a piece of lined paper perfectly folded into quarters.

The receptionist studies John closely as he unfolds and reads the note. John reads the note a second time and turns ashen.

"I take it you didn't win the million-dollar lottery?" Joe Montana queries, his eyebrows arched high as if he were peering over glasses. "Johnny, Johnny, Johnny, Johnny, Johnny," he intones in a deep voice, as his eyes survey the lobby.

John ignores the receptionist and starts in the direction of the elevator.

"Mr. Howard-Hughes, Mr. Howard-Hughes," Montana calls after him.

John abruptly stops and turns around. "What is it, Joe?"

"Nothing," Joe Montana says, shaking his head and waving his hand and fingers side to side. "Never mind."

"That guy is so damn annoying," John mumbles as he races toward the elevator and impatiently pounds the button.

John bursts into the room ahead of Ludo and heads to the space between the two beds. He is confused, as if unsure why he is there, and turns two complete circles in the small space, his arms flailing in the air like a mechanical robot whose motor functions have gone haywire. He madly searches the room for his belongings, forgetting that their suitcases never arrived and he has nothing but the clothes on his back.

"What the hell's wrong with you?" Ludo says. "You acting like a drunk Mexican jumping bean."

"What time is it?"

"About nine, nine-thirty?" Ludo shrugs. "Something like that."

"Which one? Is it nine or nine-thirty or some other time? Don't fool around with me now."

Ludo looks at a small clock by the bed. "It's exactly nine twenty-seven in the morning. What the fuck? Are our lunch reservations at the Salvation Army food line going to expire in three minutes, or what? I thought we talked about calming down, taking it a little easy. You like a lunatic, man. Too many mashed potatoes." Ludo watches his befuddled friend spin around in another circle and shakes his head in disbelief. He heads into the bathroom and closes the door behind him, his bladder near to bursting. No sooner has he started to relieve himself when he hears a frantic banging on the door.

"We gotta get out of here now!" John yells. "Stop fooling around in there. We have to go!"

"Jesus Christ, give me a minute," Ludo calls back. He finishes up and goes over to the sink.

"Tell me you're not washing your hands!" John yells from the other side of the door when he hears the water running.

Ludo steps out of the bathroom. "Can't a man take a piss in peace? What the fuck is with you?"

"I'll tell you later," John says frantically, swinging open the front door. "Let's just get out of here. Take everything. Hurry up!"

Ludo grabs his day bag off the top of the dresser, but as he exits the room behind John, its handle gets caught in the doorknob, yanking his arm and pulling him backward. Ludo retreats, untangles and sets free the handle, then hurries after John, who is already ten paces ahead of him.

"Come on already, Ludo, there's no time to waste," John calls out from the end of the hall.

"Shoot, hold on. I forgot my toothbrush," Ludo yells back.

"We'll get another one. Let's go!" John calls over his shoulder as he disappears around the bend.

"With what money?" Ludo mumbles to himself as he rushes down the hallway, wondering what catastrophic message was in that envelope Joe Montana handed to John.

John waits at the elevator, battling to keep the door open as Ludo steps past him, entering the mechanism. "Goddamned elevator," John says, as the door prematurely slams on him for the second time and then reopens. A shriveled old woman leaning on a cane impatiently bangs her cane on the ground and stares at John as he maniacally pushes the elevator buttons.

"Close! Close! Close!" John yells at the open space. The doorway, like a gaping smile missing its front teeth, remains open, as if stuck. "Damn this thing!" John hammers the first floor button four times with his closed fist, and just as the door is about to shut, he accidentally hits the third-floor button, and it reopens again.

The woman loudly bangs her cane on the ground. "Close the door, you lousy bum. I want to get out of this contraption sometime today! Stop playing around," she creaks.

"Come on, come on, come on, come on!" John yells at the door.

John keeps pounding on the open door button, until Ludo grabs his arm, reaches past him, and presses the close door button.

"Relax! Damn! What's the matter with you? What the hell is going on?" Ludo demands.

"What the hell is going on?" echoes the woman with the cane.

John stares at the button panel as the elevator starts its descent, repeatedly pushing the first-floor button like it's a speed control on a Sony PlayStation game. One floor down, the lift stops and John shoots out of the opening. Realizing he is on the wrong floor, John charges back in, just making it ahead of the closing door, which slams hard on his shoulder and reopens.

"Son-of-a-bitch!" John yells as he steps clear of the door.

"Talk to me," Ludo says in warning, but John, clutching his stomach with his left hand and pounding repeatedly on the first floor button with his right, doesn't reply. "Easy, man, you're going to bust the damn thing."

"You're going to bust the damn thing," the old woman echoes, banging her cane hard.

When the door opens on the first floor, John steps in front of the woman, cutting her off as she is about to exit, and enters the lobby.

"Where are your manners, you little manure pile?" the old woman snarls. Taking no chances that the other passenger will block her path, the woman lifts her cane and pushes the butt end of it into Ludo's stomach. She steps in front of him and slowly ambles out the door, glaring at John as she does so. She lifts her cane as if to strike him, but instead, as if the movement were a switch to release air, a loud crackling noise reverberates from the region of her hindquarters. The woman smiles wickedly and directs the air behind her toward John with a wave of her hand.

"Let's go, Ludo!" John says, shrinking back from the strong exhaust and starting across the lobby. "There is no time to waste!"

"Why you always fighting with these people?" Ludo calls out to John's back as he steps around the woman and rushes after his friend.

They are halfway across the lobby when Joe Montana, in an urgent tone, hails John from the reception desk.

"Mr. Howard-Hughes, Mr. Howard-Hughes."

"What is it?" John says, stopping sharply as Ludo smacks into his back, dropping his bag.

"Nothing, never mind," Joe Montana says, lifting his arms and shaking his head as if it were just a trifle, not worthy of mention.

"Bastard," John mutters as he snatches Ludo's bag off the floor. He hurries out of the lobby to the sound of Joe Montana's low and deep-voiced incantation, "Johnny, Johnny, Johnny, Johnny, Johnny."

A taxi idles in front of the hotel, and the driver, a middle-aged Sikh man with a thick black beard and maroon turban, nods to John as he rushes inside the cab followed by his bewildered friend. As Ludo shuts the door behind him, a long, black Cadillac bounces over the entranceway curb and screeches to a halt in front of them. John quickly ducks below the window when he sees a barrel-chested man in a finely tailored Italian suit step out of the vehicle. Ludo instinctively follows suit.

"Pull away now!" John instructs the driver. "Hurry up!"

"You got it," the driver says as he pulls to the side of the Cadillac and proceeds around the small circular driveway toward the exit.

"Just go toward the Strip, I'll tell you exactly where later," John calls out.

"What was that all about?" Ludo urgently asks John. "Who was that guy coming out of the car? Why are we hiding under this seat? What the fuck is going on? Is Knuckles and the rest of them coming to get us? What? What? What?"

"It's not them, somebody else," John says, clutching his stomach with one hand and holding his head with the other.

"If it's not those hoodlums," Ludo whispers, his head bent at an uncomfortable angle, "who the hell is it?" He peeks a glance at John, but all he sees is the back of John's head pushed against the seat.

"I can't talk now. I have to concentrate."

John notices that the taxi has stopped moving and impatiently waits for it to proceed. Further irritating him, the cabbie begins humming a tune and tapping his fingers on the wheel.

The cabbie watches vehicles speed by, looking for an opening to enter traffic. After a few more cars pass, the driver turns the volume up on his radio, changes the station to music from his native country, and starts singing along in a loud cheery voice.

"What's the problem?" John calls from below.

"What?" the cabbie yells. "I didn't hear you."

John groans in frustration. "Why aren't we moving?" he cries. He is afraid to lift his head for fear Versachi might spot him.

"Buddy," the driver says annoyed, yelling over the music, "taxis in Las Vegas have special rule which tourists may not be aware. We only merge onto street when such act won't cause accident, okay?" The driver glances in the rearview mirror, but cannot see either passenger. He starts singing again with renewed vigor, the back of his head bobbing up and down.

"Hey," John whispers, "we still have twelve dollars left, right?"

"Exactly twelve. You holding it," Ludo says. "Tell me what the fuck is going on. Are they after us?"

"Let's get out of here first. We'll talk about it later," John says, gripping his stomach now with both hands. He would pay one hundred dollars for a bottle of Pepto-Bismol if one miraculously showed up in the taxi—that is, if he had the money.

———————

Versachi hustles out of the hotel and back into the waiting Cadillac. He was right, the fleeting figure that ducked into the cab was John

Howard-Hughes. But the quick foray into the hotel hasn't cost him. Across the street, just two blocks away and facing in the direction of the Strip, John Howard-Hughes' taxi is stalled at one of Las Vegas' interminably long lights. Versachi's driver pushes the pedal down hard and the black Cadillac hurdles over the curb and bounces onto the street. The driver makes a quick U-turn over the lane divider, cutting off oncoming traffic, straightens out in the left lane, and then slows to a crawl about a block behind the cab.

A few minutes later, after inching along in traffic, the taxi carrying John Howard-Hughes and Ludo Garcia pulls into the Big Diamond Hotel and Casino, followed discreetly at a safe distance by a long, black Cadillac. Playing it carefully, Versachi instructs his driver to stay well back in the long entranceway. He doesn't want to be discovered while Howard-Hughes is still outside near the taxis. Versachi is afraid he will lose him in street traffic if Howard-Hughes jumps back into a cab. Or, just as bad, if Howard-Hughes knows he is being followed, he can easily give him the slip and get lost in the casino among the hordes of tourists.

Versachi is counting on the element of surprise at close quarters. And he is close. Very close.

And closing in.

———————

While John settles with the cabbie, Ludo heads into the casino and checks his knapsack at the bellman's desk. He gets ticket stub 1313 in return. Ludo stands in front of the counter, staring dumbstruck at the ticket stub as if it were a pariah in the world of receipts. His eyes are bloodshot from lack of sleep and dark circles are formed around them.

"Is there anything wrong?" the bellman asks. Ludo is blocking the exit path in front of the worker, looking like a customer who has been given the wrong coat, but isn't sure.

"No," Ludo mumbles.

"If you don't mind?" the bellman says, motioning with his hand.

Ludo blankly stares back at him, the number 1313 pounding like a poisoned mantra in his head. When the bellman motions again, Ludo, trapped in a stuporous trance, unconsciously steps aside to let him pass.

———

John stands outside the taxi, frantically searching his pockets for the twelve dollars to pay the fare. After digging into each side twice, John pulls all his pockets inside out, discovering the elusive bills bunched into a deep corner of the front right one. He sticks his head back into the door of the cab and doesn't even hear the taxi driver say "Twelve dollars and twenty-five cents" when he passes him the wrinkled bills, the last of their money. John's thoughts are overloaded with the frightening image of Versachi barreling out of the limousine in front of their hotel, bringing back haunting memories of the massive manager hurdling over tables after him in the restaurant, the ensuing chaos, and John's subsequent panicked flight. John is consumed with the pressing necessity to escape into the perceived safe confines of a big casino filled with people, and is relieved when the stray bills finally appear.

"You cheap bastard," the driver yells at John over his music. "You no tip me, you short me twenty-five cents. This no right. I do extra things, I do speeding extra fast and you treat me like this, I do U-turns—"

"Sorry, that's all the money I have, really," John calls over his shoulder as he quickly heads toward the revolving doors of the casino and the anonymity of the crowd. "Sorry!"

"You get back here," the driver yells after John, doubly annoyed when he has to step out of the vehicle to shut the door John left swinging in the breeze.

John dismisses the driver's angry words. He's given the man all the money he's got: there is nothing left. Not even a penny. The yelling gets sealed off when the revolving door of the casino swings behind John and the ambient sounds of the Big Diamond Casino take its place. John feels mentally drained, the pressure of his troubles and lack of sleep beginning to overwhelm him. He can see by Ludo's posture and the black circles under his eyes that his friend, who is standing by the bellman's desk with a distant, confused expression, is no better off.

"What are you doing?" John says. Ludo looks lost, like someone unexpectedly dropped him on the planet. He doesn't respond, just keeps staring at something in his hand.

"Ludo?" John says, waving his hand in front of his friend's face, trying to break his trancelike stare.

"Look at this," Ludo finally says, showing John the ticket stub.

"A receipt for a bag, so what?" Ludo lifts it higher and John reads, "One-three-one-three." John shrugs his shoulders. "I still don't get it."

"Double thirteen," Ludo says.

"Not this again," John says, rolling his eyes. He watches a man walk by combing his hair, but decides not to mention it to Ludo.

"Thirteens are no good, homes. Especially not two of them together."

"Listen . . ." John starts. "Forget it." John moves his gaze to the ceiling, glancing at a pair of massive chandeliers whose light reflects a rainbow of colors from thousands of pendulant crystals. "Check out those light fixtures," he says offhandedly. "How would you like to have those in your room?"

"Why don't you start by asking me how I would like to even have a room, you know, one we can sleep in tonight?" Ludo says moodily. "That would be a better question. And the answer is, yes, I would like to have a room to sleep in tonight."

John slowly blows air out between his lips, as if exhaling cigarette smoke, and rubs his foot along the imported light marble tiles flown in from Northern Italy. They are freshly waxed and polished, and it looks like they have been laid and spit-shined that very morning. "Just the same, this place is something else. Lots of fancy money in here."

"And none of it ours."

A noisy commotion ensues by the entranceway as a group of black men, some dressed in workout sweats and others in expensive suits, many wearing thick, ostentatious gold jewelry, enter the lobby from the restaurant area. There are about fifteen men in the group in the middle of which is Mike Tyson, smartly dressed in beige linen slacks and a white polo shirt.

Tyson sees John and Ludo and walks over to them. "What up, brothers?'" he says, exchanging fisted fives with them.

"Hey, Mike, what's going on?" John says.

"What up, champ?" Ludo says.

Tyson stands there quietly, a perplexed expression on his face. "Hey, guys," he finally says, "I have to ask you something."

"Well, shoot," John says.

"Did he eat it or not?" Tyson asks John.

"What are you talking about?"

"The pie. Did he eat the pie?"

John steps closer and gives Tyson a quick smile and a friendly pat on the shoulder. "Catch you later, champ," John says, walking past him and heading into the casino area with Ludo.

Tyson returns to his entourage, shaking his head in dismay, and says to a tall man standing beside him, "They didn't tell me if he ate the pie."

The tall man looks at the ex–heavyweight champion of the world and simply shrugs.

———————

The lobby serves as a viaduct for the gaming area on one side and a lavish flower garden ringed by restaurants on the other. Women decked out in a surprising amount of gold, diamonds, and precious and semi-precious stones for this early hour parade back and forth between the areas, as if on display. John and Ludo pass from the hard marble floors of the lobby into the plush golden and red carpeting of the casino. As if they are entering a completely different world, the sounds change as well, from the sedate ambience and hushed tones of the high-ceilinged and spacious lobby to the tumultuous pounding and frenetic activity of the casino area, where people are packed shoulder to shoulder. They weave their way through the congested aisles, ending up in front of a sports bar, where it is quieter.

Ludo leans on the railing that separates the sports bar from the casino floor, still clutching the ticket stub tightly in his hand.

"You still with that ticket?"

"Double thirteen, homes, even worse then a regular thirteen. It's not good."

"That's so ridiculous, it's ridiculous."

"You say what you want, but every time we been around that number, something bad happens. So don't tell me I'm superstitious. I'm just being practical."

"No, that's being superstitious. Mumbo-jumbo."

"Practical, homes, practical. Bad enough that number thirteen keeps showing up, now we got the double whammy. Everything going wrong for a reason."

"Whatever, just put that receipt away before you lose it."

"I don't like this double thirteen business," Ludo says, putting the ticket stub in his pocket. "It means more bad stuff be coming." Ludo looks around the casino as if it were a vast desert with nothing but sand for miles. "Now what?"

"I don't know. Maybe I'll give ZZ a call, she might be able to help us out somehow."

"She got another room full of killers we need to meet or maybe knows another poker game with some local action?" Ludo sees John's pained expression and softens his tone. "Sorry, homes, go ahead, just getting a little testy here."

"You good for a few minutes?" John asks.

"Yeah, I'm cool. Take your time, Casanova. I'll sit in the sports bar here and chill out. I'll catch up on some baseball scores and everything while I wait for you."

"Okay, see you in a few minutes." John is about to leave, but Ludo seems perplexed, like a turtle that has been spun around three times and can't figure out which way it is going. "What's wrong, Ludo?"

"Nothing, man," Ludo says, his expression vacant and his hand fingering the double thirteen ticket stub deep in his pocket.

Chapter Seventeen

Versachi waits for Howard-Hughes to enter the casino before exiting the long, black Cadillac, instructing his driver to keep the car running and ready. There is no sign of Howard-Hughes in the lobby, so he turns right, past a group of black men sporting lots of bling, and heads into the gaming area. With experienced eyes, Versachi methodically scans the crowd and soon finds what he is looking for: John Howard-Hughes is passing a sports bar about one hundred feet away, wearing the same blue sport coat and beige shirt he wore at the restaurant.

Versachi hurriedly weaves through the crowd, but gets stalled behind a cluster of Japanese tourists, losing sight of Howard-Hughes. He clears the group and soon reaches the sports bar where he last saw his prey. There are only a few patrons in the bar, and Versachi sizes them up at a glance: a couple drinking Bloody Mary's and screwdrivers, and a guy wearing a dark red bandanna, loud multi-colored shorts, and high-top black Converse sneakers, sitting at an empty table watching a ball game, not even giving the bar the courtesy of a token drink order. Versachi glances again at the freeloader with the bandanna, and their eyes meet briefly.

Versachi has temporarily lost track of John Howard-Hughes, but he knows he is somewhere not far away in this casino. He continues his way through the crowd in the direction he last saw his target heading, his eyes methodically and carefully watching everyone and everything.

Ludo is exhausted from his interrupted sleep of the night before and his sleepless night the one before that. While sitting isn't the same as sleeping, relaxing in the sports bar and taking a load off his feet feels pretty good nonetheless. The bar area is nicely air-conditioned, a welcome respite from the relentless heat outside. There is nothing he would love more than an ice-cold refreshing beer, but unable to afford even a tip—let alone a drink—he turns his thoughts instead to his favorite activity, eating. How good would a juicy steak cooked medium-rare to perfection, some mashed potatoes, and a solid green vegetable taste right now? Just the same, Ludo keeps his mind free of worries, the Ludo Rule in action. It's chilling time for him; he'll just hang here, watch some baseball, and take his mind off the terrible predicament he and John have fallen into. No need to worry about that group of poker-playing killers or what is going to happen next until John returns. They would deal with it later. Meanwhile, to accompany that steak meal, he also fantasizes about how good a cold brew would taste swirling in his mouth.

Ludo turns his attention back to the television monitor. The Yankee game, which started earlier on the East Coast, is on the large central screen in the bar. The Bronx Bombers have the bases loaded with just one out in the top of the first inning at Fenway Park. Playing against their traditional rivals, the hated Boston Red Sox, the excitement level is as high as it could possibly get in a regular-season baseball contest, and Ludo's eyes are riveted to the screen.

John finds a house phone just outside the poker room and asks the operator to dial ZZ's number. He had left his cell phone in the hotel—he knew he had been looking for something back in the room, though he couldn't think of it at the time. But no matter. The batteries had already run out and his phone charger was with his lost luggage so the cell phone was worthless to him anyway. And he had bigger problems, much bigger problems, than worrying about a lost cell phone that wouldn't work anyhow.

"Hi, it's John," he says when ZZ picks up.

"Who?"

"Doc, ZZ, Doc. Remember?"

"Where are you?" ZZ asks. "I called the hotel and they said you were no longer there. Is everything okay?"

"No, everything is not okay," John says rapidly. "In fact, everything is so messed up, you don't even have a clue. All I can tell you is that I'm screwed like a broken light bulb stuck in its socket. The whole situation is a mess. I don't know what to do."

John is hyperventilating and he bangs his hand against the telephone box. "I really don't know what to do."

"Calm down! What's the matter?"

"Calm down?" John screams. "He called me at my goddamned hotel!"

"Who called you?"

"Who do you think I'm talking about—Peter Pan? The restaurant manager!"

"What! That fat guy in the Versachi-whatever suit from the restaurant? How does he know you're staying there?"

"My name is on my credit card and I remember telling the waiter where I was staying."

"That was dumb. Why'd you do that?"

"I don't know, I was just talking. Who would think it would lead to this?" John says excitedly. "I guess they put two and two together or maybe he overheard us talking, maybe he just called around. How the hell do I know? I just know that I got out of that hotel just in time. I mean, literally, seconds after I walked out of the hotel, that guy, Versachi, you know, the manager, shows up."

"He came to your hotel?"

"Yes, he's hunting me for chrissakes! And any time now those guys at the poker game will be coming after me too," John whines, banging the phone box again. "A vacation, ZZ. All I wanted was a Las Vegas vacation. It's turned into a living nightmare!"

"That's not good. I'm so sorry."

"Versachi's got my credit card," John continues, "so he can figure out where I live, and the guys at that poker game have my business card so they know where I work. I can't even go back to New York now!" John's words come out in rapid bunches. "I have no money. I have no credit card. I have no plane tickets to even get out of Las Vegas. Knuckles, Harry, and the rest of them took care of that. Versachi is crawling all over the hotel so I can't even go back to my room, so now I have no place to sleep. And who knows what the police are up to, but I'm sure they're looking for me also. They had a video clip of me on TV for chrissakes!"

"What are you going to do?" ZZ says.

"I was going to ask you that. You got me into this, I—"

"Don't put your mistakes on me!" ZZ's voice has reached a fever pitch, and she is screaming into the phone. "Nobody twisted your arm to do what you did. I didn't leave your credit card on the table and mess up the restaurant or whatever the hell you did in there, and I didn't sit you down to play poker and lose all that money. Grow up, Doc."

ZZ is yelling so loudly now that John holds the phone a foot away from his ear. "Just don't blame me for your fucking life. I don't ever want to hear from you again. Fuck you!" ZZ slams the phone down so hard that John feels the reverberations seconds after the line is disconnected.

John gets the hotel operator back on the phone, but he speaks so fast she dials the wrong number and he ends up with an auto mechanic at a muffler shop. "Dammit!" John yells as he bangs the receiver back into its cradle. He picks up the phone and again asks for the operator.

This time the operator sends him through to the correct number.

ZZ picks up on the first ring. "What?" she says.

"I'm sorry, I really am. I apologize for saying those things to you. I'm just upset," John says, desperately hoping that ZZ will forgive him. "I'm really sorry, I really am."

"Just don't blame me for all your problems, Doc, I don't have to listen to this."

"I told you, I'm sorry. Please, ZZ, it's just that you're the only person I know here, I mean . . ." John's voice trails off, and a heavy silence hangs over the conversation.

"Do you think we can get together later?" John blurts out abruptly into the silence, the fear of ZZ cutting off communication with him making him even more anxious. She's his one bastion of hope in a raging sea of confusion, chaos, and calamity.

"Tonight's really not good for me. I'm busy with things."

"Can you make time for at least thirty minutes somewhere?" John pleads. "I would really appreciate it."

"Okay," ZZ says with a sigh. "Meet me around eight o'clock at the corner of Flamingo and Sandhill. There's a convenience store there. When you get there, give me a call and I'll come over and get you. But I can only meet you for a few minutes, okay?"

"Corner of Flamingo and Sandhill at eight o'clock. So that will work?"

"Yes. Maybe I have an idea to get things settled," she says. "I'm not saying it's a great idea, but we can talk to my ex-husband. He's good at unwinding things."

"Unwinding? What? This is the guy you think is the worst person on the planet? The guy who's a criminal?"

"Harry just got into trouble once, that's all. He has his good side too."

"Wait—Harry? The same Harry from that poker game is your ex?"

"You didn't know that?"

"Oh my god, I can't believe this! Harry is your ex?"

"I just told you that, yes. Calm down, Doc," ZZ says. "You're always so nervous, you don't even know what you're saying."

"I don't know what to do," John moans.

"Will you stop worrying? I'll see you later, okay?"

———

John puts the receiver down and leans against the wall, closing his eyes and burying his head inside the crook of his arm as he takes in this new piece of information. Harry—the short, beady-eyed, chain-smoking creature that collected his money at the poker game—is ZZ's ex-husband? What is going on here? Is this whole Las Vegas fiasco—the dinner hijinks and the disaster with the killers at the poker game, all of which occurred through direct association with ZZ—something she had been involved in before, and is it just a little too convenient to be random?

He sorts through the few facts he does know, but all it does is bring up more questions. ZZ takes him to an apartment that doesn't appear to be hers. But why? She was married to this sleazy rat who runs a poker game for professional hit men, but how did she get caught up with this group? And then there are these mysterious plans, whether at five-something o'clock in the morning when she had to charge out the door for some mysterious purpose and destination, or even yesterday afternoon when she was "busy." But busy with what? What does she do? Where does she go? John just can't bring himself to believe there is an orchestrated plan behind all this, but still these possibilities creep around in the back of his head. Further, there is that veiled innuendo from Harry, the two-legged rat, her ex-husband—and who knows her better than him?—warning him to be careful and stay away from ZZ. A circumstantial accusation to be sure, but just the same, hearing it, however suspect the source may be, gives John more fuel for doubt and apprehension. He starts to wonder: Was he set up?

John's head is spinning, and he can't make sense of any of it. He's confused, he's tired, he's under enormous stress, and he wishes he could talk to someone about it, but there is only Ludo—and the last thing he needs now is a lecture from his friend. He cannot imagine Ludo's reaction when he hears about the rat. Actually, the problem is, he can. Ludo would blow his stack with this piece of news about Harry, of all things, being ZZ's ex-husband! Perhaps it's better if he just leaves it be and doesn't say anything. There are already enough straws on the camel's back. And Ludo doesn't even know about the debacle at the restaurant, Versachi, the police, and that whole set of problems!

John picks up the receiver to call ZZ again, then changes his mind and replaces it in the cradle.

Ludo asked him before, "Now what?" John, thinking about the question, asks himself the same thing: "Now what?" Hunted by the mob. Hunted by killers. The police are after him. No place to go. No one to turn to. Broke. And not even plane tickets to get out of this newfound hell. If he even could get home—and he has no idea how he would manage that—they'd come looking for him there. John pushes himself off the wall, opens his eyes, and stares blankly at the swinging cord of the phone as if it were a hangman's noose out for a trial run.

Jesus Christ. *Now what?*

His bladder, full to bursting, at least gives him a temporary plan. He walks over to the bathroom door, pushes it open with both hands, and relieves himself in a large white urinal for what seems like a full two minutes. With all the commotion of the past hour, he hadn't realized how badly he had to go. John carefully washes his hands, then turns off the hot faucet and runs the water till it's as cold as it will get, splashing the cool liquid on his face. Looking at himself in the mirror, he sees the results of too little sleep and too much anxiety. A two-day-old stubble looks back at him, and his eyes are ringed by dark lines and pouches of flesh.

"Beautiful," John thinks, "just beautiful."

He throws more cold water on his cheeks, forehead, and hair, and straightens out his back, letting the water slowly drip off his face.

———————

Versachi weaves his way out of the narrow slot machine aisles and into the broader open spaces where table games are lined up one next to the other and where it is easier for him to get a good line of vision. Having difficulty picking out any one person's face from the crowd, he looks instead for the telltale blue sport coat John Howard-Hughes seems to wear like a second skin. He parks himself behind one of the blackjack tables, giving him an excellent view across the blackjack pit itself and further on into the casino. Versachi looks far away first, doing a point-to-point distance wing search so that if Howard-Hughes is on the outskirts of the vision line, he can be spotted before crossing out of it. Then he scans left and right, and up and down, doing a cross-matrix search. Nothing yet.

Versachi is wondering if indeed Howard-Hughes has given him the slip when he spots a blue sport coat directly across from where he's standing, not thirty feet away.

It is exactly the color and style of coat Howard-Hughes wears.

John exits from the bathroom slightly rejuvenated from the cold water but wearing exhaustion and frustration about him like a heavy coat. He turns left out of the bathroom, toward two long rows of blackjack tables, and he is tempted to sit down except for two things— one, he has no money, and two, Ludo is waiting for him. But just the same, he decides to watch a couple of blackjack hands, figuring that a few minutes of watching cards being dealt would help take his mind off the worries in his head and relieve the churning, acidic pain in his stomach. Like Ludo says, he has to stay positive somehow.

Distraction is good.

John watches as a rugged man in his fifties gets dealt a pair of nines and decides to split them into two hands against the dealer's seven. It is the wrong move. John knows that from the blackjack book he uses as his gambling bible, and he wants to warn the man that it's a bad percentage play. However, correct table etiquette says to let every gambler play his own hand and suffer his own results, win or lose, so John says nothing. After all, it is the man's money to blow as he likes. John watches the player bust out of the first split hand with a five followed by a ten and then draw a seven on the second hand. The man, gun shy from his first bust, incorrectly stands on sixteen, an even worse play than splitting his nines to begin with. The dealer turns over a ten and stands on seventeen, beating the sixteen held by the rugged man. The player should have just stood with his eighteen to begin with; instead, he wound up with two losses when he should have had one win. A big swing in his bankroll. John shakes his head: To be a winner in blackjack, you've got to play the percentages, and that means making the correct play on every hand.

Watching this terrible play makes John unaccountably tense, so much so that his heart starts racing. He feels a heavy pounding in his chest. Boy, he thinks, am I that much on edge where a complete stranger's misplaying of a blackjack hand would upset me like this? John gets a strange feeling, almost as if he is being watched. Maybe the pressure and angst is getting to him. Maybe that's it. John lifts his head up just as the dealer collects the player's chips, and his eyes freeze in their sockets. Standing straight across the aisle, separated by two blackjack tables, is a big, brooding, barrel-chested man in a hand-tailored Italian suit looking him dead in the eyes, very bad mojo so clearly expressed on his face it may as well have been tattooed there.

"Oh my god," John says.

Chapter Eighteen

Versachi looks up and bingo—Howard-Hughes is there in the flesh, looking right at him! They are separated by two curved rows of eight blackjack tables, each table connected to the other by a theater rope, forming an oval area in the middle called the "pit," where the "pit boss," a supervisor, watches over the action from this employee-only section. Rather than going around either end of the row, which might give Howard-Hughes enough time to escape, Versachi removes a rope and heads right through the blackjack pit, figuring correctly that the shortest and quickest distance between two points is a straight line. Versachi brushes past an indignant pit boss and removes the connecting rope on the other side, cutting the distance between himself and John to a mere fifteen feet.

John feels the innate fear of a gazelle running for its life from the claws of a fast-approaching hungry lion with a meal on its mind, knowing he needs to hightail it out of there quickly. And he does.

The lion is coming.

John rushes into the slot machines aisles, maneuvering around gamblers milling about or playing. He figures that he can take better advantage of the narrow spaces and shifting sands of people here than the bulkier man. With a little luck, Versachi might get caught behind a crowd long enough for him to slip safely away. But there is a downside to this approach—not that there is a choice—John could just as easily be caught in the congestion long enough to be overtaken. And with Versachi not that far behind him, that is a scenario he fears. One mistake now and he is a goner.

Versachi gets stalled behind an elderly couple, costing him valuable seconds. Worse, he temporarily loses his sight line of Howard-Hughes. He decides he has to take a chance and doubles back around the other side of the aisle, gambling that Howard-Hughes chose that direction to elude him. And the gambit pays off—he has Howard-Hughes dead in his sights, his prey directly coming toward him down the aisle. Howard-Hughes is so focused on glancing behind, where he expects to be followed, that he doesn't see Versachi bearing straight down on him, just seven slot machines away. Versachi pushes people aside in his progress up the crowded aisle. He smells blood.

Time for a reckoning.

Howard-Hughes is so shocked when he looks up and unexpectedly sees Versachi coming at him that he stares back frozen, unable to move. Twenty feet, fifteen feet, ten feet, five feet. John Howard-Hughes backs up like a frightened dog as the big man closes in. The only obstruction now between Versachi and his prey is a stout woman and her frail husband, a couple in their late forties who have just departed their machines in a foul mood—leaving their gaming bankrolls behind in the beasts—and who stand in the aisle, blocking Versachi's progress. Versachi, the beginning of a triumphant smile touching the corners of his mouth, steers the husband aside with the back of his hand, and with his other hand, reaches over the stout woman's shoulder.

John instinctually leans back like a boxer eluding a jab, barely escaping the thick outstretched fingers that scrape off the lapel of his blue blazer. The terrible fright of the large predatory hand coming within inches of his face stuns John like a clap on the side of his head from a boxer's hook. He stands there dumb and paralyzed with fear, a salmon almost caught in the clutches of a massive grizzly. John is unable to move, his nerves rattled and fried, as he stares into the feral eyes of Versachi, the scraping sound of the big man's paw against his blazer a harsh rasp in his ears.

Versachi reaches across again; however this time, ready for the rude encumbrance on her space, the incensed woman bats his hand away. His efforts to move her aside with the back of his hand also are fruitless—unlike her frail husband, the woman stands her ground with the immovability of a cast-iron tub. Short, massive, and built like a Sherman tank, the stout woman shoves Versachi back. Unable to pass around or through the redoubtable woman, Versachi instead reaches over her shoulder and grabs hold of John's collar with his big right fist, the cloth bunching in his grip.

John is pinned in Versachi's grasp with the stout woman sandwiched between the two like a thick pile of meat in a Jewish deli sandwich.

"Get out of my way," Versachi sneers to the woman.

"Back off, fatso," the Sherman tank replies. "I'm warning you once." She cocks her fist, ready to strike, and is about to let loose with a haymaker when Versachi releases the grip on John's jacket and defensively backs up two steps. The woman, more indignant and furious than earlier, moves her husband aside, a wispy twig barely half her weight, and steps forward, her wide frame clogging the aisle like a wedged tree in a floodgate.

"Who do you think you're fooling with?" the woman bellows at close range, her eyes fiery with anger. On her clenched fist, an enormous ring with a polished green stone protrudes at least three-quarters of an inch from its silver base and lurks in front of Versachi's face like a small cannonball. The woman, her lips curled in a menacing scowl, advances another step forward, ready to duke it out with the barrel-chested man who thinks he can push her around.

Versachi watches as Howard-Hughes, set free from the big man's death grip, finally gets his wits about him and backs down the aisle. At the end, he turns right, slipping past a slot machine spitting out coins for a lucky player, and makes his way around the corner and out of Versachi's line of sight.

The valuable seconds given John by Versachi's confrontation with the stout woman are enough to provide him two valuable commodities: time for his head to clear, and breathing room to gain distance. He zigzags down one aisle of slot machines, maneuvering his way past the congested aisles of players and onlookers, and up the next line of machines. If he can gain enough distance, John feels he has an excellent chance to elude Versachi and escape from his clutches. As it stands now, he is almost tasting freedom like fresh, spring air blowing through a veranda window.

But it is not going to be that simple. Freedom earned that easily would be too much good luck for John Howard-Hughes. Way too much good luck.

John cannot believe what he sees, and he stops cold in his tracks. Clogging the end of the aisle just a few feet in front of him is the form of a very big man, all too familiar looking. The man is stuffed so tightly into his suit that the seams appear ready to burst, and he is scanning the crowd as if searching for someone. Even from behind, the big shoulders and large head leave no doubt—it is Rock, the enormous and brooding killer who had threatened to rub John's life out over a simple innocent question. And now it is worse than a simple question taken the wrong way: John owes the man money—real money. If Rock was furious yesterday at an innocuous query about the amount he was betting, then now, with a day to let the debt fester like rotted meat in his kitchen, John shudders to imagine what his reaction would be if he turned around and saw his debtor standing in front of him, conveniently within throttling distance.

Next to Rock is a bald man with one cheek pushed out like a squirrel overstuffed with acorns. More trouble: It is Apples, the poker player who used the cutting motion with his fingers to describe a technique for ridding John of his manhood. If they turn to face back into the aisle, which could happen at any moment, John figures he's a dead man. And there is no way past the two killers. John does an about face, but it is no better there. Versachi has just gained the other end of the aisle, and he too stands with his back to John, scanning the various aisles, not yet noticing that his prey is just twenty-five feet away, staring fearfully into the back of his suit jacket.

John is trapped between Rock, Apples, and Versachi. He must act quickly before he is spotted.

And he does. There is an opening, a seat, between two enormous brothers weighing well over 450 pounds each. Huge, rolling masses of blubber protrude off either side of them, forming almost a solid wall of flesh that John hopes he can hide behind. Like an NFL fullback seeing a hole in the line, John heads for the tiny bit of space, pushes his way through untold pounds of human fat that sway and give upon his entry, and gains the other side, enough yardage for a first down and a new set of plays. Behind him, the blubber closes around him like Jell-O. John hurriedly removes his telltale blue sport coat, folds the inside over the outside so that the blue is no longer visible, and shoves the balled-up blazer between his legs, sitting quickly so he can fit in unobtrusively as just another slots player at his machine. He prays that his mostly obscured position, bookended by the massive brotherly walls of fat behind and on either side of him, plus his altered look—the beige of his shirt instead of the bright blue of the coat—will act as camouflage and allow him to escape detection from the predators at either end of the aisle.

The brothers, in their own world, take no notice of their new slots neighbor. They giggle uncontrollably like little kids, their giddiness fluctuating between high-pitched wheezes and roaring hysterical laughter. Tears pour down their cherubic cheeks, rosy red from guffawing, sounds that are punctuated by the rousing, bubbling, and reverberating explosions emanating out of the space between their prodigious bottoms and the stools they sit on, which look like children's seats under their massive frames. Their bodies heave up and down each time they guffaw anew, and rolls of fat shake like waves across their bodies. The laughter presses on their bloated stomachs, forcing out more southern wind, which in turn makes them roar with laughter again, which causes still more farting. The gas from the farting makes them even giddier, and they laugh more and fart more, a self-perpetuating chain reaction of farting, giddiness, and uproarious belly laughter.

But to John, it is no laughing matter. He is being hunted and he's trapped, stuck in a cave of fat, with nowhere to run if he is discovered. The only way out is the same way he came in. And now, short of breath and faint with fear and the noxious fumes of the brothers' ripping explosions, he nearly gags from the vapors produced by the more than fifty dishes consumed by the brothers at their last buffet, a three-and-a-half-hour orgiastic feast where they made sure to get their money's worth. The air around John and the brothers is filled with a foul compost of sweet-and-sour pork, baked beans, macaroni and cheese, honey-rubbed ribs, fried onions, beef tacos, orange chicken, nachos, fresh roast beef, pepperoni pizza, meatballs and spaghetti, turkey with all the fixings—including an apple-based sausage stuffing and gelled cranberry—house-special fried rice, a heaping of mashed potatoes, nine sugar-free desserts, four double-chocolate brownies with frosting, three triple-portions of vanilla ice cream with all the toppings, and a myriad of other foods partially digested and expelled into the air through their rectal muscles.

The odors waft into John's nose, smelling like a mix of ethanol, muriatic acid, rotten eggs and, hideously, the sweetened sickly aroma of rancid apple. John does all he can to maintain consciousness against this rank fusillade.

The brothers, getting higher by the minute off their own powerful fumes, are in an intoxicated frenzy. One long continuous gurgling explosion lasting almost a full half minute ripples out between the cheeks of the brother to John's left. The rat-tat-tat of the emission sounds like a machine gun strafing a field and sends both brothers into a prodigious and hysterical laughing fit.

"Oh, that was sweet, that one there, Elwood, sure was. I think you mowed down a few that time," the brother to John's right howls in a southern accent as the strafing farter lets loose another long ripple, redoubling the frenzy of the siblings.

John sits, stuck in a cauldron of suffocating exhaust, gasping for breath, clinging to a thread of hope against detection by the ferocious men in the aisle, his fear of death a strange juxtaposition to the roaring laughter of more than nine hundred pounds of farting and giggling human flesh.

———————

The sports bar where Ludo waits for John is elevated a few feet off ground level from the rest of the casino floor so that patrons, after taking a brief respite from gambling or as a prelude to getting their feet wet with some action, will have a clear and tempting line of vision to the nearby table games and slot machines. John leans forward around Elwood's substantial girth, frantically trying to catch Ludo's attention, but it is of no use; his friend is engrossed in an exciting bases-loaded situation between the New York Yankees and the Boston Red Sox. Ludo has no idea that the real spellbinding drama at the moment is not between two rivals on the television monitor above him, but on the casino floor off to his left starring his best friend, John Howard-Hughes, who is hanging on for dear life in a precarious situation surrounded by brutes, killers, and farting behemoths.

Though John is separated from Ludo by a mere seventy-five feet, for all the good it does him at this moment, he might as well be on the far side of the moon.

Out of the corner of his eye, John spots Versachi coming toward him, slowly making his way down the aisle, just twenty feet away. Perilously close. Versachi is lost in thought and, turning his head back and forth, is peering carefully between the machines to the banks of slots on the adjacent aisles. Like a turtle retreating back into the safety of its carapace, John quickly pulls his head back into the protected shell of his area. He's partially obscured by the prodigious mass of the two brothers, but still, with danger lurking and getting closer, John feels vulnerable and exposed. With every step Versachi takes in his direction, John's heart races a little faster. John needs more to pull this off: a disguise, something to blend into his background like a white ptarmigan against the arctic tundra. To become invisible at a glance.

There's precious little time and John needs a plan. Any plan—and right now.

His eyes whirl about looking for ideas, taking in his surroundings in quick frames like a camera shutter. Click, click, click. In the next aisle, between John's slot machine and Elwood's, he sees a slot player's face obscured by a low-lying baseball cap; next to that player, a young woman, faceless under a broad low-lying floppy hat. And, like bookends on either side of him, the brothers' matching painter's caps are worn so low over their foreheads that, except for their gargantuan size, they too appear nondescript and faceless. An idea congeals from the amalgam of quick snapshots of his neighboring players: He needs to cover his head as a disguise! That's his only hope to avoid being discovered.

John unconsciously runs his hand over his uncovered head, then looks over at the blue kerchief peeking out of Elwood's back pocket. His eyes return to Ludo sporting a bandanna on his head and then back to Elwood's posterior, from which a newly reverberating sound erupts from behind the blue handkerchief, causing it to flutter ever so slightly.

No, John thinks, shuddering! I can't do it.

Versachi is slowly approaching, looking between the machines into other aisles, getting precariously closer with every step. There is not much time.

No! No!

John's eyes desperately flip back to Ludo's bandanna, tied low over his forehead. His focus pings back and forth like a pinball striking rubber bumpers—man with baseball cap, woman with low-lying floppy hat, Ludo with bandanna, Elwood with fluttering handkerchief, Ludo with bandanna. Ping, ping, ping.

No! No! No!!!

In an act no rational man would ever contemplate except under the most dire of circumstances, John Howard-Hughes, having no other choice available to him, grabs the tip of the blue handkerchief with the very edge of his thumb and index finger, and snakes the blue cloth out from Elwood's back pocket. Like an overfilled air tube whose plug has been withdrawn, a long bubbling flatulence resonates loudly off the seat below like a trumpeting of Gideon at the open gates of Jerusalem, and a gust of stale, fetid fumes from the smorgasbord of decaying and digested buffet food is propelled into the air. John quickly affixes the blue handkerchief over his head in the style worn by his friend Ludo. The moist bandanna clinging to John's forehead overloads his senses, and a gurgling stream of vomit surges up his throat. More than the nauseating warmth of the hankie or the pungent effluvium gathered in its folds, it's the repulsive dampness of the clinging blue cloth that overwhelms John. He does all he can to clamp his mouth shut and keep from spewing forth an unwieldy load of vomit.

———

Sensing that something is off and feeling a slight pressure against his buttocks, Elwood slowly twists his prodigious frame to glance behind him. Seeing nothing of note, he slowly turns back again, but not before John, shifting his far shoulder to block the other brother's view, seizes the opportunity to borrow a handful of coins from the well of Elwood's machine, tokens he needs to play the part of a slots player.

Elwood reaches back to pat his pocket and notices his handkerchief is missing. Not believing this, he feels his back pocket again. Still no handkerchief. Puzzled, he looks over at his new neighbor and sees on the man's forehead a blue kerchief in the same style as the one that was previously in his pocket. Elwood sits there scratching his head, a confused look on his face, before he shrugs and goes back to farting and playing slots.

———

For some strange reason, in a world full of inexplicable occurrences, unimaginable coincidences, and strange happenstances, Versachi randomly stops behind John's seat and leans over the fraternal walls of fat to watch his slot machine. John hears the big man's heavy breathing just behind his right ear; worse, he can feel the heat from the exhalations. Reflecting off the polished metal of his slot machine are Versachi's eyes—dark, black orbs that peer over his shoulder, revealing a curious fascination of the three spinning reels. John holds his breath as if his own expulsion of air might give him away. Danger hovers too close, one short fried calamari and garlic marinara–scented breath away. But to complete the picture and pull off the illusion of a slots player, John's got to fit in and *look* like the real deal, be one of the players who habituates the machines and works its mechanisms.

He's got to play.

John nervously clutches his handful of coins, afraid to loosen his grip lest they tumble to the floor, but doing so is the only way he can get access to an individual coin he needs to insert into the coin acceptor. The bank of machines in this aisle are throwback slots that the casino installed for the old-time players who loathe the newer credit-only machines and still want to play by hand, featuring longer, more suspenseful spin cycles, manual coin-play, pull handles, and payouts that clatter loudly into the metal well below. Any misplay here and Versachi may see that something is off.

It is the moment of truth.

Trying to act casual but with hands shaking almost uncontrollably, John attempts to insert a dollar token into the machine with his right hand, but he can't get it in and the coin noisily clanks off the metal and onto the floor. He quickly grabs another coin and tries again, glancing upward and seeing in the reflection near the coin slot two dark pupils watching his every movement. This time, after his shaking hand rattles the token a few times off the metal around the hole, he is able to force the reluctant coin into the machine. John quickly pulls the long, black-tipped silver-armed handle of the slot machine and nervously watches the symbols through the display glass, and above them, on the reflective part of the metal, still fixed on the action, he glimpses the feral eyes of Versachi, who is strangely fascinated with this particular slot machine.

Three reels are set in motion and, after a whirl of spinning and the concurrent buzzing sound of the mechanism, the moving parts come to a halt. It's a bar and two lemons. A loser.

"Son-of-a-bitch," Versachi angrily calls out, laying a heavy hand on John's shoulder.

He is done for! The gig is up. He has been found out and is going to suffer the consequences. A rush of adrenaline shoots through John's body as the weight of the hand, which feels like a bear's paw, presses against him. John stiffly waits for that hand to slide over a few inches, curl around his throat, and tighten.

"You can't beat those bastards," Versachi pronounces.

A loud, rotting flatulence erupts in stereo from the brothers, a long chorus that causes them to roar with laughter and slap their thighs with merriment as foul gas pours out of their smokestacks. The fumes and tumult send Versachi scurrying four feet over, where Rock and Apples had stood earlier, leaving unsaid any additional thoughts he had about John's luck. The brief distraction over and now out of the direct line of fire, Versachi scans the wide aisles in all directions. His prey appears lost. But like a lion hunting a wildebeest that has wandered outside the herd, he is patient and ready to set himself in motion if the wind changes and the scent of his prey drifts downwind. He is a man accustomed to using his instincts, and he just knows he'll get another shot. He feels it. John Howard-Hughes cannot be far, of that he is sure.

Little does he know how close he is to Howard-Hughes, just one stool and 450 pounds of farting brother away.

———————

John just needs Versachi to extricate himself from his command post at the end of the aisle and move away so that he can get the hell out of the casino and out of this predicament. But backing out of the seat now would be premature, no matter how tense he feels, not with Versachi one short stride away. He's got to stay patient and continue playing the role just a bit longer.

"Just take it easy," John says to himself, eyeing Versachi out of the corner of his eye. "Just keep playing, be another player at a machine."

John drops another coin in the slot and pulls the handle. Suddenly, a cacophony of wailing sirens, screaming bells, and the pounding of coins crashing into the metal well of a slot machine startles John. He spins around wondering what has happened, only to find that players nearby are getting out of their seats; in fact, everyone in his immediate area is looking in his direction. And then it hits him: It's his machine! John has hit the jackpot. Three sevens are lined up, a rare and beautiful sight for a slots player.

But for John, this ethereal slots sight is not paradise found, it's a disaster. He stands up, red-faced and embarrassed. As if pulled by a magnetic force, he looks over in Versachi's direction. Their eyes lock, and as recognition comes over the big man's face, John, as broke and bereft of money as a beggar on the street without a tin cup, takes one last longing glance at the windfall pouring into the well. The slot machine appears to mockingly smile at him, its front teeth three beautiful sevens, the money pounding into the metal well below enough to take care of all his and Ludo's problems with the poker players. John doesn't have a second to waste. He hurriedly squeezes back through the brotherly walls of fat, the layers of blubber swaying against his force, sidesteps the gathering crowd watching the slot machine spit out its beautiful bounty of coins, and with Versachi hot in pursuit, runs for his life, the sounds of coins hitting metal and loud farting ringing in the air behind him.

And off they go again, pursuer and pursued weaving their way down row after row of slot machines through the throngs of gamblers, big cat after little mouse. John hustles past a woman clapping her hands exuberantly, beseeching a Wheel of Fortune machine to reward her with a thousand-times payout, and by five elderly ladies lined up in a row casually chatting with one another. He clears the rows of slots and gains the long row of blackjack tables where he was first discovered by Versachi. Glancing back, he sees Versachi doggedly in pursuit, but the big man is temporarily stuck behind one of the old ladies who has gotten up to stretch her legs, buying John extra seconds to choose between two options. He can head back toward Ludo at the sports bar near the front of the casino, but that risks getting trapped again in the clogged aisles. He also fears running into the arms of Rock or Apples, who he last saw heading in that direction. His other choice is to go deeper into the casino toward the shopping arcade where the crowds are thinner and a sudden burst of speed might enable him to elude Versachi in one of the stores. Then he can slip around behind him, redouble his way back and get the hell out of the casino, alive and well—hopefully.

The thought of getting trapped and grabbed by Versachi in the congested aisles of the slot machines casts his decision; John quickly decides for the open space. He throws his jacket back on and hustles down the corridor of the shopping arcade, desperately trying to rid himself of the disgusting hankie he has just removed from his head. He spastically shakes his hand, looking like a cross between a cheerleader pumped up on LSD waving a pom-pom and a rabid lunatic needing a straightjacket, but for the life of him, the foul cloth sticks to his hand like gummy snot to a pinky finger—and won't come off. He rushes past shoppers who, seeing this madman in the blue jacket waving his arm wildly about, step aside and pull their children closer.

Up ahead, the hallway bends left, and John goes with it.

———————

Versachi had lost sight of Howard-Hughes at the last turn, but when he sees the waving handkerchief by the twenty-one tables heading toward the farther end of the casino, he knows he's back on track. He follows the sight of the wildly waving hankie past the gaming tables and into the shopping arcade, knowing that, at the base of this inexplicably strange display, it is John Howard-Hughes.

———————

A small Chinese boy watching the action in the corridor is amused by the gesticulating clown in blue waving the blue flag as he weaves down the hall, another fun event in his day full of wonderment, and he smiles with delight as John approaches. And there's even more fun. The clown holds out the squarish blue cloth to him, and like a runner passing a baton in a relay race, the child takes the bait and grabs the handkerchief.

The child's parents, window-shopping at a clothing store, are busy examining the cut of a summer jacket and are oblivious to their son's transaction and his subsequent struggles to rid the cursed blue handkerchief from his tiny hand. Stuck with this smelly cloth, the boy holds his nose with his free hand while he tries to shake the handkerchief loose with his other. But it is not cooperating. Frustrated by his lack of success, he finally grips the edges of the cloth with his teeth and pulls it free from his hand.

The mother's face fills with an expression of horror when she turns and sees this stained kerchief dangling from her child's mouth. She quickly pulls it from his teeth and disgustingly flings it to the ground. The child watches with fascination as a big man running past steps on the discarded material, the gummy cloth sticking to the bottom of his shoe and traveling down the corridor with him as he heads in the same direction of the clown who has just passed by.

Amazingly, the blue handkerchief with the brown stain that started its journey in Elwood's back pants pocket has found its fourth owner in a brief span of ten minutes.

John ducks into the first store he sees, a large clothing outlet, hoping that Versachi might bypass the shop and allow him to circle back in the other direction, on his way to freedom. However, the big man sees John enter the store, and follows in after him. John shadows his way around a tall rack thickly packed with colorful summer dresses, while Versachi, head turning side to side as he scours the store, briskly walks by on the other side, his view of John obstructed. John quietly scurries toward the exit and waves off an approaching employee with both hands, but it is too late. The salesgirl, pre-programmed with inane gibberish from the store's management, chatters out her canned speech anyway.

"May I help you with anything else, sir?" she squeals in a voice hitting the range of soprano just as John reaches the door.

John turns with the wail, as does Versachi, who immediately spots him.

As John bolts toward the exit, the girl turns to Versachi. "May I help you with—" she starts, but stops mid-sentence and jumps out of the way as the burly man nearly runs her over on his way out of the store.

John turns right and sprints deeper into the mall, dodging startled shoppers as he tries to outrace his pursuer. He has a fifty-foot head start when he turns the corner and finds himself in a dead-end hallway containing six stores. He heads into the last of these outlets, a gift shop filled with Las Vegas trinkets, Sin City T-shirts and baseball caps, newspapers, magazines, books, snacks, and assorted gambling-related knickknacks popular with tourists. John has to quickly figure out a plan because Versachi will soon be around the corner and upon him. Valuable seconds tick away as John scans the store for an exit, a back way out, a closet where he can successfully hide, even a counter he can duck behind, but there is nothing here that will work. He has one dim hope left, a long shot, but in this town of long shots and long odds, he knows that you can't win if you don't play. Sometimes you just have to roll the dice. Desperate times call for desperate plans, and John needs to make a play.

Standing a few feet away from John, a fragile-looking woman in her seventies is curiously watching him, as if sizing up his mettle and weighing its relative value. He hurriedly approaches the woman. Knowing there is little time left, he gets right to the point.

"Ma'am," John blurts out, "I know this is a strange request, but will you sell me your hat?"

The woman stares at John and says nothing, her hawklike eyes surveying him like a hovering bird of prey watches a field mouse scurry on the ground below. A large red handbag with a tiny duck logo emblazoned on it dangles from one hand, and in the other, a wooden cane the color of burnt mahogany is tightly held in her gnarled fingers. Her withered and dry face, deeply etched, reminds John of a clay pot baked in the desert sun for far too long. She has long blonde hair that is quite youthful-looking for her age, and a broad, floppy hat that hangs over her face.

"How about twenty dollars, ah, thirty dollars for the hat?" John says.

John hands are moist with sweat, and he nervously looks over the woman's shoulder. Versachi is going store to store in the corridor, and John has just seen him enter the jeans boutique across the way. Hopefully, the dressing rooms—if there are any—will occupy Versachi and buy John precious time.

"I don't think so, sonny," the woman finally says.

John talks quickly. "I—uh, you see, my mother just died three months ago and she had a hat exactly like this. Please, it would mean so much to me if—"

"Okay then," the woman says, handing John the hat. "I'll give it to you."

Her blonde hair swings free and youthfully cascades down her back. John immediately puts the oversized floppy hat on, pulling it low over his forehead, then turns his sport coat inside out and puts it back on. The jacket's lining is a checkered pattern of browns and reds, a style reminiscent of something Harpo Marx might have worn in *Duck Soup*. He is odd-looking in this getup, but if he can keep his face obscured, he's banking that his new appearance will give him a fighting chance to avoid detection. In any case, it's his only shot. Maybe if the woman stood arm in arm with him as well, it might help?

"You're such a sweet lady. Thank you so much!" John wipes away a fake tear and says in a teary voice, "Can I also ask—"

"I was able to swallow your bullshit until your rap got sappy," the woman interrupts in a raspy voice, eyeing the bizarre inside-out sport coat and flapping white pockets. "You can't con an old con. I ought to shove the gnarly part of this cane up your ass, sonny."

She had been watching John's eyes and had sized up the situation the second he walked into the store. John shrinks back as the woman advances on him with her cane raised as if to strike, and he backs into a display. Two packages of potato chips knock loose and fall to the floor. She stares at John belligerently, looking up at him from her frail five-foot frame, then starts cackling like an old chicken.

"And I'll do one better," the woman says, her eyes twinkling with delight. She grabs a handful of her hair, yanks hard, and removes the large mass of flowing blonde hair. It is a wig. John's eyes widen like a camera shutter as he is handed this golden bounty.

The woman now stands before him, her head bald as a baby's rump.

"Hurry up, sonny, and get your ass over by those books. He's coming in now. It's your best shot."

Seven seconds later, Versachi enters the gift store like a rush of bad wind. The store is L-shaped, with the back section wrapped behind the front and hidden from the counter's view. He quickly scans the front of the store, which just has one customer, a woman in her thirties with breasts too large for her slight frame, turning pages in a fashion magazine. Versachi heads into the back section, where the books, magazines, and gambling knickknacks are on display. A few people mill about; a solitary man perusing a business book, an old bald lady with belligerent features near the candy rack, and a very odd-looking woman with long blonde hair, a big floppy hat pulled low on her face, wearing a bizarre checkered jacket that appears to be more the inside of a coat than its outside, a style punctuated by white pockets and stitching, similar to a getup a bum or crazy person would wear. The odd-looking blonde woman has her back to him and stands by the book rack in the gambling how-to section.

Versachi peeks around the store, but doesn't see Howard-Hughes anywhere. He walks to the book and magazine rack and stands next to the woman with the checkered jacket, trying to collect his thoughts. He's already looked in the other five stores and he knows Howard-Hughes didn't sneak past him in the corridor.

So where is he?

John's knees feel like they're about to buckle when Versachi walks over and stands so close to him that he can feel the heat emanating from the big man's body. In fact, as Versachi reaches over to grab a magazine, their shoulders touch.

"Excuse me," says John's barrel-chested neighbor.

John mumbles back in falsetto and pushes his head forward so that the blonde hair of the wig forms a wall on the side of his face, completely obscuring it from view. With the large hat pushed down low and his inverted jacket a mélange of checkered colors, John thinks he has a chance to get by undetected if he can keep his face averted—and if he doesn't faint from fright. As a prop, he has plucked a book off the rack, *How to Win at Gambling*, and holds it unopened in his right hand. The pressure of Versachi actually touching him across the shoulder wreaks havoc on John's nerves. His stomach feels like it's twisted into a horrific knot, and it takes everything John can mentally summon to keep from screaming. The physical and emotional tension of being so close to a brute who has spent an inordinate amount of effort to catch him is enormous.

And now they are as close as two matches in a matchbook, just one strike away from flame, and then ashes.

Ludo reclines comfortably at the sports bar, enjoying the cool air, some highlights from the day's games, and an occasional glance at a cute girl playing slots across from where he sits. He has been trying to catch her eye, but five minutes earlier, much to his annoyance, a heavy woman took the aisle seat next to the girl, blocking his view. Ludo occasionally checks the slots area anyhow, in case the heavy woman moves and his view is restored.

It's been about forty-five minutes since John left to call ZZ, quite a long time considering John said he'd be just five minutes or so, and Ludo is beginning to wonder what is causing the delay. He thinks about getting up to look for him, but in this crowd it would be easy to cross paths and miss one another. And if John comes back and can't find him, they'll have the damnedest time hooking up with each other in this big casino. Neither has a phone and with no hotel room or obvious place to meet or contact one another, that really is not much of an option. No, best to remain here patiently. That's where John knows to look. Perhaps he's having a long conversation with ZZ and can't break away just yet.

Just the same, John has been gone for a long time, and Ludo is uneasy.

———————

An oppressive silence reigns in the tiny area where John, the hunted, stands side by side with Versachi, the hunter, who doesn't realize his prey is inches away, sharing the same oxygen. Time has slowed down in John's world, and he and Versachi have been funneled into a warped dimension where sounds are elongated, stretched, and transmogrified as if in an underwater echo chamber. The labored panting of Versachi, still gathering his breath from running in and out of the stores, and the jingling of the coins in John's pocket as he nervously toys with a few pieces he grabbed from the hastily abandoned slots bonanza, are the only sounds audible in this surreal continuum.

John feels Versachi's hard triceps pressed against his own and hears the two isolated sounds in this warped dimension play over and over again, like a vinyl record scratched and skipping. Inhalation of the big man's breath, exhalation of the big man's breath, and jingle, jingle, jingle of the coins in John's pocket. Inhalation, exhalation, jingle, jingle, jingle—sounds that appear grossly magnified in volume and drag along the surface of time like a steady drip of water on a tortured prisoner's forehead. He holds his breath, not daring to take in air, fearful that the breaths will hang too heavy in the quietude around him. But the tension is murderous. Silence weighs on him like seventy-five feet of underwater pressure, his brain prone to the staggers if he surfaces too quickly. John feels like giving up, throwing his hat and wig to the ground, and yelling out, "I'm here, I'm here, I'm here right next to you. It's me! Cut the nonsense and do me in already. I can't take it anymore!"

He does not know how much longer he can handle the pressure pushing against his brain.

Versachi peeks over at the woman standing next to him. Impulses flick at his brain, telling him that something is not quite right, but he cannot make meaning of them. His thoughts start to meld together, the strands wrapping around each other, forming a weave. Something about the hair doesn't look quite right, and that strange hat seems a little off, and that funny-looking jacket feels out of place. The sounds of the jingling coins, not that of the regular change a person would ordinarily carry, but the heavier, deeper sounds of something else, like coins from a slot machine. All these thoughts pull at something he can't yet identify in his consciousness, but deep within his subconscious brain, thoughts are coming together and taking shape. His face screws into a puzzled expression as diverse patterns coalesce in his brain, like the missing letters of a cryptogram coming into focus. The woman next to him jingling her coins seems too nervous. She is too quiet. And she is too still. Something *feels* wrong. Versachi slowly turns his head to get a better look at this strange woman, when an ear-splitting roar erupts directly behind his back.

"May the good lord save me!" a bald woman in her seventies loudly crows out to the back of Versachi's head. She looks like a lifelike female version of Dr. Seuss, but meaner, and is pointing accusingly at the magazine Versachi holds in his hands, *Bad Puppy*, a gay publication that Versachi has absentmindedly snatched off the shelf while he collects his thoughts. The bellicose woman, barely five feet tall, her scalp bereft of hair, pokes her bony index finger sharply into his upper arm.

"He's looking at boys!" the bald woman wails. "He's looking at little boys. May the good lord have mercy!"

Versachi turns red with embarrassment and drops the magazine like a burning chunk of coal. Flustered and on the spot, Versachi quickly snatches a *Playboy* off the shelf, but it is too late—the burning coals are no longer in Versachi's hands, but in the old woman's eyes.

"You goddamned pervert!" the old lady crows. "Now you're looking at little girls." Her bald pate radiates with reflected light from the fluorescent bulbs overhead, casting an almost bluish tint to her skin. The veins on her thin neck pulse with blood as she stares up at him.

Versachi feels like a pedophile in the playground as three more sets of eyes focus on him: the attractive woman with the oversized bust who has wandered into the back, the well-dressed man browsing the book section, and the clerk who is peering around the bend. They stare at the confrontation between the diminutive, elderly woman, and the strapping, virile man—more strange entertainment in a strange city. He drops the *Playboy* magazine like it's another burning chunk of coal from the same fire pit, grabs *Knitting Today* off the shelf, and flees to the front counter, the hunter now the hunted.

The old warhorse follows him, step for step, eyes blazing and screaming all the way. "You don't fool me—and you don't fool God either!" She waves her cane menacingly. "You'll go down with the house of Cain," the old woman warns. "Philanderers, adulterers, buggerers, sodomists, perverts. You'll all be together in the same vat of hot tar in the end!"

Versachi reaches the front and throws a ten-dollar bill on the counter. "Keep the change," he mumbles to the clerk, and hurries out the door.

"Pervert!" the old lady yells after him as Versachi scurries past staring eyes down the hallway. "Goddamned sodomist!"

She returns to the back of the store and turns to John, giggling like a little girl and grinning ear to ear. "I haven't had that much fun in a dog's age."

———————

Three men sit by themselves in the bar area, drinking mugs of beer and watching baseball games on the television monitors. One of the men, a nervous sort, withdraws a comb from his breast pocket every few minutes and runs it through his shoulder-length blonde hair. Ludo has watched each of these men reorder drafts in fresh mugs, chilled and caked with ice. Watching them take long swigs from frosted glasses makes Ludo terribly thirsty. Twice, he has had to wave off the waitress for want of money to buy a beer. He is imagining how refreshing one of those ice-cold drafts with frothy heads would taste in his mouth when a mannish-looking woman walks into the bar and comes over to him. She is wearing a strange coat with a checkered pattern of browns and reds and flapping white pockets that give the jacket the appearance of being inside out.

"How's it going, big boy?" she says in a deep voice.

"Fine," Ludo says, avoiding the woman's gaze and twisting in his seat to face another direction. He glances toward the slots area, hoping the big woman might move her hefty bulk off her seat and unobstruct his view of the cute girl he has been ogling. But there is no luck there; the woman is deeply engaged in her machine and appears settled in for good.

"Want to party?"

Ludo is about to tell the annoying woman to get lost, but the voice seems familiar and he looks up. "Homes?" Ludo says, a puzzled expression on his face. Underneath the unfamiliar hair, he is greeted by a familiar smile. Sure enough, it is John.

"What the hell is with you?" Ludo says, looking him up and down as if he's seeing a ghost, both stupefied and concerned with his friend's incredibly bizarre appearance.

"Long story," John says, the long curly blonde wig and oversized floppy hat slightly askew on his head. He is looking around the crowd suspiciously and jingling a few coins in his pocket. "Hurry up, we have to get out of here right away," he says, tugging at Ludo's arm.

Ludo lifts his nose; an odor of rotten eggs and rancid apples permeates the air. "What's that smell?"

———————

A long, black Cadillac furtively tails the taxi carrying John and Ludo to a diner some distance off the Strip. When the taxi drops off its load, the driver of the Cadillac, who alertly recognized John Howard-Hughes when he exited the casino and entered the cab—even in his strange getup—circles back to pick up his boss. He makes quick progress and is soon pulling into the entranceway of the Big Diamond Casino, where the barrel-chested man in the Italian suit anxiously awaits his arrival. Versachi is excited at the good fortune brought to him by the driver: John Howard-Hughes has been found. The big man instructs the driver to return to the diner he has just come from as quickly as he can, red lights be damned. No time is to be lost.

This time, there would be no escape for Howard-Hughes. Versachi would make sure of that.

Ten minutes later, the speeding Cadillac pulls into the diner's parking lot and positions itself in a spot a few spaces to the right of the front door. Versachi instructs his driver to keep the car running in case Howard-Hughes makes a run for it, though it is a superfluous instruction: In this desert heat, only a fool would sit baking in a car without running the air-conditioning. Versachi surveys the eatery for a few minutes before getting out of the car, savoring the confrontation just ahead of him. He carefully fixes his suit and tie, twists his head side to side to work out some kinks in his thick neck, then pushes his black hair back with his hand and walks over to the diner's entrance.

Versachi pulls open the front door, and with a jaunty bounce to his step, enters the confines of the diner.

Chapter Nineteen

John empties his pocket when the taxicab arrives at the diner. The handful of coins he collected from the slot machine is just enough to pay for the fare and allow the driver a seventy-five-cent tip. With that expenditure, John and Ludo are again flat broke—neither one of them has a dollar to his name in this town. They desperately need to get hold of some money, and immediately is how fast they need it. Work is the only way they know to accomplish that goal. Ludo had called around earlier only to find that hospital gigs require a sheriff's card—as do many other temporary jobs in Las Vegas—and to get a sheriff's card requires ID. And to get that far, which they can't, they would need money to pay the processing fees for their paperwork, which they don't have. Getting a sheriff's card requires being fingerprinted and identified downtown at the sheriff's office, which John can't do given his escapade at the Mafioso restaurant and subsequent Metro police interest.

In other words, their only solution is dishwashing and bussing at the diner—if Virgil will give them the hours.

John is taking his turn at the sink and is busy scrubbing pots, his arms covered in suds up to the elbow, when Ludo walks into the kitchen and dumps a load of plates into a deep plastic bin.

"What was up with that wig and shit back in the casino?" Ludo says. "Man, you strange sometimes."

"Never mind," John says, dismissing the conversation with a wave of his hand. A few bubbles sail off his arm and into the air. One large one, floating longer than the rest, gets good hang time and hovers above the sink. Then, alas, gravity exerts its inevitable force and the bubble crashes into the top of the stainless steel sink, its ephemeral flight over—and it disappears from existence.

Ludo still doesn't know about Versachi and that set of problems, and John isn't in the mood to enlighten him. They are already in a big-enough mess, and he doesn't want to burden his friend with another set of difficulties equally bad, maybe even worse. The soup is already boiling with too many bad ingredients. In this situation, ignorance is bliss.

Ludo looks at John and is about to press for answers, but given that John hasn't volunteered a word about his strange behavior and that bizarre wig, he figures he'll get to the bottom of this perplexing episode later. In due time. Between washing dishes and bussing plates, they have all night to talk. But still, it is obvious that something very disturbing is bothering John, and it hovers over the two of them.

"Homes, there's a big guy out there looking for you," Ludo says. "For a newbie in town, you seem to be awfully popular."

"Who is he?" John says, putting a pot back in the sink and coming over to the swinging doors near Ludo. Water drips on the floor as he wipes his arms dry with a rag.

"Beats me," Ludo says, pushing open the doors and returning to the dining room area, his tray loaded with pitchers full of ice water.

John looks through the frosted glass window of the swinging kitchen doors and sees Virgil talking to a big guy in a dark suit. The man's back is facing John, but the profile is unmistakable: It is Versachi, and he's turning toward the kitchen. John backs away from the glass in abject fear. Once again, Versachi has found him. He is cornered.

Jesus Christ, how did he find me here?

Unable to come up with a better plan and with seconds to act, John hurriedly squeezes onto a long shelf under a table where pots, pans, and random kitchen items are kept, pulling empty flour bags over himself as cover. He lies prone on the metal shelf, fear gripping him like a second skin.

———————

Versachi is about to push open the door to the kitchen when he is intercepted by Virgil. The manager puts his hand on Versachi's arm as a way of restraint.

"Excuse me, sir," Virgil begins in an authoritative voice, "you can't—"

Versachi looks down at the hand on his arm as if a mosquito has landed there and he is about to crush it, a slight smile dancing on his lips. The manager, sensing the very same thought in some shape or manner, quickly and wisely removes his hand and shrinks back.

"Stay out here," Versachi commands, and Virgil, clearly recognizing the pecking order between the two of them and valuing the preservation of his very own particular species, backs off and steps aside.

"I'm looking for the dishwasher," Versachi says to a busboy, a short Mexican man of indeterminate age, as he comes through the swinging kitchen doors into the dishwashing area. "My plate is dirty."

The busboy, intuitively understanding an unhealthy situation he wants no part of, feigns ignorance of the English language and hastily retreats back through the swinging doors and into the dining area.

Versachi looks around, determined to find Howard-Hughes. He walks over to a draped cloth hanging in front of a closet and pulls it aside, but there is no Howard-Hughes behind the curtain, just a storage rack of cleaning supplies. A thin metal coat hook to its left holds the blue sport coat that Versachi instantly recognizes.

Getting warm.

Looking down, he sees two shoes hanging off the end of a middle shelf of a long table, the feet inside of them nervously twitching.

Very, very warm.

Versachi rubs his hands together in satisfaction. Now he's got him. Finally! He reaches underneath the empty flour sacks, grabs hold of some solid material and yanks hard. Out comes John Howard-Hughes, sliding off the shelf in a cloud of white flour and tumbling hard to the floor, puffs of powder punctuating the air like pollen blown off a tree. Versachi looks down in pleasure. There he is, John Howard-Hughes in the flesh, covered in flour and resembling pizza dough before it is tossed into the baker's pan. A few pots and pans tumble out as well and loudly clatter on the tile. Versachi kicks a small pan out of his way and after two bounces, it skids across the floor, making a whistling sound until it stops with a thud against a large sack of rice.

"Well, well, well. Look what we have here," Versachi says, brushing flour specks off his suit jacket. "I've been looking for you, you squirmy peckerhead."

Grabbing a large handful of fabric on John's shirt, the material bunched in his tight grip, Versachi lifts John to his feet and then shoves him backward against the counter. He steps forward and grabs the back of John's neck with a thick hand, and pulls him closer so that they are inches apart.

"You were pretty clever back there, I'll give you that," Versachi continues, his hand feeling like five hundred pounds of lead on John's neck, "but now it's payback time."

"I can explain—"

"I suggest you shut up before I stuff you into one of these cooking pots," Versachi says, his voice booming like angry thunder. He leans over John like a whale about to snack on krill and shrimp. "You think you can scam us for a free dinner and throw it in our face, you little shit? And then make me chase you around the casinos like we're playing hide and go seek at the playground? You're fucking with the wrong boy, boy."

John begins whimpering, "Oh my god, don't kill me! I—"

"I was thinking more about twisting your head so it faces the other direction, but maybe your idea is better." Versachi, like a dragon without fire, breathes garlic onto John instead.

"Please don't kill me. I'll do anything—"

"Then start with twenty-five push-ups, now!" Versachi yells into John's face.

"Push-ups?"

"Now!" Versachi booms in a terrifying voice. John immediately drops to the floor, doing two quick push-ups. Ludicrously, a large cockroach hops onto his arm and crawls onto his back. John frantically tries to shake it off, but the bug, content in its nest of powder, doesn't budge.

"Three, four, five." Versachi stands over him and counts. "Keep going."

Ludo comes through the kitchen doors with a small, thin-handled broom held high in his hand like a baseball bat. Versachi turns to face him. Ludo, feeling foolish with a three-foot broom that may as well be a breadstick against the massively built man, immediately turns the handle over, the whisked end of the broom facing the floor, a sheepish smile creasing his lips.

"Little sweeping, man," Ludo says to Versachi, pushing the broom along the floor. He looks over at John doing push-ups. "What the fuck are you doing?"

"Shut up, Ludo!"

"Keep doing 'em!" Versachi commands. "Eleven, twelve, twelve, twelve." Versachi counts in time to each push-up.

"Wait, you missed thirteen. I—"

"Don't make me lose my patience," Versachi screams, wadding his fists into balls like wrecking irons.

"Thirteen bad luck, homes," Ludo calls over softly.

John struggles to lift himself up off the floor for another push-up, but can't manage and lays exhausted on the ground. White flour covers the floor around John, giving the impression of a misshapen ball of dough that's fallen off the cook's table.

"I can't do any more," John moans. "I can't go."

"Do 'em!" Versachi bellows.

"You got a bug on your back, homes," Ludo says.

John throws a nasty glance in Ludo's direction. He sharply twists his back again, but the cockroach doesn't budge.

"Do 'em!" Versachi repeats as he stands over John with clenched fists.

"Man, he told you to keep going," Ludo says.

"Ludo—"

"Get up then, I had enough of your fucking around," Versachi yells. "Get up!"

John scrambles to his feet, finally shaking the bug free in the process. It lands at John's feet and pauses, as if awaiting applause for its human bull ride, before scampering out of sight into an open sack of flour. Versachi advances forward, his menacing glare drilling right through the irises of his prey's eyes as John, petrified, backs against a wall.

Suddenly, the big man bursts out laughing and heartily slaps John on the shoulder, knocking him one foot to the side.

"What? What?" Ludo asks.

"Oh, man, that was funny," Versachi says, guffawing loudly.

"I-I-I-I don't understand," John stammers. "Y-You're not going to kill me?"

"Not right now," Versachi says, beside himself with amusement, his massive chest pumping up and down. "You gave a piggyback ride to a cockroach!"

John and Ludo look at each other, confused, as the big man roars with laughter. Versachi turns to see that no one else is within earshot, immediately puts on a serious face, and then whispers, "I'm agent Mr. V, FBI. We have some things to talk about."

"You're FBI?" John says, astounded with this pronouncement.

"Now we're really fucked, homes. The FBI?"

Ludo turns to Versachi. "I don't know him, by the way."

"Shhhhhh," Versachi cautions with one finger to his lips. He looks around before continuing. "Don't mention that F-word again. Nobody can know. We're not after either one of you. I'm here because I need your cooperation, cockroach rider."

"You're a G-man?" John asks, still not getting it.

"He can use the G-word, can't he?" Ludo asks.

"Just don't use the F-word," Versachi replies.

"Let me clarify," Ludo says, "just to be one hundred percent clear. The G is okay and the F is not."

"Ludo, will you knock it off!" John says.

"What's all this about?" Ludo demands, looking at John. "Where the hell did this F and G guy come from?"

"Both of you shut up," Versachi says. "I'm actually after a man named Giulli—that's right, pronounced just like the girl's name, Julie, but trust me, the resemblance ends there: The male version is a lot more violent. This guy, Giulli, happens to be the owner of Amiga Bella, the restaurant your friend here trashed yesterday. You see, when a particular fool went in and did his thing, that was fate dropping a golden boy into our lap. And guess what, cockroach rider? He looks a lot like you."

"Trashed a restaurant? What?" Ludo scratches his head, and then as recognition sets in, he looks at John. "Naaaah. That dumb ass on the video was you? Holy shit!"

"Yeah, Mr. Knucklehead of the Week is in the house, cuchifritos. Front and center," Versachi says, looking at Ludo. And turning to John, "Congratulations on making the show, bubba. And by the way, watch out for the police. I think Metro, that's the Las Vegas police department, bubba, has taken an interest in you as well.

"Now," Versachi continues, "what we're going to do is talk a little and figure out a plan to get you out of trouble, cockroach rider, and at the same time you're going to do me a little favor as well, you see? I'm going to grab a seat out there, and you'll sit down at the table behind me. Make sure to order food so that everything looks one hundred percent natural."

"But we don't have any money!" John says.

"Look, cockroach rider, don't push me. Make sure you order food so you're not sitting at an empty table. Also, act like we don't know each other, and under no circumstances," Versachi leans into John's ear and whispers loud enough for Ludo to hear, "do you mention the letters F-B-I. Never use the F-word, you got it? And that goes for you too, cuchifritos."

Versachi underscores his last statement with a hard pinch to John's cheek that leaves red indents on his flesh.

"But we can use the G-word?" Ludo says.

"That's right, but not the F-word."

"We're going to talk inside?" John asks.

"That's what I said."

"Virgil is not going to like that," John says. "The manager."

"Let's just say that Virgil and I will have a little heart-to-heart and I'll stress the point that we need a few minutes of privacy."

Versachi turns around at the kitchen doors, raises his hand as if to say something more, and starts laughing again before he pushes his way through the swinging doors and back into the diner.

————————

John and Ludo face each other across a Formica-top table cluttered with bottles of Heinz ketchup, Gulden's mustard, Tabasco, and pink packages of Sweet 'n' Low, blue ones of Equal, brown ones of raw sugar, and white ones of Domino bleached sugar. In front of Ludo sits a bowl of traditional southwestern chili with a small hill of sour cream and minced onions sprinkled on top. John has pushed his pea soup to the side, untouched, and instead empties two packages of white sugar into his coffee—even though he doesn't use sweeteners—stirring the dark fluid round and round with his spoon. Three packages of Saltine crackers lie next to his soup bowl, one stacked atop the other.

Versachi is in the booth directly behind John, sitting back to back with him. He is wearing a dark gray suit with a fine pinstripe of darker gray lines. His massive chest fills the space between table and booth, a small amount of which is perched over the table like a bluff hanging over a valley. In front of Versachi, stacked high on a white oblong plate, is a large order of chicken wings drenched in red barbecue sauce. A pile of discarded and crumpled napkins, stained reddish-brown from the sauce wiped off his mouth and fingers, is tossed haphazardly and litters the table about his plate. Versachi puts down a half-empty cup of black coffee, still steaming, and picks up the daily newspaper, the *Las Vegas Review-Journal,* holding it high in front of his face. He pulls the newspaper a little closer and leans back a bit to make himself better understood.

"Just look like you're talking to cuchifritos there," Versachi says into the middle crease of the newspaper. "And remember, we don't know each other."

From across the room, the situation is being closely monitored by a third party, Virgil. The manager paces moodily by the register, watching his two workers and the big bully in the suit suspiciously converse across two booths. He doesn't know what is going on, what a well-dressed thug would want with these two street bums, but whatever it is, he doesn't like it. This powwow at the adjoining booths has put him in a major tizzy. For one, Virgil hates when his workers take a break of any sort, which in Virgil's view, except for very brief trips to the bathroom, is never justified. The way he sees it, if you're at work, you should be working. Period. Until a worker clears the front door and is off the diner's property, he's in Virgil's domain and subject to Virgil's hegemony. But if there's anything Virgil hates more than his workers taking breaks, it is getting bullied, especially since he's a bully himself. The convergence of these two annoying and aggravating situations has put him in a very foul mood, and he blisters like a furiously boiling kettle of thick soup.

John holds the cup of coffee to his lips and whispers over his shoulder to Versachi. "We just want to be finished with this mess, get out, and be done with it."

"It's not that easy," Versachi whispers back. "You pissed off a mob guy—a made man—and trashed his restaurant. Not something I would normally advise. He's a little miffed about that, if you know what I mean. But if you scratch my back, I'll scratch yours, and we might be able to work something out."

"What kind of scratching we talking about?" John says, staring hard at Ludo.

"Why are you asking me?" Ludo says.

"Ludo, I am not talking to you."

"So why are you looking at me?"

"Because I can't look at him. We don't know him, remember?"

"Oh, right, sorry," Ludo says.

"That's right, you don't know me," Versachi says.

"And we can only use the G-word, right?" Ludo says.

"Ludo, will you stop this nonsense with the F and G already?" John says, exasperated. "I was asking about the scratching."

"Don't worry about the little things," Versachi says. "You just call me at eight-fifteen on the dot and we'll work out all the details then. No need to worry yourself about it now." Versachi turns a page in his newspaper and keeps it high in front of his face. "And cockroach rider, let me give you some free advice while I'm at it. Stay away from that girl. How the fuck a punk dishwasher like you ends up with a girl like that is beyond me. She's got a past you don't want any part of. Just a little free advice."

"You either tell me what this is about or we're out of here on this," John says, ignoring Versachi's comments about ZZ.

"Hold on, homie, I'm not done. Still food here and I'm hungry." Ludo quickly stuffs a loaded spoon into his mouth. "Where we going?"

"Damn it, Ludo, we're not going anywhere. Do you have anything on your mind besides goddamned food?"

"Eating time, man, the Ludo Rule goes—"

"I'm not doing anything unless I know what's going on," John says over his shoulder.

"That's okay, then. I'll let you take care of this on your own. Good luck." Versachi puts the newspaper down and stands up as if to leave.

"Wait, wait. Alright, let's keep talking," John says.

His bluff working like a charm—as he had no doubt it would—Versachi sits down with a wry smile and picks up his newspaper again.

Virgil rushes over to the table when he sees Versachi drop the paper and stand up, but when the big man sits again, he continues past the table as if on his way somewhere else, glaring at John as he passes.

"Homes, can I have those crackers if you're not going to eat them?" Ludo asks.

"Go ahead," John says.

"What's the big deal?" Ludo calls over to the back of Versachi's head. "All he did was skip out on some dinner bill, so what? It's like, ah, what do you call it, like, a minor misdemeanor. Like running a red light."

"Is that right, nachos con todos?" Versachi shakes his big head in mock assent. "Metro police may have a few questions about theft, destruction of property, and assault for throwing a table over on the waiter. Ask your boy a few questions about his little adventure there."

"Wow, you did all that?" Ludo ponders out loud.

"That's if they get to you before Giulli does," Versachi continues. He licks the chicken wing juice off his fingers, dries them with a napkin that he crumples up and tosses into the pile on the table, and then carefully smoothes back his thick, black hair.

"If you cooperate with the three letters we're not going to talk about"—Versachi clears his throat in a long gurgle and glances around—"then perhaps I can fix all these problems. One hand can wash the other one, if you follow what I'm saying."

"If we cooperate with the F letter, is that right?" Ludo says

"Yes, that's right," Versachi says.

"How do you like them chicken wings?" Ludo asks.

"They're pretty good. I would order them again," Versachi says.

"Ludo, will you relax on the food for a minute?" John says, his frustration mounting. He's worried about the amalgamation of threats coalescing against his well-being—Giulli, the Mafia, Versachi, the FBI, Metro police, ZZ's psychopathic ex-husband, Johnny Wonderbread, Knuckles, Rock, Apples, and the other killers at the poker game—and Ludo can't seem to take his mind off the chicken wings.

John's voice raises an octave and he turns to face Versachi. "I don't understand all this. I'm just here on a goddamned vacation. I'm not agent triple-zero-seven, James Bond in Las Vegas. Jesus!"

"That's double-o-seven, homes," Ludo says, correcting him.

"Don't look this way and lower your voice," Versachi warns, and John turns back around.

"You eating the soup? It's getting cold," Ludo says.

"Just take it, Ludo."

"Oh, by the way," Versachi casually adds, "so you get a little more educated about the local situation here, cockroach rider, Giulli happens to have old-school Italian traditions and a reputation for taking personal things personally. He's not a big fan of people coming in and redecorating his family restaurant. And he might consider that personal, if you know what I mean."

"That don't sound too good," Ludo whispers to John.

Virgil slowly strolls by the table, glowering, letting his presence be known to the two dishwashers. He is quick to move away, however, when Versachi looks over in his direction.

"You need me, so to speak, to run a little interference, cockroach rider. Remember, call me at eight-fifteen, exactly, at the sports bar of the El Dorado. When someone answers, ask for V. But before you call there, try the Hidden Treasure and see if I have left a message for you to try a different number. At that number, ask for VV. That's a double V. When you get hold of me, but you won't get hold of me, you understand, because I don't know you, I'll tell you where we're going to meet at nine o'clock, and then we'll meet at that place I tell you, but it won't be me telling you that, and it's there that I'll tell you the meeting place for ten o'clock. If you're given another number to call between nine and ten, do not use V or double V. That won't be good. We have to be careful. In that case, use the W between the Vs, that's VWV. Just those letters. Whoever answers will act like they don't understand, but they will. If they act like they understand, hang up without a word and call again to confirm. If they still say they understand, forget that plan, it's no good."

"But if they act like they don't understand, how will I know if they do?" John says.

"Because they'll act like they don't."

"But what if they really don't?"

"Then they'll act like they do. Look, cockroach rider, don't wise-ass with me. You just do what I tell you to do. Now, when you get to the party—and I'll tell you where it is, but only later—I'll go over to a quiet spot and you'll come over and stand nearby so we can talk, but we won't talk, you understand? You don't know me. And then I'll tell you what you have to do. Repeat the plan to me."

"So I'll call you at eight-fifteen to see where I should call and then you'll tell me where I should go to meet you at nine o'clock so you can tell me where to meet you at ten o'clock, and when I get there, we won't talk, but we will."

"That's right."

"And I'll use the V in the first case, the double V in the second, and if we have to use the third, then I'll use the W in between and will hang up if anyone understands, but continue on if they don't."

"I don't know what the two of you just said, but why don't you just tell us right now where he should meet you, instead of all this cock and bull," Ludo says. "Make it simple without all the F's, G's, V's, double V's and W's between the V's."

"You're not going, mofongo, so don't worry about it," Versachi says. "Just make sure, cockroach rider, that you use the W to throw them off."

"Throw who off?" John says.

"He said *them*, homes, not who. He said 'To throw *them* off.'"

"Who is them? Who we talking about?"

"Them, I told you that," Ludo says.

"But who?"

"Yeah," Ludo says to Versachi. "We worrying about them or who? Who is this other who or them we gotta worry about?"

"Not your problem," Versachi says.

"You still haven't told me exactly what I have to do," John says.

Versachi turns around and shows all his teeth in a big smile. He then stands up and shakes out his hulking limbs as if they were folded plastic just taken out of a box and flips a ten-dollar bill on the table. With his curious walk, very light for such a big man, Versachi saunters out of the diner without looking back.

Ludo lifts himself off his seat and looks over John's shoulder to see if Versachi has left any of the chicken wings, then shakes his head as he spies a plate full of bones picked clean. "Let's skip out of town, bro," he says, clapping his hands on the table for emphasis. "This whole thing ain't right. And that number eight-fifteen o'clock to call him is bad too, man. I feel it. Real close to that eight-thirteen room with that poker game, and that one didn't work out too good. Eight-fifteen is too close a neighbor, and I know what I'm talking about."

"First, eight-fifteen o'clock is not a number, it's a time. Second, there's no place to run. He knows where we live. And he has my credit card, for chrissakes," John says, throwing up his hands. "And you forget one tiny, little detail. We're broke. No, we're not broke, we're flat broke. Like squashed pancakes. We have no means to do anything anyway."

"Homes, that was my last five-hundred dollars that Godzilla and that rat took. I don't got nothing else. You know, man, my only family is that cheap-ass uncle of mine, makes your family look like they throwing money around. Getting anything off that millionaire skinflint would be harder than squeezing orange juice out of a camel's ass. Man, I already late on the rent back home to take this trip." Ludo's voice gets softer. "Your sister wouldn't advance you a couple of bucks to get us through this, would she?"

John groans. "A couple of bucks? We need, like, three thousand plus! You know the answer to that one. I'm still into her for that four grand for the car. And obviously, we don't need to bring up my father, the tightest man on the planet." John feels pangs of pain in his stomach and wishes he had a bottle of Pepto-Bismol in his hand. He'd down the entire container of pink liquid in one swig. "Forget orange juice out of a camel, try getting grapefruit juice out of that dromedary. You know how he is. I'd hear about this for the rest of my life—and still not get any money out of him. No way I'm letting him know. I think I'd rather die than ask."

"At this rate, you may get your chance," Ludo says.

"I'm not in the joking mood—be serious for a minute," John says, his hand gripping his stomach as a fresh twist of pain makes him grit his teeth.

"Let me tell you, something about this whole thing ain't right, like black chalk on a blackboard. Like, you can't see what's written even though it's marked up, you know what I'm saying? This dude is working an agenda that ain't our agenda. Like that poker game back there, we're playing in the wrong game and we can't win with their rules, and whatever their rules are, we don't even know them. We lose before we even sit down."

"What choice is there? I see no options."

"This is one fucked-up, mother-fucking, fucking crazy situation, man. Fuck!" Ludo nods his head in the direction of the bread basket. "Pass the bread, homes." John hands it over and Ludo continues. "What's this bit about your girl? What past of hers is he talking about?"

"Who knows? He's probably just trying to get me nervous."

"I don't know if it's working on you, but it's working real good on me. Both she—and I don't even know her—and he, both of them, get me nervous. Real nervous, like popcorn on a hot skillet. You get what I'm getting at?"

John shrugs and Ludo continues. "I got a question for you, bro." Ludo points his finger at John and looks at him square in the face. "How do we know this guy is really FBI?" Ludo rips off a big chunk of bread, dips it in a puddle of sauce, and begins chewing on it.

"Come on, Ludo."

"Well, what do we know about him besides his little cloak-and-dagger speech back there?"

"He showed us his ID," John says.

"He showed us a piece of paper," Ludo says, tapping on a napkin. "You ever see an FBI ID?"

"Just on TV, I guess."

"That's my point. For all we know it could be his membership to International Brotherhood of Pasta Throwers or whatever, or his ID from his four o'clock tea club. And maybe he is FBI, but how the hell would we know?"

"We could call the national headquarters and ask," John says.

"With the trouble we got, that don't sound like such a good idea right now even if we could find out anything, which I doubt. 'Cause if he is, he ain't gonna be too happy about that call. And if he ain't, we don't need to be inviting the FBI into our situation here with all our problems, you know what I'm saying? It's getting a little too complicated as it is."

"So if he's not FBI, what is he?"

"Let me tell you something," Ludo says, looking out the window and watching Versachi's long, black Cadillac back out of a space and drive off. "If I've learned nothing else here, I can tell you this. Nothing, nothing here is what it seems to be. This city is one big mirage, you know what I'm saying? I don't believe nothing in this town. Up ain't up, red ain't red. If I see an egg, I don't believe it's an egg. If I see a seven of diamonds, I don't believe it's a seven of diamonds. This spoon," Ludo says, picking up a spoon and banging it on the table, "if I see it in Las Vegas, I don't believe it's a spoon."

Chapter Twenty

Virgil has been watching John and Ludo with great impatience. They had been sitting for about fifteen minutes when they should have been working. Fifteen very long minutes. And with the thug who bullied him, no less. Virgil knows who to pick his fights with, and it certainly wasn't going to be that menacing Brutus. The manager, stewing in his own juices, has every intention of taking out his pent-up hostilities on the weaker of the parties, those vagrant dishwashers, but he is just waiting for that oversized thug to leave. Not that Virgil needs extra motivation to show his special love, since unmercifully bullying employees was what he did every chance he got, but just the same, he has plenty of extra motivation to flambé those two for his pièce de résistance.

Few of his employees lasted long, and in his perverse way of thinking, Virgil liked that. He fashioned himself after the old gunfighters he saw in his beloved Western films, marking the secret notebook he kept under the cash register with a notch for every employee who quit. Not quite the same as notching a gun barrel for every cowboy who went down to the faster draw, but for Virgil it is equally satisfying. In his seventeen years as manager of the diner, where he lords over the help like a queen eunuch in a harem, he has proudly collected hundreds of notches in the pages of his journal. It is his policy to never fire employees, and he never has, preferring to make their lives miserable to the point that they quit. It is a game he plays with the same fervor baseball players do when they tack on personal stats in preparation for upcoming contracts in their walk years, or to enhance their position in the record books. And Virgil thrives on it. Or to be more accurate, he lives for it. Once he targets a worker, the unfortunate victim never lasts long.

So Virgil, a man of contradictions, is both angry at the affront leveled at him by the thug and inwardly excited because he smells a ripe opportunity to rack up two more notches this very evening.

Finally, the hulking man in the suit leaves the booth and exits the diner. Virgil, stuck explaining a check to a dim-witted customer who can't figure out why tax is charged on all the food items, breaks free and immediately goes over to the table where the two vagabonds are idly chatting—and *not* working—one of them banging a spoon on the table.

Virgil stands over them silently, with a sinister sneer ripped across his lips, letting the full impact of his displeasure reign on the consciousness of his busboy and dishwasher team.

"Having fun, boys?" Virgil finally says, shifting his weight from side to side like a boat rocking in the harbor. His pants are pulled high up on his stomach, just below his crossed arms, and his belt, a bit too short for his girth, is clasped in the very last hole, with the end of the stiff leather sticking straight out like a woodpecker's erection.

John and Ludo silently look up at the bristling manager. Clearly, their visit with Versachi didn't sit well with Virgil and he was going to direct every last bit of bile in his system onto them if it was the last thing he did this evening.

"Now get your asses back in the kitchen and start scrubbing," Virgil orders, his voice seething with rage.

Ludo takes the napkin off his lap, crumples it up, and tosses it on his plate. It drops on a pile of leftover gravy at the edge of the dish and then slips off its side, a small ripped piece clinging precariously to the plate, as if a metaphor for the sticky mess the pair is in. Both

John and Ludo know better than to throw wood into this blaze, and they wordlessly step around the manager and head back toward their stations.

"That will be another thirty-one dollars and thirty cents to your tab, uh-huh," Virgil says to their backs with evident satisfaction. "Plus a five-dollar tip."

———————

Virgil mercilessly rides his dishwashers every time he comes into the kitchen, which is often, heaping insults and abuse on them as if the endeavor of inflicting pain and suffering is a holy mission from a higher power. The criticism rains down on them like an unending hailstorm: The dishes aren't clean enough, they are working too slowly, they are talking too much, there is too much soap in the sink, and then not enough. Real or imagined, Virgil keeps at John and Ludo with screams, commands, and criticisms so ear-splittingly loud that customers can hear his thundering diatribes through the closed kitchen doors and all the way to the far side of the diner. Versachi's visit has clearly unnerved the ranting manager, and had he begun drooling froths of foam from his mouth like a weathered horse, neither John nor Ludo would have been a bit surprised.

Despite the steady bombardment, John and Ludo keep at their tasks. They need the money. They need this job. If they were anything but flat broke, they would have quit in the face of these insufferable, tyrannical harangues. But they weren't anything but flat broke. They are, exactly, flat broke, devastatingly so, without a dollar to their name, so they stoically put up with Virgil's maniacal tirades.

Finally, at seven-thirty in the evening, when his night dishwasher arrives, Virgil calls a truce to the relentless assault and lets them off work. After deductions for their food bill, he hands Ludo thirty-five dollars for the both of them. After almost five grueling hours in the hot kitchen, being vilified and belittled, Ludo just pockets the bills without bothering to count them. Worn down and weakened, John and Ludo are resigned to the day's pay being whatever it is. They just want to get out of there. Not daring to instigate Virgil's ire further with any smart retorts—and having no energy to fling them at the manager anyway—the two sorry friends silently untie their aprons, place them on the work counter near the dishwashing machine, and head out the front door into the evening air of Las Vegas.

———————

The blast of hot air outside is actually refreshing after the even hotter air pumped out by the dishwashing equipment inside, and the fact that it is fresh, unfettered by soap, food refuse, machinery regurgitations, and Virgil's pounding voice is another welcome reprieve.

"I've never seen anything like it. That guy's a raving lunatic. He just didn't let up," John says. "Talk about earning your money, man, that was the shift from hell."

"Thirty-five dollars," Ludo says. "What are we going to do with that?"

It is still light out, the time between the closing light of the day and the incipient darkness of the night, as the two depart from their calamitous experience at the diner and head in the direction of a small retail plaza, walking slowly and digesting their newfound freedom from the banging pots and shrill screams of minutes before. They walk silently and aimlessly—since they have no place to go—individually digesting their situations and feeling the soft evening air against their skins. They traverse several blocks, pushed or pulled by fate, before John pauses and faces his friend.

"You want to talk about luck, listen to this one," John finally says. "A guy comes to Las Vegas with ten thousand dollars, gambles all day and straight into the night. His luck goes up and down and then abandons him altogether. He loses hand after hand at blackjack, increases his bets and still keeps losing. At three in the morning, he's down to his very last ten dollars." John holds up ten fingers and looks at his friend. "You know what happens?"

"You do this every time. I'm tired of it, man. Either tell the story or don't tell it. Too many dishes in my head. Too hot outside. Too many problems."

"Just guess what happens with his last ten dollars."

"I'm not playing these games. I'm not guessing." Ludo kicks a pebble, and catching the tip of it, it feebly rolls just a few feet away. "This day been too hard already. I don't want to be shot down with this nonsense."

"C'mon, just this once," John implores.

"Okay," Ludo says, "what, he wins?"

"Wrong!" John loudly exclaims, his voice echoing down the street. "He loses his last ten dollars. You're wrong!"

"Fuck you, man, with these stories. I don't have the strength for this. You promised not to shoot me down, then you shoot me down. Let's talk about something else."

"Nothing personal, but you were so wrong," John says.

"Never mind," Ludo says.

A mangy black dog slowly trots toward them, its parched tongue hanging out of its mouth, but when it gets close, it skirts the sidewalk, avoiding them as though they were in a class below its station and not to be mingled with. Ludo turns to watch the dog trot unevenly past them, then immediately dart into a driveway and out of sight. They reach a corner and stop when the light goes against them.

John leans against the lamp pole, and gesticulates with his hands. "The problem is," John continues, "he has no hotel room lined up yet and he doesn't have a penny to his name, so he ends up walking up and down the Strip for hours, just killing time, not knowing what to do. Guess what happens next. Take one shot at it."

"I don't know."

"Really, what do you think happens next? I won't shoot you down, I promise."

Ludo sighs. "Alright, someone gives him some money, and then he gets a hotel room, goes to sleep—"

"Wrong again!" John exclaims gleefully. "That's not what happens!"

"Fuck you. Let's just walk somewhere already. I'm too tired to just stand here and listen to this crap."

Ludo looks in all four directions and can't decide which to proceed in, not that they have anyplace to go. Instead, he stares down at the black asphalt of the street. After a few seconds, he says, "Let's go this way," and they continue on in the same direction as before. "So what happens?"

"He finds a hundred-dollar bill lying on the street. He goes back to the casino and gets lucky. And I mean *lucky*. He presses his bets playing roulette—doubling them every time—and wins twelve straight times betting black. He wins two-hundred-and-fifty-six-thousand dollars. True story. That's Vegas, anything can happen."

Ludo continues on for about twenty feet, silently letting John's tale sink in. But something is troubling him about the anecdote.

"Wait a second," Ludo says, and stops walking. "You didn't finish the story. Guys like that never walk away with the money."

John looks down at a crumpled sports parlay card lying on the curb near his feet, tossed away by a player like a pit from a fruit completely devoured, and doesn't respond.

"He had that thirteen sitting on him, didn't he?" Ludo continues. "That would be the next spin. It couldn't have turned out good."

"How do you find thirteens in everything?"

"Your story, man." A wry, tired smile creases Ludo's lips. "He tried doubling up one more bet, didn't he?"

John shrugs and without any further discussion, and for no reason either of them could explain, they turn right at the next corner and head in a new direction.

———————

Off in the distance they can see the neon lights of the casinos on Las Vegas Boulevard, the thoroughfare that divides the city into east and west. It is a world away from them here on Tropicana Avenue and Eastern Avenue a few miles east of the hordes of gawking tourists marching up and down the sidewalks of the Strip like relentless armies of ants on forest trails. Tropicana Avenue is one of the main thoroughfares that traverses the city east and west; Eastern is one of the main avenues that flows north and south, paralleling the Strip and, farther down, between Russell and Sunset, framing the eastern end of the airport. In this busy intersection, it is not tourists that fill the streets, but cars whizzing by on the way to their destinations.

"I'm going to meet up with ZZ for a little while," John says, the first time either of them has spoken in minutes. "I'll meet you at the mall right before we have to meet Versachi, say eight forty-five, by the Neiman-Marcus store. Give me twenty dollars for the cab, I think that's what I'll need, and guard the rest with your life."

"Yeah, exactly that, with my life, though after I get a cab, if it's my money or my life, it's not going to leave them much choice."

Ludo hands over the bills and looks at the three crumpled fives remaining in his hand, money that looks like it too has its own sorrowful story to tell. "You be cool, man. I don't mind taking a quiet break after that," Ludo says, jerking his thumb back in the direction of the diner. "I really don't mind that at all. That fifteen ought to get me to the Mirage sports book or something. Page me there and we'll figure it out."

"Didn't you bring your cell phone, Ludo?"

"I never bring it on vacations, that's why they're vacations. Anyway, they would have got that too, along with our money."

John starts walking off and stops when he is hailed by his friend.

"Hey, homes," Ludo calls out to John. "Try to stay out of trouble, okay?"

Chapter Twenty-One

John is apprehensive when he exits the taxi at the convenience store on the corner of Flamingo and Sandhill, arriving there a few minutes before eight. There is too much on his mind, and not much of it is pleasant. His disconcerting conversation with ZZ earlier in the day makes him wonder what kind of a get-together they will have and given her moods, if they will even have that rendezvous. And then there is Versachi, whose presence in his life hangs over him like an ogre's foul shadow. Which adds to the uncertainty, worry, and acidic pains in his stomach.

John pays the cabbie thirteen dollars and fifty cents for the fare and tip, and exits with six dollars and fifty cents tightly clutched in his hand—the last of his money. The taxi lacked air-conditioning so he is thankful to be out of its sticky heat and into the refreshing coolness of the store. He is dreadfully thirsty, and grabs the first cold bottle of water he sees, twisting the top off, and downing half the liquid in one long quenching gulp. The cashier rings up one dollar and five cents and waits while John examines his total savings—a five, a single, and two quarters—as if they were precious artifacts. John finally hands the clerk the five and receives three singles and a pile of change the clerk unloads on him. John dumps the coins in his pocket without counting and then slips another dollar across the counter, asking for four quarters. He is left with a pocketful of change and three dollar bills, which he tucks into his back pocket.

John finishes the rest of the water in another long gulp and places the empty container on the counter before pushing through the exit doors and into the evening. He walks over to the phone booth to make his call, feeling the hot dry air, like an oven, bake his body, and socks thirty-five cents into the slot. John hopes, as he dials ZZ's number, that she will give him a ride to the mall after they get together. In fact, he's counting on it. Three dollar bills and a pocketful of change is barely enough money to get a Las Vegas taxi down the block, let alone go any type of distance.

ZZ answers the phone on the fifth ring. Already a sign of trouble. Even in the brief span of time since John met her, he knows that five rings for ZZ is a very long time in her world, a bad augur for this phone call. She starts by dropping a bomb on him: She can't meet until later, sometime after nine o'clock. John, however, has to catch up with Versachi around that same time and he cannot be late. Versachi made that very clear. That's the minor problem. The major problem is that his paltry sum of loose bills and coins is not enough money to catch a cab, and he is stuck far away from the Strip.

In short, it's a disaster.

"Are you there?" ZZ says.

"I'm here all right, I'm all the way out here in like bumfuck Egypt or something," John cries, gripping the phone so hard his knuckles turn white. Looking around, there are no familiar landmarks: He is far from Las Vegas Boulevard and there are no casinos in sight, just two-story apartment complexes, houses built in the ubiquitous Southwestern style prevalent in Vegas, and run-down strip malls with the seemingly requisite complement of businesses—massage parlors, smoke shops, hair and nails salons, and convenience stores.

John takes a deep breath before continuing. "I don't know where I am, and I have to, I mean, I must—"

"Doc, you're so dramatic. Really!" ZZ says, cutting him short.

John can hear voices in the background and then the sound of a toilet flushing. Where was she and what was she doing that he can hear other voices and a toilet flush? "You don't understand—"

"Don't be such a drama queen! Just meet me around nine-thirty at this address I'm going to give you. Any cab can find it. It's a private house on Russell Road in the eastern part of town. But I only have a few minutes then, okay?" ZZ's attention seems to be divided, and John can tell that she is in a rush to get off the phone.

"So, about half past nine?" John says after she gives him the address. "That's good for you then?"

"Yes, Doc. I have to go. Bye," ZZ says abruptly.

"I have no money to get—" John starts, but the line is dead. He stares at the black-and-silver phone box as if the telephone unit itself had let him down and slowly replaces the receiver back in its cradle. He rips the edge off a pink piece of paper affixed to the phone box advertising escort services and writes down the address on its back with a keno crayon he had stuffed into his pocket. "Great," John thinks as he shoves the crayon stub back into his pocket. "Just great." John pushes the door to the phone booth open and wanders across the gas station lot. As he contemplates his latest contretemps, a squealing set of tires startles him out of his reverie and he barely jumps back in time. A car speeding across the lot to shortcut a red light at the corner narrowly misses him, shoots out the far curb cut with another loud squeal of tires, and then tears off down the street.

"Geez, I can't even walk across a gas station safely in this town," John mutters.

At the curb, being extra careful not to get run over, he looks both ways twice, then behind him, before hustling across the street and onto the far sidewalk. John turns onto Flamingo Road, heading east, and walks in the direction of Boulder Highway, a mile or two away. Except for the thick traffic on Flamingo, it is quiet in this part of Las Vegas, comprised of mostly one-story suburban homes and empty lots. John walks several blocks, kicking pebbles as he goes, bemoaning his latest predicament. He thinks of Ludo's parting words: "Stay out of trouble, okay?" Boy, he just can't seem to do that in this town. Everything he touches turns to problems, and those problems become bigger problems, and then more problems get piled on again like he's a plate of lasagna made with trouble pasta, trouble mozzarella, and trouble sauce attempting the *Guinness Book of Records* for the greatest number of layers stacked on top of one another. There seems to be no relief from the complications he finds or that find him, a mess that grows and gets more complicated at every turn. Even crossing a gas station lot turns into an adventure fraught with peril.

John sees a phone booth just outside a small convenience store near a corner and, just as a twisting pain in his stomach wakes him up from his doldrums, it dawns on him—he has to call Versachi! Checking his watch, John sees it's almost eight-fifteen. Yikes! John races to the phone booth, cutting off and barely squeezing through its entrance one step ahead of an elderly woman.

"That booth is mine," the old lady protests in a creaky voice.

"First come, first served," John calls back before shutting the door in the woman's face, the badly rusted hinges squeaking loudly as it closes. He doesn't intend to be mean-spirited, but as Versachi made clear, he *has* to make this phone call on time. The woman, none too pleased with John's preemptive maneuver, angrily kicks a piece of trash against the outside of the phone booth. She moves to within inches of the pane and glares at John like he's insulted her pet pink poodle.

John presses "0" on the phone pad. "Information will be thirty-five cents, please," the canned recording announces.

John reaches into his pocket for change, but his hand, balled around the clump of coins, is arrested near the opening by a loose thread entangled in his fingers and won't budge. Finally, John yanks his hand free, pulling his pocket inside out and sending the coins splattering onto the floor of the phone booth. One penny remains in his hand and he disgustedly flings it to the ground. The penny bounces off the glass and lands on his shoe. Feeling cursed by the errant coin, John kicks out his foot, dislodging the penny and sending it flying off the glass again, but at the same time stubbing his toe sharply against the wall of the booth.

"Son-of-a-bitch," John screams as he hops up and down in pain. He bangs his fist against the glass door in frustration.

The old lady angrily bangs back against the door and continues to glare at him through the glass.

"You will need to deposit thirty-five cents or this call will be terminated," the recording intones.

"Okay, okay, damn it," John yells back to the recording, so incensed that he feels like strangling the phone in its own wire until the recording can no longer spit back caustic messages at him. Versachi instructed him to phone at exactly eight-fifteen, and John, filled with anxiety at the not-so-veiled threats leveled against him by the big man, is afraid to be late for the call. As he bends to retrieve the stray coins, his rump collides with the glass wall on one side and propels his head into the glass wall on the other side, momentarily stunning him. John drops the phone and it swings off the metal cord like a pendulum, snapping sharply against the side of his head. He lets out a deep breath and stands up, banging his fist against the phone box in frustration.

"Damn!" John yells out. "Damn, damn, damn!"

John pauses a few seconds to let his head clear, rubbing the spot where it met the wall. It is sensitive to the touch, and he can feel a small lump swelling on his scalp. Checking his hand, he sees there is no blood. He also checks the side of his head where the phone whacked him; no blood either. He again bends down to retrieve the wayward coins, more carefully this time, bringing his knees and back straight toward the floor. Pushing a few pennies to the side, John fishes out the quarters and dimes, stands up slowly, and inserts one of each into the phone. After five long and agonizing rings, an operator picks up.

"Operator, can I have the phone number for the Hidden Treasure?"

"Is that the Hidden Treasure Casino or the Hidden Treasure Hotel?"

"Ah, the ah, hotel please."

"I have listings for reception, information—"

"I'll take reception."

"Please hold while I connect you to 702-648-4831."

John presses his hand hard on the small ledge below the phone as he waits for the connection. The phone rings and rings and rings. "Pick up the goddamned phone," John mutters. Looking up, he sees that the elderly lady has moved even closer and is now pressed against the glass, her pale, blue malevolent eyes magnified like fish eyes in a round bowl. John turns to face the other direction.

He is about to hang up, when a voice on the other end picks up the receiver on the eighth ring.

"Laundry services, we clean to a sparkle. Tim speaking, may I help you?" The voice is affected, very gay. Tim is sitting at a small desk, alternately filing his nails and flipping magazine pages. Behind him, dirty laundry is heaped in large piles of whites and colors, badly needing attention.

"Can I be transferred to reception, please?" John says.

"Then why are you calling the laundry?" Tim blows the nail shavings off his fingertips. "That's a question that begs to be asked."

"I didn't call the laundry—"

"I beg your pardon, poodle, but if you didn't call the laundry, why do you think you're talking to *the laundry*? Divine intervention, I presume?"

"I really don't know, Tim. It was a mistake. Can I please be connected to the reception desk?"

"Why didn't you say so in the first place, Mr. Divine? Even better, you should have called reception if you wanted them. Is there anything I can do for you before I transfer you to reception?"

John bangs the phone against the booth. "No," he squeezes out in a strained voice. "Just the reception, Tim, nothing more."

"What was that noise? Are you okay?"

"Jesus Christ, Tim! Will you please transfer me already?"

John waves away the old lady waiting for the phone. She waves back with small clenched fists and somehow edges closer. In fact, she has pressed her entire body against the glass wall.

"You don't have to be so testy," Tim says. "And by the way, is there any such thing in the order of the world as a mistake? Really? Philosophically speaking, of course. I'll transfer you now."

"Why does everything have to be so difficult?" John screams out loud while he gets transferred, banging the phone booth window with his fist.

The old woman crosses to another side of the booth and positions herself so that she stands directly in front of John. Her lips are pulled back, revealing crooked, discolored teeth. In one hand, she displays a quarter held high at John's eye level, and she taps it on the glass. Her other hand balls into a small fist and bangs vigorously on the window. John again turns away from her. His murderous thoughts of strangling the phone now include strangling the woman as well. Jesus Christ, what a nightmare!

Five long rings later, a young, cheerful woman answers the phone. "Hidden Treasure Hotel, reception speaking," the woman says.

John breathes out deeply before saying in a strained voice, "You guys really ought to do something about the laundry—"

"Laundry services? One moment please. I'll transfer."

"Wait—" John yells, but it is too late. Seven long rings later, a familiar voice picks up the line.

"Laundry services, we clean to a sparkle. Tim speaking, may I help you?"

Covering the mouthpiece with his hand, John screams in frustration, "Son-of-a-bitch!" and smacks the phone hard against the phone box.

From outside, the old lady screams back. "Get off the phone, you goddamned bastard."

John briefly turns to stare at her, and the old barnacle stares right back, her pale-blue irises reflecting light from the overhead lamp, glowing as if they are radioactive.

"Hellooooo? If you don't talk, I'll hang up." Tim starts counting in a singsong voice: "One, two, three, four—"

"Don't hang up!" John pleads, uncovering the mouthpiece.

"My, my. If it's not my old friend, Divine. We really have to stop meeting like this. We like playing games, do we now?"

John groans. "Tim, I need reception, they transferred me back here again by accident."

"Really?"

"Yes, really—"

"But think about it. Are there really accidents—"

"Tim, transfer me to the goddamned reception. Please."

"I think it's interesting that—"

John slams down the phone and thinks about choking the implement with his bare hands and donating the remains to science. He deposits another thirty-five cents and dials the operator. The old lady outside starts banging again, and John, at the limits of his patience, bangs back from the other side of the glass, the two of them staring murderously at each other.

"Operator, may I help you?"

"Hidden Treasure, ah, Hidden Treasure Hotel. Reception, please."

The call is put through and a familiar voice comes on the line again. "Laundry services, we clean to a sparkle. Tim speaking, may I help you?" Tim is prettying his hair in the mirror with some mousse and wipes the remnants of foam on a folded and laundered shirt that sits in a pile next to him.

"Damn this!" John screams while covering the mouthpiece, then takes his hand off. "Tim, this is me again. You have to find a way to get me to reception. I'm begging you."

"Divine? Very intriguing that you call again. And begging yet? Hmmm . . . Hold on."

"Reception."

"This is John Howard-Hughes. Can I get my room number?"

"We don't give out room numbers for security reasons. Just check on your phone, sir, it says the room number right there."

"I'm not in my room."

"Why didn't you say so? Your name, please?"

"John Howard-Hughes." John cups one ear as a large truck, with brakes screeching and moaning, pulls to a halt at the corner, obscuring the operator's next words.

"Excuse me, what did you say?" John asks.

"Your name, sir. I asked your name."

John tries to yell above the truck as it starts up again. "I just gave you my goddamned name."

"I'm sorry, I couldn't hear you. Your name, please?" the operator says.

"Howard-Hughes."

"Fine, and you, sir?"

"John Howard-Hughes is my *name*. Can I please speak to myself?"

"Excuse me?"

"I mean, goddamn it, I would like to check my messages."

"You need your room number. I think we've been through that. Is there anything else I can help you with?"

"What else can you possibly help me with, you dumb—"

The line goes dead. "Damn it!" John screams to the empty line. He grips the phone in his hand as if he is choking the dear life out of it. "Rrrrrrrrrrrr!"

The old lady, incited by John's outburst, feverishly starts knocking on the phone booth. Her mouth, open wide in a dry yodel, reveals a mottled pink paste of gum clumped on one side in her orifice. John waves the nasty creature away and turns. He puts in more money and tries ZZ's number. When he reaches her answering machine, he hangs up without leaving a message. Strained to the end of his limits, John doesn't think he can take much more. His stomach, tight with tension, feels as if a rogue wave of hydrochloric acid has crashed onto its inner linings. Dr. Bradley, the family physician back home, told him that if he doesn't find a way to calm his tension levels, he is going to get bleeding ulcers before long. What Dr. Bradley doesn't know is that this rate is now at full throttle in a Las Vegas phone booth out in the semi-deserted doohicks of the suburbs in a city where people want to kill him, he is broke and homeless, and every goddamned thing on the planet is going wrong for him. Forget strangling the phone booth or strangling the elderly lady—he'll go right to the source and just strangle himself.

He's got to get hold of Versachi immediately.

Bad enough the way things stand now, pissing off Versachi would just further cook his goose. He can't get messages at his hotel. He tried, but no go. He'd better try Versachi at the El Dorado; that's where Versachi told him to call. Hopefully, he is there. John picks up the phone, deposits thirty-five cents, and again dials zero.

"Operator."

"Can I get the phone number for the El Dorado Sports Book? . . . Yes? . . . Thank you." John hangs up, finds two more coins in his pocket, a quarter and a dime, and dials the number given to him.

A prerecorded message comes on: "For local calls, you do not need to dial a 'one.'"

The coins clang back into the well. John checks his watch, grabs the change from the coin return, and hurriedly drops them back into the slot.

The old lady has hit full stride. She starts banging on the door again—and this time doesn't stop.

"Stop banging," John yells out, but the old lady, in reply, blows a bubble so large that the pink gum cloud growing out of her mouth hides most of her face.

"Why me?" John yells.

He can barely make out the voice on the other side of the line over the din of the woman's banging.

"El Dorado Sports Book. Your home to the best odds and coldest beer."

"Can you please page Mr. V?" John says.

"We don't page players."

"I really need you to page him. It's an emergency."

"Hold on," the man says.

John turns around and the old lady stops banging long enough to raise her middle finger and flip him off, then resumes banging on the glass with her fist.

A new voice comes over the line. "Are you cockroach rider?"

There is a pause. "Yes, I am," John says, flipping his eyes skyward.

The old lady has taken her shoe off and is using it now instead of her fists; the pounding sounds magnitudes louder than before. The woman, incongruously, has started singing the "Star Spangled Banner" as well, and the racket makes it nearly impossible for John to hear anything else.

"Oh say can you see, by the dawn's early light. What—"

John can't hear a word the man is saying.

"Can you please speak up? I'm sorry, they're doing construction here, and they're singing to christen the new shipment of cement," John blurts out, his eyes strained upward in frustration.

"What?"

"I said, 'Can you please speak up?'"

". . . so proudly, we hail . . ."

"Someone has left a message for you."

"What's the message?"

". . . And the rocket's red glare—"

"I'm sorry," John says, unable to hear the reply over the duet of the singing and banging shoe. "Can you say that louder?"

The men yells back, "He told you to call him at this number, 833-41—"

A phone message intercept cuts off the rest of the sentence, "Please deposit ten cents for the next three minutes."

"Son-of-a-bitch!" John screams out.

He frantically fumbles around in his pocket for more change, pulling out napkins, a keno crayon and tickets, a few stray pennies, and assorted scraps of crumpled paper, which he pushes onto the phone ledge. Finding no dimes or nickels in his pockets, John bends down, pushes a small pile of pennies aside on the floor, and discovers a dime hidden among the scattered coins. As he stands, it slips out of his fingers and drops to the floor, bouncing twice. He quickly bends to get it and slams his head on the ledge in the same spot as before. Again the coin slips from his hand, this time kicking off his shoe and rolling toward the door. He agonizingly watches the coin roll under the door and outside the booth toward the old lady.

"Mother of god!" John screams, his hand shooting out to rub the throbbing pain in his skull.

"Please deposit ten cents or your call will be interrupted."

John quickly pushes open the door, but the old lady has already clamped her foot on the runaway coin. She stands over the dime triumphantly, grinding her foot into it with the determination of Joan of Arc. It is obvious that the conquistadoress has no intention of extricating her foot from her newly conquered bullion. But John is equally as determined to extract that coin as the woman is to grind it into the ground—if not more so. After all, he has the shadows of Versachi and Giulli hanging ominously over his well-being. He *needs* to make this call. The two struggle, John trying to push her foot aside and the woman stubbornly resisting his efforts, two petulant children in a sandbox wrestling over a yellow plastic shovel. John finally succeeds in moving the woman's foot and snatches the precious dime off the ground, just escaping five crushed fingers when the cantankerous woman slams her foot down.

John darts back into the phone booth and bangs the door shut. He pushes his body against the door in case the woman tries to storm the fort, which indeed she does, her body hitting the booth like a linebacker meeting a quarterback about to release the football, the impact of the frail woman's body against the door bending it back a few inches. John feels her weight push against the door, but resolutely keeps his body wedged against it to prevent her entry. John pops the dime in, anxiously hoping the connection is still active.

"Hello? Hello? You there?" John yells into the phone.

He looks over as the woman extracts a huge wad of bubblegum from her mouth and inexplicably affixes the gooey ball to the edge of her handbag, a misshapen mass that clings there like a large, pink snail.

"Still here," the man says. "You ready for the number?"

"Yes, please. What number was that?" John says back into the phone.

Temporarily, the woman's singing has stopped, though the banging has started up again. A pause while he listens.

"One more time? Thanks, I got it," John says. He fumbles around on the floor, rubbing the swollen lump on his skull as he bends, but there are only pennies, business cards for escort services, and assorted debris. Not a quarter is to be found. "Damn it again," John screams, realizing he needs change. He rushes out past the old lady who sticks out her foot, and narrowly misses getting tripped. He charges back into the convenience store, arriving like a gust of air through the doors.

"Can I get change for a dollar?" John breathlessly says to the clerk. He places a crumpled dollar bill on the counter.

A bored clerk, about eighteen years old with a white face barely darker than an albino and spotted with a bad case of acne, looks up from a comic book. "We can't give change unless you buy something," he dully replies. The clerk's skinny arms jut out like sticks from his plain white T-shirt and he wears a baseball cap turned backward.

"You're kidding?" John says.

"No exchange, no change." The clerk flips a page and resumes reading. One large pustule on his forehead glistens under the fluorescent lighting, ready to burst.

"I'll get these," John says, grabbing the first item he sees and pushing a package of Sno Balls across the counter.

"That's one dollar and thirty-nine cents."

John pulls out another dollar from his back pocket and hands it to the clerk.

"With tax, that's fifty-one cents change." The clerk counts out the coins and pushes them across the counter.

John scoops up the change and hurries toward the door.

"Sir."

John turns. "What?"

The clerk points to the purchase with his index finger. John steps back to the counter, grabs the Sno Balls and, once outside the door, throws them hard to the ground in frustration. Pink Sno Ball and white cream lay splattered behind John as he rushes back to the phone booth.

But now the tables have turned. John is on the outside trying to get in and the old lady is on the inside, holding the upper hand at the hotly contested phone booth. John looks at his watch. It is twenty minutes after eight. Five minutes late. He has to get to the phone and call Versachi. Right away. This is not good. John's stomach churns like the grinding of rusty bicycle gears. Dr. Bradley would not approve. John dances outside like a child who needs to pee. He can't wait any longer and bangs heavily on the door.

"Emergency," John yells, and the old lady, flashing a one-toothed grin, defiantly blows a big bubble. She sucks the bubble back into her mouth, pulls out the chewed gum, and slaps it onto the large gummed mass already on her pocketbook.

John paces outside the booth like a captive ape before mealtime. He has no time to ponder the woman's strange gum-on-the-pocketbook ritual; he has to make the call. "Hurry up, emergency!"

The old woman finishes her call and smiles at John like no bad blood has been spilled earlier and the two are the best of buddies—and not mortal enemies. As John smiles back, the woman rears back and swings her pocketbook hard, whacking John clean in the head as she passes.

"Die early," she shouts, hobbling away.

John steps in the booth, slightly dizzy from his assailant's forceful blow but too preoccupied with getting hold of Versachi to think about anything else. He drops a quarter and a dime in the slot and dials the number he was given earlier. He hears a voice answer the phone, but the gyrating sounds of hip-hop music pounding out of a passing car with three teenagers is so loud that he can't hear a thing. Nor can the person on the other end of the line, who thinks it is a prank phone call.

"Hello, hello, hello? Damn!" John exclaims over the ruckus as the line goes dead.

He flicks the coin return lever four times and bangs the phone booth hard, but no change comes out. Reaching back into his pocket, John pulls out a few loose coins, but they are just nickels and pennies from his recent purchase, which the clerk had loaded him up on—worthless debris for his needs.

"Damn, damn, damn!" John screams at the top of his lungs, stamping his feet on the ground like a frustrated two-year-old and throwing the useless coins to the ground.

John rushes back inside the convenience store and slides a dollar across to the pimply-faced clerk. On closer inspection, more than one of the pimples is festering. The clerk, still reading his comic, looks up.

"Can I get four quarters?"

"You know the rules." The clerk lackadaisically chews on some gum as he reiterates the store's policy.

"What's cheap?"

"There's a promotion on condoms, the pink ones, fifty-nine cents only, including tax. No guarantees."

"Give me one then," John says, passing him the dollar and shoving the purchase into his pocket. He notices the clerk staring at him while he takes the change.

"What's the matter?" John asks.

The clerk scratches his ear. John puts his hand up to his ear, feels a lump and pulls. A wadful of gum sticks to his hand.

"Son-of-a-bitch!" John exclaims, now understanding his adversary's bizarre act of slapping bubblegum on her handbag. Out of the corner of his eye, John sees a movement and notices a car pulling up to the phone booth. He desperately rushes out the door.

"Rrrrrrrrrr!" John groans.

He runs over to the phone booth, losing his balance as he skids and tumbles on the crushed Sno Balls outside the store. He gets up quickly and races past a man emerging from a car that has pulled alongside, entering the booth just ahead of the startled fellow. Closing the door, John smiles idiotically at the man and shows him the quarter he is holding, as if he's just enjoyed a grandiose victory in life that the poor wretch outside the booth has missed out on. The man, looking at John's crazed expression, the wad of pink gum affixed to his ear and the splattering of Sno Ball on his shoe, pants leg, and right arm, backs up a step, wondering whether it is safe to wait around for this madman to finish or if it is best to move on to the next phone booth.

John tries to push a quarter in the slot, but he can't get a handle on it; the coin is stuck to the gum in his hand. He glances at his watch. It is eight twenty-seven. He is now more than ten minutes late for the phone call to Versachi—not a good situation.

"Rrrrrrrrr!"

John works around the sticky glob and finally maneuvers the coin from his fingers and into the opening. But it goes no further than the edge. The quarter is gummed in and won't budge. He tries to push it in with his fingertip, but the coin moves only slightly deeper, becoming flush with the outer casing. John bangs the phone box with his open palm, but the coin still doesn't drop, so he rips off his shoe and slams the box even harder. The shrill clang of metal sharply echoes in the phone booth as he repeatedly bangs the phone box with long hard smacks. Pink clusters and white cream from the Sno Ball splatter over the booth like a hallucinogenic cake storm.

"I'm just trying to make a goddamned phone call!" John screams into the night, his face turned upward toward the sky.

The man waiting outside the phone booth is horror-stricken. Watching the crazed man slam the phone booth with his shoe and scream like a lunatic caged in an asylum is more than enough evidence to convince him that a quick exit from this shoe-banging, Sno Ball–flinging madman with gum caked on the side of his head is the most urgent priority in his life. There is no shortage of phone booths in Las Vegas, and even if there isn't another one for one hundred miles, he has seen more than enough to convince himself that he is best located elsewhere—and right away. He runs to his car, hops in, and before his door is fully shut, he jams the gas pedal to the floor. The man's car jumps the station's curb and hits the street at thirty miles per hour, quickly picking up velocity until his wife, now more alarmed and panicked with her husband's driving than with the lunatic back at the gas station, yells at him to slow down before he kills the two of them.

Back at the phone booth, John keeps banging, screaming, and beseeching whatever gods will listen. Finally, through divine intervention or the simple force of his banging, the quarter drops and then his dime, and the welcoming sound of a dial tone sings sweet music to his ears.

John rejoices like a rainman who has called for thick clouds to water his village's sere fields and now stands soaking wet in the resultant downpour. Laughing giddily at his victory, John starts punching in digits as if extracting revenge on the dial pad, his index finger pounding brutally on the numbers. But in his excitement, John hits the wrong sixth digit and has to redial. He angrily slams the phone back onto the hook. A long moment passes as he stares mercilessly at the box, murder in his eyes. He tightly grips the metal by its sides, hoping his coins will drop back into the well. And greatly to his relief, they do.

John retrieves the two gummy coins and pushes the dime and then the quarter hard into the slot, forcing them into the box with the shoe he holds ready in his right hand. He bangs the coin slot hard once, then twice, and the coins, reluctantly, drop.

He gets another signal.

John dials the number carefully this time, his frustration mounting with every push of a digit and barely controlling the urge to shove the phone handle through the dial pad and give the mocking telephone box an electronic enema. He anxiously waits for Versachi to pick up, hoping it is not too late to reach him. He shoves the keno crayon and ticket back into his pocket, leaving a handful of pennies on the phone ledge in case somehow the phone miraculously overcomes its mechanical setup and starts taking small coins. "Come on, come on, come on, come on," John pleads after each of the first four rings, his voice louder with each ring. Finally the phone is picked up.

"Talk to me," says a man's deep voice at the other end.

"Let me have the number for Mr. V please," John says, and then rethinks his request. "Excuse me, I mean VV." He has winded himself from his frenzied attack on the phone, and his breath comes in weary gasps.

"Which one you want, V or VV?"

John can't remember if he is supposed to ask for the single V or the double V.

"You there, buddy?"

"I don't remember which one."

"You're calling here, I don't have to tell you who you're calling, do I?" John hears a bunch of noise in the background, papers shuffling, people talking in low tones, and a television broadcasting what sounds like a spirited horse race.

"Okay, V then," John says. "No, double V, VV. I don't know."

"Choose."

"Give me the first one then."

"You have to tell me which one that was," the man says.

"Okay, VV," John says. "Let me have VV."

"That was the second one."

"Alright, let me have V then. That was the first one, right?"

"You don't sound so sure," the man says.

"Can I just have the phone number for him please?" John pleads. "I want V, that's who I want, I think."

"Why didn't you say so the first time?"

The man on the other end starts coughing violently, his breaths alternating in loud wheezes. John hears the phone drop and bang off a wall, and impatiently waits for the man to overcome his attack, hoping he doesn't accidentally disconnect the line. Please hurry up and get me the number, John beseeches silently, fearing the onset of the inevitable canned interruption that will ask him for more dimes he doesn't have.

"Which one did you say you wanted?" the man asks in a voice worn out from coughing. He starts hacking again, more violently this time. John hears the man's hand banging on the wall, then, as the coughing subsides, the noise of a match striking fire and the long draw of a cigarette.

"What did I say?" the man finally asks.

"You asked me which one I wanted."

"Which what?"

"Whether it was V or double V."

"Yeah, that sounds right." The man begins coughing again, alternately hiccupping, the exhalations punctuated by loud utterances that sound like "giddy-up." "You cockroach rider?"

John hesitates, pulling his eyes skyward and gritting his teeth. "Yes."

"He said to call him at a number I'm going to give you. But make sure you ask for the right person. He's waiting on you."

"Which one is waiting on me, V or double V?"

"Why you asking me?"

"Because . . . never mind. Now I have to call another number?"

"You want the number or not?" the man says gruffly.

"Hold on, let me get something to write with." John reaches into his pocket to retrieve the keno crayon stub, but it gets so awkwardly stuck to the side of his hand from the sticky mess of gum that he cannot get a good grip on it. He quickly gives up the futile exercise when he hears the man's impatient breathing and the warning signs of rogue coughs. He's got to get that number before the phone disconnects on him. Time is ticking, and he could be one coughing fit away from the ten-cent warning and a lost connection.

"Let me have that number," John says, committing the digits to memory as the man carefully recites them to him. He nods his head. "Thanks."

John hangs up and races back to the store, bursting through the door like a whipping gust of wind.

The clerk looks up at him.

"Can you write this number down for me, please?" John says to the clerk. John is out of breath and shuffles from foot to foot, his anxiety in full bloom. The hair above his ear on the right side stands straight up where the pink gum is matted, and there is white and pink Sno Ball clumped on his hand, shoe, and shirt. The keno crayon is still oddly stuck to the side of the hand holding the shoe, attached there by a prodigious wad of gum.

The clerk eyes John suspiciously, like he's a circus sideshow act who's just walked into a ladies' high tea.

"What now?" John says.

The clerk, not knowing which oddity to point out, chooses. He scratches his hand.

Realizing he is still holding his shoe, John drops it to the floor and pushes his foot into it. He looks back over to the counter. The clerk scratches his hand again.

John is so wound up that it isn't until he looks at his hand a second time that he notices the crayon stub caked with gum stuck to the side edge of his palm. He violently shakes his hand, but the crayon, like a mollusk clinging to a coral bed, stubbornly hangs on. On the third try, twisting his body as he snaps hard, the crayon dislodges and sails like a dart into brisk flight. It shoots over the clerk's shoulder and lands with a soft thud on the wall. The crayon stub with the pink gum stuck to its end has lodged on a photo of the president, a bull's-eye right in his mouth.

The clerk, watching the gyrations of his customer with arched eyebrows, rubs the back of his head as he turns around and examines the photo, a quizzical expression on his face. The gum, suspended from the edge of the crayon stub, gives the impression of an uncoiled pink tongue stuck out in jest. The clerk turns back around, picks up a pen, and writes the phone number down that John provides.

"Can I borrow thirty-five cents?" John asks.

"Sorry."

"How about fifteen cents then? I think I have about twenty cents in change."

"Same answer."

"Okay, can I use that phone there then?" John indicates the phone by the desk. "It's a local call."

"Not allowed."

"It's an emergency."

"Still not allowed. I'll buy that watch though. I'll give you thirty-five cents for that. You don't have to use all your money then."

"Jesus Christ, what are you, nuts?"

"You don't like the deal, you don't have to do it." The clerk, ending the negotiation, goes back to the comic book.

"I only need to make a local call," John pleads. "Come on! It's an emergency. You can't spring thirty-five cents for me?"

The clerk shakes his head no.

"Fifteen cents?"

No response. The clerk turns a page in his comic book, his eyes lackadaisically follow a colorful scene.

John checks the time, eight thirty-one. Now he is more than fifteen minutes late. What the hell, he thinks, it's only a watch. Much bigger things than a two-hundred-dollar watch are at stake. A pint of water could be worth a thousand dollars in the desert if it was necessary for survival, John surmises, and this phone call in the desert could certainly be valued at a few hundred dollars for the very same survival purposes. And he *is* in the desert. John must get hold of Versachi before it is too late. Too much is at stake here—perhaps his very life—to be cheap over a few-hundred-dollar watch. Versachi made it abundantly clear that John was not to miss this call. Just the same, selling his watch for thirty-five cents feels like highway robbery.

"This is ridiculous," John says.

The clerk's face is like granite; he'd make a great poker player.

There is no more time to waste. John pulls his watch off, lays it on the counter, and snatches the thirty-five cents from the clerk's open palm. He is about to leave the counter when, as an afterthought, he plucks the hat off the clerk's head.

"I'll take this too," John says. He puts the hat on his head, but unlike the clerk, wears it with the front facing forward. The inscription on it reads, "Lost in Las Vegas."

John runs back to the phone, on the way skidding and again tumbling onto the squashed Sno Balls outside the door. Inside the convenience store, the clerk, his bare head covered in short downy hair, flashes a big smile and attaches the new timepiece to his skinny wrist.

Chapter Twenty-Two

The cabbie hesitates to pick up the disheveled man frantically waving his arms in the middle of the street. He slows down and against his better judgment stops to take a fare. He doesn't feel right about this odd-looking, strange-acting individual, but the night is slow and it's better to grab a passenger, especially out here where there is rarely any business, than get nothing on his way back to downtown. But he still doesn't feel right about it.

"Fashion Show Mall, please, as quick as you can," John says as he climbs in.

The taxi speeds down Flamingo Avenue heading west toward Las Vegas Boulevard. It cuts across at Koval Lane to avoid the heavy Strip traffic and heads north, dead-ending on Sands Avenue near the side entrance of the Wynn Resort before making a left on Sands, which turns into Spring Mountain Road when it crosses Las Vegas Boulevard. It is at this intersection that the Fashion Show Mall is located.

Due to a fortuitous run of lights, the trip is made in just over ten minutes, excellent time for the distance.

"That's sixteen dollars and seventy-five cents please," the cabbie says, letting John off at the entranceway to the mall.

"I'm really sorry, I lost my wallet," John tells the driver as he hurriedly exits the taxi. Before the cabbie can say another word, John, feeling bad about beating the cabbie out of the fare but desperate and without any money to give him, closes the door and hightails it into the mall, glancing quickly at an ill-conceived saucer on a pole out front in what the mall's architects thought passed for design. After forty-eight hours in this town, with everything going wrong and the pressure of being broke and hunted weighing on him like a death sentence, John feels that at the very least, considering the enormous stakes being wagered against him, the town can give him a free ride.

John rapidly walks through the mall and up the stairs by the food court to the upper level where Neiman-Marcus is located, the rendezvous point with Ludo. He is still overwrought from his misadventures at the phone booth and subsequent conversation with Versachi, where the G-man, livid at the tardiness of his call, reminded John of the unpleasantries he would be exposed to if he were crossed one more time—something about John being the first course in a long evening meal with Mambo, a deranged sex-starved prisoner who would be his roommate in jail if there wasn't full cooperation. The last thing John heard when he hung up with Versachi was the agent humming a tune with a Latin rhythm. That didn't help calm his anxiety. Already, his nerves felt like bacon sizzled too long in a hot pan and burnt to a fragile crisp.

John gets the feeling that people are staring at him while he walks. Testing his suspicions, he quickly stops and turns. Two women turn their heads away, casually acting as if they weren't looking at him, but it is clear to him that they were. Even Ludo, who is waiting for him outside Toys 'R Us, has a perplexed expression on his face. He too appears to be examining John with a little too much interest.

"We're going to meet Versachi in the food court in five minutes, at nine o'clock," John says breathlessly, winded from hiking the stairs two at a time.

"What's with you?" Ludo says, eyeing him strangely.

"What? Something wrong?" John asks.

Ludo takes in his friend's odd appearance—the pants pocket

hanging inside out from his left side like a long, white tongue; the ill-fitting baseball cap two sizes too small sitting at an awkward angle on his head; gum-caked hair standing straight up on one side; and the buffet of food remains, a large chunk of bright pink Sno Ball with white filling caked on John's right shoe and the pants leg above it, and on his ear, a piece of pink gum clinging tenaciously like an elongated cellulose earring—and shakes his head with disbelief.

"Damn," Ludo says, "you got crap all over you. What the hell you do now?"

"Let me get this stuff off," John says, his fingers pulling off a small piece of gum from his ear. "Is there a bathroom here anywhere?"

"Over there, homes," Ludo says pointing farther down the hall. "Where did you get that hat? How did . . . never mind. I'll wait for you outside the food court over there. Hurry up. Versachi's not the type of guy we want to keep waiting."

Ludo watches John run to the bathroom, small chunks of Sno Ball littering the ground behind him. He can't understand how John manages to create or insert himself into chaos no matter where he goes.

John rushes through the bathroom door with such force that it rebounds hard against the wall and slams back into him, almost knocking him over. He stares at the door angrily, as if ready to have a confrontation with it, then straightens himself out and heads over to the sink. He is trying hard to keep calm, but the mambo tune running around his head in an endless loop serves as a grim reminder of what Versachi said he would do to him if he was so much as ten seconds late for this meeting, a vivid description of which Versachi was only too happy to outline in their earlier conversation. He had made it clear that being tardy was a sign of disrespect he wouldn't tolerate a second time. Not after being late on that phone call. Just the same, John's eyes stare into the door one more time so the wooden thing is clear as to how he feels.

Peering about and seeing no one around, John lifts his foot and sticks it into the porcelain washbasin. He uses a handful of paper towels from the metal dispenser on the wall to brush off the crushed chunks of Sno Ball and white cream residue from his shoe and pants leg. He takes another towel, wets it, and carefully rubs at the deeper traces of food stuck to his pants. Having finished with the initial cleanup, John removes his foot from the sink. His lower pants leg is wet, but at least it's clean. He has a harder time getting the gum off his ear, but with vigorous rubbing and pulling, he painfully manages to remove all clumps of the sticky substance. Thinking back to the lady's one-toothed mouth, John goes over his ear another time with a fresh wet towel, making sure to remove any trace, no matter how minute, of that foul woman's saliva.

Inspecting the results in the mirror, John sees that, other than his right ear, which is so red it looks like it's been plugged in and lit up, the visible leftovers from the woman's salivary glands have been completely eradicated. Luckily, the tiny gum piece that had clung to his hair came off easily as well. Satisfied that he is again presentable, John carefully washes his hands with soap and water and then, turning off the hot faucet, he splashes cold water on his face and hair, sighing in relief from its refreshing coolness. A large handful of water splashes off the sink and pours onto his crotch, wetting him down to the skin. After drying his hands and tossing the paper in the large pile he has amassed by the sink, John pulls out a few more paper towels and rapidly rubs his pants. But it is not enough—a large wet spot, fresh and cool, covers the area around his crotch.

A smartly dressed man with perfectly manicured nails and coiffed hair walks in and sees John vigorously rubbing the area around his zipper. Embarrassed when the man halts in front of him to stare, John discontinues the rubbing motions and removes the towel. The man smiles at John, his lips parted, and his top and bottom teeth pressed together flirtatiously in a wide grin. He takes a long, lingering glance at John's wet crotch, runs his tongue slowly across his lips and, still smiling, looks deeply into John's eyes.

John groans, disgusted and repulsed, and throws the damp paper towel in the trash on his way out of the bathroom.

Behind him, he hears the man groan in reply.

Outside the bathroom, a small girl standing by herself is crying, tears streaming down her cheeks. Her hands are clenched at her sides, and her pouting lower lip protrudes from her tiny sad face.

"What's the matter?" John says, emerging from the men's room.

"I can't find my mommy," the girl whines, and starts crying harder.

"Don't cry. We'll find her right away, okay?"

The little girl takes John's outstretched hand and grips it tight, secure in the presence of a concerned adult. John walks the girl in the direction of the food court where Ludo is standing by the entrance watching two women built like exotic dancers, both in their early twenties, parade by in form-fitting dresses. The women, conscious of the reaction men have as they wiggle along and knowing they are being watched, play up to this extra attention by exaggerating their movements. Standing next to Ludo and casually chatting with him is a uniformed security guard, similarly preoccupied with the migrating local fauna.

About ten feet before they reach the entrance, the girl cries out "Mommy, Mommy, Mommy!" and runs past Ludo and the guard into the arms of her mother, who is just emerging from the food court.

"Oh, my little baby girl, are you okay?"

"Mommy, this nice man helped me," the girl says, hugging her mother tightly and pointing at John.

"Is that so, sweetie pie?"

John has a big smile and bashfully puts his hands in his pockets.

"Thank you so much," the woman says relieved, and extends her hand for John to shake. "I was a little worried there for a minute."

As John pulls his right hand out of his pocket, the clear pink condom package he had purchased for fifty-nine cents at the convenience store tumbles out and lands on top of the little girl's shoe, looking like a colorful pink button on the child's canary-yellow footwear. The girl bends down and picks up the shiny package, smiling brightly as if John was a magician who had just performed a neat trick. She turns first to John and then to her mother, beaming with delight.

"Mommy, a balloon! A pink one, my favorite!"

"Oh, shit," Ludo mumbles to himself.

"Can you blow it up for me, mister?" the child asks, holding the condom package in her small hand. "I want to play with it."

"Oh my god!" the mother exclaims. She snatches the condom from the girl's hand, dangling the very edge of the see-through package between her thumb and middle finger as if it were dog offal she just scraped off the kitchen floor and was displaying to the penitent mongrel. The mother lifts the condom to eye level and stares with horror at the colored latex, but no manner of reexamination changes the nature of what she holds between her fingertips.

Diners at the edge of the food court, sensing a riveting act of dramatic proportions, lean forward in their seats to get a better view of the small brightly colored plastic package swinging between the mother's fingertips. They wait anxiously for the continuance of this confrontation, confident that its finale will not disappoint.

John's face turns a brilliant shade of red as he stands there, shuffling his feet, desperately looking for help of any kind. But none is forthcoming. Ludo, who has turned red as well, lowers his eyes to the ground while the security guard, equally uncomfortable, looks away when John pleadingly catches his eyes.

The mother, her mouth agape as she stares at the condom, reaches across and deposits the pink package into the breast pocket of John's blue sport coat. John glances into the woman's eyes, a flicker of confusion and fear registering in them. The woman looks back at him and then looks down at the damp circle on John's pants, and her eyes open even wider. She loudly gasps, sounding like her esophagus has just gotten choked on a chicken wing, takes her child's hand, and briskly walks off. The girl briefly turns and waves goodbye to the kind man who helped her find her mommy.

John weakly waves back to the child, and moves his hands over the wet spot on his pants, trying to cover it from view.

"I don't know how you do it, man," Ludo says. "I can't leave you alone for one minute in this town without you finding some kind of trouble. Not even to go to the bathroom."

"This is not—"

Ludo raises his hand. "Don't even explain."

——————

John and Ludo walk over to a table outside Lucky Lucky, the Chinese fast-food stall, the meeting place with Versachi. John is thankful this vendor is on the opposite side of the food court, away from the entrance where the shocked diners stared at him with disgust as he made his way past their tables. He picks up a few napkins and is trying to dry the wet spot on his crotch when Ludo grabs his arm.

"Homes, will you give it up? Just let it dry. There are children here."

"Jesus, Ludo, it's just water."

"I know, man, but they don't know, you know? Let's just grab a seat over here," Ludo says, sitting down. "Nobody be looking at it under the table."

John sits across from Ludo at an orange two-person table. He presses his pants again with a loose napkin he finds on the table, wads the damp paper into a ball, and playfully rolls it across the Formica so that it bounces softly off Ludo's hand.

Ludo is about to say something when a shadow crosses the table. Looking up, he sees Versachi combing his hair, his back to their table, and ostensibly looking at the billboard of the Lucky Lucky food offerings.

"Wait a few seconds and then follow me," Versachi says to John between a few muffled coughs, his right hand covering his mouth. "I'm going to put my right hand on the rail over there, that's your signal to get up and look at the sign. But don't get too close to me. When I remove my hand from the rail, you come over and stand next to me. But you won't know me. We'll talk there and you won't look at me, but we won't be talking, you follow me, and if I put my hand on the rail, you'll move away, but that's only if I do it heavily. If I do it lightly, then you stay there, but stop talking, and if I do it medium, wait for my next signal. That's only if it's my right hand. If I put my left hand on the rail, go back and sit down and we'll change to the Italian food vendor on the other side of the food court. If my right hand scratches my nose, it doesn't mean anything, it's just a decoy to see if I can flush anyone out. If I put both hands on the rail, ignore that too, it's also a decoy. Got it, cockroach rider?"

Versachi doesn't wait for an answer and heads over to the Chinese food stand.

"How the fuck do you understand what this guy is talking about?" Ludo says.

Versachi looks up at the overhead menu and, while waiting for a customer ahead of him to pay, scratches his nose with his right hand.

"That means I do nothing," John says.

John stands up as Versachi drops his hand. It hovers near the rail, its back resting against the metal. "Does that mean I go there?" John asks Ludo.

"I don't know, man. His hand is leaning against the rail, not holding it. Nah, I don't think so."

John sits down, but pops up again as Versachi's right hand slides over the rail and comes back to rest at his side.

"No, not yet," Ludo says. "That's a glide."

Versachi now leans forward with both hands on the rail.

"What's that?" John asks.

"Two-handed. He said that one you do nothing. It's a decoy."

Versachi pulls a tray off a stack at the counter, places it on the rail in front of him, and leans on it with his right hand.

"He didn't say anything about a tray. What do I do now?" John says.

"Well, he's leaning on it with his right hand. Doesn't that mean you should go?"

"Yeah, but he's leaning on the tray, not the rail."

"But the tray is on the rail," Ludo says.

"So what do I do?"

"I don't know, homes. But let me ask you something. You ever get the feeling something's not right with this guy? I mean, this whole thing with the nose-scratching and rail-holding, and right hand and left hand and two hands and no hands, and the tray, and the Chinese food and the Italian food. Who the fuck is supposed to understand all this shit?"

Versachi is still leaning with his right hand on the tray, and John, standing up, doesn't know what to do. Versachi picks up his right hand, puts it back down, and when John doesn't arrive, he slams his hand down on the tray. John gets the message, hurries over, and stands next to him in line.

"Listen carefully," Versachi says, looking up at the large yellow menu board behind the counter. "What you're going to do at this party is casually go up to Giulli, see, and just make some small talk as if you don't know who he is. I'll be off with a different group and then come by."

"And then?"

"We'll play it by ear, puppy."

"You crazy? What if he kills me?" John says, taking a big step backward.

"Get back here," Versachi says.

"You said to move away if your right hand leaned heavily."

"That was a medium hand lean. Don't wise-ass me, cockroach rider, or I'll stuff that tray of slop on the other side of the counter down your throat till you choke to death or die of food poisoning."

"May I help you, please?" says the diminutive Chinese woman behind the counter, her mouth filled with silver teeth.

"Give me an egg roll," Versachi says.

"And your friend, please?"

"I don't know him," Versachi says to the lady.

"Give me a minute," John says to the attendant, whose silver teeth hold a strange fascination for him. He has no money and would love something to eat. Actually, he's starving. He says quietly to Versachi, "Hey, you think you could spring for a few more of those?"

"Forget it, cockroach rider, hunger keeps you sharp," Versachi answers from the side of his mouth. He raises his right hand over his lower face, as if scratching his cheeks and talks from behind his palm. "He may try to kill you. And that's the break we need."

"He's going to *kill* me?"

"Just a manner of speaking," Versachi says.

The thought of being murdered has temporarily dulled John's appetite. Versachi leans all the way forward with both hands as if contemplating other items to order from the eight bins of steaming, greasy food in front of him. John follows suit, leaning forward as well, studying the selections, and getting closer in case Versachi whispers something else.

"Don't do what I do, you're being obvious," Versachi says, so John leans back and looks at the lady. "And don't stand there like you're doing nothing either, anyone can spot that. Look like you're looking at something."

"What you want?" the Chinese woman asks when she sees John staring at her.

"One more minute. I'm still looking," John says.

Versachi orders two more egg rolls to keep the woman busy, and John, with some sustenance becoming a possibility in his immediate future, salivates at the idea of food. Given his hunger, the painful thought of dying at Giulli's hands—a reality he does not have to face at this moment—is quickly mitigated by the prospect of the two extra steaming egg rolls Versachi has ordered, presumably one each for him and Ludo. The big man has a little heart after all, he thinks.

Watching the proceedings from the nearby table, Ludo rubs his hands together, seeing a little well-needed feast about to come his way.

"You see, we need Giulli to make a big move," Versachi says, his hand covering his mouth from view and staring at the menu as if contemplating further orders. "And for him to make a move, we need a catalyst to, ah, get the action going, shall we say?"

"But I don't want to get killed!"

Versachi pushes his tray to the side and leans forward with both hands on the rail. This confuses John. He can't figure out if he should leave, stay, be quiet, or go get the Italian food.

"What do the two hands on the rail mean again?" John whispers.

"Don't push me," Versachi mutters menacingly out of the side of his mouth. "You see the deal here, cockroach rider, Giulli is not going to grind you up in little pieces and kill you slowly. I was just playing with you. This guy's gig is insurance fraud. He likes to run his mouth, and that's what you're here to do—to help run his mouth. Then we got him."

"You mean I would have to testify to that?"

"That's all I need, bubba. You do the right thing and all your troubles might just go away. And if you don't volunteer, well, like I told you, I know a three-hundred-and-sixty-five-pound psychopath with nymphomaniac tendencies downtown, name of Mambo, that would just *love* to have a little company for an evening or two, if you know what I mean."

Versachi pulls out his wallet and gives the Chinese woman three dollars for the egg rolls.

"Here's what's going to happen at the party. You just keep your eye on me. When I take a drink, I'll point at Giulli with my little pinky so you'll know who he is. Then you'll do your thing. And tell mofongo there," Versachi says, indicating Ludo with a backward shake of his head, "to go get some nachos or something. I don't want to see him around or *he's* going to be dancing with Mambo, got it? This party is invitation-only, so make sure to give this name at the door," Versachi says, dropping a small piece of paper on the tray. "Later, pumpkin."

Versachi takes the bag of egg rolls from the lady at the Chinese counter, walks over to a table about ten feet away, and hesitates, a devilish smile dancing across his thick lips. He gingerly pulls out an egg roll and makes an exaggerated show of chewing it as if the deep-fried greasy appetizer is the rarest of delicacies. Versachi slowly licks his lips and then each finger carefully when he's finished.

Like two domesticated canines at mealtime, Ludo and John hungrily stare at the bag of food hanging from Versachi's fingertips, watching every motion and nuance in his dramatic act. There are two egg rolls in the bag, one for John and one for Ludo, and they await a signal to go fetch them.

Versachi sticks his nose in the bag and sniffs at the egg rolls as if savoring them for the very first time. He then dangles the bag in his hand, letting it rock back and forth, watching to see if John and Ludo might salivate like Pavlov's dogs, which, in their state of hunger, they everything but do. Back and forth, the bag swings from his fingertips, and John and Ludo slowly turn their heads in cadence with every motion. Versachi opens the bag once more, carefully savoring the aroma and studying the egg rolls, and then, with Ludo watching in horror, he crushes the paper bag in his big hands and tosses the crumpled egg rolls in a nearby garbage can. Versachi then turns and with his graceful walk, surprisingly light for such a big man, glides out of the food court and out of sight.

"Why he have to do that?" Ludo moans, staring at the garbage can.

"Ludo," John says forcefully, "Ludo!"

"What?" Ludo is still staring at the refuse container, expecting the egg rolls to somehow resurrect themselves and march over to their table.

"He told me that this guy, Giulli, the owner of the restaurant where that thing happened, that he might kill me. I should say that he casually mentioned this possibility."

"Holy smoke, homes," Ludo says, his attention snapped away from the egg rolls' final destination. "He's going to kill you?"

"Well, he joked about Giulli killing me, but I don't think he was joking," John says. "He wants me to meet Giulli, tonight, at a party, by 'accident.'"

"That's crazy. You can't do that! That's the last person you want to meet, homes."

"I've got no choice!"

"Okay, then, so what time we gotta be there?"

"Eleven-fifteen, that's the time. But not we—*me*. You can't be at that party. If Versachi sees you there, you'll be dancing with Mambo."

"I'm already dancing the meringue. This is just so much fun playing homeless and broke and having people try to kill us that all I want to do is dance the night away."

"Ludo, Mambo is a three-hundred-and-sixty-five-pound psychopath with nymphomaniac tendencies, and he happens to reside in jail with a spare cot in the cell. Versachi's not talking about dancing to music."

"Oh."

"He wants me to walk over to Giulli like it's casual and everything and strike up a conversation or something. What am I supposed to say, 'Ah, remember me? I'm the guy with that crazy girl who ordered every appetizer on the menu, stiffed you on a meal, trashed your restaurant, and then threw it in your face. Oh, hi, how are you? Oh, yeah, I almost forgot, it was so much fun, I also busted up your fifty-thousand-dollar vase that was probably passed down from your great-grandmother in the old country and is your most treasured family heirloom.'"

John buries his face in his hands and groans. "What am I going to do?"

"I'll get in that party somehow and we'll figure out something. I don't know how, but we'll get this worked out. Things will find a way."

John takes a deep breath and blows the air out slowly. "I don't know, maybe you shouldn't go. Bad enough I got myself in this mess, Ludo, but these are my problems."

"Homes. Here's how it goes down. One, I'm broke and I got no place to go. Two, I'm homeless and I got no place to go. Three and four is more of the same of one and two in one variation or another. And five through ten, no matter what, I'll be there tonight."

Ludo shifts his view from the garbage can and looks at John, a pained expression on his face.

"Why he have to throw out them egg rolls?"

Chapter Twenty-Three

At nine twenty-seven in the evening, John's taxi turns onto Russell Road and pulls up in front of a small one-story stucco house badly in need of repair. The garage door adjoining the left side of the structure, as well as the front door itself, are made of pressed wood, the outer layers of which are peeling off in long strips. The grass out front, in uneven areas that alternate with weeds and bare patches, has long since withered and turned brown, in sharp contrast to the luxuriant green lawns of the neighboring properties. The cabbie asks for fourteen dollars for the fare. John tells him to wait and heads down a narrow concrete pathway covered over with weeds, and presses the small button next to the door. Inside the house, loud reggae music blasting from a stereo and louder voices trying to be heard over the tumultuous din seem to compete with one another. Not sure if the bell is working or if the people inside can hear it, John bangs hard on the door, feeling the thin wood give against the contact. He soon hears ZZ's voice and then sees her face as the door opens. A redolent, musty aroma, the smell of burning ganja, wafts from the open door. The air behind her is thick with smoke.

"Hi," ZZ says, letting John peck her on the cheek.

"Listen, I hate to ask you," John says tremulously, "but can I borrow fifteen dollars?"

ZZ looks past John at the waiting taxi. "Okay," she says, "hold on a sec." She comes back with a ten and a five and John runs back to the curb to pay the cabbie.

The gathering in the house is surprisingly small, about fifteen people, fewer than John would have guessed from the noise. Most of the partygoers stand between the foyer and the kitchen, laughing and talking in loud voices. John follows ZZ into a small family room to the left of the entrance, where three men are passing thickly rolled joints back and forth. A low-slung couch and a love seat surround two sides of a small wooden table in front of them. On the love seat, two of the men, both large, one a heavily tattooed Latino, the other a smiling black man with dreadlocks, sit stuffed together in the small space, looking like they are locked in place and will have trouble extracting themselves to stand up. On the sofa, an obese man wearing a neck full of colorful glass peace beads sits on the side closest to the others, his legs lazily splayed out in front of him and his body sunk deep into the soft cushions. He is smiling at nothing in particular, appearing to be in his own halcyon world. Maybe those beads do work.

ZZ grabs John's hand and leads him over to the couch, where they sit holding hands. The obese man leans over and passes her a joint, carefully handing it to her by the base. She takes it, and without putting it to her lips, tries to pass it on to John, but he waves her hand away.

"Try it, honey, come on," ZZ says. "Let's do a little hit and then I'll take you to that meeting you have, okay?"

"No thanks, I'm alright."

"Just give it a little try, like this. Mmmmh." ZZ purses her lips as if smoking and playfully waves the joint in front of John's face.

"Not for me. You can do it if you want, I don't mind. Hey, I'm happy to see you. Did you have a good day?" John takes the joint from ZZ's outstretched fingers and passes it along to his neighbor on the love seat.

The black man with the dreadlocks finishes a long toke on the thick joint and starts coughing, smoke spilling out of his mouth with each cough. "That's some strong shit," he says. "It's got that little extra something in there, that *oomph*, you know what I'm talking about it?"

"Yeah, this stuff sends you traveling," the Latino replies, his eyes far away and thoughtful. "Like to the moon."

The Latino is wearing a sleeveless shirt, and his heavily muscled arms are covered with tattoos of naked women, sailing ships, and gang slogans. The love seat where he and the black man are sitting is draped with a worn Mexican serape, many years past its prime.

"Aye, pato," the black man croons. "You got that right."

"Oh, come on. Just take a little toke," ZZ says to John. She rubs his arm playfully, her flirtatious eyes big as a nuzzling doe's. ZZ gestures to her lips, mimicking a deep puff with her mouth puckered up.

"Put it right here and puff on it, just a little bit. Come on, Doc, let's loosen up and have some fun!"

"No, I really don't want to. I'm okay, really."

"Don't be so close-minded," ZZ says, raising her voice. "I'm only asking you to try it. I don't see what the big deal is!" ZZ turns her body away from John, but keeps her face angled in his direction.

"No thanks, I don't do drugs."

John nervously looks at the Latino across from him. He has just taken a huge hit on the joint and sits with eyes opened wide and cheeks drawn in, as if his face has suddenly frozen.

"I'm disappointed in you. Very disappointed. I thought we were going to have fun tonight."

"We are having fun, I mean, this is a good get-together and I'm happy to be with you."

"I see."

"Aren't you having fun?" John asks. He stares at the Latino, fascinated by the length of time the man can hold his breath. Maybe he really did freeze.

"Don't take that tone with me," ZZ says.

"I have no tone. I'm okay. Really. I'm happy to be with you. Everything's great, it really, really is."

"That's good," she says coldly. ZZ completely turns to face the other direction and removes her hand from his.

"Oh come on, don't be mad at me," John beseeches.

"I'm not mad. I think I'm tired. Why don't I take you now?" she says, moving farther away from him. "I'm sorry you're not having a good time. You obviously don't want to be here with me."

"I do! Why are you saying that? Just because I don't want to take a puff? That's not fair."

"Let's not talk about it anymore," ZZ says.

"Will you let me—"

"I don't feel like discussing the same thing over and over again. Okay? Let's talk about something else."

The Latin man still hasn't moved, and John is now getting worried. With his luck, the way things are going, the man could be dead and the blame would somehow find its way to him. He could imagine the headlines: "Brooklyn-based man drugs and causes innocent tattooed Latino at local Las Vegas party to overdose and die. DEA also involved in the investigation." Just what he needs: one more set of troubles to add to his pile and another law-enforcement agency or two after him.

"Alright, I'll try it," John says, hoping that will break the ice.

"You will? Really?" ZZ is excited and beams with pleasure at her little victory, thrilled to push the envelope further with John.

"Okay, baby," says the Latin man, finally releasing a long plume of smoke into the air and, to John's massive relief, taking a breath. "Time to teach your boy to be an astronaut." The Latino, exhibiting great endurance, takes another long toke on the thick joint, and then leans across the table and hands it to John. He winks at John as he settles back and returns to his trancelike state.

"Heh, heh, heh, heh," the black man with the dreadlocks chuckles. "Pato is gone for a trip again, folks. That boy likes space fishing."

ZZ looks at John. "Just put it in your mouth and take a little puff," she says, giggling. "Just go ahead. A little one. Come on."

John holds the joint between his fingers like a cigarette and barely inhales on it, a weak pucker like a prepubescent boy reluctantly kissing a girl for the first time and not quite knowing what to do.

"See, that wasn't so bad!" ZZ exclaims, suddenly alive with energy. She rubs John's back excitedly. "Do it again, but a big one. Do it for real this time. A real big one and hold it. Mmmuh."

ZZ sucks the air, pantomiming a long and powerful inhalation.

With the joint still in his mouth, John looks across at the Latino, still deep into his trance, and inhales fully as he saw the man do before passing the doobie. The smoke tunnels its way into his lungs and he immediately starts coughing, a gagging sound emanating from deep down in his chest. Ganja smoke and regurgitated air explode from his lungs as he hacks away, tears forming in the corners of his eyes.

The Latino, his eyes registering the action, nods over at John and smiles.

"Wheeeeee," ZZ shrieks, laughing and clapping her hands. "You're a pro now!"

John nods, an earthy taste in his mouth and his face enveloped in a cloud of smoke.

"Do it again!" ZZ says.

———————

ZZ whips through the streets like a racecar driver trying to set new records, running red lights and two debatable yellows with abandon. John marvels at her capacity, whether walking or driving, to move at breakneck speeds, as if she were a projectile that can only proceed forward at dangerous velocities. She arrives at the Venetian Hotel and Casino without incident, ignoring the stop sign at the entrance as she pulls into the property. Being no more cautious in the casino's parking lot, ZZ speeds down a long aisle of cars, narrowly missing a man who jumps back in the nick of time and flips her the finger as she passes. She makes a new spot at the end of one of the rows, parking crookedly next to a silver Land Cruiser, her car partially jutting out into the aisle.

"Are you sure you can park here?" John asks.

"Stop worrying, Doc."

"Just asking, sorry," John says, desperately trying to maintain her good graces. "Hey, do you want to walk around for a few minutes? We're a little early."

"Okay," ZZ says, quickly exiting the vehicle and charging across the parking lot before John has even put his feet on the asphalt. "Hurry up, Doc," she calls behind as she briskly moves toward the entrance.

They enter the casino with John trailing behind her, passing the gaming tables and slot machines to get to the shops situated in the rear. ZZ races ahead, maneuvering deftly around people like a character in a video game. When they arrive in the shopping area, and stores replace gaming tables and machines, her pace slows and John is able to view something of ZZ other than her back.

"Geez, do you ever do anything slow?" John says, finally catching up.

ZZ laughs. "Do you feel the funny stuff?" she asks.

"No, I feel the same as before. I don't see why everyone makes such a big deal about it. Might as well be smoking oregano if it doesn't do anything. I don't get why people would want that stuff in their system anyway."

"I heard it takes a little while, maybe forty-five minutes or an hour to kick in. At least you tried it though," ZZ says. "I'm proud of you!"

"I don't know," John says. "What's to be proud of smoking pot or crack or whatever? I only did it because of you."

"Are you blaming me again? Because if you're blaming me for everything that's gone wrong in your life, I don't have to hear it. You made your own problems, Doc, time to be a big boy and accept that. Maybe I should go—I don't need to get treated like this."

"I didn't mean it like that."

"No, really, Doc," ZZ says, her voice rising. "I did you a favor and drove you here. I didn't have to, you know. But if you're going to yell at me—"

"Okay, okay. I'm sorry."

"I just don't want to get blamed for everything. I'm your only real friend; everyone else you know is using you."

"That's not true, really."

"Wake up, Doc, don't be so naïve. Everyone is using you for something. I'm the only one who truly cares about you. And here you are, not being nice to me."

"Okay, please, I'm sorry, can we be friends again?"

"Just don't blame me anymore for your problems, and don't yell at me."

John breathes in deeply. "My fault. Please accept my apology. I don't want to fight with you."

ZZ's focus seems far away, as if she didn't hear John's last words. Her pupils are like tiny specks of accelerated neutrons darting menacingly around a core of charged uranium.

"So what are you up to tonight?" John asks, trying to steer the conversation to a bland topic.

"I'm not going to *that* party, that's for sure," ZZ says tersely. "Since no one invited me."

Bad topic. John feels like he has carelessly treaded on the wrong person's lawn—and it's his second offense. "For me it's not a party. You know that. I have to go or Versachi will throw me in with Mambo."

"Mambo? What are you talking about again? I don't understand you."

"It's this psychot . . . never mind," John says, quickly realizing he had better move off this subject. "So really, what are you up to later?"

"Can you not grill me like that, okay? Can't you just relax and let us just enjoy things? You're so uptight."

"Sorry."

"No really, Doc. You get so uptight, how can anyone be around you?"

"Okay, okay, I get the idea. You're beating that dead horse again."

ZZ smiles weakly, and John feels the tension ease. "I was thinking that we better not get Harry involved," ZZ says. "He's not a good person."

"I definitely get bad vibes around him. That's for sure."

"He doesn't like you."

"Likewise."

"No, I mean he really doesn't like you. I think he's jealous. He gets crazy sometimes."

"What do you mean?" John stops walking and faces her.

"Nothing," ZZ says, suddenly quiet. She is looking in the direction of a statue, either watching water spout out of its mouth, or farther away, in some dark recess where John cannot see.

———————

John and ZZ stand close together, their shoulders touching, looking in the window of a women's shoe store. ZZ points to a shoe patterned in leopard skin and turns to John.

"What do you think of those?"

"For you to wear or how they will look if put back on the animal?"

ZZ giggles. "No really, silly. Do you like them?"

As John leans closer to get a better look at the shoes, ZZ's phone rings. She pulls the phone from her purse, her back stiffening when she checks the caller ID. ZZ stares coldly at the number display before she answers. John has a premonition that this won't be pretty. And he is not wrong; the explosion comes immediately.

"What the hell do you want?" she screams into the phone with an immense volume that stops John cold in his thoughts. And he is not alone. As if cued by the director on a large movie set, every person as far as John can see turns in their direction and stops as if frozen in frame, extras in a surreal scene playing itself out before their eyes. The mall becomes eerily quiet; only a nervous cough or two punctuate the air. Even the nearby gondolas stopped moving, the gondoliers and their passengers rapt and still. With no place to hide and no way to intercede, John, red-faced and silent, helplessly waits for this one-act play to unfold.

The screaming of an enraged man on the other end of the line resonates through her cell phone. His high-pitched voice comes through the tinny speaker like an operatic aria in falsetto. John can only make out random words, but one of them is "Cupcakes." He shudders upon hearing this reference. Apparently, he is the subject of this screaming match and is not garnering favorable reviews.

"Fuck you, you prick!" ZZ screams back in a voice that whips through the mall and off the faux-cloud ceiling like an explosive crack of thunder. "Stay out of my goddamned life! How the hell would I know where he is? And if I did, why would I tell *you*?" She impatiently listens to the high-pitched reply, her eyes bouncing wildly in their sockets, unable to fix on any one point. She is oblivious of the fact that she is the center of attention to a rapt audience that watches her with as much fascination as if she were a three-humped camel dancing ballet.

"Go mind your own business, okay? Just leave me alone!" ZZ shouts, her free hand plaintively reaching in the air. Her eyes are rimmed with tears, and the soft pastel shade of lipstick that she favors glistens harshly in her anger.

A short burst of screaming through the speaker is interrupted by ZZ's final salvo. "Drop dead, asshole," she yells, her lips quivering in anger. With those parting words, ZZ reaches back and hurls her cell phone across the corridor, the small purple unit whipping through the air and crashing into a wall like a bird into translucent glass, the unmoving object unmoving and the moving object stopping dead cold, taking its very last flight. The phone cracks harshly against the tiled wall, shattering into pieces that scatter in a ten-foot radius.

ZZ stares straight ahead like an enraged bull trying to gather its senses after a futile rampage chasing the red cape of the matador. A few seconds go by. Long ones. The eerie silence in the mall is deafening, excruciating in its otherworldly weight. And finally, like an oppressive humidity that finally lets loose its grip from a dark, gravid cloud and releases its load of rain, the spell is broken. People who had gathered to watch this spectacle pause to see if there is an encore to follow, only to realize that the last words of the script have been spoken and the performance finished. The bull stands confused and spent, no longer seeing the matador or the red cape, simply trying to gather its wits. Slowly, as if the freeze has thawed, the crowd comes alive with movement. The director has given the signal, the long frame is released, and the muted buzzing of conversations, the rustling of clothing as people walk again and go about their business, the gondoliers splashing the water, and the occasional voices of children delighted at some new discovery in their world, return to the ambient sounds of the mall.

John looks up from his shoe tops and peeks at ZZ, a wall of doubt as to where things will go from here. The tornado has just laid waste to the village, and John waits to see what remains in the wake of its destruction.

ZZ's foot carves a lazy circle around a tiny imperfection on a marble tile, then comes to rest on top of it. She speaks softly, as if pushing the words past her lips is a monumental effort. "I don't know if it's good that we see each other anymore," ZZ, suddenly sedate, says without looking up.

"But why?" John asks.

"I just don't think it's a good idea." ZZ is sullen and her eyes aimlessly scan the floor. "Harry's not a good person, and he's a little upset about the other day." Her eyes flicker up at John. "It's probably better if you don't get involved with these people."

"It's too late for that now. I'm already involved, like it or not. I owe them money I don't have." John moves his hands around, as if trying to form his thoughts in the air. "I don't understand this whole situation. What does your ex have to do with you and me? I mean, I guess you work with him or whatever, but that's just that, isn't it?"

"What am I supposed to do? I don't see anyone out there taking care of me," ZZ says pensively, slowly swinging her small handbag by its handles. Her voice drops to a whisper, and John leans forward to hear her words.

"I don't say I like the way things are," ZZ continues quietly.

"Things can change in life. With a little luck . . ." John trails off, having no finish for the sentence.

"You're a good person, Doc, but . . . I don't know . . ."

"But ZZ, I mean, we get along good, don't we?"

"You're funny," she says flatly.

"But don't we?"

"Well," ZZ says, pausing as she brushes a few strands of hair from her eyes, "maybe it's best we just say goodbye. I have to go." ZZ seems ready to burst into tears and turns to leave. Before taking a step, however, she does an about-face and throws her arms around John. She kisses him once fully on the lips, turns again, and briskly walks away. She stops after five steps and looks back. "Call me later," she says with a sad smile and hurries down the corridor.

John stares at the pieces of the broken phone scattered along the ground. The cell phone is the only number he has for her.

Chapter Twenty-Four

Fear can do funny things to a person. And John Howard-Hughes is filled with it. His breaths come in shallow draws as if he can't pull enough oxygen into his lungs. And his heart pounds inside his chest as if it wants to burst out of its cavity, hobble down the hall away from this mess, and leave John to his own devices, as if to say, "Bye, bye, Johnny. Best of luck, see you later."

John feels dizzy and his mind is a garbled crochet of thoughts and fears. He is just not feeling right—is it the marijuana scrambling his thoughts and making him, suddenly, ferociously hungry?—and leans precariously against a wall for support like a rickety lean-to trying to weather a windstorm. He worries not only about what might transpire inside the party, but whether his legs, which feel disjointed and wooden, can even carry his body the long twenty steps across the hall. Twenty very long imposing steps, a great distance for someone in his condition. He wishes he could simply turn around, go home, and put this entire mess behind him like it never happened. But it did happen. Either he goes into that party tonight and a solution presents itself, or he lives in fear, waiting for the day they come for him. He's got to face the music. And thus, John finds himself struggling with his own personal

Armageddon, stalling, trying to get up the mental and physical strength to make it across the hallway and confront his demons. He dreads the impending rendezvous with Versachi and Giulli. He is sandwiched in the paradox of having to go in, yet at the same time, frightened at the consequences of a meeting that cannot possibly bode well for him. He certainly doesn't like any of the scenarios that run through his head. But if he turns around and hightails it out of here, there is Mambo to worry about and later on, Giulli and the mob. If Versachi doesn't find John in Las Vegas, then he will find him later in Brooklyn. He has to deal with this now; somehow he has to get out of this mess.

But how? That is the quandary.

John is unclear where the greatest part of his fear lies—with Giulli, and all the things Versachi said Giulli might do to him, or with Versachi himself, a wild card of unknown and dangerous quantity. Versachi claims to be an agent of the FBI. But is he? And what about Giulli, a reputed violent mob boss John has never met? What is his agenda? And what is supposed to transpire between him and Giulli when Versachi walks over? John can't make heads or tails out of these unknowns. Nor can he make sense of Versachi's obtuse and cryptic communications: *Call me here at this time and then call me there so you can call me here and meet me there and my right hand on the rail is this, but not both hands and then I'll meet you here and you can use the G-word, but not the F-word and we'll talk, but we won't talk.*

What the hell is he saying?

Giulli, as Versachi has made abundantly clear, is not one to be trifled with. He is a mob boss, a killer and hirer of killers, and John has pushed cake in the man's face and made this event personal. The debacle of the nine appetizers, the parade of returned food going back and forth, and running out on the bill was bad enough. But trashing the restaurant and destroying a fifty-thousand-dollar family heirloom was like taking the cake he pushed in the Mafioso's face and then smearing it across the man's clothes with a brazen wipe. Disrespect in those circles is not a good thing. And as much as John mistrusts Versachi, he appears to be John's ticket out of trouble. Or is it his ticket deeper into trouble? As

Ludo says, there is something going on with Versachi's agenda that they cannot see. And while John wants no part of Versachi's game, one with rules he doesn't understand and players whose roles are enigmatic, he sees no other choice. Nor is he in any condition right now to do even the simplest thing. He returns his gaze to the entrance, measuring what it would take to get his body over there. And it seems a daunting task.

Two tall security men with grim faces flank either side of the party's entrance, eight-foot doors draped by heavy, dark purple velvet curtains that hang from ornamental gold fixtures above. The guards are dressed immaculately in black tuxedos and shiny shoes and scan the halls periodically as if to detect danger before it gets near their station. The taller of the two doormen notices John leaning oddly on a wall across the hallway. His eyes briefly linger on him, sizing him up before they return to the clipboard in his hand and the next guest waiting in front of him.

John stands in a cold sweat watching the guests steadily arrive: first, an elderly couple, the woman decked out in a flowing gown and diamonds and the man in an expensive summer suit; then two clean-shaven men wearing matching ties and pastel shirts. Next to arrive are five women in their early twenties to mid-thirties who flirt with both doormen before entering. They flash ingratiating Las Vegas smiles, the kind that grow in brightness as money and its accoutrements water and nourish them like rain on garden flowers. All five women wear low-cut tops that reveal ample amounts of cleavage, tight, short skirts hiked well up on their thighs, and stiletto heels at least three inches in height. John notices that, unlike the previous guests, the doormen wave the bevy of women through without checking their clipboards. John wonders about the role of these women, the ones who are not subject to the guest list. Just out to have themselves a little fun—a thought John has trouble conceptualizing on this evening fraught with fear—or to meet a rich boyfriend or husband perhaps? Or are they a particular species of Las Vegas fauna that follow the money to see what portion of the green they can add to their own coloring book?

What John does know is that for him this party will not be about fun, and it will not be about him being festive, nor will it be about networking as it might be for others. No, it will be about survival. Getting out alive. For him, this is no party—it's an ordeal. He'll be walking on hot coals before running a gauntlet of fire.

Finally, taking a deep breath through his nose and exhaling through his mouth, John begins the long march across the hallway. His legs move stiffly and precariously, as if they were decayed wooden sticks disassociated from the rest of his body, yet somehow affixed to his trunk as a crude afterthought. They feel unfamiliar, like they're peg legs hastily borrowed from a stranger. The problem is that he hasn't quite learned to use these wooden stumps, and their added length lifts him to an unwieldy height. But move he does, ungracefully, a clunky robotron, fearful that any imperfection in the floor might send him toppling to the ground in a disastrous crash of rotted and splintered wood. John glances up and sees the doorman watching his awkward peregrination across the hall. It makes him even more nervous than he already is. He tries to concentrate on staying calm, but it is difficult under all this pressure. Meanwhile, first things first: He has to get across the hallway and to the door, and then through that door, which is not an easy task at the moment.

One step at a time.

John feels like he is being pushed off-balance by a strong wind as he walks, like he's a ship listing in a gale-force storm. But he's indoors—there can't possibly be any wind. Or could there be? He finally makes it to the entrance without incident—in what seems like a semi-eternity—and stands stiffly before the taller of the two doormen. He feels self-conscious and, leaning at an odd angle, looks up into steely intimidating eyes.

"Howard-Hughes," John says in a clipped voice, using all the forces of his concentration to maintain equilibrium and stay on his feet.

"Fine," the doorman says grudgingly. He looks at John like he's a box full of cat litter unwittingly found at the foot of his bed. The guard doesn't like him, John can see that. "This is invitation only."

"Howard-Hughes," John slurs. He concentrates on balance. It's difficult to stand on wooden sticks, and he doesn't want to crash to the ground.

"'How are youse' is not the right response, bubba. It's not how I am, it's how you're going to be if you don't move along. Get lost."

The doorman straightens up, a maneuver that makes him appear even taller. Either that, or John's borrowed stilts are sinking into soft ground. John is concerned that one side of the floor is lower than the other and he is afraid of toppling over, but he dares not look down and lose his stasis. Taking no chances, he shuffles over a step. If he only had a wall to lean on to support himself, that would make all the difference in the world. John feels like he's swaying or maybe the wind has picked up again. Whatever it is, something is off, that's for sure, and on top of everything else, he's fighting off the onset of vertigo from his unnatural height atop the wooden stilts he's hoisted upon. Maybe the floor *is* uneven. To steady himself, John concentrates his vision on the man's bowtie, using it as a visual anchor.

"Howard-Hughes, that's my name. Starts with an 'H.'" John wants to ask the doorman not to move, but he is worried that the man won't understand. Best to say as little as possible. More words could only make things worse here. As it is, the doorman is leery of him. John takes another step to his left, playing it safe. With his eyes, he still maintains an ironclad grip on the doorman's bowtie.

The doorman checks the guest list, turning a few pages on his clipboard, and sees no Howard-Hughes. The bowtie moves with him as he lifts his head, making John's vertigo worse. He turns to his right, facing John in his new position. "I didn't think so. You're not on the list. Why don't you scram, buddy?" he says.

A small crowd forms behind John, waiting to get in.

"Wait," John says, desperate. "I have to get in. I mean, I'm on the list."

"I'm going to tell you one more time, nicely—*Mister How Are Youse*—to vacate my line of sight."

Then John remembers. He reaches into his blazer pocket and pulls out the piece of paper from Versachi. It is folded neatly into four perfect

quarters. John unfolds the note and reads the name to the doorman. "J. Bond," John says.

"J. Bond?" The doorman scrutinizes John suspiciously, then checks the guest list.

Under his breath, John curses Versachi's twisted humor. Yeah, John thinks, triple-zero-seven, or was it double-zero-seven? He forgot what Ludo told him. Double zero, triple zero? It's hard to concentrate with the doorman's bowtie moving all over the place.

"I see you're a guest of Mr. Giulli," the doorman says, his eyes weighing the merits of this new information. A fear of death pours over John like he's caught under the front end of a wheat thrasher. This is the first time he has heard Giulli's name mentioned by anyone other than Versachi, and being uttered by a complete stranger makes John's situation that much more real. And that much more frightening.

Now he is on the mobster's personal guest list!

But that's too much to think about now. He must concentrate, maintain his balance, hang in there. Deal with the present situation, as Ludo tells him. He can't afford to fall—he will need his legs in case he has to make a run for it—but the ground is still slanted, threatening to throw him off-kilter. John shifts over another step to his left. As he moves, so do the doorman's eyes, warily, watching him with a little too much interest. Following him. In a bad way, maybe a very bad way.

Maybe John is reading too much into it?

"J. Bond," the doorman repeats, a smile creasing his lips. Why is the doorman smiling? Is it a smug and mocking grin because he is in on this too, or is he just being friendly due to John's newfound and elevated credentials with the mob boss himself?

"Calm down," John says to himself.

Maybe the pot is kicking in? John has heard it makes people paranoid, but in his shoes how would he even know the difference between real fear and paranoia anyway? They *are* out to get him, not just Giulli and Versachi, but Knuckles, Wonderbread, Rock, and the other killers at that poker game. And then there's Harry, ZZ's psychopathic and jealous ex-husband. The FBI. The cops too. What if there was a problem back at that party after he left? The DEA might get involved as well. It seems half the town is out to get him. And really, why *is* the doorman smiling like *that*? The Latino guy at the party, the one with all the tattoos, mentioned something about the stuff having "that little extra something in there, that oomph, you know what I'm talking about it?"

What was that about?

A shift comes over the doorman's eyes, a new respect as if this guest, like the bevy of five women earlier, has a meaning different from others on his clipboard.

"Have a good evening, Mr. Bond," the man says, inviting him in with a sweep of his hand.

Chapter Twenty-Five

John does everything he can to hold his equilibrium. To not panic. To keep it together. It is all too much to absorb in his condition: the cacophonous assault of noise from the hordes of blabbering people talking at once, the claustrophobic tightness of the almost one thousand guests packed into the large ballroom around him, the swirl of colors from the décor and revelers' clothing—all of it. It cramps him, pulls air out of his lungs, overwhelms him. He really wants to drop to the floor, collapse into a fetal position against the wall, and crawl back to where he came from, to a dark and comforting place where the world around him is compact, warm, safe. No light, no people, no worries. Just the womb. "Mommy, Mommy, Mommy," he can hear himself say from inside the cave of nascent life. "Mommy, Mommy, Mommy."

But not this. He is not prepared for all this.

John sweats profusely, streams of perspiration sliding down his forehead. The heat, the lights, the people, the noise, his nerves. He tries to hang in there, to maintain. But the room is far too bright, the overhead bulbs burning into his skull like cooking lamps slowly roasting him alive. He has to stay inconspicuous, blend in. Study the situation, see what he'll do. John stands blocking the doorway, as if cemented there, oblivious to the people impatiently bunching up behind him. They want to get past and into the festivities. After repeated requests, John finally understands what they are jabbering about. With some effort, he moves out of the way, hobbling ten feet into the room, next to two large, red clay planters. Each one is filled with a large plastic plant about seven feet high—or is it a tree? He examines the thin, dark knobby trunks and the green foliage on the branches. Real? Fake? He stands there unsteadily, his stilts beginning to wobble, and he grabs at the nearest plant for support, shifting his weight against it.

A loud cracking sound splits the air as the spine of the plant snaps. John goes down like a sawed-off tree, collapsing through the green foliage of the two plants and taking them both down with him as he crashes loudly to the ground, momentarily stunned from the sudden fall. He lies sprawled on the ground in a heap of two cracked clay pots, fake ground shrubbery, two plastic plants, and real dirt, a giant mess splattered over ten square feet.

Jesus Christ, what was that?

John clears dirt out of his eyes and off his face. Looking up from the ground in a mass of tangled plastic twigs, branches, and leaves, he sees a crowd of people staring at him like he's an alien that just crash-landed into the flowerpots. He struggles to disentangle himself from the plastic foliage wrapped around his limbs, and after two false starts finally manages to extricate himself from the mess. He picks himself off the ground, dirt raining off his clothes and littering the ground. Self-conscious about the massacred plants, John's foot halfheartedly pushes a small pile of dirt and shrubbery back into the largest piece of the cracked pots. He bends to pull a plant into a standing position, but the effort throws him off balance and he again goes down with the plants. So it's not a real tree? John struggles to his feet, cursing his bad luck. Trying to be inconspicuous is not working. He is self-conscious about the crowd eyeing him like a lost species that has resurfaced and is being displayed in a freak show. Seeing that the plastic foliage is hopelessly shattered and clearly beyond repair, he quickly gives up on righting it, leaving the broken plant bent over at a grotesque angle. The dried brown dirt splattered on his beige shirt gives him the mottled look of a camouflaged infantryman who has just climbed out of a foxhole.

Shocked partygoers continue to stare at the bizarre mixture of plastic plant, dirt, and man, but John ignores them and concentrates on trying to regain his composure. He is way past embarrassment tonight, and he has bigger things to worry about than a snapped plastic bush or tree, whatever it is.

This is not a good night to be running solo, not the way he feels, not in this crowd, and certainly not under these circumstances: broke, hunted, desperate, covered in dirt, and making a grand entrance by annihilating fake plants. He feels like he's in a chess match with the wrong number of pieces on a chessboard with the wrong number of squares. He really wishes Ludo were here to help and hopes his friend can get in past the tall, forbidding doormen. John tries to remember what Ludo had told him about getting in, but his mind is a jumble of synapses. He can't string thoughts together. It is too hot. His legs are too unsteady. And the walls of the room feel like they're closing in on him. Unable to grab onto one thought, his mind cycles and spins like a washing machine in mid-cycle. Dangers swirl around him: Versachi, the menacing FBI agent whose shadow hangs over him like a heavy winter coat; Giulli, the local Mafia don whose restaurant he trashed and who now, as Versachi insinuates, contemplates killing him for revenge; Harry, ZZ's psychotic ex-husband who is making not-so-thinly veiled threats through ZZ; the police, waiting to get their hands on him for mayhem, theft, and destruction of property, perhaps to throw him in with the dreaded Mambo; and Wonderbread, Apples, Knuckles, and the rest of the poker-playing murderers, any of whom might express their particular artistry if he doesn't come up with the money he owes them.

And how is he going to come up with that money? Heck, he can't even afford an egg roll.

It is difficult to stand. He is unsteady, and his eyes come in and out of focus. This thing with Versachi doesn't make sense to him. This plan about Giulli. Versachi wants John to be a guinea pig to draw him out. That's suicide move number one, a course of action that could get John maimed, killed, or thrown into Lake Mead with custom-made weighted shoes before the evening was even spent. Or buried in the Mojave desert. And then he wants John to testify against Giulli—if he even lives that long. Suicide move number two. And if he leaves without cooperating, Versachi threatens to lock him up behind bars in a horrifying tryst with a gigantic psychopath. Or abandon him to Giulli's vengeful wrath if he goes AWOL. Or Giulli can come after him in Brooklyn if the poker-playing killers don't get him first. But rat on a Mafia boss?

Damned if you do. Damned if you don't. Or just damned.

The small piece of light, the little kernel he could extract to even deem good news, is that he is alive. Where there is life, there is hope. They say.

John's options are limited. Being broke and homeless reduces those few options even further. With no other plan, he has to play out the evening. No, not with no other plan—with no plan at all. Zero. And all this on wooden legs no less. He has to get over to the side of the room where it is less hectic and the crowds won't swallow the space around him. Or gawk at him like he's a perverted plastic plant killer. A serial shrubbery sociopath. He needs to gather his thoughts without being pushed aside by arriving guests, falling through plastic foliage, or being pulled into a vortex of people taking the oxygen he needs out of the air. He needs to survey the situation from a safe harbor and plan a course of action before it's too late and the action takes him along like a helpless twig into the treacherous current of the evening. If he gets sucked into the maelstrom of Versachi's plans, the eddies might take on frightening speed. Best to work his own plan on his own terms.

If he can somehow come up with a plan.

John walks slowly and carefully, afraid his legs will buckle like snapped twigs and he will crack and go down like that plastic plant. He is burning up from the heat; he's got to get out from under the direct glow of the bulbs. Only two steps into his forced march, he becomes aware that a big man in a dark suit, standing among a group of people, is staring in his direction as if sending a message. John rotates his head behind to see who the man is looking at—it is too difficult to actually turn his body—and seeing no one in particular, he continues walking. He is having difficulty getting his timberlike legs to cooperate properly, and they advance unsteadily, stiffly, one in front of the other, ungainly, like a poorly made toy. John wobbles forward and bumps into a man, then continues on and bumps into another man. This second man angrily says a few things, but John can't understand the words. Is it English, Spanish, Russian? The KGB is here too?

Got to keep moving.

John sees a good wall, not too crowded. That's his target. Start from there. But he needs something to drink. Something cool. Anything. He's hot, he's parched, and he's faint. He's got to get out from under the direct glare of the overhead burning lights. Get a drink. More than anything. To cool himself down. To help steady him. John would dip his face into the toilet bowl if an ice bag was emptied into it, heck, even if a few crisp cubes were thrown in there. Dive in there headfirst.

Calm down.

John looks over at the bar, desperate for that stiff drink. But it is three deep in people. Too difficult. He'd never make it through. Not in this condition. Not now. His throat is so dry, John doesn't think he can speak if he has to. He sidesteps a small gathering of people and hobbles his way to a quiet section. Be inconspicuous, keep a low profile, that's the plan. But people are staring at him oddly, like he's holding a confederate flag at a union rally. He looks up—no wonder, a branch from the plastic plant is still grasped tightly in his hand, extending two feet above him into the air like he's carrying the flag into the battle of the trees. The plastic branch brigade. He tosses it away; Jesus, was he carrying it around all this time?

Damn, he is hot. He has to get a drink. With ice cubes. He finally gets the Ludo Rule: Worry about what he has to worry about only when he has to. Or something like that. Maybe it's his frayed nerves. The life-and-death stuff could wait. Yeah, the Ludo Rule. Get some liquid, cold liquid, an ice-cold drink. He needs to quench his thirst before the burning heat of the lights melts him like a snowball and turns him into a puddle on the floor. John finally gains the wall and leans against it, relief, trying to focus, trying to think. A long, low table six feet in length separates him from two couples nearby. They chat happily, the pitter-patter of partygoers without a care in the world. Their conversation sounds like a hum, a buzz, a chattering vibration of insects in a big swarm. Locusts. One woman, frivolous and modern, wears a bright summer dress of yellows and reds. The man with her, smartly dressed in a light blue-striped seersucker suit styled from the forties, evokes a more classic theme. The clothing of the couple is oddly matched, two different eras transposed into one. The man in the seersucker suit places a large golden-colored drink filled to the top with ice behind him on the table while he uses both hands to adjust his tie.

Eureka!

Bells go off in John's head and his eyes light up like a flashing jackpot when the golden glass of fluid, like manna from heaven, appears in his sights. Without thinking, John reaches across the table like a stealth plane ripping through the midnight sky, grabs the drink, and downs it in one long gulp. In almost the same motion, he drops it back where he found it.

The elixir of life. Just in time. John breathes in deeply, breathes out. Finally—cooled down. Refreshed.

After elaborately undoing and redoing his tie, the man in the seersucker suit reaches back and lifts his glass off the table. His drink is empty and he stands there perplexed, looking around and seeing no departing waiters. His wife happily chats on, pleased to hear her own voice, oblivious to her husband's quandary. The man in the seersucker suit replaces the glass behind him, but still not convinced, turns around once again to examine it. Empty. He shakes his head in confusion, excuses himself to his wife, and heads off to the bar to get another drink, still shaking his head in disbelief.

Suddenly, a blur comes in from John's left side. A big man in a suit, the one who had been looking in his direction before, nonchalantly walks by, as if on a leisurely stroll to the other side of the room. "Five minutes to showtime," the man says out of the corner of his mouth as he passes.

The sight of this man jolts John like an electric prod has just touched the raw skin of his privates. The imagined danger that was lurking somewhere in this crowd is no longer imagined, no longer in the realm of the theoretical. It is real.

Versachi is in the house.

———————

John worries about Versachi. The man seethes raw danger. It is wrapped around him like a dark, brooding shawl. It drips off him thickly like fat on a suckling pig turning slowly on a spit. John fears that the barrel-chested man with the light gait might kill him if he bolts this party without playing his dangerous game of Russian roulette. And he's also concerned that if he leaves, Giulli will also come after him. Double jeopardy. It's scary enough to hear the chamber spinning when there is one live bullet, but when a second is added, the spinning sounds louder and the odds become worse for the player. Exactly twice as bad. Even in John's confused state, he can add up those numbers. John needs a plan, any kind of plan at all, but what could he possibly come up with?

Just five minutes, Versachi said.

———————

About ten feet away, John notices a woman subtly wiggling her fingers around a drink she is holding, as if signaling him. She is wearing a long red dress that falls from her big shoulders like an ill-fitting drape, and her face, heavily caked with makeup, is broad like a man's. She holds a martini glass filled to the top with translucent pink liquid. Next to her, also drinking out of martini glasses filled with pink liquid, two curvaceous women in their early twenties wearing matching baby-blue-and-pink cocktail dresses, whisper and smile to each other. They too look at him and twirl their fingers flirtatiously in tremolo motions, as if playing the flute. John doesn't know what this is about. This whole evening is already too surreal for him. And too real. What would this big woman and her two winsome companions want with a wooden-legged J. Bond hanging on for dear life in a party, fighting claustrophobia, fear, vertigo, wooden legs, and shattered nerves? Versachi is here, Giulli is here somewhere, the police are probably undercover here as well, likely the FBI, and earlier, was that Russian he heard that group of ominous men speaking? The KGB must be here for him too.

John's vision wanders in and out of focus, and he squints his eyes for a better look. The golden, bountiful blonde curly hair that cascades over the big woman's shoulder doesn't seem right on her; it somehow doesn't match her features. And there is something odd about her, mannish almost. John has the feeling that he's met her before. The hair also seems familiar, but familiar in a strange way, as if he's seen that hair separate from the face and body currently underneath it. Then again, this is a strange evening on a strange trip in a strange town. But on the other hand, how could he forget luxurious plumage like that?

The bizarre thing—and John can't believe what he thinks he's seeing—is that the woman looks a lot like Ludo, so much so that she must be his twin sister. Ludo never mentioned a sister, much less a twin sister. In fact, he never mentioned any siblings at all. Maybe they were separated at birth, a twin Ludo has never met? What a town of hard-to-believe coincidences and one-in-a-million possibilities, a spinning roulette wheel of the preposterous, unfathomable, and bizarre, and the things that just cannot be believed if they were not seen with one's own eyes. Wait until Ludo hears about this; he'll have to tell him if he lives long enough. Imagine—Ludo has a twin sister he didn't know about!

The big woman, less subtle this time, throws John a big wink and points at him with the index finger of the hand holding her glass.

It must be the pot kicking in, John thinks, or whatever the hell that stuff was. The dreadlocked one or the Latino, John can't remember which, said that smoking that stuff could take you on a moon voyage. Well, he wasn't on the moon, but he did have wooden legs. Is that kind of the same thing? And he is witnessing sights and thoughts as

strange as he has ever seen or imagined. Weird enough that he finds a
woman who looks like Ludo. But to be familiar with the hair on his
friend's twin sister's head? That's just not right. It must be the drugs.
Ludo's look-alike twin sister is flirting with him no less! Actually waving
him over. John shakes his head no and waves for her to come toward
him. The two women next to Ludo's sister begin giggling and start
motioning him over as well. He has to find out. John treads unsteadily
and carefully to where they stand. It is difficult to walk those twenty
feet, the floor is slanted or something, but he gets there. He is in shock
when the woman in the red dress opens her mouth. Not only does she
look like Ludo, she sounds and talks a lot like him too! John shakes
his head violently to clear his thoughts as Ludo's sister addresses him a
second time.

"Yo, homes, what the hell's the matter with you?" Ludo's sister in
red says in a conspiratorial whisper. She is wearing thick red lipstick and
purple eye shadow, and her face, more heavily caked with makeup than
it appears from afar, gives her an almost ghostlike appearance, like she's
a made-up voodoo queen at a Mardi Gras ball.

"You look so much and sound so much like someone I know, it's
uncanny," John replies, wondering why they are whispering.

"Maybe it is because I *am* someone you know."

"Ludo?" John says, stupefied.

"I'm hear to back you up, man."

"Where did you get that dress?" John runs his eyes up and down
the dress and he shakes his head.

"The girls with me happened to have an extra-large-sized dress they
packed as a practical joke, so I used it to get into the party. I don't want
Versachi seeing us together. So far he hasn't made me. We'll talk later."

Ludo moves off with the two girls who John now recognizes as the
sunbathers from the pool.

John remembers why the long blonde curly wig on Ludo's head
looks so familiar. It is the very same head of hair he himself wore this
morning to escape Versachi. And before that blonde wig adorned John's
head, it was worn by the old woman who had passed it on to him. John

wonders how many times three different individuals of different sexes and age brackets, no less—all in dead earnestness—wore the same head of hair in one day.

Las Vegas, what a strange town indeed, John thinks.

A man backs into John, slightly bumping him. "Excuses me," the man calls over his shoulder without turning. The voice causes John's breath to involuntarily halt and sends chills up his back. The voice has the gravelly resonance of a chain-smoker and is all too familiar. But no, it *can't* be. John peeks around to verify what he already suspects. The man with his back to John is built like an upright boss bull, with broad shoulders that roll animatedly as he speaks and a large head that bulges out of a thick neck. He is wearing a form-fitting pinstriped gray suit that hugs his massive frame like a lambskin glove. He is conversing with a shorter man, slight of build and with only a half crown of hair remaining on his head. The disparity in size between the two men makes the bigger of the two appear that much more imposing.

"Youse gotta look at what youse doing, youse always gots to," the big man in the suit says to the smaller man. "Let's says that youse gots five of dem youse got to deal wit', right?"

At first, John isn't convinced about what is clearly evident even though everything in his senses tells him it is what it is—what were the chances of *that* man showing up here?—but when he sees the speaker's hand punctuate the air to stress an emphatic point in his story, with the letters H-A-T-E inscribed on the fingers in uneven blue ink, the shock hits his senses like a dose of muriatic acid fumes invading his nostrils. He can barely get enough oxygen into his chest, and he feels like he's competing against a pump disgorging air out of his respiratory system at a pace faster than he can draw it in. The external sounds of the room become overtaken by a loud staccato buzz, the chopping sounds of helicopter blades. He becomes dizzy and watches, transfixed, as the man's hands raise up and down with the visual explanations of his story. John sees the letters L-O-V-E go up in the air, then H-A-T-E. The blades chop faster. L-O-V-E, H-A-T-E, L-O-V-E, H-A-T-E.

Whatever paranoia and premonitions John felt before entering this party have just been fed a giant bowl of food.

A third bullet is in the chamber: Knuckles is in the house.

Chapter Double Thirteen

John needs another cool beverage. Right away. With lots of ice. If it doesn't show up soon, somehow, some way, John is prone to hitting the ground like droppings from a plump pheasant. He's got to move. He's got to get away from this spot. Whatever relief the tall iced drink had given him earlier is gone. Shocked out of his system. He starts to walk, clumsily, his lumber legs stiffening up, two poles seeking traction on an uneven trail full of rocks. He's wobbly. Hot. The heat. Desperately in need of replenishment. A car's overheated radiator trying to leg it out of the desert, its water evaporating fast, columns of smoke billowing out of its system into the stifling summer sky. Time is working against him. He needs coolant. Any brand, any type. He's got to refill the tank.

John makes his way over to where he started, across the table from the couple. Back up, regroup. They're still there, the man in the seersucker suit and his wife in the brightly colored dress, happily chatting with another couple and seemingly unconcerned with anything but the trivialities of the moment. They are separated from him by a six-foot table so geographically close, yet at this juncture of time in the continuum of life, a world of reality away. They, a blithe pair of robins in song worrying about their drinks, and he, John Howard-Hughes, a scared swallow with worries of a far graver nature—the fear of an abrupt curtailment of his life.

Sand is spilling from John's hourglass. Pouring out. Lacking any better idea, John keeps moving.

The man in the seersucker suit holds a tall drink full of ice with mint leaves and a sprig of sugarcane jutting from the top. He puts his drink behind him on the table while his hands paint an elaborate scene for his wife. John passes by at that very moment, his eyes lighting up at the fortuitous bounty laid out in front of him. A godsend, a pirate's treasure. He grabs the drink, a tall refreshing mojito, drains it in one monstrous gulp, and puts it back on the table.

And keeps going.

"Kaboom!" yells the man in the seersucker suit as he finishes his anecdote with a flourish by throwing both his arms into the air. Grinning triumphantly from the masterful telling of his story, he reaches behind to grab his glass. "Kaboom!" he yells again, his voice filled with pleasure. He lifts the glass before him, preparing to imbibe the cooling refreshment, when his face goes blank.

While his wife regales the foursome with her own story, a tea party where a long out-of-touch girlfriend unexpectedly shows up, her husband, with his eyes open so wide they look like saucers, stares at his glass in disbelief. He looks about him and, seeing no one around, looks back at the glass. It's empty and the man in the seersucker suit just can't understand it.

It's bad enough to speculate on Versachi and Giulli, but with Knuckles, there is no speculation. He's a known killer who doesn't like to be owed money. And John owes him money. He shudders as he remembers Knuckles' hard stare when he exited the poker game and then the flash of a sadistic smile as the killer held up his right fist, its knuckles inscribed with the letters H-A-T-E.

The tall mojito, filled with rum, ice, and sugar, quenches John's thirst, but just as quickly reveals his next carnal need: food. He's hungry, dreadfully so. John moves shakily across the room and stops in front of a long buffet table covered with a white cloth. There is a lump underneath the cloth, suggesting that there might be something below it to give him strength. He crunches the last of the ice cubes from his drink, his mouth a cool delight, and lifts the edge of the cloth. He's in luck. Underneath is a large rectangular platter of succulent oysters resting on a layered bed of wilted kale. Decoratively cut lemons garnish the four corners of the plate, and are flanked on either side by miniature Tabasco bottles. John peels back the cellophane wrap and in quick succession slurps down six large oysters. He prefers his oysters cold; in fact, he always remembers them served on a bed of ice. These, however, are lukewarm, and it makes them taste spoiled. Just the same, it is sustenance, and John is badly in need of that even if they don't taste as good as when they are chilled.

A passing headwaiter spots the exposed shellfish and cuts in front of John.

"Excuse me, sir," he says, and then, yelling at a junior waiter next to him, "Rudolfo, get these damn things off the table so we can put down the food. Why didn't we throw these out yesterday? Get rid of them before someone gets sick."

The warning is too late. A wrenching pain immediately grips John's innards: The spoiled oysters have wasted no time. They efficiently burrow their way through John's intestines at breakneck speed, causing him to groan out loud from the sudden pain. Jesus, why didn't he think before eating them? John looks up and spots Versachi trying to signal him from about twenty feet away.

Not now.

John needs time to think. He turns his head to the side, as if he hasn't seen Versachi. Open space is no longer his ally; he's too vulnerable there.

Better to move.

John weaves his way deep into the crowd, twisting and turning around the small clusters and cliques of people, changing directions, hoping to temporarily lose Versachi, so that he can think, figure out something—anything—extricate himself from this mess. He tries to get his mind back into focus, but his thoughts remain a cycling patter of unrelated ideas. And he's dizzy. He wanders into a small circle of men. Finding one of the group smiling at him, he nods back. The man comes forward, talking rapidly, his sentences and utterances coming in rapid bursts, like a forty-five RPM record being played at seventy-eight speed.

"Hello, my good man, I'm Paddock Rockfelter, sort of like Rockefeller, if you will, you know, just to help you remember, though that is a good association, mind you. I can see by your cut of clothes, you're the artist type, *artiste* type I would venture, that blue blazer of yours, so retro, so evolved, you know, creative, oh absolutely, a man who takes chances and all that. Not the norm, you know what I mean. My friends call me Paddie, much easier it is than Rockfelter, besides I always go by that."

Paddie's face is bright red as if he had sat too long in the sun or had had too much to drink—or both—and there is a slight slur to his voice. He extends a hand, and John, grabbing it to shake, notices its plumpness, like a gorged goldfish. He hangs on to John's hand, enthusiastically pumping it multiple times in a pulsating rhythm.

"Heart Association," Paddie screams out, then dropping to his knees and still holding John's hand, he bobs his head back and forth, flaps his arms wildly, and squawks like a chicken. "Bahhhk, bahhhk, bahhhhhhk. President of the Chicken Association," Paddie intones from his crouch.

He gets up and slaps John heartily on his upper arm. "Oh, you're great fun, old boy. Great fun you are indeed! And what's your name, pray tell, my artist friend?"

"I'm John Howard-Hughes, sort of like Howard Hughes Junior," John weakly jokes back, his mind spinning. He manages a smile through gritted teeth, his stomach twisted with pain. The oysters are back at work.

"Quite the breeding, I say. Well, while Hughes is richer, Howie is easier, more informal anyway among friends—Howard is just too formal, too high-tea, crumpets and all that—and Junior, no sense calling you by your father's name completely, Howie is the way to go, you're so right about that, you artists have to stand on your own, not borrow from the paternal, just the same, might as well take the easier path in life, I've always said that. The pleasure is mine, all mine, Howie. I do love that blazer, really."

Paddie clears his throat extravagantly, almost like a primal scream, and a few people turn around to stare. Paddie barely stops, spitting out sentences in long breaths.

"Howie, this is the 'round table' as we're known, not King Arthur's, of course, really the 'circle,' we call ourselves this, either one you like, round table or circle, all the same, the same, the same, you know like rain in Spain, never mind—my friend Robert Casagrand, real estate, this is Benjamin Hartly, textiles, and finally, my good friend Shaun DeRosa, let's say, in the happy business." Shaun is dressed in an immaculate white suit and polished yellow shoes, more reminiscent of Miami couture than Las Vegas business-casual, while Benjamin and Robert are more formally dressed in dark blue suits. An older man, wearing a conservative gray suit and with a full head of silver hair, is in the group as well, but John cannot make out his face; his back is turned and he is busy conversing with a very tall man from another group.

"John is the name—" John says.

"Easy, fella." Shaun smiles and pats John on the back. "Howie, you really can call me John if you insist, quite cute the way you say it, but my name is *Shaun*, not John, though they do sound quite close, I'll give you that. Shaun as in Shaun as in Shaun, a rose is a rose is a rose, but not quite the same number of zeros as a Hughes, Howie, but we do what we can, you understand."

"Yes, right he is," chimes Paddie with a chuckle. "Shaun is a real dandy though, watch out for him, a real zero-monger as we say." Paddie loudly clears his throat, a raucous booming gurgle that lasts several seconds, and people around them again turn and look.

Shaun elbows John in the ribs. "Nothing personal, poodle, we have a running little joke about those zeros. Where you sit in certain circles depends on how many zeros you have." Shaun rolls his tongue along his mouth, smacks his lips in a popping sound, and smiles his pearly whites.

"Oh," Paddie says in a high voice as the older man with the silver hair turns back into the group, "let me introduce you to Giulli. He likes us to use the 'J' in the name, J-U-L-I-E, or is it a 'G,' whatever G or J, oats or hay, what was I saying, oh yes, a variance for the circle, you see. We call him Mister Giulli, he's a restaurateur deluxe." Giulli has fierce-looking features highlighted by dark, depthless eyes and a grim demeanor, in sharp contrast to his more benign-looking companions. His smile, if it could be called that, barely creases his lips. He appears out of place among Paddie, Shaun, Benjamin, and Robert. Under his conservative gray suit, his collared shirt is blood red, a sobering color.

John doesn't get the connection between this intimidating man with the suit and blood-red shirt and the circle, but he gets the name— Julie, or Giulli. Whether with the "J" or the "G," this has to be the same Giulli who owns the Amiga Bella, the Italian restaurant John destroyed when he skipped out on the bill. John drops his glance to avoid eye contact, and with sweating palms, shakes hands with the restaurateur. Giulli's clasp is cold and strong, like a metal vice. He holds John's hand an extra second before letting go, as if to let him know he knows and there would soon be more to talk about. John shivers as he imagines how that strong grip would feel wrapped around his throat, and he unconsciously stretches and twists his neck as if to free it from Giulli's deadly grip.

How did he manage this? He scampers across the room to avoid Versachi and manages to run smack dab into Giulli! John looks up and is surprised to see Versachi a few groups over to the right, still trying to catch his attention. And not far from that menace is Knuckles!

How did this happen?

Surely the restaurant owner has seen that videotape Ludo described from the television show—with him wearing the same blue sport coat he has on now! And what are they all doing at this gathering and on this side of the room?

By the wall, not far away, John sees the man in the seersucker suit tightly gripping a new drink with both hands and nervously looking around, his face pale, as though an apparition had chased the color out of his complexion. And now John understands what happened. He has navigated himself in one big circle, being barely fifteen feet from the point where he started, but in a worse position than before—stuck in a dangerous Bermuda Triangle between Giulli, Versachi, and Knuckles. Whether from raw nerves or the action of rotten oysters burying themselves deeper into his bowels like parasitic worms, John's stomach takes a turn for the worse. It feels as if two rusty screws have just poked through his intestines and are viciously twisting deeper with every movement he makes.

The group of men chuckle and smile at John like he is their old friend, but John is distracted by the writhing pain in his gut and the field of unknown horrors that could occur if the paths of Versachi, Giulli, and himself intersect in the same time and space. That's Versachi's stated plan, and instinctually, John knows that's exactly the scenario he does not want to occur. John's got to remove himself from Giulli's vicinity before Versachi comes over.

"Say there, old chap, are you okay?" Paddie asks.

Shaun slaps him on the back, pushing the rusty screws deeper through his stomach lining. "Howie, you are looking a little wan. Can I call you Howie, would that be a dandy roger since we're all getting familiar?"

"A little dyspeptic, that's all." John's voice is strained and an octave higher. "I could use—"

"Say there, Howie," Paddie cuts in, "you seem like the sporting type, you really ought to join our cricket game. There are some small stakes involved, but only enough to keep it interesting, if you follow me?"

"New blood is always good for the vultures," Giulli says, looking directly at John.

The room is getting hotter, and the twisting pressure in his stomach intensifies as if two intertwining cords had just yanked tighter. Involuntarily, some gas whisks out of John's nether regions and he can smell its foul presence, a cross between bad egg and dead oyster. If he doesn't get to the bathroom quickly, it may get worse than bad gas.

Shaun sniffs the air, his face holding a quizzical expression, and looks around suspiciously to see if he can identify the source of this odiferous fragrance. Discovering nothing, he turns back to the group.

There is a brief uncomfortable silence, broken when Paddie grabs John by the elbow, steering him and the group along to one of the nearby walls.

"Hey, come over here, boys, let me show you this lithograph by Gauguin, a beautiful piece, very evocative of the South Pacific before the place lost its native charm, *very* you understand. And the really interesting thing is that when Gauguin painted it, the area hadn't changed much since Captain Bougainville first went there more than two hundred years before, you know they named the flower after him, Howie, but why they called it Bougainvillea and not Louis de Bougainvillea or Captain B, I really don't understand, you know what I mean, sport, you see I always believed this, if you're going to do it right, then just do it right, why mess around, you know in my first marriage, and this is really before it turned into a horrid affair, I mean a horrid affair with dish-throwing, though that was a fun day actually until she clocked me over the head with my grandmother's serving plate, knocked me right out it did, seven stitches as well, they say first marriages are always dreadful anyway, but let's not dwell on that one . . ." Paddie comes up for air, clears his throat, and looks around like a twittering bird before focusing his eyes on John's and continuing ". . . nor the second and third marriage either, but I haven't given up yet, you don't believe in giving up so easy do you, Howie, old boy, but then again you didn't have to live with those witches anyway, that's why I was always so glad to go on those worky work vacations, get away from it all, oh, okay, there actually was a fourth time around, but we don't count that one, do we, my, you do look pale, dear, dear, are you okay?"

John is panicking. Versachi is on his way over, pushing his way through a crowded area, barely thirty feet away. And he must get to the bathroom quickly. "Men's room?" John says in a weak voice.

"Quite at the other side of the room," Paddie says, pointing to an opening framed in huge ornate drapes, in the same direction as the oncoming Versachi.

"Excuse me," John says, heading the other way, departing seconds before Versachi arrives. John skirts his way through the crowd, walking like a bent-over simian from the excruciating pain in his stomach, first taking a wide swath around Versachi, then weaving back through a cluster of people to avoid Knuckles. John is obsessed with the immediacy of one need: He's got to quickly get to the bathroom.

———————

Versachi is seconds too late to nab Howard-Hughes, so he continues on, nonchalantly, as if he's taking a casual stroll through the crowd. Stealth is key to his mission, and he doesn't want anyone connecting Howard-Hughes and him in any way; he also doesn't want to attract undue attention by chasing him through the crowd. Versachi circles back and returns to where he was, clenching and unclenching his leg-of-mutton-sized fists. His eyes follow Howard-Hughes' path as he weaves unsteadily through the crowd, moving like a drunk against a shifting wind. He's a strange nickel, that Howard-Hughes. In the casino, running around with his wildly waving hands and that gruesome hankie; in the diner, secreted among the flour bags and bathed in white powder; and here, bent over like a dyspeptic ape. He watches Howard-Hughes move in a big semicircular pattern, running the last few steps in a bent-over sprint where the crowd thins out by the door, and then disappearing through the ornate drapes and into the bathroom.

He's a strange nickel, a very strange nickel. But just the same, he'd better start playing ball. And he'd better start real soon.

Cockroach rider is beginning to piss Versachi off.

———————

After several miserable minutes on the toilet and three industrial flushes, John emerges from the stall and heads to the sink, turning the cold nozzle on as far as it will go. He lavishly splashes cold water on his face, letting rivulets stream down his temples with water he doesn't bother to dry off. When he goes to lean against the bathroom's door, he misjudges the distance, and barely misses falling over, catching the edge of the frame in the nick of time.

———————

"Dear me," Paddie says, "I hope we didn't wear him down with all that marriage talk, got him so discombobulated that he went the wrong way, but there he is now, I see him, goodie, he's back in the right direction, but they were dreary that group of wives, one of them even tried to, oh, no matter I suppose, they ah, never mind, anyway, quite a nice chap, that Howie."

"Quite a nice chap, I say," Shaun chimes in. "These artsy types though, very sensitive, very sensitive. Weak bladders I hear, that's the word anyway."

Paddie sees John returning toward the group, gulps down a full martini in one swallow, and rushes over to meet him, grabbing him before Versachi can get away from the group of three people he is idly conversing with. Paddie leads John through the crowd, talking nonstop as they maneuver around clusters of stationary people and head back to the circle. "Are you the dabbler in diverse painting styles, cubism, modernism, the impressionists perhaps? Museum quality, of course." Paddie is animated and talks in quick bursts. "I just wanted to hear it privately, I know your type is shy about those things in public, dear me, would hate to put you on the spot, you sensitive artist types and all, but you are an artist, aren't you?"

"I love painting—" John says absentmindedly, keeping an eye out for Versachi. The room feels like a treacherous snake pit with little room to move and more snakes to move around.

"So you do paint, Howie, ol' boy? An artist deluxe. I knew it! I just wanted to hear it out of your mouth."

"Paddie, it's *John*."

"Oh, please, Howie. *Pa-lease!*" Paddie says and drops his voice to a whisper, his eyes wildly looking around, his breath smelling like grain alcohol with a hint of olives. "Shaun over there, might as well call him Shaun, not John, though maybe it's your accent, a painter's accent, I mean an artist, *artiste's* expression so to speak, the boy would like to think he can paint, you can call him John if you want, your prerogative, you artist types all have that little eccentricity, nonconformity, way of looking at things, whatever, anyhow, part of being creative I guess, me, not one inch of creativity, but *palease*, Shaun is so pedestrian in his art, not like you Howie, pure genius, I'm sure, you know, no imagination really though he tries. Now I *know* you can paint. That blue jacket gives you away, those buttons even, only an artist would wear them. The disheveled look, the casual clinging dirt, only a true virtuoso can pull it off. I've been around the art world too long, you can't fool me, Howie boy. I may not be able to wield a paintbrush myself—swish, swish, swish," Paddie makes three brush strokes with his extended arm, "but I can recognize a good artist like a mouse can spot a chunk of cheese, I don't even have to see their art. When a bear wears his fur, you know it's a bear. I've always said that."

Paddie, breathless from the long rant, downs the other drink he is holding.

"I've never painted a thing in my life. I can't even fill in connect-the-dots with color," John says painfully, his eyes scanning the crowd. He can't see Knuckles or Versachi, but the pain in his stomach, temporarily relieved by his trip to the bathroom, begins to worsen again as the oysters go back to work.

Paddie lets out a wild howl and shakes violently with laughter. Finding his circle of friends nearby, he grabs John by the elbow and pulls him into its midst. "He kills me, Howie does. He's so droll! So modest. No really, you have to show us your paintings sometime, you really do!"

"You really do, cookie." Shaun rolls his tongue around again.

"I really can't paint though," John says.

"Oh, he's too much, Howie is," Paddie screams, throwing his arms in the air and jerking his forehead skyward. "What a rock star! He's probably one of the great contemporaries. So modest."

"Maybe not one of the top three though, I would venture to say that," John quips quietly, his lips pressed tight with growing pain.

Again, Paddie lets out a howl. "I love the self-deprecation! A true sign of an artist. Really great!"

John's bowels can't hold much longer. "You'll have to excuse me for a minute. My stomach is a little weak today," John says, quickly exiting the group and heading toward the toilets. Seeing Versachi approach from the corner of his eye, he zigzags his way back through the crowd, avoiding the big man by a wide margin.

"Hurry back old chap, hurry back!" Paddie yells after him.

"Yes, do!" Shaun says.

John clears the crowd and races into the bathroom and the first stall, dropping his pants in the nick of time.

————

Versachi's careful watch of the bathroom is momentarily interrupted by an inebriated woman who takes a spill at his feet. As he bends to help her, John wobbles out the door and disappears into the crowd.

Versachi rights the woman, but it is too late—Howard-Hughes has blended back into the crowd, eluding him once again.

He is beginning to get pissed off.

————

Stuck in a mass of people and confused, John's thoughts cycle in rapid succession. A combination of the fetid oysters and stuff with the extra "oomph" has made John disoriented, his brain a frenzied mass of bouncing electrodes. He can't figure out which way to go or why he would go there in the first place. He is lost in his tracks, a lamb stumbling among a large herd looking for its mother, not knowing what to do or which way to turn.

A live band composed of five black men with outsized afros and matching sequined outfits has finished setting up and begins playing Motown classics from the sixties. The music and the energy flowing from the upbeat band kick-starts the party and energizes the crowd like a spark zipping its way along a gas line. The dance floor quickly fills with inebriated partygoers gyrating wildly to the music. They are whipped into an early frenzy, inspired by a seeming madman, who, like a top spinning out of control, weaves in and about the dance floor, spinning, jumping, and flailing his arms in the air. As the man spins wildly, his face momentarily flashes in John's direction—it is Paddie. Revelers hook arms and spin each other in giddy circles. John is pulled into the drunken mass and gets passed elbow to elbow, round and round, a cork sucked into the vortex of a whirlpool, until the woman who looks like Ludo pulls him out of the whirling eddy and off to the side.

The woman who looks like Ludo—now John remembers, it's Ludo's twin sister—has a worried look on her face and is about to say something, but the last turn on the dance floor has sent paroxysms of pain shooting through John's bowels, and he runs, doubled over and gripping his stomach, back to the bathroom.

———————

This time, there would be no escape.

As John finishes washing his hands and splashing cold water on his face, he is grabbed by the lapels of his jacket and thrown against the outside door of a toilet stall. "Look, you little pissant," Versachi says, his face drawn taut with rage and his index finger pointing between John's eyes like a loaded gun, "I'm not playing games here. You get your ass out there *now* and start talking to Giulli and get down to business. Giulli's wearing thick black glasses, lots of gold jewelry, and a green buttoned-down shirt with large star-shaped cuff links. Here's what we're going to do. You come toward where I'm standing and I'll point him out to you. You got it? And then we'll take it from there."

"What do I do about the right hand and the rail?" John asks innocently. The spinning and frenzied dancing has further scrambled his thoughts, and he struggles to get the right words out. "You know, the right hand and the left hand? And what about the egg rolls?"

Versachi grabs hold of John's collar, bunching up the material in his big fists, and pulls him closer. "Don't fuck with me, cockroach rider. This is your last warning." Versachi lets go of John's collar when he hears the bathroom door open, walks over to the exit, and brusquely shoves a drunk out of the way as he leaves.

John staggers out of the bathroom and, as instructed, heads toward Versachi. But he can't remember the signs he was given. Right hand? Left hand? Rail? Versachi raises his hand to scratch his head and subtly points with his little finger. What did he say about the pinkie again? To make matters more complicated, the man next to Versachi coughs into his fist. There is also a woman in the group who switches her drink from one hand to the other. They are all looking in his direction and signaling him at the same time. John feels like a base runner trying to pick up signs from three third-base coaches frantically sending him differing instructions at the same time—and he can't figure out what to do. Versachi is still pointing with his little finger, but John is distracted by the other third-base coaches and can't remember if it's Versachi who has the real signs for the play or one of the other coaches who is sending signals. Two of the three are decoys, but the question is, which ones?

If this were the food court, he would know to skip the Chinese stand and go right to the Italian vendor. Or was it the pretzels? John's attention goes back and forth between the coaches, not sure where to look and who to follow.

Versachi scratches his head again, then uses his whole hand to point. John just can't make sense of it and stares blankly at him. Didn't Versachi say something about not coming over if he took both hands off the rail or was it if the right hand was on the rail? Wait, there are no rails. Did he mean the drink in his hand? And now the woman next to Versachi switches hands on her drink again. Who's giving the signals? Hit and run? Sacrifice? Take a pitch?

A sudden craving for an egg roll consumes John's thoughts. When he looks at Versachi's pointing hand, he imagines a large egg roll slowly and tantalizingly dangling in front of his eyes. And he gets hungry for it.

John can't figure out what Versachi wants him to do, so he guesses. He picks a random group of people in the general direction of Versachi's pointing finger and walks toward them, still struggling to remember what to do about the rails and the hands. If Versachi shows up with a plate of chow mein, that will really throw things off. He finds himself next to a young couple, unsure what to say to them. He looks back at Versachi for guidance. The big man angrily shakes his head and putting all pretenses aside, points with his whole arm at a different set of people.

John glances over. Two muscular men with slicked-back hair stand like bookends on either side of a shorter man who is wearing an untucked green shirt and gold chains. Versachi did say something about a man in a green shirt, but what does that have to do with egg rolls? Wait! The man in the green shirt is signaling something. John watches him take off the thick black-framed glasses, blow twice on each lens, and clean them with the bottom of his shirt. John looks questioningly back at Versachi.

What does that mean?

Snapping back to attention with Versachi's threatening look, John suddenly remembers what was reiterated with brutal clarity in the bathroom—that the man in the green shirt is Giulli and Versachi wants him to go over there. John unconsciously straightens the collar of his blue blazer where Versachi grabbed him with his big hands and starts walking toward the man in the green shirt. He is less than ten feet from Giulli when Paddie races over from the dance floor, grabs his elbow, and pulls him to the side. Paddie appears to be even drunker, as if the mad, gyrating dance earlier had ignited the alcohol and made the particles in his brain more chaotic.

Paddie blathers animatedly at a pace even faster then earlier, a cavalcade of words that bursts forth in one long breathless canter.

"There you are, old chap. Now, Howie, I would want your expert opinion, from an *artiste* point of view, as a man of fine sensibilities, exalted tastes, and the fine eye of a painter who can wield the delicate feather of the brush, the hues, the swathes and touches of detail, the infinitesimal fine points of a subpixel. A man of chartreuse, dandelion, fuchsia! I can't really trust those stodgy crumpet-eaters, oh, that was some great dancing out there, you see, when I was in Africa, pounding drums, stamping feet with the savages, ceremonial paint on and all that you understand, witch doctors, chiefs, and the lot, wearing those native charms and googoos and voodoos—didn't find out till later that they were reformed cannibals and I was the symbolic feast, dancing to my own dinner, no less—but there for big-game hunting, we used to use twelve-gauge guns, but I liked the more sporting weapons, long, pointed shooters, carbines, muskets, the order and species of all those types of rifle instruments is what I am getting at. Wild music, dancing, flavor of the senses, letting it all go, Howie, my dear! But you see, organization and organization, that's what I'm talking about. What is the organization *is* the question. No guess? Time's up. Give me your hand for a sec."

Paddie grabs John's hand, extends it in a long line so that the elbow is straight, and positions himself underneath John's arm as if it is a rifle. "Rifleman's Association. Got you there!" Paddie says, red-faced and giddy with delight as he races back into the crowd.

A woman who looks like Ludo is standing next to Paddie, but with long curly blonde hair. John does a double take. He thought he was imagining this earlier. How could this be? The woman sounds a little like Ludo too, only her voice is more strained than Ludo's, like she's a nervous sort full of anxiety. John turns his head away and peers at the woman from the side, like a pelican. This is too strange, and John doesn't know what to make of it, especially on an evening like this. The Ludo woman grabs his arm and pulls him a few steps farther away.

"Step over here for a second," the woman whispers out of the side of her mouth. Over her shoulder, John sees Versachi violently push a pointed finger into the air three times in harsh succession. "Listen to me," the woman's voice continues. It is deep, quite masculine for a woman. Come to think of it, the voice is just like Ludo's.

John suspiciously eyes the speaker.

"Homes, you're not going to believe what is going on here."

John turns and faces the speaker. No doubt now. It is Ludo. "Why are you wearing a dress?"

———————

Ludo is talking to John, but his words sound like a jumble of flapping wings. John looks over Ludo's other shoulder, fascinated by the wallpaper, and understands where the noise is coming from. The wallpaper has thousands of seagulls designed into its fabric, and they're working their wings. Ludo tugs harshly on his sleeve, and John looks back at him.

"You see that old guy over there with the thick glasses and green shirt?" Ludo says. "The one with the guys on either side of him?"

John nods. It is the man surrounded by the two bigger men with slicked-back hair, the one who was cleaning his glasses.

"That's Versachi's Giulli," Ludo says. "I recognize him from the TV show. And the one over there, that guy in the light-pink shirt next to the woman with the big hairdo? That's Giulli's Giulli, the real one."

"What?"

"One of them is real, the other one is not."

"One of them is fake?" John asks. He can't understand what Ludo is saying about one Giulli there, and a second Giulli, a Giulli's Giulli, over in another spot, but that one of them is fake. John looks back at the two Giullis, first the one in the green shirt, then the one wearing the light-pink shirt. Both Giullis look real to him. And then there is even another Giulli Ludo didn't mention, the one back in the circle with Paddie and Shaun's group, the elderly man in the gray suit and blood-red shirt. John has already spoken with that Giulli, so he knows for sure that that particular one is real. John wonders how many more Giullis are in the room.

"Anyway, I just spoke to Giulli, man. You won't believe what's going on," Ludo says.

"Which Giulli? There's three of them here." John watches a seagull fly around the room and hears the flapping sound again. How did it get off the wallpaper?

"What's the matter with you?" Ludo looks at John funny. "The owner of the restaurant you trashed is what I'm talking about. Giulli don't care about it. At all. You have no problems with him."

"With who?"

"Giulli, man. Who do you think we're talking about? He's covered under insurance, you know, the restaurant. You actually did him a favor. The vase wasn't really real; it's a fake."

John's head is spinning. Ludo's talking about fake Giullis and real Giullis, and vases that are fake and not real, but he's been strangely quiet about his twin sister in the red dress.

A heavy man walks by, the rolls of fat on his neck forming three fleshy chins over a white shirt stained off-yellow at the neck from sweat. He stops behind John, facing Ludo, holding a tall martini glass in his left hand. With the thumb and middle finger of his right hand, the man, holding Ludo's gaze steady in his own, extracts an olive from his drink, slowly licks the alcohol off it, and crisply pops it in his mouth. When the man starts licking his lips, Ludo, who has been staring in disbelief, faces a different direction and unconsciously fixes his dress, aware that the man hasn't shifted his gaze.

John is looking over Ludo's head. "You see that seagull?"

"You high, man, or what?"

Ludo looks behind himself, avoiding the gaze of the three-chinned man, and sees the patterns on the wall. "Oh, the wallpaper. Listen, I don't know the deal with this guy Versachi, but we're clean, man, with Giulli. We're clean with the police. It's Versachi we have to worry about. I don't know what his gig is, but make no bones about it, homes, we gotta stay away from that guy."

John is still engrossed in the Giulli mystery and wondering how many more Giullis are floating around the room. So far he has identified three of them. It is a world full of Giullis.

Versachi is out of patience, and he doesn't like what he sees with the manly looking woman in the red dress. Something is not quite right. Doesn't she have the beginnings of a beard forming? He starts over in their direction.

"Homes. Homes!" Ludo says, grabbing John's arm and watching in alarm as Versachi makes his move.

"What?"

"We got to move from this spot. Now. Oh shit!" Ludo says, taking John's arms and steering him to their left. "What the fuck is Knuckles doing here?"

John looks at Ludo. "You really didn't see that seagull flying around?"

Ludo quickly leads John through the crowd, abruptly changing directions to skirt around both Versachi and Knuckles, and finds temporary sanctuary in the midst of the crowd. But they can hide for only so long. Ludo's got one thing on his mind now, just getting them out of this party safely. The good news: It's a big party and they might be able to lose them in the crowd long enough to gain the exit. The bad news: Versachi is on to them and won't make it easy.

"Can we get a quick drink?" John says to Ludo. "I'm dying of thirst."

"I know that voice. I know I know that voice, that voice I know!" exclaims a man who maneuvers himself right in front of them, blocking their path. He is wearing a pastel-pink shirt and white linen pants with creases so crisp they look like a person's fingers would get cut if they ran down them too rapidly. The man, all smiles, holds a reddish-pink drink in a martini glass. John instantly recognizes the voice; it is Tim from the laundry.

"Why, if it isn't Divine," Tim says. "Sooo nice to meet in person, especially after our whisperings, shall I say, on the phone. And to think, somehow ordained by fate, we meet. Still think it's a coincidence, Divine?"

"Not now, Tim," John says. "Not a good time." John steps around him and continues walking.

"Aren't you going to say hello?" asks Tim's companion, the voice vaguely familiar.

John waves his hand in greeting without looking.

"Johnny, Johnny, Johnny, Johnny, Johnny," the voice calls out, as if possessed.

"What's that kook doing here?" Ludo says.

"Mr. Howard-Hughes, Mr. Howard-Hughes."

"What is it, Joe?" John says.

"Never mind," Joe Montana says with a devilish smile and a side-to-side shake of the hand.

"How the hell do you know so many people here?" Ludo asks, as they hurry through the crowd. "And did that one guy call you Divine?"

———————

Two doors located about forty feet apart from each other along the same wall lead out of the banquet room. Versachi has strategically stationed himself between the two exits like a sentry on alert, and stands defiantly, hands on hips, waiting for Howard-Hughes or his buffoonish friend, cuchifritos, in the ridiculous red dress, to show their faces.

———————

John feels a few fingers tapping him on the shoulder, but he ignores them, hoping the fingers will go away. The fingers keep tapping and John turns. It is Tim again.

"I feel like we're old friends and we hardly know each other. Isn't that funny?" Chirping like a bird in spring, Tim drops his voice to a more serious tone and continues. "Divine, how are you, *really*?"

"Just hanging, Tim," John says without turning.

"I dare say." Tim makes a popping sound with his mouth and taps his fingers a few times on his glass.

"I like the bold red color of your dress," Tim says to Ludo. "Not the shy one, eh?"

"Thanks," Ludo mumbles. He looks warily at Knuckles' back, not twenty feet away. The killer is deep in conversation with a heavy-breasted woman wearing a low-cut red dress, the same color as his own.

"Maybe we can all go shopping sometime?" Tim continues.

Ludo subconsciously smoothes out some wrinkles on the front of the dress and whispers to John, "Remind me to hang myself if one of these guys out here doesn't kill us first."

John swallows hard when he looks up. Knuckles has turned around and starts walking in their direction. He stops perilously close, just five paces away, and stares over John's shoulder. John jumps as a hand grabs his shoulder from the other direction and spins him around. It is Paddie, red-faced and excited, rubbing his hands together like two sticks of wood being used to spark a fire.

"Howie, did I tell you I was affiliated with the Railroad Association?" Paddie yells out drunkenly. Paddie's hands flutter in fast motion.

Ludo quizzically looks at John. "Howie? Divine? What's with all these names? How do you know all these people?"

John doesn't respond and stands like a zombie, too frightened to move or reply. He stares transfixedly at Knuckles, who is standing at such an alarmingly close proximity that it immediately sobers him up like a bucket of cold ice dumped on two fighting dogs. Ludo, following the path of John's eyes, turns around as well. He too freezes, a jolt of adrenaline doubling his heart rate. The killer is focusing on something behind them and hasn't noticed them yet.

"Perhaps you don't know the secret handshake? Grab my hand," Paddie says. John absentmindedly holds his hand out. Paddie grabs it and bends down so that his knees are just off the ground. He pumps John's hand back and forth like pistons on a locomotive, singing out,

"Choo-choo, choo-choo, choo-choo," as he energetically pumps their arms. "Railroad Association!" he gleefully announces.

Standing up to his full height, Paddie releases John's hand and howls with laughter again, throwing both arms in the air. "Good one! Oh, what a gamey audience," he yells, clapping John briskly on the shoulder. "I love that guy, great chap," Paddie says to Joe Montana. "Great chap!"

Knuckles had been smiling at some joke, but when he hears Paddie's exuberant laughter and catches John's eyes, his smile quickly disappears. There is no doubt now, he has made John. His shifting eyes settle on the red dress as well.

"Oh shit," Ludo says softly. It is too late to move.

Knuckles slowly cracks the knuckles on each of his fingers, the joints under the letters of love and hate making a popping sound, and starts walking toward John.

"Paddie," John says desperately, gesturing over his shoulder, "show him one of the handshakes. Please."

Ever eager to accommodate, Paddie intercepts Knuckles, grabs his hand, and whirls him around in the other direction before the big man can react.

"I have a suggestion to make," Joe Montana says, stepping between John and Ludo, taking each of their arms and rapidly steering them toward the exit. "There is a big bully-type coming this way—no, don't turn around—he's the one who left you that envelope the other morning. I think that, well, if I were you, I would make myself scarce and do so very fast. In fact, Tim and myself are going bye-bye at this very moment—Johnny, Johnny, Johnny, Johnny, Johnny—we'll give you a ride if you'd like."

"Yeah, we'll take it, thanks a million," Ludo says, hurrying behind them.

The tall man at the door briefly acknowledges John and says with a smile, "Have a good evening, Mr. Bond."

Ludo stares in amazement. "Mr. Bond? Homes, what's with all these names?"

The four—Tim, Joe Montana, John, and Ludo—with a clear path in front of them, hurry to the exit. The last thing John hears before they escape out the doors is Paddie's voice rising above the crowd, yelling something about the Corkscrew Association.

Chapter Twenty-Seven

Tim's pink Monte Carlo convertible lurches to a stop at the intersection of Fremont and South Main Street across from the Plaza Hotel and Casino in downtown Las Vegas. It is one o'clock in the morning, and the invigorating breeze generated by the convertible's open top as it whips through the streets is replaced by the stilled hot air of night.

Tim turns to the back seat and hands John two silver-dollar coins. "The ninety-nine-cent shrimp cocktails at the Golden Gate just down Fremont here are heavenly for the price. It's a longstanding downtown landmark. On me," Tim says.

"Thanks so much for everything, guys," John says. "You really saved our ass."

"There's a thought," Tim says, smiling at Ludo. "*Pa-lease.*"

"Touchdown!" Joe Montana calls out from the passenger side as the Monte Carlo pulls away amidst a cloud of blue exhaust fumes.

The cashier takes John's two dollars and lets him slide on the tax, taking the change out of her tip jar to make up the difference. She grabs two shrimp cocktails, generously pours the red cocktail sauce on top, and pushes them across the counter.

"Don't worry about it, dear," she says knowingly to John after he fumbles in his pockets and comes up empty. "We've all been there." She glances at Ludo's dress, trying to figure out what that is about, then back at John, his crumpled clothes hanging off him like they had been fished out of a dirty laundry bin. You can never tell with people, she thinks, how they got to where they are, but usually, once they are there, you can figure out where they are heading. Here, before her, were two leftover fish dredged out of the mud when the shallow pond water evaporated. They are an odd-looking couple, one in a bright red dress and the other in a blue blazer. Combined, they look like a red-and-blue-striped neon tetra fish minus the fluorescent glow. But these two fish not only lack luminescence, their trip has ground them down to the dull patina of dead fish skin exposed to air, and they seem to have trouble even finding a tank to swim in.

John and Ludo huddle around a small table, picking at shrimp drenched in red cocktail sauce in an old-fashioned sundae glass. Their servings are filled to the top with tiny succulent shrimp, a foodstuff locals and tourists in Las Vegas ingest daily by the tons. For John and Ludo, this modest feast is one to be savored, because they don't know when they'll get their next chance at something to eat.

"That's what I call splurging, when you spend your last dollar on an appetizer," Ludo says, gloating over the shrimp.

John warily eyes the seafood, hoping they take to his system better than the rotten oysters he foolishly gulped down at the party. He had been able to void the fetid shellfish in his many trips to the bathroom earlier, and his stomach has returned to some semblance of normal, though for him, normal isn't very good, not with all this tension. But at least the paroxysms of pain have passed.

"These shrimp cocktails are good, man," Ludo says, licking his lips. He picks at the tiny shrimps one at a time, enjoying each morsel to its fullest. "I'm never looking down on homeless people again. You just never know."

"No kidding."

"So what's going on with you and your girl?"

"I guess we broke up. It's finished. We kind of said goodbye this evening."

"Kind of?"

"She said it's best we don't see each other anymore, starts walking away, you know, like goodbye, see you in the next life kind of thing. Then she changes her mind or something, turns around and offhandedly says to call her. But I don't have any way to call her. So what does that mean?"

"She can always call you at our hotel," Ludo says.

"Come on, it's not funny."

Ludo tries to spike a shrimp slightly larger than the others, but it pushes deeper into the glass. He eyes another one, successfully impales the tiny crustacean, and eats it. "So you don't know where she lives, where she works, what she does, even what her last name is?"

"No, nothing. I really know very little about her."

"But I thought you had her phone number, home boy."

"Here's the crazy part, I didn't tell you. She—"

"Something you didn't tell me?" Ludo says, snapping to attention. "Wait a second. Now what are you going to spring on me? What did you do now?"

"Give me a break, Ludo."

"No, listen to me. Crazy and this girl, and crazy and you, can't seem to separate from one another, man, like you all intertwined or something. You're like a disaster-making, tornado-creating machine that can't seem to go ten minutes in this town without touching down and unleashing some kind of mayhem or whatever. You're walking trouble, homes. You find it all—cops, FBI, poker-playing killers, gangsters, hit men, angry mothers in malls, crazy girls with psychotic ex-husbands, TV shows featuring criminals, pink condom balloons, mambo-dancers, and who knows what else—and we in trouble with all of them. This just in two days. What's left? The U.S. Army is after us now?"

"Alright, so I got into a few mishaps." In the back of John's mind, he worries about the KGB as well, remembering that foreign language he heard at the party, and the DEA, in case the Latino or black man at the party overdosed and his name came to light; but he thinks better of adding it to Ludo's list, not that it would matter at this point with all the trouble they have.

"I'm glad they were just a few trifles. I'd hate to see what happens if you get in some real trouble." Ludo snaps the thin wooden shrimp fork in half, puts the pieces in the empty shrimp cocktail glass, and pushes it to the side of the table. "What do you say we turn in now and catch some shut-eye?" Ludo continues. "Maybe we can get comfy under some nice clean sheets at the hotel—oops, I forgot, we have no place to go. Maybe we can roll a few bums out of their boxes, sort of piss on some bushes and mark our territory, and hope no bigger wolves come by and piss on us." Ludo shakes his head side to side. "I just don't get how you always find so much trouble. You like a genius with that, the Einstein of atomic explosion problems." Ludo sighs deeply and looks John square in the eye. "Let's get to it already. What were you saying before?"

"Well, when I was with ZZ, you won't believe what happened earlier."

"I never do with you, and my bad luck is that I'm always right. I can't wait to hear this." Ludo leans back in his chair and crosses his arms. "Go ahead," he says when John hesitates.

"Okay, so we're walking in the mall and her ex calls, which sets her off. She starts screaming at the top of her lungs. It was the most embarrassing thing I've ever seen. ZZ gets madder and madder, yelling and screaming the entire time, then flings her phone against the wall so hard it shatters all over the place. Then she breaks up with me, but before she leaves, she tells me to call her. One problem—the only number I have is in plastic pieces all over that floor. On one hand," John continues, "she seems to really like me, but then without warning her mood swings one hundred and eighty degrees and it's like another person steps into her skin. I've never seen anything like it." John finishes eating and pushes his dish to the side.

"I hear you," Ludo says. He pulls John's cocktail glass closer, peeks inside, and then pushes it back to where it was. There are no shrimps left; John ate every last one of them.

"What are you doing?" John says.

"What are you talking about?"

"You know what I'm talking about."

"Homes, you doing this cryptic stuff again."

"Don't play all innocent with me. You know exactly what I'm talking about," John says, his voice rising.

"You got something to say, just say it. Stop with these games. How am I supposed to know what you're talking about? You ain't said nothin' yet." Ludo raises his voice as well, and now both of them are arguing loudly in the ninety-nine-cent shrimp cocktail area at the Golden Gate casino in downtown Las Vegas, two old fighter ships facing each other broadside with their cannons out.

The cashier looks over at the two bums arguing. Not the first time she's seen this type of thing. Accustomed to the dregs and down-and-outers of downtown with not much to do except survive, she's seen a few ne'er-do-wells go at it. She dispassionately watches the two strange fish argue, mild entertainment to help the late hours pass. Just another night in paradise.

"Don't play innocent with me," John says angrily. "Like I don't know what you're up to."

"Give your brain a rest, man. You talking nonsense again. Them shrimps got to your head."

"I saw you look inside that shrimp cocktail." John points accusingly at the glass.

"You're talking about this empty glass over here?" Ludo pulls John's glass over and looks inside. "Yeah, it's empty, so what?"

"Don't act like you didn't look inside to see if I left over any shrimps. I saw you pull over that glass. I'm sitting right here. It was right in front of my eyes."

"I was just tidying up the table a little bit," Ludo shoots back. "There's nothing wrong with a clean table." He crumples his napkin into a ball, and pushes it into the cocktail glass. "See, all cleaned up."

John and Ludo stare moodily at the empty shrimp cocktail glass with the crumpled napkin in it, neither looking at the other. If the cocktail glass had legs, it would pick itself up and change tables.

"Yo, maybe we're a little cranky, homes."

"You're right."

"No biggee, just some shrimp."

"Yeah, just some shrimp," John says, starting to get angry again. He opens his mouth to say something, but decides to let it go. No sense to continue arguing over this nonsense.

"Just some shrimp," Ludo repeats.

They look at each other a few seconds, the air heavy with tension, mentally digging in for another round of sparring over the ninety-nine-cent shrimp cocktails.

John looks hard at Ludo, tempted to say something after Ludo's last word on the shrimp, but decides not to take the bait. "There's another thing," John finally says, looking at the shrimp glass. "I think her ex was threatening me on the phone and that's why she broke us up. Maybe that's what it was. To protect me."

"Yeah? Why the hell she have us go up to that hotel room, not show up, and two hours later, they got every last dollar out of you and me? Huh? The last thing we see is that guy Harry with the contents of our wallets, like everything we got. We lucky we still got our skin and bones. If they weren't attached they would have taken them too. Damn! She should have started protecting you back then. We could have met her anywhere, a bar or a coffee shop, why there of all places? Unless we were set up. That's what I don't understand. It makes no sense to me."

"I just don't think that's what happened," John says.

"Is that right?"

John sits silently, looking down at his hands.

"Wait a second," Ludo says, looking intently at John. "What's this crazy thing you started talking about before? Don't be springing no more surprises on me. Better I find out now before things get worse."

John groans.

"Give," Ludo commands.

"Well, that guy, Harry."

"Yeah?"

"That's ZZ's ex."

Ludo looks at John to see if he's joking, but there is no humor in John's face. Ludo shakes his head silently, tapping his fingers on the table. Long seconds tick off the clock as Ludo digests this new piece of information. "You're shitting me?" Ludo finally says.

"She told me earlier. I couldn't believe it either."

Ludo bangs on the table and the two shrimp cocktail glasses jump. "If we didn't just get bamboozled by those two, then can I wake up from this nightmare? Hello! What the fuck do you think happened? We got fleeced like a couple of patsies, and the only thing we got left to our name is a couple of empty one-dollar shrimp cocktails, excuse me, ninety-nine-cent shrimp cocktails that we didn't even have enough money to pay for by ourselves. And we just finished them, so they ain't worth nothing now. Jesus Christ! What's wrong with this picture, homes? You tell me. If it wasn't for her, we wouldn't be neck deep in this shit."

"I know what you're looking at, but I just don't think she set us up. I mean, I don't know her that well or anything, but I do know her a little bit, and she really is a sweet girl inside."

"Sweet is not an adjective I would have picked."

"Hear me out," John says. "Somehow in her life, I mean, I don't know what happened, but she got mixed up with the wrong people and I guess I stumbled into that mess. It was only after I insisted we get together that she told me to meet her in that hotel room."

John lifts his water glass a few inches off the table, shakes it, and watches the water swirl around.

"She tried to get me to change the plans. That's a fact, Ludo. I just wish things had turned out different."

"Well, maybe it's for the better, homes. Things always seem to work out that way." Ludo stares at his hand and shrugs his shoulders. "What the fuck do I know anyway?"

"Things happen in life, maybe she's just got some serious problems she can't deal with, that's all."

"I think *we* got serious problems, if you ask me," Ludo says, getting riled up. "You better wake up to that one."

"I don't know what's going on exactly, but I bet her problems center around that ex."

"That two-legged slimy rat?"

"That's my guess. You know, sometimes in life, people get into trouble, and well, maybe they're not as good as you and me in getting out of it."

"Now, there's a convincing point," Ludo says. He looks at the empty shrimp cocktail glass with the crumpled napkin inside and at his friend's bedraggled appearance, shaking his head meditatively as he reflects on John's last thought. He then looks deeply into John's eyes. "Homes, what you don't quite seem to get is that we're fucked. I don't know how we could possibly get into more trouble or sink lower down in the levels of human worth. The only group of organisms in this town that aren't after us are stray fucking tail-less, three-legged, one-eyed street midget mongrels. And they don't even want anything to do with us. In the pecking order here, the only things lower than us are the ninety-nine-cent shrimp cocktails in this joint."

"Come on, L—"

"Hold up, homes, let me tell you something. You know you're in real trouble, forgetting anything else, when you count Virgil as one of the people around you that you like the most. Now that's fucked up."

"We agreed we were going to stay positive," John says. "In our situation, we have to make the best of things, and being negative is not going to help. You're the one always telling me that." He looks at the bags under Ludo's eyes and the dark shadows caused by sleeplessness and imagines he looks no better off.

"Being homeless, without money, and on the run from criminals, hoodlums, and lowlifes out to kill me usually makes me a little edgy. I mean, what the fuck are we going to do, wander the streets all night?" Ludo looks over to the food counter. The cashier is absentmindedly buffing its surface with a damp rag. "Alright, man, I'll drop it. We just gotta get some plan going. Something. Like some real chow, maybe a place to sleep—and I don't mean curbside housing or a cardboard box. But what you got to get through your head, homes, is that we're not only homeless, we're flat-out fucked."

John drops his head into his hands, letting the full gravity of their predicament settle in. They have no place to sleep and are without money, friends, and credit cards in this town, no options, especially in the middle of the night. Until Ludo mouthed the word "homeless," the thought hadn't really struck home.

Now it does.

"What do you suggest we do?" Ludo says into the top of John's bent head.

John moans from behind his hands in reply.

"Homes, that ain't doing us any good. It's tough enough as it is."

John lifts his head up, the bags under his eyes like old leather change purses. "I don't know, Ludo. I really don't know."

Ludo pulls the shrimp cocktail glass in front of him and is about to take another peek inside, but when he looks up and sees John glaring at him, he pushes it back to where it was.

There is a long silence as the two searchingly look at each other. Ludo opens his mouth to speak, but changes his mind and closes it.

"Alright, tell me, what is it?" John says after a long yawn.

"Man, we need a place to crash. Maybe you can call that girl of yours."

"That same one you said I shouldn't talk to again?"

"Desperate times."

"It's like, you know, one forty-five in the morning. I can't call this late."

"You gotta do something, homes. There's only so long we can camp out in the Garden of Eden here. The natives are getting restless." Ludo nods over to the wall by the casino area. A security guard has been watching them for a while and now conspicuously positions himself against a nearby wall, his muscular arms crossed, letting the two know that they may have exceeded their welcome. The burly man's gun prominently sticks out from his hip holster, and his uniform, of a starched light tan issue, is crisp. His grim demeanor sends a message in much the same way that pit bosses send messages to card-counting blackjack players the casino no longer wants at their tables. In the parlance of blackjack professionals, this is called "heat," unspoken signals that cross-armed, hard-staring, and firm-standing pit bosses, floormen, security guards, and upper management somewhat subtly, at least in the first stages, communicate to card counters, a warning that their next move will be throwing them out—forcefully, if necessary. Even the Golden Gate is only so grateful for a few spare dollars. And these two itinerants crowding the empty space are already pushing their luck.

John looks over at the security guard and shakes his head. "How am I going to call? We don't have any money."

"The house phone, man, local calls are free." Ludo points to a beige phone with a long dangling cord affixed to the wall just outside the eating area. "Just dial and let's hope she picks up."

"Her phone's busted."

"Homes, that was earlier. Maybe she fixed her phone or got a new one by now. Takes a few minutes in one of them stores. That ain't that hard to do. What's with you? Just try, it can't hurt. It's our only hope."

Ludo glances over at the guard. A second one has joined him and also watches them with folded arms.

John has misgivings about calling this late, especially considering their disastrous meeting in the mall, but knowing that they have no other shot at a room and a bed, he figures he's got to try something, no matter how desperate. He wearily gets up and walks to the house phone, the long dangling cord slightly swinging in its place. Both security guards watch his every step. Impulsively, like a six-year-old, John sticks his tongue out at them and wiggles both hands by his ears. The first guard, his annoyance spiked by this vagrant's puerile gesture, stiffens up and whispers to his colleague.

"Knock it off, homes," Ludo calls from the table. "We already in enough trouble. Just call her, man."

John picks up the phone handle. It is warm and clammy, as if it was just used by a person who held the phone too desperately in his grip. While he waits for the house operator to pick up the line, John turns his attention in the direction of a few stragglers playing at a nearby one-dollar minimum blackjack table. The Golden Gate, a friendly grind joint for locals and tourists with not much money to burn, deals modest-sized games, outlasting its patrons a few dollars at a time. The results are inevitable. If the casino doesn't get them one hour, they'll get them the next, or the following day, or the following month. Time is on the casino's side. The longer the clock ticks, the more the casino adds to its coffers.

"Hi," John says to the hotel operator when he hears her greeting, "can you connect me to an outside line?" John gives the woman the number and the connection is made. Each ring increases the tension John feels, ratcheting it up one more notch. His instincts tell him not to call, to hang up the phone, that this is the wrong time, but nothing seems to be at the right time on this trip. What if she's out and her ex-husband, for some reason, is with her? Or she has other special friends in town and is not alone this evening? Or if she's in the same dark mood as earlier when she flung her phone in the mall and told him it might be best they not see each other any more?

By the sixth ring, John is about to hang up when the line crackles with life. There is a long pause before John hears ZZ's greeting.

"Hello," ZZ says, her voice groggy and thick with sleep.

"Hey, this is John."

"Who?" ZZ says.

"Doc, John, you know, Doctor McDreamy. You forgot me already?"

"Oh, what's up, Doc? Did I miss an appointment?" ZZ says, thinking it was a reminder call from a physician. Her voice is distant, some thirty-seven winks away, as if this conversation is among complete strangers with nothing in common but a forthcoming doctor's visit.

"What's up, Doc—that's pretty funny," John says.

"Who is this?"

"It's Doc, you know, Doc," John repeats for lack of anything else to say.

"Oh," she says, her voice heavy.

"I'm just saying hello. I see you got your phone working again," John says, still not sure she knows it is him. ZZ doesn't say anything, so John continues. "I'm surprised you were able to glue all the pieces together so fast. You must have been good with models as a kid," he nervously adds.

"What?"

"The phone, you know, gluing the phone back together. Just a joke, sorry."

"Whatever," ZZ says dully. "Why are you calling so late?"

John doesn't feel comfortable broaching the subject about his homelessness and tries to buy a little time. "Do you think we can talk a little?"

"We are talking. What's the matter with you?"

"I mean, you have a few minutes. Is it okay to talk now?"

"It's the middle of the night, Doc. Is everything okay? You sound down."

"I just wanted to say hello."

"You already did that. Can't we talk in the morning?" ZZ's voice is slow and sounds like she could fall back asleep at any moment.

"I have to ask you something," John says.

"What is it?"

"Well, I just wanted to see how you're doing. I was thinking about you."

"You keep saying the same thing over and over again. Are you on one of those downer moods again? How do you expect anyone to be around you like this? Where are you?"

"I'm downtown, just walking around. Not doing much."

"You with that friend of yours, what is it, Pluto?"

"It's *Ludo*, not Pluto. He's a good guy."

"Pluto," ZZ repeats, her voice drifting.

Ludo calls over from the table in a loud whisper, "Come on, homes, stop jerking around. See if we can stay over there."

"Can I just ask you a little favor?" John says.

"You're like a broken record, saying the same things over and over again. Just call me in the morning, okay?" ZZ says, her voice sluggish and barely audible.

John hears the phone drop and scrape along the floor. ZZ has fallen asleep.

The two security guards have lost patience and escort John and Ludo out to the street, more flotsam and jetsam to float in the stream of life outside. A few dollars' worth of patronage will buy time and a leisurely chat in the Golden Gate's deli, but with these two thin bones sucked dry and clean, a few hours of stirring empty ninety-nine-cent shrimp cocktail glasses with little wooden sticks was pushing it. There are places for vagrants to congregate downtown; the Golden Gate is happy to help out for a while, but it is not a venue for the homeless to pass their time, especially when the particular dead-enders start arguing loudly about their empty shrimp cocktails—for the third time.

The air outside is stifling, as if someone has choked the oxygen out of the night and left John and Ludo gasping for the leftover scraps. They are weary from the last few couple of long and hard days and nights, the psychic weight of their energies a ball and chain manacled to their souls. They trudge down this street of neon lights and bright façades, seeing little but the despair around them and the even deeper despair within. Faced with the stark reality that they are penniless and have no place to go, outcasts to a society that used to welcome them, they move slowly, their tired legs feeling like they carry extra ballast on a portage that is already far too long and way too arduous. They move aimlessly past the small casinos and gift stores that line both sides of Fremont Street, impervious to the dazzling casino marquees flickering and shimmering in the night. They pause in front of the legendary Horseshoe Casino, birthplace of the venerable World Series of Poker. Here is where all-time great champions such as Doyle Brunson, Johnny Chan, Johnny Moss, Amarillo Slim, and Stu Ungar—who died miserably in a rent-by-the-hour motel room in a seedy section of Las Vegas—duked it out at the no-limit hold'em poker tables and played their way into poker history.

The tourists left milling about at this early-morning hour are lighthearted and laughing, or drunk and rowdy. The booze and the excitement of the gamble make them feel bigger while the cash is in play, like blow-up dolls pumped overfull with extra air. But when the last chip has been taken off the felt, it is like the air has leaked its way back out again, and the dolls shrink and shrivel until they are spent piles of old plastic, something that has been used up and no longer exhibits any recognizable form. With less money than they started with or all of it gone, flushed down the toilet of false hope, the gamblers' brief thrill at the gaming tables and machines is replaced by a quiet and soul-lonely desperation.

For gamblers, while the chips and coins are in play, the drudgeries of everyday life go away. It's about the gamble, a trigger of an atavistic urge that kick-starts the adrenaline juices when the bones are thrown, the cards are dealt, or the wheel of life's fantasy is spun. Action is the operative word. *Action.* Players pay the admission price, enter into the house of fun, and take their chances. And when they're done, they go back to where they're from, hungover perhaps, poorer for the excursion perhaps—or richer, with more acorns gathered into their pile—but satiated. Maybe over-satiated, filled, gorged, flagellated, and self-flagellated.

For locals making this a ritual, it is dead-end alley—stop and don't pass go—a game that ends when their paper money runs dry, the casino has all the green houses and red hotels, and their wallet is nothing but leather on leather, or more precisely, a dried out rubber band with no elasticity, though there is nothing left for it to hold anyway. They sleep with that harsh reality and wake up to it too, the new day bringing only more hours with the same nothing. Tourists out to have fun can take their drunken and happy bodies back to their lodgings at the end of the night and lay their heads on feather pillows in beds made and prepared for them, leaving the reality behind and taking the fantasy to their dreams. When they awaken, the morning sunshine brings the promise of a new day.

But this forlorn pair, John and Ludo, colored like clowns in blue jacket and red dress, no longer are a part of the feathered and made-bed world. They have been relegated to the side streets and dark alleys the tourists don't see, where the less fortunate congregate. This is a different part of Vegas, where the other half lives—the twenty-five-dollar-a-night flophouses filled with floozies, hustlers, pickpockets, petty thieves, whores, winos, weirdos, people down on their luck, deadbeats, misfits, vagrants, migrants, junkies, crackheads, tweakers, dealers, desperados, and degenerates. It's the side of the city where a dentist finds fewer teeth per mouth, lawns are weeds poking out from concrete slabs, and an evening's repast is likely to be cheap and fast—Big Macs, oversized hot dogs, greasy Chinese takeout, sixty-nine-cent tacos, and perhaps stale popcorn to accompany bottom-of-the-barrel beer in a cup.

And on this side of town where fewer teeth chew on cheaper food, Ludo and John can't even afford a flophouse. And desperation, in a town used to seeing so much of it, won't buy them special sympathy. Downtown is a place that sees them and their type day after day, an endless army of ants that, after a while, look like an endless army of ants. Move out a thousand, another thousand come in to replace them. One down-and-outer is the same as another, one sad tale may as well be another—the stories have all been heard over and over.

And no one wants to hear them again.

The pair wanders on silently, two war-weary soldiers on a long march to nowhere. Circling around a long, lonely block, they arrive back on Fremont Street among the stragglers still kicking air, and then push themselves down Casino Center Boulevard. For lack of a better idea, they enter the Golden Nugget casino. Earlier, the rush of cool air greeting them as they pushed through the doors would have been refreshing. Now, neither the hot nor the cold fazes them. They are the walking dead, marginal players hovering about like discarded paper scraps half floating and half sinking in a fetid pond.

A security guard eyes them, but they mean nothing to him one way or the other. He's seen these down-on-their-luck washouts every day for years. What's one more set of broken players to him?

The hapless duo wander past the lobby and turn right, passing aisles lined on both sides with slot machines before reaching the table games. They drift past a busy craps table, but the hollering, laughing, hooting, and inebriated energy of its players after a winning roll of the dice gets them even more depressed, so they trudge through the Fremont Street exit and return to the street. They walk a few blocks east on Fremont, away from the heart of downtown and its cluster of casinos, to where the crowds are thinner, humanity lives closer to the ground, and there is less to laugh about.

There is a casino there, the Green Clover, a rundown club that caters to locals who see their paychecks ground down week by week, never getting wise to the fact that their pursuit of the life-changing get-rich-quick win is buried so deep into the slot machines they play that they'll never see it in real life, no matter how many times that illusory vision appears in their daydreams and fantasies, and no matter how many times they push their sweaty bills and moist coins into the omnivorous beasts. The only thing that's going to change in their lives are the days of the calendar, each one peeled off after the other like an old movie showing the passage of time. The days pass from coin to coin, button to button, paycheck to paycheck, a slow march of minutes and hours. Time, precious time. Grinders play each week until their bankroll is sucked dry and then wait until their next paycheck when more funds will be available to piss out of their lives. One day these players will wake up to find another commodity missing, one that is not fungible and whose unit of currency is not measured in dollars, but in heartbeats. Tick by tick by tick. That is when their hearts stop beating and the game is over. The shells that hold their spirits will have emptied and turned stone cold dead.

Blinking white bulbs on the billboard outside the Green Clover advertise two beers for one dollar, a good deal down here. John and Ludo enter the casino's confines, but it is too cramped for the way they feel. They are in little mood to mingle or be jostled by crowds. And not being able to buy a beer, even at the bargain-basement prices available downtown, depresses them even further, so they push their way back out through the doors, their footsteps grinding harshly on the cement sidewalk. They just want to sleep, close their eyes, and let this whole nightmare disappear behind their lids. Being inexperienced at getting turned out of society, they don't know where or how to look for a place to get the shut-eye they so desperately need. John and Ludo are too despondent to even think of a plan and, as exhausted as they are, it is easier to walk than to stop, so they continue on like two mechanized zombies wound up and forced into the night.

"Let me tell you what I think," Ludo says, the first words either has spoken in many blocks.

"Yeah, what?"

"I don't know what the fuck I think. That's what I think."

They change directions, moving aimlessly, two plucked feathers shifting in the wind. Drawn by the lights, they head back toward the busier end of Fremont Street, where the downtown casinos butt one against the other—the Plaza, Golden Gate, Four Queens, Fitzgerald's, Las Vegas Club, Golden Nugget, Fremont, and Horseshoe.

They are most of the way down Fremont Street when a barker in front of a flashing sign that reads "Girls of Glitter Gulch" stops them. "Come on, big boy, free admission. Check it out. The most beau-ti-ful women in the world. And I said *beau-ti-ful*. Come on inside," the man intones in a deep and guttural baritone, the sound coming out as if chiseled and tuned from the smoke of a lifetime of high-nicotine cigarettes.

"I don't know," John says to him.

The barker, a short man in his forties dressed in a tuxedo, grabs hold of John's upper arm and pulls him closer. From up close, the pomade on his hair glistens black with shades of deep blue reflecting off the neon above. A mole just above his left eye catches the red and flashes like a stoplight. The man doesn't even look twice at Ludo in the red dress and floppy hat. He's seen it all on these streets—transvestites, hermaphrodites, homosexuals, butches, bestialists, sadists, masochists,

pimps, queens, and cross-dressers of every stripe and color. To the
barker, they are one and the same as anyone else, just different-colored
fish in the same night tank, competing for the same food tossed into
their water. The bigger and stronger fish snatch the larger flakes by the
top, grabbing the best morsels for themselves; the scrapers and bottom-
feeders take whatever is left over that sinks to the bottom—the crumbs,
the dregs, the refuse. This pair of tetras, in their blue jacket and red
dress, apparently didn't get the bigger flakes.

"Come on in," the barker says to John. "Bring your girlfriend.
Enjoy the rich sights of downtown, the music, the most beau-ti-ful
women in the world. Check it out, my fine friends, you've got nothing
to lose. I repeat, you have nothing to lose by having a gander."

"He's got a point," Ludo says, and the two walk by him and into
the club, figuring that, if nothing else, they can soak in some air-
conditioning and take a load off their feet. They pass through a dark
velvet curtain split in half and enter into a large room filled with the
dank air of old beer and stale cigarette smoke. After the bright lights
that make the night seem like day outside, it is hard to see anything
except the few dimly lit bulbs that reflect off their corneas. John and
Ludo stand next to one another as their eyes adjust, feeling like two
strangers who have intruded yet again into someone else's premises,
where, likely as not, they will not be welcomed.

About a dozen girls are lounging about and only a few customers,
so when they walk in, they are eyed rapaciously by a few of the dancers
looking to bump and grind their way out of this slow night with at least
a few more bucks. These new visitors don't look like they have much,
but when Las Vegas Vinnie is able to entice some bait into the club
from Fremont Street, the circling fish have to at least see if the chum is
worth taking off the hook.

It is already past three in the morning, and John and Ludo drag
themselves forward like two disillusioned and lost hikers on an endless
march they wish they had never undertaken. Worn down from one
defeat after another, they can barely scrape enough energy together to
shuffle their feet forward, let alone ogle any night birds in this dark
club. On another night these girls might have drawn some interest from

them, but tonight, the best-looking bottoms in this club are not of the flesh-toned and shapely variety, but flat and of a dark red hue—the empty and inviting soft-cushioned chairs. Seeing two plush candidates nearby, they drop into them as if the chairs were the holy grail of body-relieving comfort. As their worn frames soak in the padding of the seats and their legs get welcome release from carrying their loads, the two sigh with relief.

Three girls extract themselves from a nearby bar and walk over. An overly thin girl with stringy yellow hair and large firm breasts pushing out from a diaphanous halter top arrives first. She positions herself behind Ludo and starts rubbing his shoulders. The brunette next to her, a tired-looking girl with pouting lips and worn-out blue eyes, sits on Ludo's lap and grabs one of his hands, playing with him like he is her long-lost little doll that grew up, and here, after all these long years, has come back to say hello. The third girl, on the far side of thirty pounds overweight and with a face devoid of any enthusiasm, coos at John like he's her little lovebird that has come back to the nest. It doesn't take long, just two or three minutes, for the girls to realize that these are just a couple of dead sticks with no leaves on them, barren twigs with no fruit to drop. They retreat back to the bar, lazily making their way across the floor with fluid, smooth movements like cigarette smoke wafting out of an ashtray. Another girl walks by, eyeing them like a hungry mouse sniffs at cheese, but she passes without a try, seeing that what's left is just rind and wax.

Soon, it is management's turn to have a look. Realizing that these two deadbeats aren't going to part with anything but soiled oxygen, a burly manager in a tuxedo moves them out swiftly and firmly to churn with the dwindling masses back on the street, and to let them blow their broke and discarded air out where no one else has to breathe it.

The barker eyes them on the way out. He knows the score and throws them a friendly wink. "Come back some other time, fellas," Las Vegas Vinnie says, his deep, baritone voice magisterial and rich, like an actor who could command an entire audience with his majestic vocal cords.

Across the street, two drunk men in their early twenties weave their way out of a casino, and the barker, seeing more fish to reel in, bellows out to them.

"Walk on over here, my friends, and see the most beau-ti-ful girls in the world. The most *beau-ti-ful*."

John and Ludo turn away from the strip club and rub their eyes against the bright neon casino lights of Fremont Street, two pariahs churned out once again by security. Desperate for a place, any place, with air-conditioning to take the heat out of the night and a chair to rest their weary bones, they continue their downtown migration, looking for a low-key shelter of some sort that might allow them time to reconnoiter their predicament. The precipitous downward spiral has driven John and Ludo so far below the line of where they'd ever imagined, and they have become so quickly accustomed to its vagaries, that they have become part and parcel of the rejectamenta of downtown Las Vegas.

In short, two bums.

It is approaching four in the morning when this forlorn duo, who find unwelcome signs at every turn, drop into a pair of chairs in the front row of the keno lounge in the Five Aces Casino, a few blocks east of the main casinos on Fremont Street. Three long rows of chairs face the counter, behind which a monotone-voiced keno teller does the double duty of calling games and taking bets.

The only other player in the lounge, also in the front row but on the opposite end, is an old man with a five-day growth of gray whiskers. He is bent over like a miner who has spent fifty years working coal in a cramped shaft, and now, half a century later, has been spit out like a dried chicken bone with its skin, sinews, and fleshy meat picked clean and sucked off. He slowly works his way up to the counter on arthritic bowed legs, moving as much sideways as forward like a two-legged upright crab, and his eyes, clouded with a soft film, seem in desperate need of cataract surgery. One old gnarled hand, rimmed with protruding veins, pushes a keno ticket to the clerk along with a crumpled one-dollar bill that looks like it has been fished out from his socks. But that's clearly not the case, as this piker wears no socks, and his shoes, cracked black leatherette wrapped around his bony ankles, barely hold together enough to even be called shoes.

The keno clerk takes the dollar without emotion, processes the bet, and pushes back a marked duplicate, the man's receipt for the game.

John watches the old-timer slowly ease himself back into a chair with an audible groan and wonders how many keno tickets this geezer has played in his life, or even in the last few days. He speculates that the man spends the entirety of every Social Security check on rent, keno tickets, and cat food. If the casino would allow it, the man's food stamps would likely go toward a keno ticket as well; as it is, the keno games for this compulsive piker are vapor dreams that dissipate daily into the stale casino air, and leave him with nothing more than he started. But as down and out as the old-timer might be, John doesn't think of him as being a bum, just another down-and-out guy like himself and Ludo trying to catch some luck in the keno lounge. Actually, the real truth, as John sees it, is that the old-timer has it better; at least he has a few bucks to play with to try to catch a break, while he and Ludo sit there empty-handed. Presumably, when the old-timer walks out of the keno lounge, he has a place to go, regardless of how lowly that dwelling might be, which is a lot more than they have going for themselves.

John and Ludo listlessly watch endless cycles of numbers light up on the keno board as game after game after game is played. Every third game, the old man, either due to superstitions surrounding the number three, his budget for lasting all night at the game so he has a place to be, or simply the amount of walking his legs could sustain between breaks, would crab his way to the counter and push another bet across its surface.

"Homes," Ludo whispers.

"What?"

"Is that what I think I see?" Ludo points to the floor at the base of the keno counter. Next to an old newspaper and littered among a few discarded keno tickets is a partially obscured five-dollar bill.

John's eyes glitter with light like a video poker player who has just seen his machine kick out a royal flush. He pulls himself into a standing position and starts toward the money. But before he can get there, the old man, who had seen Ludo point as well, springs out of his chair. Moving surprisingly fast for a cripple, he outraces John to the bill, and firmly stamps his foot on it. The old geezer, his face unshaven and grizzled, and with a full head of thinning and unkempt white hair, looks up at John and opens his mouth wide. It appears to be a grin, though John cannot be sure. There is not a tooth in the man's mouth, and what resides in that dark orifice John cannot make out or even want to imagine. The geezer starts laughing, a nickering wheeze that rattles off the phlegm in his throat.

John stares at the toothless old creature, his foot tightly clamped on the five-dollar bill. It is another humiliating defeat in his newfound and downtrodden life, and he returns to his chair in the same condition he left it: exhausted, broke, and with a feeling somewhere between despair and disgust. He watches the old man slowly and painfully bend down to pick up the bill and then head over to the counter to bet it all on one keno ticket.

"We have no goddamned luck in this town," John mutters to himself, still staring at the spot where the old man, ever alert for any possibility of advancing his meager means, beat him to the bill, testament to the crusty geezer's many years of survival skills and a truth known on the streets down here: When you're down and out, experience is a better asset than youth.

A security guard, who has been watching the luckless pair for a while and has had enough, walks over and plants himself in front of John. "Buddy, this area is for keno players only. Why don't you take a walk?" He stands there with hands on his hips, his chest puffed out with machismo and tight against his uniform.

John is thinking of a reply—but he's too tired to be clever, let alone bicker with this bloated turkey—when, in the cup holder of the chair where the keno crayons and tickets are kept, he sees a shiny object that appears to be a coin. Pushing aside a bent rate book and a discarded ticket, John fishes out exactly what he thought he saw, a silver dollar.

Like a little boy showing off his entrance ticket to the fair, he holds it up for the guard to see.

"We're playing!" John exclaims, tapping the coin against the armchair for emphasis. He slowly walks over to the window, randomly marks off nine numbers on a keno ticket, and hands it to the teller with his one dollar. John returns and falls heavily in the seat next to Ludo, wiggling the marked ticket in the air for the benefit of the security guard to prove that he's a player who deserves that seat.

"I'm keeping an eye on you," the security guard says, moving away. He crosses to the edge of the lounge, and banking his head sharply from side to side, works out some kinks. Feeling good after flexing his arms and checking the tightness of his biceps, the guard daydreams about pushing it hard the next day at the gym and pumping up his biceps another notch. After a last glance at the sorry pair, he returns to his rounds on the casino floor. He'll be back in a while to check on these two.

"It was our only dollar! What'd you do that for?" Ludo cries.

"What else are we going to do with one miserable dollar? I'm so tired," John says, his eyes heavy with sleep. "And we need these seats." He leans back in the chair, his body melting into the fabric, and closes his eyes.

Ludo glances over at the old man. The geezer is leaning forward and squinting at something behind the keno clerk. Ludo follows his line of vision and sees numbers light up on a squarish board and realizes that the game has begun.

"Fifteen, seventeen, seventy-three, two, sixty-six," Ludo reads off. "What numbers we got? Yo, homes."

John opens his eyes. "What? I have no idea. Here, you check it out." John hands him the ticket and leans forward, resting his chin on his hand and closing his eyes. He is just getting comfortable when a sharp elbow from Ludo jolts him back to consciousness.

"We won, we won!"

"You're kidding?" John says, his eyes closing tight.

"Yeah, we hit a number."

"Oh," John groans, "one number is not enough. Give me five minutes."

Ludo pushes John again.

"One is not enough, I told you that," John says irritably, opening his eyes.

"No, we got six right. It says on the pamphlet that we won fifty-eight dollars. It's a special promotion this month on playing nine numbers."

"Fifty-eight dollars? What the hell we gonna' do with those crumbs? We need real money. Throw it away," John mumbles as he slumps over. Within seconds, he is back asleep.

Ludo collects the money at the counter and declines the invitation to replay the ticket. He pockets the fifty-eight dollars and drops back down in the seat next to John. Soon, closing his eyes as well, Ludo is deep into his dreams, floating along with soothing visions of waves as they roll into shore, one after another, a pleasant memory from a trip he took to Hawaii with a girlfriend some years earlier.

Ten minutes later the security guard returns to the lounge. He waves to the keno caller, who tiredly nods back, and goes over to the two slumping patrons, who are fast asleep. A keno crayon hangs precariously between Ludo's middle and ring fingers, and a few keno tickets, unmarked, are scattered on his lap. He is snoring loudly, resting peacefully on a beach in Maui. John opens his eyes momentarily and stares blankly ahead at the security guard, as if not noticing him. He is in the middle of a different type of dream, a disturbing one: ZZ is alone in a dark room with a weak bulb barely illuminating the dank walls, and there are bars on the door. Solitary confinement. She sits on a cold floor, hair matted and disheveled, malnourished, rail-thin arms jutting out of prison garb. Her face is drawn and stained with tears. She has just exhausted herself crying and screaming into the darkness, and now, with burning tears running down her face, repeats over and over in a despairing, helpless voice, "Why did they do this to me?"

Just as John's eyes close again, he feels something kick his feet.

"Get up. You can't sleep here."

John opens his eyes and sees the security guard standing over him with his feet squared and his hands on his hips. John is groggy and about to close his eyes again when his repose is again interrupted by a kick on his feet.

"And tell your buddy to get out of here as well."

John nudges Ludo.

"What?" Ludo says with eyes closed. John nudges him again, a little harder.

———————

It is past four-thirty in the morning on their sojourn through downtown when John and Ludo are unceremoniously escorted out of the casino, the third time they have been kicked out of a downtown establishment on this long, oppressive, and torturous night-turned-early morning. The security guard, only too glad to do something to break the monotony of the graveyard shift, walks them all the way to the exit, giving them a little shove at the door when they reluctantly stall in its threshold. The hapless duo stands just outside the casino, dead-tired, and with no clue which way to turn or where to go. Ludo looks up into the glare of a bright streetlight and beyond it to the dark sky filled with stars, aware of how far out of his reach those stars are for him. Heck, even earthly things seem to be beyond his grasp. John looks down, examining his own shadow cast by the casino's neon lights, fascinated by the insignificance of the small dark area created by his presence. Near and far, at a darkened spot in the cement and at the glistening stars of the heavens, the pair stands there ruminating, the minutes eating away at them.

Lost in Las Vegas.

Noticing that the bums haven't moved from out front, the security guard sticks his head out the door. "Move it," he says.

Like robots following a programmed command, the two stragglers amble across the street and down a few blocks. Seeing a two-foot-high cinder block dividing wall, they sit and through bloodshot eyes look at the dark asphalt of the street in front of them. A black cat warily looks at John and Ludo, giving them a wide berth as it passes by.

"We got to get out of this town," Ludo says, shaking his head and watching the cat continue down the street. Bad enough with all the thirteens that find them—Ludo doesn't want to add to his friend's own dark thoughts by mentioning the significance of a black cat crossing their path.

John sits quietly and plucks a stray hair off his pants. He lets it catch a breeze and watches it take off in a swirling motion.

"We got fifty-eight bucks, homes, enough for a hotel. Let's just grab something and close our eyes."

"What, are you nuts? We get a big windfall like this and now you think we're millionaires?"

Ludo scratches his head, the words "windfall" and "millionaires" juxtaposed with their desperate situation as wandering vagabonds in downtown Las Vegas befuddling his thought processes. He kicks his foot, loosing a stray paper that has blown against it, and watches it sally past him down the street in the direction of John's recently freed hair, discarded jetsam off to play in the winds, glad to be detached from their homeless way stations.

"I can see," John continues, "how all this money changes the way you think. You've become blinded by all the riches. It's a typical syndrome of people, who, like us, suddenly come into money."

Ludo looks at John—the dark bags under his eyes, the lines creasing his forehead, his slumped shoulders—and reconciles this against his friend's words. "You out of your mind, homes? What riches you talking about?"

"Trust me, I've read about this, people who can't deal with big money. Like those athletes who start out in the slums and suddenly get multimillion-dollar contracts. They don't know how to deal with it and lose it all. Right now, we can't afford that kind of luxury. That stack of bills we got is our ticket out of town."

"We can't afford it? Man, it's like twenty-five bucks or something for some old el cheapo room. We got fifty-eight. I've got to get some sleep, man. I'm so damned tired. No, not tired, wasted. We can't keep going like this."

"So we go a little longer without some sleep. We have to think long term. We need that money for getting us on a bus and getting us out of here."

"Fifty-eight dollars ain't getting us on a bus back home."

"Maybe not, but it's just not worth paying all that money just to close our eyes for just a few hours," John says. "That would cost us about half of what we got. And for a fleabag? We're above that. Come on, Ludo."

"All that money? We're talking chump change!" Ludo pulls the money out of his pocket and shakes it around. "Get a good look at this, homes. Fifty-eight dollars. That's it. All of this ain't much, and half of this is half of ain't that much. At this point, we ain't above nothing."

John takes the money from Ludo's hand and waves it in his friend's face. "This windfall is ruining you, my friend. I can't let that happen. I read too much about this, I've seen it in my business with clients that waste good money with frivolities they could do without. Lucky for us, I can steer us through these tough waters with experience, a clear head, and sound fiscal principles. I just can't let this windfall destroy everything we've just built up."

Ludo stares at John, his eyes bloodshot and ringed by dark circles.

"I have to look out for you, Ludo," John continues. "The stress has clearly taken its toll. You're not thinking rationally. The money has gone to your head and made your brain drunk. We're probably better off ripping this up and throwing it away. I would make that sacrifice for you, my good friend."

Before John can get his other hand on the money, Ludo, who has visions of feather pillows, a thick mattress, and a steaming plate of Chinese food flash through his head, quickly snatches the bills from John's hand and stuffs them safely back into his pocket.

"Homes, you were actually going to rip up the money?"

"Ludo, just throw it away. Let's get that stress out of our lives. Hey, you taught me that."

Ludo looks at his friend. "What the hell you talking about with all this gibberish?"

A grinding noise erupts behind them, the prolonged rattle of metal, and they both turn to look.

"It sounds like the sprinklers," Ludo says.

John looks up at the dark sky, tracing the outline of the Big Dipper, and starts laughing.

"What's so funny, man? I don't get the joke."

There is more grinding from behind, like rusty cylinders banging against each other, and Ludo again turns to see.

"Don't you get it?" John says.

"Get what, man? Only thing I get is that we're being hunted like dogs with a disease, we're homeless, and we're lucky if we get out of this town alive. What the fuck is there to get?"

"It. All that!"

"You're fucked up, man."

The sprinklers come to life, raining water down on them in a high arc. John and Ludo hop off the cinder block dividing wall and out of reach of the cascade of water, their hair dripping wet, their shirts soaked to the skin. John points up at the rivulets of water coming off Ludo's hair and onto his shirt, shrugs his shoulders, and begins to laugh again. Ludo still doesn't get the joke, but he laughs as well.

Soon, John and Ludo are laughing hysterically, tears rolling out of their eyes.

"What the fuck is so funny?" Ludo says.

Chapter Twenty-Eight

Ludo sits in a smoky haze among chain-smoking gamblers in the sports book of the Lucky Charm Casino, crossing and uncrossing his legs. Every few seconds, he impatiently looks in the direction where his best friend went fifteen minutes earlier to see about the cost of getting plane tickets out of town. He is long past caring that he looks odd wearing a dress in public—and a badly wrinkled one at that; in fact, he is so worn down by the implosion of his life over the past forty-eight hours that he's not even cognizant that he is wearing one. After a night living like a bum, he starts to feel like one, thinking more about what he has to do to survive in Las Vegas than what he looks like doing it. The small sports area is squeezed in among the rest of the casino's offerings, appearing to be more like an afterthought to the original design. One large projection television, positioned in the middle of a wall, shows highlights of the day's baseball games. On either side of this screen, mounted with heavy steel brackets, are three smaller monitors displaying various sporting events the casino is able to pick up on cable. Seven tiny, round cocktail tables are laid out in front of the screens, exactly as many tables as there are televisions. Two or three chairs made of pressed wood are clustered around each of them. On the opposite end from Ludo, five locals are bunched around two tables they have pulled together, drinking Coors out of cans and watching a baseball game, a Dodgers-Giants rerun from the evening before.

Normally, Ludo is easily entertained by baseball, but the calamitous collapse of this vacation weighs on him. He feels edgy, the rhythm of his thinking out of kilter. A long sleepless night aimlessly wandering downtown and getting kicked out of casinos and clubs like a degenerate has done little to improve his outlook. This following a night in which he barely slept and another when he didn't sleep at all. Being broke, hunted, and facing disappointment and defeat at every turn didn't help either. At least the lucky keno win gave them enough money to buy food, but it was only a sampling, a taste that gave him a ravenous yearning for more. They had compromised and limited their expenditure to just five dollars between them, including tip, sharing a day-old croissant and a juice that tasted more like the plastic it was packaged in than the orange derivative it advertised on the label. This purchase had reduced their bankroll to fifty-three dollars, a stake that John hoped to build upon.

John and Ludo had taken on a look of sorts, and rather than blending in seamlessly with crowds it was the opposite—they stuck out like two dull-colored caricatures marring a bright and colorful drawing.

Ludo spots John farther down the casino, finally, walking slowly toward him. John's blue blazer is badly wrinkled and has taken on a darker hue, as if a paste of dirt, sweat, and the burden of a long night had redyed the fabric. Like Ludo, he sports a three-day-old growth of beard and heavy, bagged eyes. The thirty seconds it takes for him to reach the sports bar seem like long minutes to Ludo, who stands up as John approaches, an anxious expression on his face.

"Well?" Ludo says.

"Plane tickets are one hundred and sixty-nine dollars each, three hundred and thirty-eight dollars total. That's what it will take."

"You said one hundred and sixty-nine dollars each?"

"One-six-nine, yes, for each of us."

"One hundred and sixty-nine?"

"Yes, Ludo. How many times do I have to tell you the same thing; one hundred and sixty-nine dollars? What's so hard to understand about that?"

Ludo looks hard at John, his face creased in deep thought, and shakes his head. "I don't like that number."

"What's wrong with you now? That number happens to be our ticket out of town."

"You didn't say one hundred and sixty-eight or one hundred and seventy? You said one hundred and sixty-nine."

"Yeah, so?"

"One hundred and sixty-nine happens to be thirteen multiplied by thirteen. It's a curse, man. Some kind of bad mojo, dark magic, dead chicken, black cat, thirteen-mongering Las Vegas voodoo witchcraft on us we can't escape no matter what we do. And now them thirteens are multiplying by themselves, propagating all over the place like some mutant disease or something."

"Ludo, thirteen is just a number, nothing less, nothing more."

"Numbers just ain't numbers, especially when a thirteen is blowing its hex all over us. Them thirteens like some psychotic bad luck plaguing everything we do on this trip." Ludo mumbles something additional under his breath that John cannot make out.

"Never mind, this whole conversation is ridiculous." John waves his right hand to dismiss the discussion. "I don't know why I always argue math and logic with a guy that's superstitious."

"This ain't math, home boy, that's what you don't get. This is *numbers*. You may know your math, but I know my numbers. You always looking at what you see and can never see what you can't see."

"How can you see what you can't see? That makes no sense."

"See, that proves it. Right there you make my point. You can't even see it."

"See what?" John says incredulously. "How can I see what I can't see? Can you see *it*?"

"Of course I can't see it. But I can see it."

"Why don't I learn?" John says to himself, throwing up his hands.

"Well, like it or not, Ludo, one hundred and sixty-nine dollars—one-six-nine—that's what the ticket costs. How much we got?"

"Fifty-three dollars, Mr. Math. Now we need a way to turn fifty-three dollars into three hundred and thirty-eight dollars. We gotta figure that one out."

"If we can get unlucky, maybe we can get lucky too. It can work both ways. Luck balances itself out. All I know is that we have to get out of this town—and soon."

"I hear you on that, homes. I just don't like them thirteens all over the place on us; more scary when they be multiplying with each other like they some kind of freak aliens or something."

John is about to say something, thinks better of it, and runs both his hands over his face, taking a respite from the world for a few seconds.

———————

John is marching up and down the long row of blackjack tables at the Four Queens Hotel and Casino in downtown Las Vegas, observing the various tables in action. He is two paces ahead of his friend when Ludo rushes forward and puts a firm hand on his shoulder, stopping him in his tracks.

"Will you pick out a goddamned game already, homes?" Ludo says. "You been up and down these tables like fifty times."

"Only twice."

"Three times, homes. You been procrastinating all over the place. Look, we don't have a lot of time before we too late to get those tickets and get on the plane. Take this one here," Ludo says, indicating the table in front of them. "We got to get out of here and our only chance is if you play. Stop fooling around. We can't win by you walking a hole in the carpet."

"You can't just play at the first table you see."

Ludo slaps himself on the forehead. "The first table you see? You been looking at every table like a dizzy banana. What's wrong with this one?"

"I don't know. A table has to feel right."

"I thought you were all about math, homes. What? We got to sit cross-legged on a floor with a Ouija board to figure this out?"

"That's something else."

"You're something else," Ludo says, pushing John forward toward a table. "Stop fooling around and take this one."

"But Ludo—"

"This one's good. It feels right to me. Just sit down and if the guillotine is going to have our heads, let's get it over with already."

John sighs and pulls back a chair, occupying the center seat directly in front of the dealer. He pushes fifty-three crumpled dollars forward, all their money. The dealer spreads the bills across the table so it is clearly visible to the eye in the sky above, then collects them together and deposits them into the drop box to his right. He plucks two green twenty-five dollar chips from the rack in front of him, places them next to three blue one-dollar chips he extracts from the same source, and pushes them across the table to John.

"Good luck, sir," the dealer says.

Two other players are seated at the table. The player to John's right, a frail-looking, white-bearded man in his seventies, pushes out one black chip as his bet. To his left, in the third-baseman's seat—the last position to get cards before the dealer takes his allotment—a man flamboyantly attired in an electric-blue dress shirt with the two top buttons undone and a jet-black silk blazer sits with almost a dozen stacks of black and canary-yellow chips in front of him, coolly watching the action. Two pit bosses positioned behind the table carefully watch every move of the player seated at third base, now and then whispering among themselves.

Ludo, in his red dress and floppy hat, leans over John's shoulder and mentally adds up the third-baseman's table stake. The black chips, piled high in multiple stacks, are worth a hundred dollars each, and the canary yellow chips, stacked in three smaller piles of uneven height, are worth one thousand per chip. "That dude must have twenty, thirty thousand dollars there. You see that?" Ludo whispers, ogling the wealth of chips.

"The only thing I see is that we need to get out of here before we get killed. That's what I see."

"Okay then, bet it all, man, let's just do it," Ludo says.

"No, Ludo, you can't just bet it all on one hand. That's too impulsive for a correct long-term strategy. Trust me, I know all about this. Remember, I've been studying those blackjack books."

"What long-term you talking about? If Knuckles or Versachi catch up to us, or the police, long term has a short-term meaning, you know what I'm saying? Besides, if we're going to get on that plane, we got forty-five minutes to get this done or we ain't getting out of here today. Everything's booked, there's only that one flight available. And if we don't make it, that ain't good."

The dealer, a tall man well over six and a half feet in height with a name tag that identifies him as "Bert" has been waiting for John to place a bet and finally says, "You gentlemen care to make a wager?" His voice is smooth and the fingers of his right hand, the one not holding the deck, dance in the air.

John pushes three dollars worth of chips onto the betting spot in front of him. "Let's just get our feet wet first," John says to the dealer.

"Excuse me, sir." The dealer points to a placard. It reads *Fifty Dollar Minimum*. "The dollar table is that one over there," Bert says nodding to the next table on John's right. "If the duckling wants to wet his feet, I suggest he stays out of the big duck pond over here."

Ludo whispers to John, "Don't take that crap. Bet the fifty. Show him who's got the big money!"

John runs his thumb up the side of the three blue chips, letting each chip click on the one below. He looks over at the bettor on his left and sees several thousand dollars in the betting circle, a large bet even for that player, then at the dealer, who is watching him. John removes the three dollars from the betting circle and pushes out his two green chips instead, making a fifty-dollar bet.

"That's it, man, let it fly," Ludo says.

"Don't break the bank, boys," Bert says as he gives two cards to each player and himself.

The player with the large stack of chips to John's left turns over a blackjack and gets paid off immediately. The dealer stacks a few piles of yellow and black chips next to the bet, paying him at three to two on his wager. The flamboyantly dressed man in the electric-blue shirt pulls the chips back in front of him and neatly adds them to the top of his stacks.

It's John and Ludo's turn. They have two tens, good for a hand of twenty, and the dealer shows a six as his upcard. John confidently slides the cards under his chips, signaling that he'll stand with his total.

"Excellent, a twenty!" John says. "You like *those* numbers, Ludo?"

"That's good then?"

"That's very good. Start counting your chickens." The two slap each other five.

"I'll work with you on that number then," Ludo says. "Cock-a-doodle-doo!"

"That's a rooster."

"Rooster just a chicken with a funny beard, that's all."

The tired-looking player to John's right stands pat with his hand, slipping his cards under his chips, and now it is the dealer's turn. Bert turns over his downcard, a five. He has eleven points.

"Damn!" John mutters. If the dealer draws one of the many ten-value cards in the deck—a ten, jack, queen, or king—he'll have a twenty-one and they will lose everything but their three blue one-dollar chips.

Bert, moving slowly for the maximum dramatic effect, turns over a two. He has thirteen points, and by the rules of the game, he must draw again.

"The dreaded thirteen," Ludo says. "We're screwed."

"That thirteen is good, not bad. Any nine or above, we bust him and we win."

"Them thirteens are never good—you can't seem to get that through your head. We're cursed with that number; it don't leave us."

John and Ludo tensely watch the action. The dealer turns over an eight, for a perfect twenty-one. John and Ludo watch, horrified, as Bert collects their fifty-dollar bet.

"Tell me that didn't happen," John says. He stares blankly at the empty betting circle, his eyes glued to the spot where the two green chips had resided as if staring long enough would replay the hand in his favor and make the chips come back.

The dealer collects the losing hands from the table and joins them with the discards in the clear plastic tray to his right. He begins shuffling the cards with fanciful flourishes and sharp riffles, putting on a show as he mixes the cards with great fanfare. Bert's hands move fluidly, and the cards, like magic, flow between them.

"You two are bad luck. I can feel it," says the frail-looking player on first base as he collects his chips and leaves the table.

John looks up plaintively, as if beseeching the gods hidden in the eye in the sky, and says out loud to no one in particular, "All we asked for was one card. That's it. And we can't even get that. This town can't even give us one lousy, crummy, crappy, puny, pathetic, miserable little card. Not one!"

John drops his head, mumbling quietly to himself. His reverie is interrupted by the dealer, who is waiting on him.

"What did you say?" John says.

"Your play, duckie." Two cards have been dealt to John, and Bert is pointing at them indicating that it is his turn to play. Two green chips are on his betting spot. He has been dealt a twenty, and the dealer shows an ace.

"I thought we lost. Where did that come from?" John asks.

Bert jerks his head toward the third baseman, the man with the stacks of black and canary yellow chips. John looks over at the man, speechless.

"Wow, man, thanks," Ludo says.

The third baseman coolly stares ahead, a wry smile barely perceptible on his lips.

The dealer sings out, "Innn-surance?" The completion of the first syllable of "insurance" takes a full three seconds for him to finish enunciating and another two for the rest of the word to follow gracefully along. Bert's voice is melodic, like a professional actor gracefully performing songs in a stage production number. He looks at John to see if he elects to make the insurance wager. John shakes his head no.

"No blackjack, no blackjack, no blackjack," John chants softly, invoking his best mantra for good luck.

The third baseman lifts two fingers and shakes them side to side, a universal blackjack signal letting the dealer know that he doesn't want insurance either.

Bert checks his hole card and looks up at John as if he has bad news. "Blackjack," Bert says crisply.

"Bullshit!" John screams out. He pushes his chair from the table, disheartened and angry with the dealer's automatic win. He gets up and turns from the table. "That's bullshit!" The money is lost and all their hopes are ruined. Everything. That's it. John doesn't have the heart for it anymore. He can't take another defeat. Versachi, Knuckles, whoever, whatever. They can have him already.

" . . . is not in the cards," the dealer calls loudly after him.

John stops in his tracks. "What did you say?" John asks, turning.

"No blackjack," Bert sings out, smiling broadly at his own joke. "Sit down and play on. Your hand is still live, duckie. Let's have your decision."

Stunned, and with his heart still racing, John returns to his seat and picks up his cards. He has been dealt a ten and a five for a fifteen. He takes a deep breath and looks at Ludo. Not good. He scrapes his cards against the felt surface, indicating a hit, and he receives an ace. Sixteen points.

"We have to go for it," John says resignedly.

"You sure, homes?"

"No choice; we have to play the percentages."

John taps on the table and another card is dealt. It's a four, and once again John has a twenty. It is the dealer's turn. Bert turns over a five. The ace can count as one point or eleven, but either way the dealer has to draw again with this hand of soft sixteen. He deals himself a ten and now has a hard sixteen, less than the seventeen points required for a dealer to stand. Accordingly, Bert deals himself another card. It is a four. He also has twenty points and the hands are tied.

"*Puuush*," sings Bert for a full four seconds, the word hanging in the air like morning fog on the coast.

"We can't even win with a goddamn twenty!" John cries.

"We lose?" Ludo asks.

"A push, a tie. We didn't lose, but we should've won. He had a twenty, again, and we didn't win. No goddamned luck. None at all. It's just ridiculous."

Ludo edges to the table and moves the bet to a spot in front of him. "Let me try, maybe it will change our luck."

Bert deals Ludo an ace and a seven. He gives himself a ten of spades for an upcard. Ludo looks at John for guidance.

"I'm not sure what to do. I can't remember," says John.

"Think man, think. You're always reading that book by that blackjack guy," Ludo says. "What does that book say to do?"

"*Todaaaay*," the dealer calls out and taps the spot in front of Ludo.

John looks over at the player with the large pile of chips. He looks back at John's cards passively, his expression unreadable. The man with the chips then scratches the felt subtly with his finger, the signal in blackjack letting dealers know that a player wants another card.

"*Tooooo-dayyyyyyyyyyy*," Bert sings in the air.

"Take a card. Now I remember!" John exclaims, getting the hint. "The book says to hit soft eighteen against a ten. Ask for a card, Ludo."

Ludo signals for another card and Bert deals him one.

"You got a three," John says excitedly. "We have a perfect twenty-one!"

"Throw a screwball on them cards," Ludo implores the dealer as John flips his eyes skyward.

The third baseman stands. The dealer nimbly turns over his downcard, a ten. He again has a twenty, a very strong hand, but a loser to Ludo's twenty-one. Bert places the fifty dollars in winnings next to Ludo's bet.

"That's one hundred dollars! Hoooooome run!" Ludo screams out, and he and John high-five each other. "That Cardoozi or Cardini or whatever the name of that guy that you read, he's the god of blackjack. That was the play, man! That was the big play! That time we got them chickens to cock-a-doodle-doo!" Ludo excitedly imitates the crow of a rooster and flaps his arms like a chicken. "Cock-a-doodle-doo!" Flush with the excitement of the big win and feeling the tide of their luck turning, Ludo, over John's feeble objection, lets the hundred dollars ride. He feels hot—and he is. He is dealt a blackjack. The $150 payoff gives them a total of $253, ten bright green twenty-five-dollar chips plus the three blue chips. Ludo bets another one hundred dollars and again wins.

"That's it," John says, reaching over Ludo's shoulder to haul the chips in. He gets a twenty-five-dollar chip colored into five red five-dollar chips and flips one of them back to the dealer as a tip. He plays one more hand for ten dollars—the dealer allowing them a one-bet exception to the table minimum—wins that, and sings out, "We got it, we got it, we got it! Three hundred and sixty-three dollars. That's two plane tickets to New York and twenty dollars for the cab ride. Exactly."

"It's all there? You sure? Count it again, don't take any chances," Ludo says.

"Already did. Done deal. Let's go."

"Oh, man, we appreciate that so much—" Ludo says, turning to thank the third baseman. He looks over, but the man with the chips is gone and all they see is the third baseman's long dark jacket, looking like a black cape from the distance, disappearing into the crowd down the aisles.

Ludo looks at John. "Yo, homes, remember that blackjack book you had, the picture on the cover?"

"Yeah, why?" John says.

The two look at each other, thinking the same thing.

"Holy shit, wasn't that Cardoozi, Cardini, whatever the hell his name is?" Ludo says.

Chapter Twenty-Nine

The taxi weaves around two lanes of double-parked cars and pulls up in front of the overhanging Jet Blue sign at McCarran International Airport. With their nonrefundable one-way vouchers from Las Vegas to New York in their hands, John and Ludo only need to pick up their boarding cards at the ticket counter and they'll be on their way. A porter waits outside the door of the cab with a long flat luggage cart and opens the door for them. Ludo steps out first, while John reaches into his pocket to pay for the fare.

"May I help you with any bags?" the porter says.

"Yeah, find them," John says.

"Take it easy, homes, not his fault the bags didn't make it."

Ludo turns to the porter. "No, we're cool, man."

The porter looks at Ludo with raised eyebrows. Apparently, it's not often that that he sees a traveler in a red dress with hairy legs and a three-day growth of beard.

"Is there a problem?" Ludo says, staring belligerently at him, and the porter moves on without another word.

"That's twenty dollars even," the cabbie says to John.

John hands the cabbie the three five-dollar bills and five crumpled singles he had gripped tightly in his sweating hand for the entire cab ride. Once again, they have parted with the last of their money. The cabbie counts the bills twice, ascertaining that there's no tip, and shakes his head. He had sniffed out these deadbeats as soon as they hopped in the cab.

At the check-in counter, John and Ludo nervously wait in line. They worry about Versachi showing up here even though they have no particular reason to believe he knows where they are. However, they have learned not to underestimate his sixth sense, especially with the uncanny knack he has shown for tracking down their whereabouts. Ludo pulls his floppy hat down lower and adjusts the long blonde wig on his head. His dark eyes scan the crowd looking for any suspicious signs. John's baseball cap with the inscription "Lost in Las Vegas" is pulled low as well. They figure the best chance they have to make it through the airport undiscovered and without incident is to keep their profiles as low as possible.

In this town, accustomed to the garish, the bizarre, and the out of place, where Elvis impersonators perform matrimony services, where outcasts and outlaws from other states are given a new start in life, and where behavior deemed outrageous elsewhere is accepted if not embraced, it takes a lot to look out of place. However, John, scruffy-looking with the wrinkled and stained blue blazer that is already becoming threadbare, and Ludo in his red dress, blonde wig, and unshaven face, manage to stand out like two shifty vagrants trying to get into a millionaire's ball. It's one thing to fit in with the madness and fantasy world of the casinos where everything goes and bizarre can be normal; it's another to fit in with the staid environment of McCarran Airport, where bizarre looks bizarre. John and Ludo, looking out of place to begin with, don't help matters by their nervous mannerisms and furtive glances around the terminal. They are so far gone at this point after not having slept for almost three days, they don't realize they're about as inconspicuous as two clowns in loud colors, exaggerated ears, and red bulbous noses among a party of white-gowned bridesmaids.

"We better get on that airplane, homes, that's all I'm telling you."

"We got the vouchers, they're already paid for." John waves the stiff white receipts in his hand. "We're getting on that plane."

"Homes, until we're on that plane, we ain't on the plane. You know what I mean? Damn, look at all these security guards and police. It makes me nervous."

"There are just as many as when we arrived a few days ago. You're just being paranoid."

"I'm not one inch paranoid, man. I'm just afraid of that FBI goon showing up here."

John rolls his eyes. "That's good. I was afraid you were being paranoid. Let's just play it cool, there's just two parties ahead of us. We're number three. We're almost there."

"It's going too easy, man. Nothing goes this easy for us in this town. Everything is a motherfucker. I don't trust it. And I don't like that number three where we standing. Not the way things are. It's the back end of a thirteen, you know what I'm saying?"

"Are there any numbers that don't look like thirteens to you?"

"Yeah, numbers that don't look like thirteens. Them numbers."

A woman in her mid-forties standing in front of them and wearing a white tennis outfit turns around and stares bewildered at the husky voice coming from the dress. Ludo glares at the woman and she turns back around, moving a few feet forward as well.

John turns to Ludo, looking him up and down like a guy sizing up an attractive girl, and shakes his head approvingly.

"Cut it out, man. I'm in no mood for this," Ludo warns John with a pointed finger.

An elderly attendant finishes up with a married couple and two children and waves the woman in the tennis outfit and her companion over to the counter. Another attendant just coming on duty, a pouty-looking woman in her mid-forties, indicates she'll help John and Ludo.

"Keep your voice low," Ludo warns John as they walk over. "Don't attract attention. We don't want no one hearing us. And be cool about this. Just let me do the talking, you too nervous."

"Hello. Welcome to Jet Blue. Where are you flying to?" the attendant asks.

"New York," Ludo says to her in a barely audible voice. The lady raises her eyebrows at the deep masculine voice coming from the customer in the dress, and Ludo, remembering what he's wearing, raises it an octave. "There's two of us, Ludo Garcia and John Howard-Hughes."

"Excuse me?" the woman says, holding her ear and bending forward.

"Ludo Garcia and John Howard-Hughes," Ludo says again, his voice so soft that the attendant still can't make out the words.

The attendant holds her ear with one hand. "I'm sorry, I can't hear a word you're saying. Will you please speak louder, uhh, ma'am, I think?" The woman turns red, not sure whether she should address Ludo as a man or as a woman.

Ludo looks around to see who might be listening and gets elbowed aside by John. "Excuse me, sweetie," John says to Ludo, and steps up to the counter.

"My girlfriend is a little hoarse today," John says to the attendant, "aren't you, dearie? We're a little tired, aren't we? Yes we are. Why don't you just let me take care of this, honey buns?"

Ludo stiffens his back and stares at John. "We'll talk about this later," he mutters in falsetto.

"That's Ludo Garcia and John Howard-Hughes," John announces to the attendant. "I'm John, of course."

"Keep it down, man. What's the matter with you?" Ludo whispers to John. "And screw you with this honey buns crap."

"That's Ludo Garcia and John Howard-Hughes," the attendant loudly repeats back to John. "Is that what you said?"

"Yes ma'am." John nervously looks around, hoping the loud mention of their names isn't heard by anyone too interested. Two men in dark suits stand a few aisles away, but they appear to be legitimate passengers in line waiting for tickets. John makes a mental note to keep an eye on them.

"Sir," the attendant says.

"What?" John turns back around.

"Tickets, please."

Ludo hands her the vouchers, quickly pulling back his big hands. She looks up at Ludo, still not sure what to make of him. Ludo smiles back at her.

"Photo identification, please," the attendant says to John.

"I don't have my ID with me," John says. He thinks for a moment and then adds, "We have the tickets, ma'am, we just need the seats."

"Without identification, you can't fly. Standard security measures. Maybe your, ah, girlfriend has the ID?"

"I don't think he does, ah, she does. We're supposed to be on that flight."

"Not without ID you're not," she retorts, getting irritated with the antics of these two.

"And he's not my boyfriend," Ludo says. "And I'm not she . . . never mind."

The attendant looks at the pair quizzically. Didn't he say this was his girlfriend just a little while ago? She glances over at the next agent, unsure what to think. Judging from her colleague's expression, she is not alone in believing that something about these two is amiss.

Ludo nudges John and says quietly, "Homes, we ain't got no driver's licenses! What we gonna do?"

With his hat worn low, Ludo turns toward the attendant and says in a high squeaky voice, "What do you mean? We can't fly?"

"You *can* fly if you have identification. That's all I'm saying. I told your boyfriend the very same thing."

"Boyfriend? What—" John says, looking at Ludo. "Oh."

"He's not my boyfriend," Ludo says, trying to keep his voice high-pitched. "I already told you that."

"Shut up, Ludo."

The attendant's face screws up in confusion. She can't quite make out what is going on with these two oddballs and has just about had enough of them. Something is clearly wrong. She tries to get a better look at John's face, but when she does, he pulls the cap down lower.

"We bought these tickets back at the hotel, and I want to get on this plane," John says to her. "That's all I'm saying."

John looks off to the side and catches a movement. "What's that?" he says to Ludo. John sharply jerks his head toward the right. Ludo looks in that direction. At the end of the terminal, a big man with a surprisingly light gait is walking briskly in their direction. No doubt about it—it's Versachi.

"Holy mother of roast beef sandwiches!" says Ludo in his regular voice.

"Sir, I'm sorry, but without identification for the two of you, we are not—"

The attendant stops in mid-sentence. Her two customers have abruptly departed the ticket counter and are heading rapidly toward the exit. She calls after them, but they continue moving at a brisk pace toward the door.

John and Ludo rapidly head toward the exit, desperately hoping to avoid getting caught by Versachi. A security officer follows right on their heels, the click-clack of his wingtips making rapid taps on the tiled floor as he jogs after them. In front of them, by the exit, another security officer solemnly stands with arms folded, his gaze focused on them.

"We're fucked!" Ludo cries softly to John just as the officer catches up to them and grabs each by the arm.

John gulps, thoughts of Mambo, the three-hundred-and-sixty-five-pound homosexual psychopath, rushing through his brain.

"We're finished, homes, they got us!" Ludo whispers. "Whatever you do, don't try to bribe them and make this worse."

"Yes?" Johns says tremulously to the officer.

"You left your tickets, sir," The security officer points to the ticket counter where the attendant is waving two vouchers in the air.

"We'll get them later," Ludo replies. The nonrefundable vouchers are good only for this flight and worth nothing to them if they can't get on the plane. And with no ID, they'll never get their money back anyway. However, their big concern at the moment is Versachi—he has found them again.

"Thanks anyway, sweetie," Ludo says, blowing the shocked guard a kiss as he and John rush out the exit.

———————

Versachi has stopped about thirty feet away and watches to see where the confrontation with the security guard will go. When John Howard-Hughes and his friend in the red dress pass by the guard and out the exit, Versachi, cursing loudly to himself, goes outside after them.

The luckless duo catch a shuttle just outside the door, hopping onto it just before the back door closes. They peer through the dusty window in the rear as the bus pulls away from the curb and goes on its way.

Versachi has just emerged from the terminal and is staring straight into the back window of the bus.

Chapter Thirty

When the driver announces the last stop, the Lady Luck on Ogden and Third one block off of Fremont Street in downtown Las Vegas, John and Ludo exit the shuttle bus after riding the entire way in a harsh silence. They are afraid to give verbal form to the horrible reality they find themselves in. They are back to square one: broke, homeless, and without options. On top of that, they are disheartened from their terrible defeat at the airport. Their Las Vegas trip has lasted less than seventy-two hours, yet it seems like this vacation from hell has lasted for a lifetime, an eternity even. Their realities and thoughts are so far removed from their everyday lives in Brooklyn that their memories of home seem abstract, distant, fabricated remembrances of a faraway land, like a dream they have had; nay, a nightmare.

"Damn, we were so close," John says as they start walking down the street. "So close."

"I told you I didn't have a good feeling about that," Ludo says. "We had that thirteen multiplying itself all over us."

John abruptly stops. "Ludo, will you take off that goddamned dress already? Don't you have your shorts on underneath or something?"

"What? Oh, I hadn't even thought about it," Ludo says, abashed.

He pulls the dress off over his head, unzips his small bag, stuffs the dress into it, and they continue down the street.

"And the hat," John says, "and wig."

Ludo removes the hat and wig and also stuffs them into his little bag, then straightens out the red bandanna that was under the wig. John and Ludo look at one another anew. They are dressed exactly the same as when they originally arrived in Vegas—John in his khaki pants, beige dress shirt, and blue blazer, and Ludo in his colorful Bermuda shorts and short-sleeved red polo shirt—except that three days of hard wear and tear on their clothing and harder wear on their person have given them a desperate appearance. They have the look of two guys who try to hustle luck any way they can but seem to lose every time. The casual observer, however, would be unable to guess that it's the other way around—luck has hustled them and left them stranded like whales washed up on the beach, hoping a fortuitous tide will take them back to the deep waters of the ocean.

Dapper, they are not.

"There's got to be a way to get out of this town," John says.

"You would think so, homes, you would think so."

They walk north on Sixth Street, quietly lost in thought, their shoes crunching softly on sand speckles blown in from the desert. They're back on their downtown hegira with no destination in mind, only this time not in the dark abyss of a mean and unforgiving night, but the bright sun of the day. They pass a tourist shop hawking Indian jewelry and artifacts and a pawn shop advertising watch batteries for two dollars before heading down a side street with multi-floor garages the casinos maintain to accommodate their customers and employees.

"What do you think about water?" John says.

"I don't think anything about water, I just drink it," Ludo curtly replies. He is staring straight ahead at the view leading out of downtown, past the elevated I-95 freeway that wraps around a few government office buildings and connects with I-15 south continuing all the way through Nevada to San Diego, until connecting to I-5 and the Mexican border at Tijuana. There is a cluster of stores near a corner—a fast-food fried-chicken joint, a liquor store, and a self-serve laundromat—and beyond, a gas station and some nondescript one- and two-story office buildings that have seen better days.

"Why do you think I'm asking you this question?" John says.

"How the fuck would I know why you're asking me this question?"

"Well, I must be asking for a reason."

"Usually things you ask have no reason," Ludo says, "so why don't you either tell me what you got to say or let's change the subject."

"Why don't you ask me then?"

"Why don't I ask you why you're not asking me? That don't make no sense. There's something wrong with you. The sun baked your head or something."

"But don't you think I have a reason to ask? I'm the one asking."

"And I'm the one being asked to ask, but ask what? Whether to ask you what to ask or to ask whether you have a reason to ask? I don't know what the fuck you're talking about."

"Just go ahead, I'm asking you. Ask me."

"Okay, I ask."

"What are you asking?" John says.

"What the fuck is wrong with you?" Ludo screams, throwing his hands in the air. "You ask me to ask, and I ask, then you ask me what I'm asking and I don't know what the fuck I'm asking. Something the fuck about a glass of water is how this started. I don't know." Ludo snaps off a twig from a bush they pass and flips it to the side. "Fuck you, by the way."

They turn a corner and head back toward Fremont Street, the center of downtown Las Vegas.

"Hey watch out—" Ludo grabs John just before he trips over the extended feet of a panhandler who sits with his legs splayed out on either side of a coffee can and his back propped up against a wall. A small placard leaning against the can reads, "Needz Money for Pot." The man has two large floppy straw hats perched on his head, one atop the other, and without taking his eyes from the book he is reading, *The*

Great Gatsby, says, "Got two bits, fifty cents, one dollar for a worthy cause, my fine fellows?"

"I don't get it when guys perfectly able to work beg for money," John says loudly enough for the bum to hear. "That's ridiculous. And for drugs, no less." Out of curiosity, John pauses, leans over the man's feet and looks into the can. There are just a few coins in it.

The man lifts his head to look at them, one hand holding his place in the book, the other supporting the spine of the novel. His eyes are luminous and blue, and his teeth are perfectly white and straight. He is somewhere in his mid-twenties, freshly shaved, and incongruously dressed in a clean button-down shirt and shorts, like a freshly scrubbed frat boy two years out of college. He looks John and Ludo over. They look like street people themselves, ones who are clearly not only failures in the game of life, but at panhandling as well.

The panhandler directs his gaze at John. "The redoubtable brothers of fallen fate on their myopic peregrination get stuck in the miasma of life's abyssal labyrinth, but staring into the shallows of the shadows they forgetteth that a good cleansing of the spirit includes one of the sacred skin to complement the curb walking—may I call you Curbie for short?—and ease the olfactory burden," he says, looking at their soiled clothes and exaggeratedly sniffing the air.

"Same to you," John calls back to the bum, who watches them pass with great amusement.

———

John and Ludo push through the doors of the Troubadour, hoping that the relaxed setting of this small casino will allow them a quiet place to relax and think things through. They head into the keno lounge and settle into the last row, studiously avoiding the front and its vulnerability to kicks on their soles from testy security guards. One nondescript straggler marks out keno tickets near the front, but otherwise, there is no action here early in the day. Most of the patrons are elsewhere in the Troubadour, pushing coins into machines or grinding out their luck at table games. A burly security guard watches them with arms crossed, his expression not overly inviting. Still smarting from their previous evening's troubles, John mugs his face at the guard.

"Will you chill out, man? We got enough trouble," Ludo says.

"Yeah, but—"

"Just forget about him, homes, leave it. He ain't nothing to us. We're just sitting here."

John watches the security guard relay something through his walkie-talkie and then return his gaze to them. "He's got the whole casino to look at. Why does he have to watch us?"

"We better keep moving; they already looking at us too closely. We stay too long here, they going to make us move. Better to get going now before we get comfortable."

John and Ludo wearily pick themselves off the keno chairs and slowly trudge past the small gaming area of the casino—two aisles of slot machines, one table each of roulette and craps, a few scattered tables of three card poker and pai gow, and three blackjack tables. John pauses by the last table, a single-deck blackjack game without any players, until Ludo nudges him and they exit through the back door of the casino and into the pool area. It is late morning, about eleven-fifteen, and the sun, still rising, continues its unmerciful assault on the mortals below. The pool area is crowded with sunbathers alternately dipping in the pool to cool down from the intense summer heat, and then heating up again in the sun on their lounge chairs. There are no lounge chairs available, so John and Ludo stroll slowly along the pool looking like two bums who have drifted in off the street, which, indeed, is exactly what they have become.

"No chairs, man, none," Ludo says, scouring every last occupied chair for an open place.

"Not even one. Screwed again. Screwed at every turn here," John says. "It's unbelievable. We can't catch one break in this town, not even the smallest one. It's like every single thing in Las Vegas is conspiring against us."

"Homie, I don't know about you, but we smell like two street people.

We need to get these clothes clean, get some showers or something. It's bad enough to be homeless, but to get dissed by a street bum of all things, saying we stink, how low is that, man?"

John has stopped by the deep end of the pool and is staring at the water. He turns to look at Ludo, a strange expression dancing on his face.

"Oh no," Ludo says. "I don't think so."

"I think so."

John pushes Ludo, and Ludo in turn grabs on to him as the two tumble into the pool with a giant splash, screaming like children and showering the guests around them with heavily chlorinated water.

———————

The front door of the Troubadour opens and John and Ludo, soaked to the skin like drenched hamsters—but nonetheless feeling refreshed and clean—are unceremoniously shoved outside the casino and into the street by the burly security guard who had been watching them earlier. Still dripping water and leaving a wet trail behind, the down-and-out friends turn left out of the casino and head back toward Fremont Street in the same direction from where they came earlier. The panhandler sits there cross-legged, the two straw hats still atop his head, but with a new message selected from the stack of signs kept to his side. This one reads, "Money for Beer."

"I see the chlorine brothers have made arrangements," the street person says, sniffing the air in the same exaggerated manner as before. He looks directly at John and says, "Afternoon, Curbie, nice of you to visit."

John walks past him without a glance, shaking his head. He's not going to get into it with this bum.

"How about some coinage for the realm?" the man calls after them and rigorously shakes his cup of change at John, a broad smile spreading across his lips.

John and Ludo find a bench two short blocks away and drop themselves down heavily upon it. Riverines of chlorinated water drip from their clothes and form small puddles around and beneath them.

A teenager wearing a baseball cap pulled backward, cut-off jeans, and a white T-shirt with no sleeves, pulls up to the bench on a bicycle and stops right in front of them. His pale face is riddled with acne, and the thin arms resting on the handlebars look like two pistons in a gear shaft. He chews gum loudly and stares blankly at the pair.

"Go away," Ludo says, waving his hand in dismissal. John is staring at the ground, mired in his reveries, and pays no notice to the visitor.

The kid on the bicycle doesn't say anything, just sits there staring at them.

"I said, go away. We don't want to be bothered."

"Got change for a dollar?" the teenager asks. His voice is flat and his face registers no expression.

"No," Ludo says.

"Got the time then?"

"No, we don't have the time either," Ludo says.

"Well I do," the teenager says, shaking his wristwatch. The watch has a unique design Ludo has seen once before, but he cannot place where. He stretches his arms behind him on the bench and rolls his eyes.

"Why don't you just keep riding up the street there?" Ludo says, indicating a direction with his hand. "Go bother someone else."

The kid remains in front of them, passive, his expression flat.

John looks up and the teen suddenly comes to life, flashing a big smile when John notices him. He then bicycles away. Ludo looks over and sees recognition in John's eyes. It is the kid from the gas station.

"You know this freak also?" Ludo says, bunching up his eyebrows and looking at John's bare wrist. "Homes, is that your watch he's wearing?"

Just as the scorching heat of the day sucked the moisture and coolness out of their clothes and began to remind them that the desert is unforgiving, a long, black Cadillac that had followed the shuttle downtown skids to a halt in front of the bench. Before Versachi can get his ample frame out the door, John and Ludo take off running in the opposite direction. Behind them, they hear a car door slam shut and the frantic screeching of wheels as the Caddie makes a K-turn. They round a corner and seeing the panhandler in his usual spot, John and Ludo throw themselves down on either side of him. The beggar's newest sign reads, "Change(d) for the Deranged."

"The night riders on the wrong side of the orbit," the panhandler says in greeting.

"Hurry up, Ludo," John says, stripping off his jacket and shirt. "We need some kind of disguise. Be quick about it." John grabs the top straw hat off the panhandler's head and plunks it down on his own. Ludo follows suit with his shirt and the second hat the panhandler is wearing, and they each grab a placard from the pile. Ludo ends up with a sign reading "Nickels in Trickles." John's sign reads "Money for Cocktails," but his hand covers the last five letters. To a passerby, if there are any doubts about the authenticity of the three bums on the street, those doubts would center on the middle one of the group, the clean-shaven one reading *The Great Gatsby.* The other two, with scrubby beards, unkempt appearance, cheap straw hats on their heads, and the look of two vagabonds that have gone a few too many rounds in life's underbelly, appear to be the real deal.

The bum in the middle, the well-groomed one, is eating a banana. He says without missing a beat, "The excommunicados hath joineth the pismires and plebeians of the hajj in deep philosophical matters in the adytum of ticking eternity as the unholy one descends upon Eden."

"What the fuck did he say?" Ludo whispers across to John.

"How the hell would I know?"

Seconds later, Versachi comes running around the corner, sweat dripping from his temples, and stops in front of the bums, winded and breathing hard. The Cadillac, following behind, idles in the street, its dark tinted windows reflecting the sun back onto the ground.

"Which direction did they go?" Versachi says to the one in the middle. John and Ludo have their hats pulled low and their eyes face

the ground. All they see are the tops of Versachi's shiny black shoes.

"How about fifty cents, one dollar, o corpulent one?" the bum says.

Versachi smacks the sign out of the bum's hand. "Answer me quick, lowlife, before I ram that coffee can up your ass."

"They may have gone out yonder way over there," the bum says and points with his left hand held high. With his right hand, he flips the peel of the banana in the direction he points.

Versachi turns and on his second step skids on the peel, banging heavily into a parked car before falling to the curb. "Son-of-a-bitch," he yells from the ground. Versachi pulls himself up, quickly dusts off his suit, and then trots off in the direction pointed, his suit pants ripped at the knee and thigh areas and a noticeable limp in his step. The Cadillac speeds off down the street, surveying a different route in the hunt.

John and Ludo wait until Versachi and the Cadillac are out of view, then place the placards back in the pile.

"Thanks, bub," Ludo says as they stand up. "We owe you."

The bum shoves a few bills in John's pocket. "Here, you need this more than me."

"I can't take this," John says, but the bum pushes his hand back and motions him to start moving.

"Thanks a ton," John says, and he and Ludo flee down the street, still wearing the bum's straw hats on their heads.

"Fear not the ephemeral ubiquity of moving inertia, irradiated abyssal shallows, and pre-posthumous existential reverberations," the bum calls after them before returning to his book.

Chapter Thirty-One

Ludo removes his bandanna and wipes a large swath of sweat from his head. It is 105 degrees under the protective canopy of a city bus stop where he sits next to John, taking shelter from the harsh glare of the sun. A bus slows, thinking they want to board, but Ludo waves it on.

"Man, it's hot," Ludo says. "We like two turkeys in the oven."

John clears his throat and turns toward his friend. "How are we going to get out of this mess? We need two thousand, eight hundred and eight-three dollars to get these guys off our back," John says. "What are we going to do?"

"It's two thousand, eight hundred and seventy-three dollars. You still forgetting that the rat added it wrong."

"Jesus, not this again. Forget about that goddamned ten dollars already. We need real money to get the hell out of here."

"Ten dollars is still ten dollars in my book, homes."

"Do you think we have more important concerns than a ten-dollar addition error?" John says, his voice a taut guitar string twirled an octave tighter.

"I ain't arguing that, I was just bringing it up to keep things straight, that's all. You the accountant, man, you should know the right numbers more than anyone."

"We have bigger things to worry about than fighting over a pointless, ridiculous, stupid ten dollars. I don't know why you keep arguing about this."

"I wasn't arguing nothing, just mentioning, you know," Ludo says, stubbornly crossing his arms. "You the one arguing, because you talked about it after I talked about it. The first one to bring something up can't be the one arguing."

"The second one can't respond to anything unless the first one starts it, so if we were arguing, you started it." John leans back, his lips pursed like a petulant child.

"Mentioning is just mentioning. There's a difference. It ain't arguing. Arguing is when you argue, not when you mention."

"Forget it." Beads of perspiration are gathering on John's forehead. "Let's just forget about the ten dollars. It makes no sense to argue over this ridiculous thing."

"Agreed. I won't say more about that ten dollars."

"But you just did! You just mentioned it again," John says, pointing his finger accusingly at Ludo.

"You're the one keep bringing it up. I was done with it already, now you fanning the flames."

"You had to mention ten dollars one more time, get the last word in. You couldn't just let it sit or we'd be done with it already. Instead, you wanted to argue about the ten dollars. That's my point."

"You still talking about that ten dollars?"

John opens his mouth to reply, but thinks better of it. He watches a couple of winos stumble past them, reeking of body odor and cheap vodka. The two sit silently for a few minutes, the shorted ten-dollar issue hovering over them like a threatening rain cloud that just won't break. He breathes out deeply, blowing his breath into the hot air. "We just can't get out of here washing dishes. Those peanuts Virgil pays us can barely get us a taxi ride across the street."

"No kidding, homes." Ludo watches sweat drip off his arm and immediately evaporate on the cement below.

"We have to get money somehow," John says. "We have to come up with some kind of plan, something."

"Can't you just call up and get another credit card? I never could get no credit cards, but isn't it that easy when you already have one?"

"The problem is that by the time they send me another credit card, it will be another week. And where are they going to send it anyway? Care of the soup line, tenth bum from the back? Special delivery to the third cardboard box under the bridge? We need money fast. That's not going to do it. And I have no ID to even pick it up anyway. That's a dead end."

"I got you," Ludo says, dropping into thought. "How about this? Can't you ask your sister or whatever to wire some money?"

"Jesus Christ, you crazy? I still owe her four grand from the car."

"Yeah, that car thing didn't work out too good," Ludo says, shaking his head.

"Every day I have to hear about it. Every single day. The car, the money, the car, the money, the money, the car. How I'm irresponsible. How I'm this, how I'm that. It took one month's begging just to get her to lend the money to me in the first place. I did everything but get on my two knees for that loan. Damn, that was the biggest mistake of my life."

"I know she a little uptight and everything, but hey, this is an emergency, you have to try."

John traces a long line running across his palm with his index finger until it runs out of room by the base of the thumb.

"Well?" Ludo says.

"She'd kill me if she thought I was in trouble. Thing is, we wouldn't have to worry about Knuckles or Versachi or the rest of them doing us in if I get her involved. She'll do it herself," John continues. "I can't ask her. No matter what, that's just not an option."

"What's the what, homes? We need it for legitimate reasons."

"Legitimate? There's almost nothing that's considered legitimate in her eyes. Bella's just not going to send me the money. Plain and simple. When she hears three thousand dollars or whatever the hell we need, she's going to think I'm in trouble and that I should get out of it myself as a lesson on how not to get into it in the first place. Bella would sooner flush the money down the toilet than bail me out of trouble I got into because she thought I acted irresponsibly."

"That's pretty harsh, man."

"She thinks I always manage to get into trouble. Can you believe that?" John is staring at Ludo's blank expression, as if waiting for his friend to concur in some form.

A few seconds pass with no response, so John continues, "I mean, what could I possibly say to justify her giving me that kind of money?"

"Just tell her the truth. What's wrong with that?"

"You mean, I should tell her that the police, the FBI, six poker-playing killers with names like Knuckles, Apples, Rock, Joe Popcorn, Wonderbread, and Joey Cleaners, a psychopathic ex-husband of my sort-of girlfriend who I just met and don't know her last name or what she does for a living, Godzilla is chasing us all over town, *and* a Mafioso owner of a restaurant where I skipped out on a bill and caused fifty-plus-thousand-dollars worth of damage to his place are all after me and that's why I need the money?"

"Well, yeah. It's the truth. Why not?"

"Come on! How is she going to believe that? It's so far-fetched, I don't even believe it!"

"Well, don't tell her all that. I don't know, tell her it's two million thousand degrees outside and we're stuck on a bus bench in the desert watching winos wander by and we're being cooked alive in our own sweat like, ah, what do you call it, them self-cooking things, I don't know, Jiffy Pop or whatever. Yeah, the popcorn. But don't tell her it has anything to do with you getting in trouble."

John doesn't reply, so Ludo continues. "Well, tell her just the part she needs to know."

"Which part? Being chased down the street by a three-hundred-pound gorilla who turns out to be an FBI agent who's hunting us like we're deer in season? A professional killer who threatened to cut off my nuts and then chuck them out a window because he thought I was bluffing in a game of poker? Borrowing a wig from an old lady to use as a disguise? A psychopathic nymphomaniac named Mambo who's waiting for us in a jail cell? Having no place to stay and wandering the streets like a homeless bum? Not having two nickels to rub together? Who could possibly believe any of this?" John throws both his palms open and looks beseechingly at Ludo.

"Yeah, you got a point." Ludo scratches his head and watches while another bus approaches the stop. He waves it on and follows its progress down the street before turning back to face John.

"Hey, you hungry?"

"Ludo!" John growls by way of warning.

"I can't help it if I'm hungry, man. Don't be getting on me," Ludo says. "Just like a little hamburger or some mashed potatoes sounds pretty good to me. Actually, an ice cold beer with the whole plate—cool us down with this heat, man—maybe throw in some good French fries with it also, sounds even better right now. I'm still thinking about that meatloaf I didn't get—"

John stares at Ludo, his eyes bloodshot and his forehead creased with furrows of frustration. His head is moist with sweat, and a large drop forms on his temple before running down his cheek and dropping off by his feet.

"Alright, alright, man. Listen, how about you tell her you lost your money on the street or it got robbed out of the room. Yeah, how about that?"

"What room? We don't have a room anymore. We don't have anything," John says quietly, his voice bathed in futility. His forehead glistens with sweat, and when he leans back a few more drops cascade down his cheek and onto his pants.

"Pull it together, homes, I know we're a little short on a place to stay. Just tell her anything, I don't know. Make up something good. We got to try."

"Nothing I can tell her will explain how I need that kind of money. I might as well say we're starting a business selling hot dogs from a corner cart."

"How about asking your father?"

"You kidding? He's tighter than a clam's ass that's been soaked for two days in Super Glue. That's a dead end. You know that."

"Yeah," Ludo says, "I hear you on that, but we got to run through every possibility no matter how far-fetched. Man, my uncle's been soaking for decades, the glue in his rear end already like petrified ass wood. And that's the only family I got unless we're talking about some cousins I ain't seen in a decade and some. We just got to do this by ourselves. That's what we gotta do, bro."

"How? What can we do?"

Ludo lifts his index finger up in the air as if he's a sailor testing the wind direction while he thinks. His eyes scan the street and stop, as if resting, on the faded façade of a building across from them. "Hold it, homes, you had a point before about them hot dogs," Ludo says, snapping his fingers together.

"Please, stop with the food. I'm not in the mood."

"No, no, it's not about the food part, it's about the cart. Listen, you know that expression, 'Don't put the cart before the food?'"

"It's before the horse. 'Don't put the cart before the horse.'"

"Yeah, whatever, but listen to me. The cart is the idea, man. Tell your sister you're investing in, ah, what do you call it, a business or something. Yeah, how about that?"

"What are you talking about? I'm going to suddenly quit working with her and my father so me and you can sell hot dogs on a corner in Las Vegas? She's not going to believe that for a second. *I* wouldn't even believe that for a second."

"Just let me finish here, okay? It's just an idea, a little stretch maybe, but it can't hurt to listen. We desperate, man, keep that in mind. We have to keep an open mind, you know what I'm saying?"

"I'm listening." John looks at Ludo suspiciously.

"Here's what you tell her. First—" Ludo stops when he sees the expression on John's face.

"Go ahead," John says.

"You're going to shoot me down, I haven't even said nothing yet. I can see it coming."

"I'm not going to shoot you down, Ludo."

"Don't be shooting me down now, not in this heat, man. You know I'm sensitive on that."

"Come on already, out with it."

"Okay then, so here's what you do. First, you tell her about this incredible opportunity you came across."

"Yeah?"

"You're looking at me funny," Ludo says flatly.

"How the hell am I supposed to look?" John says, throwing up his hands. "This is how I look. Will you tell me the goddamn plan already?"

Ludo studies John carefully before continuing. "Well, you tell her it's a golden opportunity and she gets interested right there. Who doesn't like a golden opportunity?"

"My sister doesn't. Bella doesn't believe anything, especially if it has something to do with me."

"You at least pique her interest a little, homes."

"Mentioning a golden opportunity certainly won't."

"So you present it different, in a way she understands, you know what I'm saying?"

"Go ahead."

"Okay, man, it's a good business."

"What business?" John says sharply.

"You're shooting me down, I can see it coming."

"I am not shooting you down. Will you get this over with already?"

"The balloon business."

"The balloon business? I'm supposed to tell her I'm going into the balloon business?"

"Yeah."

"That's the dumbest thing I ever heard."

"You said you wouldn't shoot me down."

"But that idea is so stupid. Balloons? What are you, crazy? Where did you get this ridiculous idea from?"

"I was flashing on that mall thing. You remember how excited the little girl got when she thought you gave her a balloon?"

John groans, flashing back to the pink condom that landed on the little girl's foot. "Why do you have to bring that up for?"

"You asked, homes. That's where the idea came from. But the beauty of the idea is that the balloon thing is so unbelievable, your sister might go for it. If you go with something believable, she won't believe it. We know that. So you go the other way with the unbelievable, that's the thing. If she won't believe the believable, then she'll have to believe the opposite, the unbelievable. That makes perfect sense, you know, if one thing is one way, then the other thing has to be the other way."

"If she can't believe it, she won't believe it, plain and simple. That's just logic."

"That's your problem—logic doesn't always make sense and you don't get that. And that's how you get your sister. Through the back door. You make it something she can't believe, that's why she'll believe it. If she believes it, it's only because she can't. You see? It's too obvious if it's believable and she'll see right through it. So you use double reverse psychology so she don't know if she's looking at the mirror or at the reflection of the other mirror in the mirror, and that's why she'll believe the unbelievable. And that's why this balloon idea is so perfect."

"I don't know how any of this makes sense."

"See? That's my point. It already worked on you. Is it believable that we're sitting like two broke roasted ducks at a bus stop? No, of course not, but that's the way it is just the same. You see, the more unbelievable, the more she's going to believe it. You give her something believable, she won't believe it. You know what I'm saying?"

"It's too hot for this, Ludo," John says. "Let's just forget about it."

"Hear me out, homes. So you tell her you can get the rights to balloons that, when you let out the air, it makes different noises, depending on which ones you buy."

"What kind of noises? You mean like animal sounds—dogs barking, roosters crowing, that kind of thing?"

"Not exactly."

"Then what?"

Ludo looks down at his hands, abashed.

"I'm waiting," John says.

"Farting sounds," Ludo says quietly.

"Excuse me?"

"Yeah, farting sounds, different ones. Loud ones, long ones, little cracklers." Ludo laughs out loud. "Kids would love 'em. It's funny, man. Farting balloons."

"Tell me you're not serious."

"I'm dead serious, homes. Hey, man," Ludo chuckles, "we could be farting balloons dot com. Yo," Ludo calls out in a mock street pitch, "anyone want to buy from the farting balloon man?"

John looks at Ludo with a flat expression.

"Well, homie, what do you say?"

"Are you out of your mind? Who would possibly believe that?"

"That's my point, homes!"

John drops his head and rubs the back of his skull with both hands. After a few seconds, he looks up at Ludo's triumphant grin, streams of sweat pouring down both sides of his friend's face.

———————

John stands in the phone booth next to the bus stop and listens while the operator announces the collect call to his sister. After a long hesitation, causing the operator to ask if his sister is still on the line, Bella accepts the call.

"Yeah?" she says.

"How's it going, Bella?" John says.

"What did you and your idiot friend Dildo do now?"

"Why would you say that? I'm just calling to say hello, see how things are going."

"You wouldn't call me from Las Vegas collect just to chitchat. What happened to your cell phone? And doesn't your hotel room have a phone? Stop wasting my time and get to it. Must be a doozy."

"Well, I lost my phone and ran into a few—"

"Just get to the point. I don't have all day for your stories."

John doesn't know why he plays these games with her. It must be old habits carried over from when he was a kid. Bella, fifteen years his senior, was his surrogate mother after his mom died. She is overbearing in her relationship with John, a suffocating abuse that isn't confined to the house but carries over to the workplace. She nitpicks and criticizes everything he does, making life around her miserable. When he graduated junior college, he reluctantly joined the small family accounting practice under pressure from Bella, a decision he regrets daily. Yet, even with Ludo's encouragement, he never works up the courage to go out on his own.

"How much?" Bella says, short-circuiting the process. "I know it's about money. Did you and Dildo blow it all on one hand or something?"

"I'm a little short, that's all."

John hears Bella's caustic laugh on the other side, then the sound of a bubble being blown and popped.

"I see," Bella says. "How short?"

"Just a couple of bucks," John says, "if you could help me out. I have a great business idea."

There is silence on the other end of the line. John can picture her sitting in the living room of her apartment, her large bicep muscles flexing out of a sleeveless T-shirt and her shaved head reflecting light off the overhead lamp. He hears her jaw working on a wad of gum.

"You're a beauty, Baby Cakes," she finally says.

"Do you have to call me that name? You know I hate it."

"Well?"

"It's an excellent idea, very exciting. I mean, really exciting."

John hears Bella working the gum harder. "Really?" she says. "You know, I got this kind of a phone call when you went on that Mexico trip with Dildo. And you didn't forget about that four thousand dollars, did you?"

Bella is not making this easy for him, not that he expects any different.

"I didn't forget." John's hands are moist with sweat. The phone booth feels like a sauna, even with the door propped open.

"What's this thing you're talking about?" Bella says.

John breathes in deeply and then quickly presents Ludo's scheme about the farting balloons. Bella listens in complete silence while John sums up the plan. "So," John continues, "after the kids blow up the balloons they let out the air and out comes these big farting noises. It's very funny. The good thing," John continues, scrambling to retrieve Ludo's convoluted logic, "is that it's one of those ideas you can't believe."

"Un-huh," Bella says in a noncommittal tone.

"And that's why it will work, because it seems like it can't be believed, so you can believe it, and that's the beauty of the disaster," John says, unable to remember how Ludo phrased the scheme. In his panic, he has no idea what he is saying anymore and how Ludo's explanation went— did he really say "disaster?" Now, as he explains Ludo's farting balloon scheme aloud, the scheme seems even more ludicrous and preposterous to him than when Ludo first proposed it.

There is a long uncomfortable silence on the other end of the phone, as if the line has gone dead. John feels like a bucket of water has just been dumped over the coals in the sauna, intensifying the heat. Sweat drips off his forehead, and a pool of perspiration gathers and makes its way down his back.

"Bella?"

John finally hears her measured breathing, then her voice.

"Are you on drugs?"

Chapter Thirty-Two

John takes a seat on the bench next to Ludo, dropping heavily onto the wooden slats. For ten minutes, neither one says a word. They stare at the hot asphalt feeling like they're staring at a pair of one spots on the come-out roll, two dice players with everything on the line who have just crapped out. Snake eyes. Their last hope of outside help, small though it was, is gone.

After watching another bus slow down and waving it by, Ludo glances up at the burning sun, then addresses John. "Now what the fuck we do?"

"That's a good question," John says.

"I'm glad that's a good question, but it don't exactly answer anything by telling me it's a good question. We better start getting real here, bro. Between us, we don't have enough money to even get on a city bus. That's if we even had a place to go, which we don't." Ludo wipes more sweat off his brow. "Fucking heat."

"They should have advertised, 'Experience a Las Vegas nightmare,'" John says. "Some vacation." He kicks a few pebbles and watches one with a little more giddyup than the others hop a curb and land on the street, bouncing a few feet farther before stopping cold on the hot asphalt.

"Yeah, some vacation, man." Ludo says. "Talk about a cooked goose and everything, we stay out here much longer, homes, people be looking to serve us with gravy. Maybe there's another thing that—" Ludo stops and shakes his head, leaving his words hanging in the air. "Never mind."

"What now?" John asks.

"Nothing."

They watch a few cars go by, then Ludo turns to John. "Wait a second, homes. How long were we in that diner for? Six, seven hours?"

"Something like that."

"And we owed, what, thirty-five dollars for the food?"

"Yeah, so?" John says.

"We got shorted! Since when they lower the minimum wage to like, whatever dollars an hour or something. That's fucked up. We ought to go back and give Virgil a piece of our mind."

"I think we got more pressing problems to worry about than being a few dollars short," John says.

Ludo contemplates for a minute, then smacks himself in the head. "What the fuck was I thinking?"

"What is it now?"

"I got us a plan, homes. I'm feeling pretty good about it."

"Yeah?"

Ludo watches a drop of sweat roll off his hand and evaporate on the ground. He opens his mouth to talk, but changes his mind and doesn't say anything.

"Let's get to it already, Ludo, I don't have all day for this."

"What, you in a hurry to go somewhere? The next corner got a one-hour special on curb space where we can sit without security guards with big chests kicking us out?"

"Can you just goddamn tell me what it is and stop all this nonsense?"

"Now I'm not going to tell you. That's it."

"What do you want me to say, hallelujah, we have a plan, one that's even better than the farting balloons?" John says.

"Okay, forget about it if you don't want to hear it," Ludo says, crossing his arms.

"Forgotten."

They sit silently, watching a bird amble in circles across the street before flying away, and then stare hard at a discarded newspaper yellowing from the rays of the sun on the other side of the street. Ludo, fidgeting anxiously on the bench, finally says, "So you want to hear it then?"

"After all this build-up, I can't wait to hear—go ahead. Like you said, something is better than nothing."

"Okay, homes, when I called about planes the other day, I also checked on buses to New York, just in case. I found out that we can get one-way tickets for eighty-five dollars each. They got a special. That's one hundred and seventy dollars total. We don't need no ID neither."

"Uh-huh."

"So we make the money, get on a bus, and get the fuck out of here."

"Right, okay," John says.

He waits for Ludo to say something more, but when he doesn't comment, John says, "Yeah?"

"Yeah, what?" Ludo says.

"Yeah, like I hear you," John says, irritated. "What else? What's the plan?"

"That's it."

"You mean that's the whole plan? The entire thing for this big build-up is that? So, the money just shows up, poof, right out of a genie's bottle, and then we sit on a bus for four days and four nights with a bunch of homeless types who can't afford to travel any other way?"

"That's right, with people like us."

"And how do you suggest we get that one hundred and seventy dollars? *That's* the plan we need."

Ludo looks at John long and hard as a way of answering.

"You're not suggesting we go back to being the dishwasher and busboy brothers?"

"That's right," Ludo replies doggedly.

"No way," John says, crossing his arms and shaking his head. "Not a chance in hell."

Chapter Thirty-Three

The money the panhandler had given John is enough to get them two bottles of cold water at a convenience store. These they drink with great gusto. It had been a long walk to the diner, made worse from exhaustion, lack of sleep, hunger, and their unenthusiastic outlook on life. The real problem, however, is the unrelenting heat. After two hours of walking in 113-degree temperature, their throats are parched and their lungs sore, as if they had been sucking air out of a furnace pipe. Finally, they reach their destination, wearily push open the front door of the diner, and feel the refreshing air-conditioning against their overheated skin.

Virgil is standing by the entrance, leaning against the outside counter of the cash register when John and Ludo walk in, their faces flush from the effects of too much sun and the unrelenting heat of the day. The manager pulls his pants up so that the belt line is barely below his chest and stares at them like they're vermin on his piece of pizza. "Look what the wind blew in," he says with evident satisfaction. "If you're looking to homestead here, we're full and there's a waiting list. Come back early tomorrow, first two homeless people get to share an extra carrot stick."

Virgil's mouth is formed in a shape that on just about anyone else might be called a smile, but on him, it is an expression somewhere on the scale of human emotions between amusement and a grimace.

John and Ludo look around. The diner is busy as usual at this early-afternoon hour, but it is a large place, and there are still plenty of empty tables. They stand silently in front of Virgil for a few seconds, and Ludo clears his throat.

"You still need some help?" he asks.

———————

Ludo finishes scrubbing a pan, dips it twice in the clean-water basin, and slides it down the counter with a little spin. It pings off the back face of the counter, dives over the edge, and lands on the floor, clattering harshly off the painted cement surface. Virgil walks in as the pan crashes to the ground, disapproval written all over his face. He looks forward to the challenge of making these vagabonds' lives miserable, and when the day is done, perhaps adding a few notches to his notebook. Without a word, Virgil plucks the pan off the floor by the edge of its handle so as not to sully too much of the skin on his fingers and flips it back into Ludo's sink, the water and soap bubbles lifting up in a wide arc and splattering onto Ludo's apron. He then heads out the kitchen door.

Ludo watches Virgil pass through the swinging door and back into the dining area and shakes his head.

"I love this job," Ludo says as he dips the pan twice more and slides it down the counter again, this time with less force so it doesn't carom off the backsplash. "My mamma worked hard to give me an education. Too bad she's not around to see how far her boy moved up in the world." He grabs a large frying pan and forcefully works steel wool into its surface.

"Ludo, we'll never get out of here at this rate. Virgil is going to give us food and thirty-five dollars each for this shift. That's what, a hundred dollars short for those bus tickets?"

"Exactly one hundred short, homes. To the penny. And at this rate, that's a lot of time for us to get to know our good buddy Virgil real well."

"I think I'll lose it if I go one more night without sleep. I can't do it. I just can't do it," John says.

"Neither one of us, bro."

"But if we spring for a room, even a cheap one, there goes our money and we become like permanent vagrants here," John says. "I don't think I can do that either."

"Something to think about," Ludo says.

"Yeah, something to think about."

Ludo puts the pan and steel wool down and looks over at John. "Hey homes, I been wondering," he says. "How did you come up with Cupcakes?"

After stocking a tray with freshly filled salt and pepper shakers, John hoists it up in the air, balancing the load against his upturned right palm. "I don't know, just sitting there with those guys, I kind of panicked and that's the first thing that came into my head."

"Just wondering, homes."

"The funny thing is, Ludo, I hate cupcakes," John says, and heads back into the dining area.

John has made up his mind. He's going to try ZZ one more time and see if they can get together later. He tightly grips the thirty-five cent tip left earlier by a grizzled man with unkempt hair who had sipped on a single cup of coffee for almost two hours before leaving—a tip the waitress didn't want to bother taking and told John he could have—and walks past Virgil's vigilant eyes over to the phone booth. John is hoping ZZ will put Ludo and him up for the evening. Another night wandering the streets downtown is too much to face. But how to explain the situation in terms that will make sense to her? John has trouble enough understanding the whole predicament himself, and while he cannot guess what ZZ's reaction will be, he has to at least see if there is any way she can help them. With ZZ, it is impossible to predict anything. If she could be set off by a simple friendly response of "no" as to whether he wanted dessert or not in the Italian restaurant, how would she react to a complicated explanation of why he and Ludo are broke, homeless, and need a place to sleep?

He'll find out soon enough.

John drops the coins in the slot and dials ZZ's number, waiting impatiently for the phone to be answered. Each ring feels like an eternity under Virgil's hateful stare. John can see Virgil's ire fire up like a furnace steadily stoked with shovels full of black coal.

Virgil watches John walk over to the payphone, licking his chops in anticipation of an infraction of his work rules and the fallout that will occur. In Virgil's world, nothing should interfere with work, not friendly banter, not an overly long bathroom break, and certainly not a phone call on company time.

Fifteen-minute coffee or fresh-air breaks or even a quick two-minute phone call? Not in Virgil's house.

Two waitresses and one cook who have worked alongside Virgil at the diner for more than a dozen years wait for the impending explosion. Like battle-weary soldiers accustomed to combat on the front lines, they have witnessed the parade of new recruits coming and going with grim amusement. As he has been doing for years, the cook sets up a betting pool every time a new employee walks in the door, booking wagers with the two waitresses and other interested parties on how long the new worker will last before quitting. Results usually came quickly: The majority of new employees lasted but a week, a few days, and in some cases, just a few hours. It usually didn't take long for Virgil to get to them. Several years back, a nervous sort who clearly didn't have the moxie to handle the abuse hadn't even tied his apron on before Virgil exploded in a tirade, driving the poor fellow, quivering and shaking, into a nervous breakdown. The broken man was out the door before he had even gotten his hands wet. The cook had been gravely disappointed: He hadn't even had time to set up the over/under line before the newbie quit, a good betting opportunity missed. He had seen a quick exit coming and thought he could squeeze in a nice profit on the under.

These new workers were evidently turning into favorite targets for Virgil—it was clear Virgil had it in for these two—so the bookie and his bettors didn't expect a long shelf life under the manager's tenacious grip. The cook set the over/under on how long this ragged pair would last at three shifts. He had originally set the line at five shifts, and then four shifts, but when there were still no takers, he dropped it to three. All agreed that three was the magic number for the wager. It was obvious that Virgil was going to spare nothing and go at these two with all his force. He hadn't hiked his pants up this high in many months, Virgil's tell that things were going to get hot in the kitchen.

Virgil walks over to a table near the wall phone acting busy, but John knows the only thing he's busy with is watching him and putting pressure on his phone call. Almost nothing goes on at the diner without Virgil, who is constantly on the move to all parts of the establishment, having his beady eyes active and involved. The call connects on the fifth ring, followed by a few seconds of silence, the phone sounding as though ZZ had dropped it on a soft surface and it is now being fumbled in her hand.

"Hello," ZZ finally says, sounding distracted.

"Hi, it's Doc calling."

"What's up?"

"I'd like to see you later if possible. Do you think you can meet me at the Railbird diner?"

"I can't make it tonight. Maybe tomorrow, I have to see. We'll talk in the morning, okay?"

"You don't understand. I might be leaving town soon," John says, holding on to the possibility that somehow they will be able to scrape together enough extra money to get a bus ticket out of town and put three thousand miles between their reality and this nightmare. "It has to be tonight or we might not be able to see each other for a while."

"You're so dramatic, Doc, such a drama queen. I told you, you need to calm down. You're leaving just because I can't see you tonight?"

"No, it's not that at—"

"Really, I don't understand you. Suddenly, you get into a mood or something and you decide to go? It doesn't make sense."

"It's not so sudden. I—"

"You just said it was sudden, like you might go tonight." ZZ talks fast, her words formed at a fraction of the speed of her thoughts. "Tonight is pretty sudden in my book, Doc. You're really hard to figure out. These ups and downs, you should get help or take something. I don't—"

"ZZ, please, can I talk for a second? You're not giving me a chance. You're jumping the gun on things here."

ZZ giggles and suddenly sounds giddy. "I guess you're right. Go ahead," she says, dropping her voice to a sexy tease.

"You remember I said that I live in New York. Right?"

"Yessss," ZZ says, dragging out the "s" sound in a flirtatious purr.

John's pulse quickens when he looks over at the manager. Virgil never stands anywhere for very long, and he has been staring at John for more than a minute now. Not a good sign. He feels like a ship in harbor with the big guns of the enemy aimed broadside.

"I'm just here on vacation. I have to go back eventually. You see, it makes sense, right?"

ZZ giggles with delight. "I guess I could see you quickly if you make it worth my while." ZZ lowers her voice to an alluring whisper. "You in your place?"

"My place?" John is distracted by the sight of Virgil edging closer to the phone. He is momentarily confused, wondering why ZZ thinks he's in his Brooklyn apartment.

"Your hotel, silly."

"I can't go back there."

"You can't go back to New York? To your hotel? I don't understand," ZZ says, getting agitated. "What are you talking about?"

"No, I'm not in my hotel. I'm helping out at the Railbird diner."

"You're what?" It is ZZ's turn to be confused.

"I'm doing some extra work here. A few things came up so I'm over here, you know, for a little bit and everything." John realizes that it doesn't sound good, but he doesn't know what else to say.

"Did you say you're working in a diner? I thought you were here on vacation."

John wants to say that he thought he was coming to Las Vegas for a vacation, all right, but not the vacation from hell. "Well yeah, you know, uhm, I'm like, ah, you know, ah, just picking up a little extra money, you know, a few extra bucks," John says, realizing that this can't possibly make sense to ZZ. It doesn't even make sense to him. But it's too late now, he can't take the words back. Maybe mentioning the vacation from hell would have been a better explanation.

"You're doing accounting at night? That's weird." ZZ thinks for a moment, but lets it pass. "Okay, I'll be there in thirty minutes. Let me get ready—"

"Wait, hold on. It has to be a little later than that. Is that okay? I'm still in the middle of things."

"Do you want to see me or not?" ZZ says, greatly agitated now. "I don't understand you sometimes. You make things so difficult."

"Of course I want to see you! It's just—"

John glances back at Virgil. The manager tries to hike his pants higher, but they have reached their physical zenith and don't move. Virgil's face is drawn taut, like a pressure cooker with the lid straining at its limits. John can see that if he doesn't get off the phone soon, the cover will explode off the pot and become a lethal weapon in flight.

"Look, if you don't want to see me, then forget about it." ZZ's voice has become loud, and she sounds like she's one small provocation away from blowing her own lid. John doesn't know how to explain that he is washing dishes, but Virgil, his temper escaping in a boiling froth, soon clears up that problem.

"Get your ass back in the kitchen, you loafer. We got dishes to clean," Virgil screams, unable to contain his anger any longer. His right hand quivers epileptically by his waist as it futilely tries to pull his pants up higher. "You're being paid to wash the goddamned dishes for me, not chitchat with some floozy on the phone."

"One minute, Virgil, I'm finishing up," John says, quickly covering the mouthpiece on the phone. It is too late. ZZ hears the exchange between him and Virgil. The word "floozy" could not have earned him brownie points.

"I thought you were an accountant in New York, Doc," ZZ says in an accusatory tone. "Or is it a doctor?"

"I *am* an accountant in New York!"

"But you're doing dishes in Las Vegas? In a diner? Is that what you're doing there, washing dishes?"

"Well, yes—"

"So this whole thing is just a lie, like you're a doctor also. I have to go—"

"Wait," John screams into the phone, desperate, his last flicker of hope in Las Vegas fading like batteries sputtering on a dying charge. His eyes nervously flick up. Virgil has moved closer, to within inches of the phone, the end of his belt pointing at John's chest. "It's not like it seems! Hold on, give me a second, let me explain. Please ZZ."

"It *will* be like it seems," Virgil screams, "when I kick your ass out the door like bad dishwater. This is not tea time, Cupcakes."

ZZ simultaneously yells over Virgil's voice. "What is it? Are you a baker, a doctor, an accountant, a dishwasher, a sicko, who the hell are you?"

"I'm dishwater, ZZ, dishwater! I mean a dishwasher!" John blurts out, not knowing what he is saying. "Goddamn it, I'm not dishwater, I'm a doctor, I mean an accountant. I—"

"Don't yell at me, Doc," ZZ yells. "I'm not the one not making sense with ten jobs at the same time all over the place."

"I'm sorry, listen to me, I'm under so much pressure. Just trust me, please."

"I just don't know, Doc, Joe, Bob, or whoever the hell you are," ZZ says, her voice suddenly sedate, like a tire going flat with just enough air to hold its form and continue down the road.

"Will you listen to me?" John is pleading. His relationship with her is quickly slipping out of his fingers, mercury that slithers away as he squeezes it tighter.

Virgil is so close to John's face, he can see the manager's pulsating acne and smell the baloney and mustard he eats every day for lunch between two pieces of white bread. "Move your ass already and get off the phone!" he yells. A few customers turn and watch the red-faced manager shaking with anger. The end of Virgil's belt, as if ready to spew forth venom, shakes like a rattler's tongue. "I don't want to have to fire your lazy carcass. Don't be testing me, Cupcakes, I—"

"Maybe we shouldn't talk. I really don't know about you anymore," ZZ says.

"Okay, okay," John whispers to Virgil, pushing his hand down to calm the infuriated manager, a gesture that further incenses him. Virgil is so close to John, he might as well be on the phone himself.

"Alright," ZZ says, "if you say 'okay' just like that and that's what you want, bye then."

John hears the phone creak as ZZ pulls it away from her ear. "Hold it," he screams, "I wasn't talking to you." He hears the phone come back to ZZ's ear.

"So you're not talking to me, is that it?" Virgil says, his voice dropping to a menacing tone.

"Who is that guy yelling by the phone?" ZZ says.

"He's nobody," John says. "Don't worry about him."

"Nobody, you say?" Virgil queries.

"Well," ZZ says, "I don't like playing games, Mr. Whoever-You-Are. I don't know, this is too spooky—"

John is getting hammered on both sides of the phone and clenches his fist in frustration.

"You said *nobody*?" Virgil growls, his hands dropping to his hips.

"Oh my god," John groans, getting more and more frustrated by the twin conversations.

The manager stares at John, his tiny brown eyes counting a victim soon-to-be for his little book under the register, baloney congealing in his stomach.

"I'm real, ZZ, I am what you think I am, I mean, you know, what you thought I am, was. I don't know what I'm saying anymore." John is getting confused, and his head feels like it got dipped into the slop sink and got clogged with suds. "There are these problems—"

Those are the last words ZZ hears before the connection is sharply broken by Virgil slamming his hand on the receiver's cradle, his eyes looking like they're ready to pop out of his skull and dance an angry hip-hop on the floor.

"Now, *that* is *that*, Ro-me-o," Virgil says, his voice strained like thin spaghetti just out of the pot. He slowly enunciates every syllable, as if painfully. "Jul-i-et is waiting in the kitchen for you to rinse her pretty metal pot–scrubbing fat ass. Start operating back in the room there, Doc. I'm warning you, don't test me."

John trudges back into the kitchen, plops a tray full of cups into the sink, and silently swirls them around under the suds.

"You called her, didn't you?" Ludo queries.

"Yeah."

Ludo can see by John's pained expression that the conversation didn't go well. "Not too good, huh?"

John slowly nods his head in assent. "Not too good doesn't even begin to cover it, Ludo. A complete utter disaster. I didn't even know what I was saying to her before she hung up. We're through, that's it. Nothing goes right for me, I mean, nothing. Now she doesn't know who I am, I mean, can you believe this? She thinks I'm a dishwasher, of all things!"

Ludo looks at John bent over the sink, his arms elbow deep in suds, and says nothing.

Chapter Thirty-Four

The kitchen doors swing wide open, banging off the back walls, as John rushes through them. He is out of breath, as though he has just run a quick sprint, and he stands by the door, the tray dangling from his right hand.

"Hey, Ludo!"

"Yeah?" Ludo is taking his turn at the dishes while John does the bussing. He looks up.

"How much is the bus?"

"Fifty cents, a dollar, ten cents? How the hell would I know what a local bus costs? I'm just the dishwasher here. We can't afford it anyhow."

"No, I mean the bus to New York."

"Oh, the dream bus that we'll never get out of this diner alive enough to see? That's eighty-five dollars per ticket, probably more if we go out in a casket. You prefer plain pine or a nice walnut? Or will a cremation and a fancy urn be more your style, sir?" Ludo disinterestedly turns back to the slop sink and rinses his hands.

"Come on, how much?"

"We're not even close, man. After this shift, we'll still be one thousand pots and one hundred dollars short."

"Well, guess what?"

"Not this again."

"Just guess."

"I'm not in the mood for this, homes." Ludo picks up a rag, dries his hands, and looks over at John.

"You'll never guess what just happened," John says.

"I already got that part figured out. If you're going to tell it, man, just tell it. This day's been too hard for these games. I don't have the strength for this."

"Okay," John says. "This guy walks in with a big ten-gallon hat and with an even bigger smile, has a cup of coffee—nothing more—and asks me in a thick Texas drawl, 'Are you the busboy here?' I say, 'Yes, can I get something for you?' He shakes his head no and tells me that his name is Doyle Brunson and he just won one million dollars in a big Texas hold'em game. And then he says, 'I was down and out a time or two. I see you could use a good break and I'm going to pass my luck on to you. You look like a fine fellow.' And then he walks out the door."

"So?"

"Well, guess?"

"Homes," Ludo says warningly.

"He gave me this as a tip," John says, pulling his right hand from behind his back.

"Holy shit!" Ludo says. John is holding a crisp one-hundred-dollar bill.

"One hundred dollars!" John exclaims. "Read 'em and weep!"

"Man, that's unbelievable! That gives us exactly enough money with what we'll get on this shift! What time is it?"

John looks at the clock on the wall. "It's ten o'clock. Shift over in ninety minutes."

"That cross-country bus leaves at midnight. We just have to figure out, first, how to get to the bus station; second, how to avoid any catastrophes between here and there; and third—no matter what, no matter how, no matter anything—how to get our goddamned asses on that goddamned bus and get the goddamned hell out of here. At midnight, I want my Brooklyn ass planted on that bus seat. Period."

Virgil walks into the kitchen on the tail end of the conversation and has a bemused grin on his face. "Oh, is our favorite dishwashing and busboy team making big plans for a vacation with all the profits from their hard work?"

John walks by Virgil, pats him on the shoulder, and says, "Maybe so, Virgil."

———————

"How much more?" Ludo asks as John comes in from the floor.

"Forty-five minutes to take-off. It's eleven-fifteen," John says looking at the clock. "Ludo, you've asked me that ten times in the last ten minutes."

"You're sure it's that long?"

"I'm staring at the clock. It says eleven-fifteen. You can see the same time as easily I can. What do you want me to say?"

"Well, what time is it now?"

"Ten seconds after the last time," John says with a sigh. He drops off a plate of dishes and goes back through the swinging doors and out on the floor.

At eleven seventeen P.M., a man walks into the diner dressed in nondescript clothes you wouldn't remember ten seconds later. His face, however, is one you'd never forget—if you lived to tell about it, that is. On the left side, a deep scar runs vertically from high on the forehead all the way to just above his chin, and on the other side, three scars of various lengths cross the skin and catch pale light in carved furrows. He walks with a slight limp, almost imperceptible, and though his figure isn't imposing, his presence is. Even a house cat could sense that you didn't want this man in your home uninvited.

"We're not used to seeing you here in the evenings," Virgil says to the newcomer.

"Mixing things up a little," the man says in a deep but quiet voice, his eyes unflinching, like frozen marbles.

"The usual spot?" Virgil asks.

"I think I'll try a new table. This one, right by the door."

"I'll send someone over to clean it right away."

A middle-aged waitress who looks like she has served a life sentence of hard time at the diner goes over to Virgil and stands with one hand on her hip and the other holding a pair of menus. Her hair is piled high in a large bun, and she is loudly chewing on a hunk of pink gum with her mouth open.

"Becky just quit," the waitress says to Virgil. "I think she had enough of scarface, something about a large hunting knife and . . . forget about the rest."

"Send her over here," Virgil says.

"Too late, she's gone. By the way, you may want one of your newbies here to serve up Becky's tables. I'm not going near that," she says, and walks away.

John runs into the kitchen and his hands are shaking. He is breathing rapidly and opens his mouth to say something, but nothing comes out.

"What is it, homes?" Ludo says, turning to face him.

"Wonderbread is out there."

"What do you expect in a restaurant, homes, Martha Stewart's homemade butter rolls? Or you think this is a Jewish deli and they should have rye bread? What the fuck is your problem?" Ludo points to a tray full of dirty dishes. "Yo, pass me that tray, homes, and stop talking nonsense."

Virgil comes running into the kitchen yelling at them. He's in a good mood because the waitress has quit and he can't wait to mark the notch in his book. But he's in a bad mood also, because now he is short-staffed. "How many times do I have to tell you vagrants to work more and gab less?"

"We're working, man, we're working. We getting it done," Ludo says.

"Tell your friend, Doctor Cupcakes here," the manager says, indicating John with his thumb, "that we got a table to clear now. We're backed up and need to get moving."

Virgil turns to John, screaming and stomping both feet on the ground like a little child. "Get your homeless vagrant no-good lazy ass out there now! We have a customer waiting. Work to be done. Table. By the door. Now!"

John reaches into the bin piled high with dirty dishes and dips his finger along the flat part of a plate filled with leftover black beans. He smears the paste above his mouth, forming a dark mustache, and grabs the straw hat off Ludo's head.

"Wonderbread," John calls across to Ludo in a hoarse voice, sounding possessed as he rushes through the doors and returns to the dining area.

Ludo and the manager stare at John as he exits, the kitchen doors swinging hard off the wall behind him.

"Something off with your friend upstairs, you know what I'm saying?" Virgil says to Ludo as his index finger makes a circular motion by his forehead. "Cuckoo, cuckoo, cuckoo," the manager adds, not looking like his own deck has a full complement of fifty-two cards.

Ludo just shrugs as Virgil follows John out onto the floor.

John emerges from the kitchen with Ludo's straw hat pulled low and a dark, uneven line painted over his upper lip. Though there are plenty of clean tables set and ready to go, Wonderbread has chosen the only one in the section that has not yet been bussed. It is the table closest to the ingress and egress of the diner, and Wonderbread sits facing the door. He holds a long knife in his right hand and is cleaning dirt from under his nails with the blade. A family of four sat there previously, and the table is littered with dishes, glasses, silverware, soiled napkins, and food scraps. John, his hands shaking and damp with sweat, is stacking the plates, bowls, and cups, one atop the other. He keeps his head down, averting eye contact with the killer, but his eyes are riveted to the long blade in Wonderbread's hands, which the killer works in slow methodical motions like a sushi chef carving slices of soft fish flesh. The scraping sound of metal against fingernail unnerves John, and in these close quarters, excruciatingly long seconds feel like minutes. He feels the laserlike intensity of the killer's eyes boring into his skull. From up close, he hears Wonderbread's clipped breathing, the ghastly sounding intakes of air and the murderous exhalations, and it makes him think of the final breaths of a dying man.

John fills a tray with the dirty plates and glasses from Wonderbread's table, the sound of each stacked dish magnified in his ears. This process seems to take forever; finally, to his relief, he gets the table cleared and carries the loaded tray over to the bussing station across the way, in his nervousness almost dropping the entire load when he misjudges the distance and barely catches the lip of the counter. With shaking hands, he pushes the tray deeper onto the flat of the counter, avoiding an embarrassing catastrophe that would focus Wonderbread's attention to him. Not what he wants. John returns to the table with a damp rag and wipes it clean, suddenly realizing that he hasn't breathed in a very long time. He wipes the surface quickly, avoiding Wonderbread's eyes, although he can't take his own eyes off the long, sharp knife in the killer's hands.

John turns to leave, but his upper arm is grabbed from behind and held in a vicelike grip. Wonderbread's fingers dig into his skin like the talons of an eagle holding onto a doomed rabbit.

"Hey, you," Wonderbread says, his voice low and raspy.

John's heart is pounding so hard he thinks he can hear it beating. He looks down, self-conscious about the unevenly lined black-bean mustache and cheap straw hat. "Si?" John says, without looking up.

"Get me a glass of water, lots of ice."

"Right away, señor," John says in a Mexican accent so fake he doesn't even fool himself.

"Busboy, I like lots of ice. You got that?"

Wonderbread releases John's arm after he nods his head in agreement and turns his attention back to toying with the knife gripped in his hand.

John makes it back to the kitchen, his hands frantically trying to speak and his mouth futilely trying to move. He is hyperventilating and stands in front of Ludo, his arms flailing in the air.

"What's with you, homes? Calm down, man."

Ludo can't figure out what is wrong with John, but clearly he is losing it. The nightmare of their trip and three days with almost no sleep have obviously sent his friend over the edge.

"It's Wonderbread, Ludo. It's Wonderbread," John finally blurts out.

"So what the fuck do I care what kind of goddamned bread they serve in here?" Ludo says. He points to his own upper lip and asks, "What the fuck is wrong with you, and what the hell is this shit? We need this job to get out of here. Don't fuck it up."

Virgil comes into the kitchen, but before he can say anything, John rushes past him on his way back to the dining room.

John returns to Wonderbread's table with a glass of water. His hands are shaking so badly that water spills over the edge and onto his fingers as he almost misses the table, barely landing the glass on the very edge of its surface.

"Busboy," Wonderbread says, before John can escape.

"Yes? Si?"

"I don't know you, do I?" The voice is hard and menacing, as serious as a bullet piercing a man's heart.

"I don't think so, señor," John says, shaking his head and turning.

But Wonderbread is not finished. "You seem familiar, but you're new here, isn't that right?"

"Yes."

"In my business," the killer says, "I don't forget people."

John shrugs and goes two steps before he is again halted. "I asked for more ice, busboy."

"Right away," John says heading back to kitchen. From the corner of his eye, he sees Virgil watching his every movement.

"Ludo," John says as he enters the kitchen, frantic and shaking like a sparrow caught in a frost, "I can't go back out there. Wonderbread is suspicious of me."

"*I'm* fucking suspicious of you. Lay off this bread shit here, man, you're getting me more nervous than I already am."

"Come here," John says. He grabs Ludo, pulls him over to the glass lookout in the kitchen door, and points to the table by the entrance.

"Oh, shit!" Ludo exclaims. "What the fuck is he doing here? Fuck that. What the fuck are we doing here? Why didn't you tell me he was here? Fuck!"

"Who did you think I was talking about?"

"Holy mother-fucking banana-eating chicken-scratching shit on a double-toasted bagel."

"I think he recognizes me. I can't go out there. Take this," John says, stuffing the hat on Ludo's head. "You'll need it, trust me. And bring him a glass of icewater."

Virgil enters the kitchen just as Ludo, wearing the broken straw hat, brushes past him. Virgil watches Ludo's back as it passes through the swinging doors into the dining area and then he looks over at John, his eyes resting on the strange black line painted on John's upper lip.

"What's with you two?" Virgil says.

Ludo approaches the table where Wonderbread sits and can't believe what he sees. The killer has a large knife in his hand and is using it to carve designs in the paper napkin. Immediately, his underarms get moist with sweat. One drop travels down Ludo's side, tickling his skin uncomfortably. He carefully places the glass of water on the table and feels two more drops of sweat work their way down the same path.

"Hey, you," Wonderbread says, his face as expressionless as a dead animal on a cold winter day.

"Sir?"

"I asked the other one for ice. Twice. Can I get some goddamned ice around here or what? Surely there is enough ice in this place."

"Will get right on it, sir," Ludo says, his heart racing. With shaky legs, he walks over to the water pitcher and fills a glass to the brim with ice cubes and water.

"Having fun with scarface?" the waitress says without sympathy as she passes by Ludo.

Ludo ignores her and returns to deliver the water. He carefully puts the glass down by Wonderbread's hand, but the glass is filled high with water and a small amount spills on the killer's fingers. Ludo pauses and looks up in fright.

Wonderbread stares at him silently, then turns his hand and watches the water drip off its side.

Ludo is unsure what to do and he slowly backs away from the table, keeping his eyes on Wonderbread's knife. The killer continues to watch the liquid drip off his hand, fascinated by the drops as they crawl down his skin, as if they were the last specimens of blood dripping off a fresh corpse. Ludo backs into a customer, the water turning red in his imagination, then turns and passes by the register, where he is stopped by Virgil.

"What gives with you and Cupcakes? What's with the tag-team act? What the hell is going on here?" Virgil demands in a whisper, his eyes whirling around as he keeps watch on his customers and his help on both sides of the diner.

Ludo opens his mouth to talk, but nothing comes out. The image of Wonderbread and his expressionless face watching the liquid of life drip off his hand chokes the words right out of his throat. He tries again, and this time there is sound to his voice. "Nothing," Ludo says hoarsely, finally getting his wits about him. The color has run out of his face, and he is unnaturally pale under the fluorescent bulb above. "My hand was getting that waterlogged fungus stuff so I took a break from the dishes."

A patron walking over to pay his bill looks up with alarm upon hearing this predicament. Virgil hitches up his pants and glares at Ludo before addressing the customer.

"Oh, yeah, that was *fungus for us*, a company joke. We had a small company party last night, some free stuffed mushrooms and food for the help—unless of course they couldn't pay for it—and we had them wash dishes instead," Virgil says, laughing in an exaggerated manner.

"That's a good one," Ludo says, patting the manager on the back and dryly chuckling along with him. "Too bad management didn't throw in a free twenty-five cent cup of coffee. That's also a company joke."

The waitress swings by after the customer pays and departs. "Virgil, tables need to be cleaned over in the back. I'll need a little help here if you can send someone by."

The manager snaps at Ludo in a low voice. "Now get your ass moving, freeloader, and start spreading your coffee-for-free dreams over there," he says, pointing toward a group of tables filled with dirty dishes.

Ludo moves in a daze, the manager's words drowned out by a primal pounding in his head as he thinks of the long knife and the chill he felt standing just two feet away from Wonderbread. No wonder John was acting so strangely. Ludo starts toward the back, but does an immediate about face as the full force of his encounter with Wonderbread holding a knife in his hand—and watching the water drip off the killer's hands like blood—hits his consciousness, the impact like a brick landing on his head. Instead, he walks directly into the kitchen, past the angry face of his manager, who is busy at the cash register ringing up a customer with one hand and hiking up his pants with the other.

"Hombre, it's fucked out there. I almost shit in my pants. Why didn't you tell me he had a knife?"

"'Cause then you wouldn't go."

"Good guess." Ludo stuffs the hat back on John's head. "I'm not going near that again. A table on the right side needs clearing. Your turn, bubba."

Virgil enters the kitchen and this time it is John, not Ludo, who rushes pass the startled manager. Ludo is back at the dishes, elbow deep in suds. Virgil pulls up his pants and rubs his head in disbelief.

"Hand's feeling better," Ludo calls over, and raises his arm to show Virgil.

———————

At eleven-thirty, Virgil comes in with a small wad of cash in his hand, and gives each of them thirty-five dollars. "Shift over, another one in the books. You boys are strange, but you work hard and did a good job," he says.

John and Ludo watch Virgil exit through the swinging doors into the dining room. It is not elation they feel at having enough money to buy a bus ticket out of town, but abject fear, for on the other side of the door, a cold-blooded killer they owe money to sits there waiting for them with a knife in his hands, one large enough to carve up a big-game animal. They take off their aprons, pull over two milk crates, and sit wearily upon them. Neither one knows what to do about the imminent danger terrifyingly close to them.

"We go out there, man," Ludo says, "Wonderbread going to cut us up with that knife."

"Did you see how long that thing is? It's not good. They've come to get us, Ludo!" John holds his face and then looks up at the clock. A minute has passed and it is eleven thirty-one.

"What time is that bus?" Ludo asks.

"Twelve o'clock, exactly. We got twenty-nine minutes to get there. The question is—how?"

"I don't know, homes. I just know we got to get by Wonderbread somehow and then we got to find a way to get to that bus station."

"We need a few bucks for a taxi," John says. "You think we can sweet-talk Virgil into spotting us a few?"

"Virgil wouldn't give a plucked feather to a naked chicken."

"What are we going to do?"

Chapter Thirty-Five

John and Ludo are still sitting on the upturned crates staring at the wall clock when Virgil walks in and looks up at the clock. "It's eleven thirty-five. You boys can go anytime, the shift is over, you been paid. Unless you enjoy my company that much."

"We're just taking it easy for a minute."

"Suit yourself," Virgil says, and leaves.

John gets up, pacing back and forth in front of Ludo, alternately sighing and mumbling to himself.

"Sit down, man. You're getting me nervous," Ludo says. He is watching the second hand tick slowly around the clock.

"I can't take this anymore," John says, gripping his stomach. The acids are heating up and churning with the tension.

"Hang in there, man, we'll figure out something."

"I don't know, Ludo, I just don't know."

"If we're going to catch that bus, homes, like it or not, we're going to have to bust a move soon," Ludo says. "We gotta just go for it. There's no back way outta here. That back door is padlocked from the outside, there's only the front. We just have to deal with Wonderbread, no other choice."

"You're right," John says. He peers through the round glass window in the swinging doors. "He's still there."

Neither one makes a move, however, and instead, paralyzed by fear, they watch the second hand go fully around the clock as another minute ticks off. One less minute to work with. It is now eleven thirty-nine. That leaves them just twenty-one minutes to catch the bus, if they can even get there.

"I'm going nuts just doing nothing," John says. "Let me clear a table or something, shake some cobwebs out, maybe I'll think of something."

"Hurry up, homes, the clock is ticking," Ludo says as John pushes through the kitchen doors, leaving Ludo to stare at the second hand going round and round and round.

Outside the diner by the front door, the driver of a beat-up 1970s Thunderbird convertible is leaning heavily on the horn, honking nonstop, the blaring noise causing everyone in the diner to turn and look. The driver of the long, black Cadillac parked next to the Thunderbird, a short stocky man with hair cut short military style and a bulge the size of a gun pushing out of his jacket, is fed up with the honking and gets out of his vehicle. He goes around to the driver's side of the Thunderbird and motions with his hands for the honking to stop.

John looks out the window to see what all the commotion is about. The driver of the Thunderbird, a woman with long dark hair parted off to the side, stops leaning on the horn and, with a big smile full of white teeth, waves to him. It is ZZ, and she honks twice more in greeting. John waves back, raises his hand to indicate he'll be out in a minute, and hurries back into the kitchen.

John pushes through the swinging doors and yells over to his friend, "Ludo, Ludo. Get up! ZZ is outside in a car! We got a ride!"

"Unbelievable, man!"

Checking his excitement for a minute, John says, "What do we do about Wonderbread? How are we going to get past him?"

"Now or never, homes. Let's roll the dice. Let's just put our stuff on and hope for the best."

"Here goes nothing."

John rushes over to the closet, pulls out the blonde wig they stashed there, puts it on his head, and covers it with the straw hat he borrowed from the panhandler. Ludo throws the red dress back on and rips open a package containing a new mop head and puts it on, the white tendrils looking like bleached dreadlocks. He throws the other straw hat on top of the mop head, pulls it down low, and grabs his small day bag. They're strange-looking and transparent disguises, but after three sleepless days and nights under the constant strain of living like hunted animals, neither John nor Ludo has the capacity to understand that they couldn't fool a retarded dog with this getup.

The pair walks through the kitchen, past the astonished chef and short-order cook, and enters the dining room from the waitress station. They pass a few tables in the back, the occupants gawking at this bizarre duo, then by Virgil at the register, who stares speechlessly at them. However, the aisle near the front-door exit is blockaded, and John, in the lead, stops dead in his tracks. Wonderbread stands in the middle of the passageway with his feet spread apart as if planted there, impeding their progress. They had naively thought their makeshift disguises would make them look like different people, but Wonderbread, seeing the ludicrous sight of a wig and a mop on the heads of these two clowns, one in a stained blue blazer that sorely needs ironing, and the other in a wrinkled, ill-fitting red dress that looks like it has just been uncrumpled from a ball, is not fooled.

The killer steps forward to less than a foot away from John, imperceptibly nodding his head as he carefully studies John's eyes to see what kind of grit lies behind them. The scars on Wonderbread's face are the color of dead fish and his eyes the pale gray of tombstones with a morbid quality that would give the grim reaper pause in a staredown. John feels a pulse throbbing hard in his neck and he swallows painfully, a big lump of fear catching in his throat and barely making it down. Behind him, Ludo is shaking with fright, his gaze transfixed by the killer's depthless eyes. Wonderbread's hands are clasped together in front of him, the hunting knife no longer in sight. But that is of little comfort to John. In fact, there is nothing comforting as he stares into Wonderbread's eyes from nine inches away. The killer's pupils have the morbid quality of an abyss, a bottomless pit of emptiness, a dark eternity that's cold, unforgiving, and hollow. But more than anything, John feels an abject cold tingling, what a dying man must feel as the blood that heats his life runs out of him and his last thoughts are those of impalpable terror.

Wonderbread reaches into his coat pocket and as he slowly pulls his hand out, John shrinks back. He sees death looking at him, cold and gray and eternal. This is it, John thinks, the game is over. Fear washes cold over his entire body, and then hot, as sweat gathers on his skin and pours down his spine. Ludo's comforting hand against his back, a brief bridge to life, helps bolster his legs from imminent collapse as he watches Wonderbread's hand slowly draw out of his pocket. He sees a glint of metal and his mind races. Knives are made of metal, flesh is soft, and the meeting of the two is often mortality's last dance. But the killer removes only a monogrammed handkerchief from his pants, the metal of his platinum ring catching the light, and John breathes again.

Not yet.

The killer is toying with him, playing games, in no rush to make human sushi. Wonderbread dabs at the corner of his mouth before replacing the handkerchief in his pocket, his unmerciful eyes locked into John's. He lifts his hand and points at John's heart like his index finger is a gun, cocks his thumb, and fires, the sound "pshhhhh" escaping his lips as if the speeding whish of a bullet has been slowed down to allow its velocity to be heard and admired before metal splits skin, bone, and organ.

Wonderbread smiles, a lurking line that cuts across his mouth like the jagged edge of a butcher knife, and then steps aside to let them pass.

But it's not going to be that easy.

Chapter Thirty-Six

John and Ludo have no sooner emerged from the diner, barely catching their breath in relief from the frightful experience with Wonderbread, before a further danger shocks them: a long, black Cadillac idles ominously just outside the diner's entrance. They see Versachi's big frame make its way out of the vehicle, the car rocking as he steps out, a menacing scowl on his face. Clearly, he's none too happy with them.

"Let's run for it, Ludo," John says as they sprint the twenty-five feet to ZZ's waiting car. John jumps in first through the door pushed open by ZZ, and Ludo, a step behind, dives headfirst into the back seat seconds before ZZ sets the car in motion.

ZZ immediately sees the nature of the situation, first jamming the gearshift into reverse, then into drive, as she maneuvers the car in the direction of the street. She tears out of the driveway with a hard right turn, tires screeching and leaving a wide swath of rubber on the edge of the diner's parking lot. When she hits the open air of the street, she jams the pedal to the floor, the Thunderbird convertible feeling its oats and shooting forward in a burst of speed.

Versachi quickly reenters his vehicle, the Cadillac peeling out of the parking lot in pursuit of the old Thunderbird, quickly gaining speed into the night and hurtling down the street right behind it.

The chase is on.

"Hi Doc!" ZZ calls out, exhilarated, as if the chase is but a game, a diversion from reality. She steers hard to the left, crossing several lanes of traffic ahead of oncoming cars, races down a narrow street, and comes out again on a straightaway, jamming the accelerator to the floor and picking up speed. The black Cadillac, screeching loudly on the hard turns, is equal to the task when they hit the avenue and keeps pace behind them, its dark windows giving it the look of a gruesomely grinning shark gone night hunting. "Wheeeeeeeee," she exclaims, giggling, as she fakes a turn to the left and then to the right, with the Cadillac behind them swerving in response. ZZ sits upright, checking both the rear- and side-view mirrors as she swerves around turns, her face flush with excitement.

John and Ludo are still in shock from their close-range confrontation with Wonderbread just minutes earlier. Now, the sudden appearance of Versachi and the suicidal car chase overload their senses, and they hang on tight to the armrests, speech playing hide-and-seek with them—and doing a good job of hiding for the moment. Death is courting them, with many interested suitors, and they can't seem to shake it. John just nods back in response to ZZ's greeting as she weaves through the streets at dangerous speeds. The last thing he wants to do right now is distract her and have the car crash head-on at these dangerous speeds. John thought for sure Wonderbread was going to carve them up like strips of beef jerky, and then for no reason he can figure Wonderbread let them pass, as if it was a cruel joke, a little game he was playing. Like a tag team of bad luck and hard luck, they get past Wonderbread only to find that their nemesis, Versachi, is laying in wait for them.

Ludo sits wild-eyed in the rear seat, petrified by the dangerous chase and ZZ's maniacal maneuvers to elude the black Cadillac pursuing them. He wonders if they have jumped out of the proverbial frying pan and into the fire. John was right when he said "a lot of trouble"; that was verified within seconds of meeting ZZ. Ludo is just righting himself from the floor when another hard turn sends him sprawling again. He finally gains the seat and exchanges glances with John.

"ZZ, we need to get to the bus station in, like, ten minutes," John yells over the wind, finally catching hold of his senses and his voice. "Can you do it?"

ZZ jams on the brakes, leaving a trail of rubber for twenty feet, and then jerks the wheel hard to the left, sending the car fully around in the opposite direction, a perfect one-eighty. Ludo is again thrown to the floor of the back seat and John onto ZZ's lap, and then they are thrown sideways as she floors the accelerator and zips by the black Cadillac coming the other way, honking her horn at the vehicle and screaming with delight. She reaches the corner and whips around the edge, leaving another long trail of rubber before pushing hard on the gas. She makes the next corner at almost fifty miles an hour, hits the brakes, and then whips the car to the right, the tires squealing loudly in the night air and sending the car's passengers careening against the doors. ZZ then straightens the car out and darts down a long street, giving John a moment to catch his breath and glance behind them. He watches the road carefully for signs of the Cadillac, but it appears that they have lost Versachi.

"This is fun!" ZZ exclaims, decelerating the vehicle and smiling wildly. "I'm ZZ, by the way," she calls over her shoulder. "Don't be so rude, Doc. You should introduce us."

"We didn't quite get the chance yet," John says, taking a deep breath, his fried nerves short-circuited. "That's Ludo, my buddy from New York that I had told you about."

"Hi, ZZ, nice to meet you," Ludo says over the noise of the whipping wind. "We appreciate the ride. You came along just when we needed you."

"Nice to meet you too, Pluto!"

"It's Ludo," John yells.

"What did you say?" ZZ yells back, unable to hear over the noise as the T-Bird skips through a gravelly stretch, the fast-spinning wheels grinding on its surface and spitting out chunks of rock.

John waits for a straightaway before speaking. "I didn't think I would see you again. How did you even know we were at the diner?"

"You told me, silly, remember?"

John doesn't remember; in fact, his brain is so shot and his body so exhausted from his nerves being ground raw over the last few minutes and the nightmare of the last three days that he can barely make sense of his thoughts at all. Everything has suddenly caught up to him; he is utterly exhausted. "We saw Wonderbread in the diner. He had a knife and I thought he was going to carve us up like a Thanksgiving turkey."

"That loser? Forget about him. There's no problems with those lowlifes anymore," ZZ says. "Don't worry about them. Things were taken care of."

"What did—"

"Don't ask, okay?" ZZ says, raising her right hand firmly, like a stop sign. "We'll be there soon. Hang tight." ZZ races around another turn, her face pensive. Two blocks later she skids to a halt at the dimly lit bus station right behind a silver Greyhound bus, its luggage racks open like a bird ready to fly.

"We're here!" ZZ announces.

"You're the best, ZZ. The best. Thanks so much for everything!" John says, reaching for the handle and throwing open the door. The clock outside the station shows two minutes before midnight, the time when their bus to salvation leaves. No time to take chances—they have to get on that bus.

ZZ grabs John's shirt before he's out the door and pulls him closer. "I love you," she says, and kisses him fully on the lips. She then lets go and pushes him back, her eyes sparkling as she nods toward the door. The next second a troubled look flashes across her face, a look John remembers seeing when her ex-husband called and she hurled her phone, splintering it into a score of pieces.

"Hurry," she says, "you'll miss your ride."

John closes the door, still savoring the kiss: soft, moist, and full of promise. In an instant, ZZ's car is off and racing down a Las Vegas street.

"I never seen anything like that, homes," Ludo says, pointing after the car. "But hurry up. We gotta get on that thing."

In front of John and Ludo, in the form of a large, silver Greyhound bus, lies salvation from a three-day apocalyptic nightmare in the dark underbelly of Las Vegas. Their dice had landed wrong when they were betting right; their roulette number came up odd when they were betting even; a mere deuce was dealt when they doubled down and needed a face card; a spade came on the river giving their opponent a flush when they held a straight. Fate and misfortune had sent them plumbing the depths of a city they thought was all glitter, only to find that each coin has two sides, the shiny one you see when it faces the light, the other hidden and dark as it lies flat on its back.

"Last call," the bus driver yells out by the luggage compartment on the side of the waiting Greyhound just ahead of them.

John and Ludo drag their beaten souls toward the bus and turn at the whipping sound of wheels racing across asphalt and the repeated blaring of a honking horn. ZZ is speeding down the street from the other direction, hair flowing behind her and an enormous smile on her face, hotly pursued by a long, black Cadillac with dark tinted windows.

Chapter Thirty-Seven

The evening is humid, unusually so for Las Vegas, and the hot air hangs heavy and oppressive. Though the sun has long descended from its zenith, turning day into night, its heat continues to bake the desert earth. The parched windless air, chokingly hot at 101 degrees, hangs motionless, as if stillborn.

It is one minute before midnight in the middle of the Mojave desert in a city carved out of a vast expanse of sand, limestone, sagebrush, Joshua trees, and tumbleweed, and watered with the rotten fruits of man's obsession with chance and money. It is a place where mislaid dreams play in a field gone sallow, where the ones who have stumbled discover that something has gone terribly wrong with their American dream along the way—moths who couldn't resist the flame and got singed or, worse, devoured by it. On the Strip, the electric bulbs are bright, lighting the desert with colored neons and fluorescents, a garish slash across the landscape. But here at the Greyhound station, the lights are muted and the night colors dull. This is the underbelly of the city, where the ones who didn't eat the buffets with the rich tourists congregate; where alcohol, rotgut versions of it, are the sustenance and fare; and where the only dreams worth thinking about are where that next bottle will come from or where some tawdry, unrequited love might be found on the cheap. Shadowy figures fill the shadows or are the shadows, and the less fortunate on this cut of sand use the big wheels of Greyhound to gain their distance, to escape from their bad beats and try their luck elsewhere, and to use the time of a long passage to parboil their solitude on the lonely miles of the open road.

A wino wanders aimlessly past them, his pants filthy and held up by a string. A couple of other derelicts, the wino's companions in misery and hard luck, occupy a bench, their contributions to the city's machinery like pigeon droppings on a statue, a blight to the finery the city of Las Vegas prefers to sweep under the rug. Near these unfortunates, another group of destitutes congregate, looking like they've seen better days. These lost souls stare vacantly into some far-off spot in their past.

John and Ludo pull themselves heavily up the three steps of the bus and trudge down the aisle, the strain and exhaustion of their odyssey encumbering their spirits like a wino's discovery that his gallon jug is empty, its last few drops already sucked dry by parched lips. They are weary as weary can be, and even the small trip up the few steps onto the bus is a Herculean effort. Their misfortunes have sucked most of the life out of them, and the only thing separating them from the drunks and derelicts on the bench is enough money for a pair of tickets that will grant them passage to a world where there are expectations and dreams beyond the grunge and dead-end hopes of the streets, to get shelter from the driftwood that's been cast aside to decay in the open desert sun. The hapless duo takes seats toward the back on the side facing the street, dropping heavily into them like potato sacks thrown onto the back of a truck.

The driver shuts the outside luggage racks, pulls hard on the handle beside his seat, closing the front door behind him, and walks down the aisle to where they are sitting.

"I'll take your fare, boys." The driver, a grizzled and rail-thin old-timer who looks like he has been around some years before Elvis was king, hovers above John, who occupies the aisle seat.

"No problem," John says. "I'm paying for two."

"Give him everything, bro," Ludo jokes weakly. "Every last dime."

John reaches into his pants pocket and pulls out a small wad of crumpled bills. He hands it over to the driver. "Here it is," John says with wearied satisfaction.

The driver makes a face as he counts out the money and then he counts it again.

"Something wrong?" Ludo asks the driver.

"No, nothing wrong at all, I'm feeling fine," replies the driver, straightening up his back. "However, you happen to be three dollar and fifty cent short."

"I counted that money seven times, and every one of those seven times I got the same amount," John says, pointing at the money in the driver's hand. "Maybe you need to count it one more time, you know what I'm saying?"

"For one, don't point at me, young fella, or I'll stuff that digit up your ass. For two, you may have counted this money every day since last Christmas, but you're still the same three dollar and fifty cent short no matter how many times I count it. Now, I don't got all day for you two. Cough it up. Three dollar and fifty cent."

"It's all there," John insists. "Every penny of it."

"Count it, man, it's all there." Ludo chimes in.

"Look, sonny boy, the fare is eighty-six dollar and seventy-five cent each, which makes one hundred and seventy-three dollar, fifty cent total. There's only one hundred and seventy dollar in my hand. What part of the three dollar and fifty cent you having a problem with?"

"What are you talking about? The fare is eighty-five dollars exactly," John says indignantly. "We called the office two days ago. We know the price."

"The fare *was* eighty-five dollar and that was two days ago. It went up one dollar and seventy-five cent per ticket yesterday at midnight. That makes it one hundred and seventy-three dollar fifty cent, which make you short three dollar and fifty cent. Now cough it up. I ain't got all day for this hogwash."

"But that's all the money we have."

"Well then, get off."

"You can't do that," John says, his voice shaky.

"The hell I can't," the driver yells. "If you can't pay the fare, get off my bus." Spittle forms at the edge of his mouth, and his whiskers appear even whiter against his reddened face.

Dejected and without any strength left for fighting, John silently sticks out his hand. The driver slaps the wad of bills back into John's palm and heads for the front of the bus, stopping briefly to chat when an elderly lady wearing an oversized hat over shockingly red hair grabs the old-timer's arm.

"Let's go," Ludo says quietly as the two wearily grab the chair backs in front of them and haul themselves out of their seats. "What the fuck did we do in our last lives?"

With heads lowered, Ludo and John silently will their living carcasses down the long aisle. By the first row of seats at the front of the bus, the driver blocks their passage. He removes his hat to comb his hair, and then replaces it on his head. John, in the lead, stops, and being too depressed to say anything, just stands there with his head down, waiting for the driver to clear the way. Ludo waits behind him.

A few seconds pass, and then the driver finally asks, "Where are you two going?"

"I don't know," John replies, looking past the driver, out the exit. "I really don't know. We just want a bed to sleep in tonight, a bite of food. Where we going? I don't know where we're going. Anywhere, nowhere. Everything has gone wrong for us in Las Vegas and we just need to get out of here and go home. That's all we want."

John looks into the driver's weathered visage, his face lined with years of hard knocks and tough gravel roads. "You know," John continues, "we're just two regular guys with one simple dream: to get the hell out of Vegas."

Chapter Thirty-Eight

"Hand me that one hundred and seventy dollar and get back in your seats."

"But—"

"Hurry up. I don't like to start late."

John reaches into his pocket and hands the money back to the driver. "Well, gee, thanks. I really appreciate that."

"Thank your lady friend back there in the seventh row." The driver nods his head toward the woman with long, red hair and a straw hat with garish ornamental plastic flowers pinned on the front.

The two look at each other and shrug, too exhausted for any more energetic reaction, then slowly retreat back down the aisle. John pauses by the lady with the bountiful red locks and gaudy straw hat. "I'd like to—" John halts his sentence as the lady removes her hat and then her wig, revealing a shiny bald pate. Ludo looks on, mouth agape.

"Somebody abandoned a jackpot between a couple of big brothers," the woman says in a voice caked with many miles, "and I was lucky enough to shoot right in there and scoop it up. 'Course, I might have left a little bit of it behind on some fun. So, I figured I would get me on the road and give some new place a try for a while. I also picked up some new upholstery for my crown. Why don't you try it on? My headdresses usually look good on you."

John takes the ensemble from the woman's outstretched hand and puts on the wig and hat. He stands without expression, the shocking red hair and flowered hat somehow looking natural on him.

Ludo looks back and forth between the old woman and his friend John, and back at the woman defiantly smiling under a bald crown—yet one more baffling episode in this strange vacation. He stares at John and scratches his head. "You know *her* too? And did ZZ really call you Doc? How do you know all these people? We just been here a few days—ah, never mind." He then turns to the lady, "You wouldn't happen to have anything to eat, would you?"

A sound reminiscent of a whinnying horse accompanies the jolt of the engine as the Greyhound slowly pulls away from the bus station. Against the backdrop of a beautiful desert sky, the bus edges its way into the emerging night, heading east and leaving Las Vegas.

Chapter Triple 13

EPILOGUE

Thirteen miles outside the city limits of Las Vegas, a Greyhound bus with license plate number NV131313 has pulled over to the side of the road, plumes of black smoke funneling skyward and dissipating into the baking hot air above. A busted gasket has disabled its engine and rendered it unable to proceed farther down the road. Two passengers inside the bus, one wearing a crumpled blue coat, bright red wig, and garish hat, the other a white mophead and an ill-fitting red dress, awaken from a restless sleep as the wheels of the bus grind into the gravel—and stop.

They open their eyes and watch the faint outline of black smoke slowly lift into the crimson desert sky.

The End